W9-AZW-632

RADIANT

Also by James Alan Gardner

Trapped

Ascending

Hunted

Vigilant

Commitment Hour

Expendable

JAMES ALAN GARDNER

An Imprint of HarperCollins*Publishers*

This book is a work of fiction. The characters, incidents, and dialogue are drawn from the author's imagination and are not to be construed as real. Any resemblance to actual events or persons, living or dead, is entirely coincidental.

HarperCollins books may be purchased for educational, business, or sales promotional use. For information please write: Special Markets Department, HarperCollins Publishers Inc., 10 East 53rd Street, New York, NY 10022.

Eos is a federally registered trademark of HarperCollins Publishers Inc.

Designed by Renato Stanisic

ISBN 0-06-059526-4

To Bill and Veronica

AUTHOR'S NOTE

THANKS to the usual people: Linda Carson, Richard Curtis, Jennifer Brehl, and Diana Gill. Every writer needs good feedback, and yours has always been great.

Some readers may ask, "Why all the Buddhism? Are you preaching something?" Not at all. First, you'll see there are schemes afoot in the League of Peoples that are deliberately exploiting differences between Eastern and Western viewpoints. (Yes, that's vague but I don't want to give too much away.) Second, I thought it would be fun to confront Festina with a sort of mirror opposite, and "opposite" includes an opposing philosophical outlook. Third, I'm tired of melting-pot futures where all the cultural differences of our present day have been homogenized into some lukewarm vanilla snooze. As far as I can see, the future will continue to contain Buddhists, Christians, Muslims, Sikhs, Neo-Pagans, agnostics, atheists, etc., as well as people who invent new belief systems, people who don't think about religion at all, and people who try to change the subject when conversation turns toward uncomfortable topics.

I'd like the League of Peoples books to reflect that multiplicity. Each story in the series shows a different slice of the universe by presenting a particular character's "take" on what's happening. All of the narrators are biased and fallible . . . but by showing the world from many different viewpoints, I hope to give readers a more varied, better rounded view of a complex future.

One last note: the narrator defines a number of Buddhist terms throughout the text. Most either come from Sanskrit or Pali, two languages used in the Buddha's day. Loosely speaking, Sanskrit was Northern India's "highbrow" language while Pali was a related language used by the common people (rather like the relationship between Latin and Italian). The Buddha generally used Pali because he wanted to be understood by the masses. However, the Sanskrit versions are often more familiar to English speakers (e.g., the Sanskrit "karma" as opposed to the Pali "kamma"). My narrator follows the fairly common practice of using Sanskrit for words that have already become part of English (karma, dharma), but Pali for less familiar terms.

RADIANT

1

Anicca [Pali]: Impermanence. The principle that all things change over time and nothing lasts forever.

SEVEN days after I was born, my mother named me "Ugly Screaming Stink-Girl."

Such birth names were common on my homeworld—a planet called Anicca, first colonized by Earthlings of Bamar extraction. Wisewomen swore if you gave your babies unpleasant names, demons would leave the children alone. In Bamar folktales, demons were always gullible; a name like "Ugly Screaming Stink-Girl" would fool them into thinking the baby was so flawed and worthless, there was no point hurting her. Why bother making her sick or nudging her in front of a speeding skimmer? She was already an Ugly Screaming Stink-Girl.

Years later, when I'd learned the proper chants to protect against demons, I was allowed to choose a new name. It happened during the spring festival: girls and boys, nine years old, giggled with their first taste of adulthood as they officially discarded their baby names. We wrote our awful old names on bright red pieces of paper, then threw the papers into a ceremonial fire.

Bye-bye, Ugly Screaming Stink-Girl. Unless, of course, the name stayed stuck in everyone's mind.

Most of the other nine-year-olds immediately announced what new names they were taking. Only a few of us couldn't decide. We tried a succession of different names, switching every few days: trying this, trying that, until we found one that made everyone forget we'd ever been called anything else.

Or until we realized we'd always be Ugly Screaming Stink-Girl, and it was time to stop pretending otherwise. Just pick a name at random and stick with it.

I picked the name Youn Suu. Simple, meaningless, easy to pronounce: like Yune Sue. But it was a label of convenience, nothing more. Like wearing a particular shirt, not because it was comfortable or good-looking, but because it didn't have obvious rips or stains. I didn't feel like a Youn Suu, but I didn't feel like anyone else either. Just a barefoot girl, anonymous.

Part of me still fantasized I'd find a *good* name—a name that was *me*—but I tried not to think such thoughts. The Buddha taught that wishful fixations were "unskillful." Wise people lived life as it was, rather than frittering away their energies on pointless daydreams. My actions counted; my name didn't.

So I became Youn Suu.

Until I left Anicca, people called me *Ma* Youn Suu . . . "Ma" being the polite form of address for an undistinguished young female. Women of high prestige and venerable old grannies warranted a better title: the honorific "Daw." But I was sure I'd never be Daw Youn Suu. I'd never win prestige, and I wouldn't live long enough to become venerable. I'd die young and unimportant, because by the age of nineteen my full name had become Explorer Third Class Ma Youn Suu of the Technocracy's Outward Fleet.

At least, that's what it said on the ID chip burned into the base of my spine. In my heart, I was still Ugly Screaming Stink-Girl.

My ugliness had a story. My life had no room for other stories—no "How I Won a Trophy" or "My First Real Kiss"—because all my potential for stories came down to "Youn Suu Was Ugly, and Nothing Else Mattered."

Like all stories, the tale of my ugliness had long roots. Longer than I'd been alive. The Bamar are a tropical people, originally from Old Earth's Southeast Asia. The British called our homeland "Burma," their version of our tribal name. Burma = the Bamar . . . even though the same region held hundreds of non-Bamar cultures who raged at being left out of that equation.

But the story of Ugly Screaming Stink-Girl isn't about Old Earth history. It's about being beautiful.

Bamar skins are like burnished copper: red-brown protection against the sun. Even so, the searing brilliance of equatorial noon could still damage our exposed skin. Bamar women therefore developed a natural sunscreen from the bark of the thanaka tree—a paste that dried to yellow-white powder. It prevented sunburn and kept skin cool. Even men wore thanaka sometimes, slathering their faces and arms if they had to work in the fields on a blazing-hot day.

By the time my ancestors left Old Earth, science had created much better sunscreens; but that didn't mean the end of thanaka. Thanaka was a symbol of our birth culture—our birth *world*. On an alien planet like Anicca, people clung to such symbols ferociously. Female Aniccans who didn't wear thanaka were thought to be rejecting their Bamar heritage. They might even be trying to look *European* . . . which was enough to get little girls slapped and grown women labeled as whores. On Anicca, decent girls and women wore thanaka.

The makeup was brushed on in streaky patches thin enough that one's underlying skin showed through the brushstrokes. A specific pattern of strokes was deemed "correct Anicca style": a single swipe of the brush on each cheek, another swipe across the forehead, and a fine white line down the nose. Thicker coatings all over the face might have provided more protection than localized daubs, but that would have defeated thanaka's *other* purpose. Thanaka makeup, shiny yellow-white on dark copper skin, was excellent for catching the eyes of men.

Far be it from me to criticize my ancestors. But there's something askew in your priorities if you keep your sunblock thin, risking serious burns, because a light dusting sets off your complexion better than an effective full-face coat. On the other hand, women have done much more foolish things in the pursuit of beauty than diluting their sunscreen and dabbing it on in dainty patches. Foot binding. Neck extension. The surgical removal of ribs. Compared to our sisters in other places and times, women on Anicca were paragons of restraint.

Even so: if a few pats of tree-bark powder hadn't become an indispensable element of beauty on my homeworld, "Ugly Screaming Stink-Girl" would have been just a childhood nickname instead of a life sentence.

Here's why. My mother was allergic to thanaka. She could never wear the tiniest beauty spot without rashes and bloating. She tried a host of substitutes, but found fault with every one. My mother refused to be satisfied—nothing but real thanaka was good enough. (Another of those fixations the Buddha called "unskillful.")

So my mother went bare-faced and became a social outcast. Or so she told me years later. How can a daughter know if her mother is telling the truth? Was my mother really treated badly for being different? Or did she just blame the normal disappointments of life on the way she looked?

As a girl, I had no patience for Mother's tales of woe. She wearied everyone she knew, demanding sympathy for the way her peers had ostracized her. At the age of fifteen, I finally had a frothing hysterical fit, screaming, "People don't hate you because of your face. They hate the way you whine! Whine, whine, whine, whine, whine. I hate it more than anyone. And I hate you. As if you know *anything* about being ostracized!"

I was more emotional back then. Subject to outbursts.

Now I've got past the rage. I've changed. But I'll get to that. At the moment, I'm explaining about my mother.

She thought her lack of thanaka had ruined her life. And before I was born, or even conceived, she decided to create a corrected version of herself, a daughter who would be beloved and popular, never suffering social rejection.

My mother found a man reputed to be an expert gene-splicer . . . even though human-engineering was illegal on my home planet and every other planet in the Technocracy. For a fistful of rubies (passed down as a sacred inheritance through ten generations and never touched until my mother spent them all), this DNA doctor promised to produce a perfect daughter who was smart, fit, and beautiful. Extremely beautiful. In particular, she would have vivid *permanent* thanaka-like beauty patches on her cheeks, forehead, and nose.

You can see where this is going, can't you? But my mother couldn't. For a woman who claimed to know suffering, she'd never learned much about the universe's love of irony.

It's no challenge to create a baby who's intelligent, robust, and exquisite. The technology is well established. Building better babies has always been the driving force behind bioengineering, even if proponents pretend otherwise. Since the earliest days of gene-splicing, scientists have muttered about "improving agricultural stock" or "facilitating medical research," but those are just side issues. The primary target was and is the production of superbabies; any other result is a lucky offshoot. Never mind that manufacturing überchildren has been banned for five hundred years. Laws or no laws, money continues to change hands to create gifted progeny who'll outshine their peers. DNA technicians have all the equipment and expertise needed to produce smart, athletic, attractive offspring . . .

. . . provided one keeps to conventional notions of brainpower, fitness, and beauty. That's what the black market does well. If, on the other hand, you make a special order—such as yellow-white streaks in specific regions of a little girl's face—then the gene-engineers have to improvise.

They have to try untested genes and histones.

They have to wing it.

Therefore:

I was born adequately bright. In the ninety-ninth percentile of human intelligence.

I was born an adequate physical specimen. Small but strong. Thin but not scrawny. By my teen years, I excelled at five forms of solo dance. I even performed, to great acclaim . . . at least in Anicca's yein pwe dances, where all the dancers wore masks.

I had to wear a mask because I was *not* born adequately beautiful. My hair was black and lustrous, my skin resembled feather-soft silk, and my body had tastefully generous curves. But I was still an Ugly Screaming Stink-Girl.

Sometime before birth, the yellow-white pigments intended to adorn my face congealed into a single palm-sized blob glaring from my left cheek. A leprous puckered livid spongelike weeping mass of tissue.

Mostly, it wept a thin, oily ooze. If I told gawking strangers the fluid was just sweat, they said they believed me. But it *wasn't* sweat. I obsessively studied biochemistry till I could determine the fluid's exact chemical composition . . . then obsessively fell into the habit of listing those chemicals under my breath, reciting their names like a chant that could drive away demons. (I'd recite them for you now, but I've given up being neurotic.)

The fluid from my cheek stank of gangrenous pus. At least it did to me. Others assured me they couldn't smell a thing, so perhaps I just imagined the stench. A psychosomatic olfactory delusion. It's possible.

It's also possible people were lying when they said there was no putrid reek of necrosis. I accused them of that many times, shrieking, "Admit it, admit it, admit it!"

As I've said, I was more emotional back then. Subject to outbursts.

Occasionally, when I was under stress or drank too much caffeine, my cheek wept blood. I still told people the fluid was sweat; then I glared, daring anyone to contradict me.

Few did.

* * *

Inevitably, my face drew the attention of the Explorer Corps. Explorers are "brave volunteers"—draftees—whom the navy sends into unknown situations. Or into known situations that are too damned dangerous for unblemished personnel.

Explorers are expendable. If someone has to die, let it be an Ugly Screaming Stink-Girl. Otherwise, there might be repercussions. Measurable drops in morale and productivity.

In Explorer Academy, we were forced to read studies that showed just how badly navy personnel reacted to the death of normal or attractive-looking crew members. Performance ratings plummeted; clinical depression became rampant; people on duty made serious mistakes from shock and grief. Why? Because modern society resembles a character from Bamar sacred stories . . . a young prince named Gotama. The prince was brought up by his royal father in a luxurious pleasure palace where he was kept unaware of old age, disease, and death. He grew up knowing only the joys of his harem, and parties and feasts and games. But the gods refused to let Gotama waste his life in superficialities. Through trickery, they showed him the ugly truths his father had concealed. When Gotama finally learned that the world had a dark side, he was devastated—affected so deeply that the experience set him on the road to enlightenment. Prince Gotama became a Buddha: *our* Buddha, the most recent in a long line of Awakened teachers who've pointed the way to wisdom.

But normal Technocracy citizens aren't ready for Buddhahood. They're not emotionally equipped to leave the pleasure palace. When confronted with anything that suggests their own mortality, they don't get stronger—they crumple.

They've never learned to live with untimely death. How could they? Old age has been alleviated by YouthBoost treatments. Disease can almost always be cured. As for fatal accidents, they're virtually nonexistent thanks to the League of Peoples. The League, headed by aliens billions of years more advanced than *Homo sapiens*, regards willful negligence as equivalent to deliberate homicide; and the League never hesitates to punish those responsible. If, for example, a corporate executive approves the design for a vehicle, or a body implant, or a nanopesticide that hasn't been sufficiently tested for safety—sufficient to satisfy the League, not just human inspectors—the negligent executive will be exterminated the next time he or she enters interstellar space. It doesn't matter if the product *is* safe; failing to test it thoroughly shows callous indifference toward the lives of others. Therefore, the League considers the culprit a "dangerous nonsentient creature" . . . and the League instantly kills any dangerous nonsentients attempting to leave their home star systems. There's no escape, no appeal, and no sentence but summary execution.

One has to admit it's an elegant way to keep lesser beings in check. The League doesn't directly govern humankind or the other alien species at our level of development. The League has no courts, no bureaucracies; it doesn't tell us what we should or shouldn't do. It simply kills anyone who isn't sufficiently considerate of sentient life. The onus falls on us to intuit what the League will accept. We receive no hints or guidelines—we just get killed when we don't do our best.

Which means every commercial product in the Technocracy is as safe as imperfect humans can make it. Also that human communities are built with the finest possible protections against fires, floods, etc. And that police forces are provided with all the facilities they need in order to apprehend criminals who might otherwise jeopardize innocent victims.

So, like Prince Gotama, people of the Technocracy are shielded from life's cruel grind-wheel. The only exceptions are the few men and women whose duties take them outside the pleasure palace, to places that haven't been "sanitized."

Men and women who land on unexplored planets.

Men and women called Explorers.

The navy's Explorer Corps takes in freaks from every corner of the Technocracy. People who can die and not be missed. People whose messy demise won't paralyze ship operations, or make normal-looking personnel think, "Someday I too will suffer and die."

Because if the person who dies has a weeping reeking cheek,

those inside the pleasure palace are less likely to identify with the victim. When an Ugly Screaming Stink-Girl gets killed, the death won't affect *real* people's performance. Why should it? She wasn't quite . . . quite. And the news services won't report her decease to the world at large, because then they'd have to publish her picture.

Nothing hurts a newswire's circulation figures like pictures of Explorers.

At least that's what we were told in school. Even back then, I wondered if there might be more to it: if perhaps somebody in the back rooms of government or elsewhere recognized that the Technocracy's pleasure palace culture was a dead end. Prince Gotama couldn't achieve his potential until he walked away from his harem and feasts.

Could it be the Explorer Corps was intended to follow Gotama's example? That we'd been sent down our difficult path because we alone were worthy? Or that the corps had been created for some as-yet-unrevealed purpose, and the popular belief that "ugly deaths don't hurt morale" was simply a cover-up for the truth?

The pampered mobs in the pleasure palace were too weak to become wise. Only those marked by adversity—running sores, deformed jaws, bulging eyes, angry birthmarks—had the strength to become fully free. Perhaps the Explorer Corps had been created so there'd always be a few of us who weren't sedate cattle. Perhaps some unknown bureaucrat, blessed with the stirrings of enlightenment, was offering Explorers the chance to Awaken.

Or was that wishful thinking? Given the stupidity displayed by people in power, why should I believe secret wisdom was at work? More likely, the Explorer Corps resulted from age-old hatreds against those who looked different, disguised as a branch of the navy because the League didn't allow the outright slaughter of pariahs.

Or perhaps it was the ultimate deterrent to discourage bioengineering: don't gene-splice your children, or we'll force them to become Explorers.

2

Klesha [Sanskrit]: Poison. Used to describe any mental attitude that leads to disruptive fixations.

I GRADUATED from the Explorer Academy four days after I turned nineteen. A week later, I was assigned to the frigate *Pistachio*. The name made me laugh when I heard it; but tradition dictated that all vessels in the Outward Fleet be named after Old Earth trees, and only big ships got majestic titles like *Ironwood* or *Sequoia*. Little ships like ours (a crew of thirty-five plus a handful of cadets-in-training) had to settle for names of less grandeur . . . and just be thankful we weren't *Sassafras*, *Kumquat*, or *Gum*.

For two months after my arrival, I did nothing except "button-polishing"—the mundane chores required to keep my equipment in top condition. *Pistachio* didn't have anything else for me to do. Explorers on a starship filled the same niche as marines on old seagoing boats: while the regular crew ran the ship, we did whatever else was necessary. Landing on hostile planets. Boarding civilian craft suspected of breaking safety regulations. Helping to evacuate vessels in distress.

But *Pistachio* never had any such missions. We were just a utility ship, running straightforward errands in the tamest regions of space—mostly transporting personnel and materials. *Pistachio*'s uninspiring work never demanded an Explorer's specialized skills. Therefore, I idled away my days like a firefighter in monsoon season, filling the time with preventive maintenance: inspecting the tightsuits we'd use for landings, calibrating my Bumbler (an all-purpose scanning/analysis device), checking the charge in my stun-pistol, and generally inventing work to keep myself from self-destructive boredom.

Despite years of rejection and being an Ugly Screaming Stink-Girl, I was still "unskillful" at finding things to do on my own. In the Academy, I'd had classwork every waking moment. I'd also had fellow students who knew how it felt to watch pleasure-palace people reel away from you in disgust. On *Pistachio*, however, I'd entered a social vacuum with no friends and no pressing duties. No mother to fight with. No coping skills.

I thought I would die from loneliness—not the sharp, aching kind but the dull, ongoing blur. It can feel like fatigue that never goes away; it can feel like dissatisfaction with everything around you; it can even feel like lust, as you lie alone in the dark and pretend someone else is there.

But it's loneliness. Deep, helpless, hopeless.

I tried to clear my head with meditation, but never managed more than half an hour at a sitting. Not nearly enough to ease my restlessness. If I'd been back home, I'd have asked a spiritual master what I was doing wrong . . . but no one on *Pistachio* could help me, and I certainly couldn't help myself.

I found myself prowling the ship corridors at night, hoping something would happen. The engines exploding. Falling in love. Having a mystic vision. Getting a nice piece of mail.

Now and then, I contemplated becoming a drunk or nymphomaniac. Wasn't it traditional for bored, lonely people to plunge into petty vice? But that was more Western than Eastern; when Bamars went stir-crazy, they usually shaved their heads, stopped bathing, and starved themselves into oblivion. Which I might have done, except that head-shaving, etc. were favorite tricks of my mother when she wasn't getting enough attention. I swore I wouldn't go that route.

For a while, I tried to exhaust myself dancing: in my cabin, in the Explorer equipment rooms, in the corridors when I was alone. But every place on *Pistachio* felt cramped, except a few big areas like the transport bay, which always had people around. I couldn't bring myself to dance with regular crew members watching. Anyway, I hadn't danced much since I'd entered the Explorer Academy. My ballet was rusty, my flamenco lacked rhythm, my yein pwe had no grace, my derv just made me dizzy, and my freestyle . . . every time I started something loose and sinewy I ended up as tight as wire—stamping my feet and shedding hot tears, though I couldn't say what I was crying about.

Maybe I cried because I'd lost the flow. Once upon a time, I'd had the potential to be a dancer. Now I'd never be anything but an Explorer.

So in the end, like most Explorers, I took up a hobby. My choice was sculpture. Making figurines out of clay, wire, copper leaf, and the small industrial-grade gems that *Pistachio*'s synthesizer system could produce. I found myself constructing male and female "Gotamas": princes and princesses trapped in ornate palaces that resembled Fabergé eggs. I molded expressions of horror on my Gotamas' faces as they looked through windows in their eggs and caught their first glimpses of the world outside.

After a while, I found myself spending so much time on art that I skimped on bathing and eating. I didn't shave my hair off, though—just cut it short to keep it out of my eyes.

I said I had no friends. That was true. I did, however, have a partner: a fellow Explorer. Unfortunately, he was insane.

He was a lanky loose-limbed twenty-four-year-old beanpole who called himself Tut: short for King Tutankhamen, whom Tut resembled. More specifically, he resembled Tutankhamen's funerary mask. Tut had somehow got his face permanently plated with a flexible gold alloy at the age of sixteen.

Before being metallized, he'd lived with a facial disfigurement as severe as my own. He wouldn't describe the exact nature of his problem, but once he told me, "Hey, Mom"—he always called me "Mom" because I'd introduced myself as Ma Youn Suu and "Ma" was the only syllable that stuck in Tut's brain—"Hey, Mom, I decided I'd rather soak my face in molten metal than stay the way I was. Paint your own picture."

I doubted that Tut had truly immersed his face in liquid gold (melting point 1063°C), but I couldn't rule it out. He was one of those rare individuals—always perfectly lucid, yet thoroughly out of his mind. If Tut had found himself in the same room as a vat of molten gold, he might well take one look at the bubbling metal, and think, "I could stick my face in that." Two seconds later, he'd be ears deep in yellow magma.

That was the way Tut's brain worked. Odd notions struck him several times a minute, and he couldn't judge whether those notions were merely unusual or utterly deranged. For example, he was obsessed with keeping the gold on his face "shiny-finey clean," so he constantly experimented with different kinds of polish—not just the usual oils and waxes, but also materials like ketchup, the ooze from my cheek, pureed mushrooms in hot chocolate, and his own semen. Once while we were talking in my cabin, he began going through my things, trying every garment I owned to see how well it buffed up his complexion . . . all while we were discussing a complicated technical bulletin on new procedures for taking alien soil samples. Every now and then, after he'd finished rubbing his metal forehead with my panties or the toe of my ballet shoe, he'd turn from the mirror and ask, "What do you think? Shiny-finey?" I'd say I couldn't see any difference, he'd nod, and we'd go back to debating the niceties of separating extraterrestrial worms from extraterrestrial loam.

In Tut's defense I'll admit he was a skilled Explorer. He'd graduated from the Academy five years before I had, and his grades had been excellent. He'd even won an award in microbiology, his field of specialization. (My specialization was biochem . . . a natural choice after all the hours I'd spent analyzing the fluid from my cheek.)

Tut was the sort to throw himself unreservedly into whatever he chose to do. He was a quick learner and possessed a high degree of patience—an *obsessive* degree of patience. I never had cause to criticize his handling of equipment or his knowledge of operating procedures.

But Tut was as mad as a mongoose. Not violently so—since he was still alive after five years in space, the League of Peoples obviously didn't consider him a threat to others. I often enjoyed his company, and found him helpful as a mentor: he'd had five years' on-the-job experience, and he taught me many things my academic training hadn't covered.

But none of that mattered. How could I trust a lunatic in life-or-death situations? Why was Tut on active duty when anyone could see he was *non compos mentis*?

I asked him that once. Tut just laughed. "They don't need us sane, Mom. They just need us ready to bleed." He chucked his finger under my chin like a fond uncle amused by his young niece. "If they rejected head cases, Mom, you wouldn't be here either."

I was so affronted by his insinuation I stormed out of the room, stomped back to my cabin, and made thirteen statues of little gold-faced men being disemboweled by tiger-headed demons. When I showed Tut the results, he said, "Shiny-finey! Could I eat one?" I told him no, but later I noticed my favorite demon was missing.

Two months and fifty-four statuettes later, we finally received a distress call.

At the time, *Pistachio* was transporting twelve dignitaries to the planet Cashleen: six officers from the navy's Diplomatic Corps and six civilian envoys from the Technocracy's Bureau of Foreign Affairs. Since Tut and I had no immediate duties, we always got assigned to play host for any honored guests who came aboard . . . but this particular group of VIPs took one look at my face and instantly became self-sufficient. My cheek had the wondrous power to make the mighty say, "No, no, I can do my own laundry."

So I'd had little contact with the diplomats on that flight. I didn't even know what their mission was. However, Cashleen was the homeworld of the Cashling race—longtime allies of the Technocracy—so I assumed this was just the routine diplomacy that goes on between friendly powers.

The team of envoys certainly didn't behave as if their trip was important. Instead of preparing for the work ahead, they spent most the voyage getting drunk and trying to seduce the better-looking members of *Pistachio*'s crew. For the entire week of the flight, Tut never went to bed alone. He told me, "Hey, Mom, everyone loves to lick gold. Did you think it was just on my face?" I consoled myself with the observation that people might be eager to sleep with him once, but nobody did it a second time.

I'd never slept with Tut myself. I'd never slept with anyone. An honest-to-goodness virgin. Not literally, of course—I'd manually ruptured my maidenhead within twenty-four hours of learning what it was . . . mostly to spite my mother, who'd given me an infuriating lecture on remaining intact. Only afterward did I stop to think: *Yes, I've done it, but how will my mother know?* Any "discovery scenario" I could imagine made me nauseated. Later on, I found that the thought of sex made me nauseated too. How could anyone want to do that with somebody who looked like me? Pity? Depravity? A lust so intense it didn't give a damn what it fucked? I couldn't conceive of a single acceptable reason why someone would sleep with me, so I fled every situation where the possibility might arise.

I was in my cabin, gouging a little hole in a Princess Gotama's cheek so I could plant a pearl there, when the message buzzer sounded from my desk. Most likely, I thought, the diplomats wanted me to fetch another case of Divian champagne. They never wanted to see me in person, but they were quick to ask for booze to be left outside their doors. Without looking up, I said, "What is it now?"

The ship-soul's metallic voice spoke from the ceiling. "Explorer Youn Suu. Captain Cohen requests your presence on the bridge. Immediately."

I nearly threw my figurine across the room. "Is there a response code?" I asked as I rushed to the door.

"No." Which meant the captain hadn't yet decided how to resolve the impending crisis. I had no doubt there *was* a crisis—not just because I'd been called to the bridge "immediately" but because the call came straight from the captain to me.

I was a wet-behind-the-ears Explorer Third Class. Tut was not only more experienced than I, but he outranked me: as an Explorer Second Class, he was my superior officer. Protocol demanded that the captain address all Explorer matters to Tut, who would then bring me in if he chose. Going over Tut's head to call me directly meant the captain thought the situation was so serious it couldn't be left to a madman.

(Cohen knew Tut was crazy. Everybody knew. They just pretended otherwise until their backs were to the wall.)

Pistachio's bridge was small, made smaller by two diplomats who filled the space with bustling self-importance.

One was a woman no older than I. Black skin, no hair, scalp bleached paper white and covered with complex abstract tattoos in royal purple. With flawless skin and bone structure, she was almost certainly a test-tube baby like me . . . but from the boutique end of the black market. Tall. Strong. Amazonian. Beautifully proportioned, but with muscles like a giant panther. She wore the gold uniform of a commander in the navy's Diplomatic Corps, plus three nonregulation diamond-stud pierce-bars mounting the bridge of her nose—a perfect example of the privileged thoroughbreds who pranced their way through the Outward Fleet's DipCor. For centuries, our military diplomats had made themselves rich through bribe-taking, blackmail, and investments based on confidential information. Then they'd established diplomatic dynasties, bringing their offspring into the corps and speedily promoting them to lucrative posts. (Nobody my age could have *earned* the rank of commander.) Over the years, DipCor had become a family-run business, full of intermarried bluebloods with inflated egos and bank accounts: the last people you'd trust to work out vital treaties. These hereditary princes and princesses didn't just live in the pleasure palace—they *owned* it. The woman in front of me turned in my direction, then quickly looked away . . . unaccustomed to sullying her eyes with beautyless things.

The other diplomat was a fortyish man, a civilian well tailored and well fed. He smelled of alcohol and his eyes were bloodshot. When he opened his mouth to yawn, his tongue was practically white, coated with the telltale signs of hangover. Or perhaps with gold dust from Tut. Unlike the female diplomat, this man didn't avert his eyes when he saw me. He glared with utter disgust, not only despising my blemished cheek but my face as a whole, the cells in my body, and everything down to the subatomic level. In his mind, I was obviously made from the wrong kind of quarks.

"You took long enough!" he growled. His voice suggested he was the sort of diplomat who eagerly volunteered for missions where he got to make threats.

"Youn Suu took a mere forty-three seconds from the time I first called her to the moment she appeared on the bridge." Those words came from the one person I knew in the room, Captain Abraham Cohen. In a low voice, he added, "Thought I should get the exact time . . . in case one of these schmuck diplomats decided to kvetch."

Captain Cohen's eyes twinkled at me. He was a delicate wispy-haired man who loved to play the fond Jewish grandpa. Often he could be charming, but sometimes I wanted to shout in his face, *I've already got a grandfather!* My occasional annoyance at Cohen, however, was nothing compared to Tut's. Tut was utterly obsessed with our captain—particularly the possibility that Cohen might be a fraud. One night, Tut had walked into my cabin at three in the morning, sat on the edge of my bed, and whispered without preamble, "Nobody's really called Abraham Cohen. It's too much, Mom. Abraham Cohen. *Abe* Cohen. The name has to be fake. I'll bet he's never even met a real Jew. He steals all that Yiddish from bad movies. You want to help me pull down his pants and see if he's circumcised?"

I'd declined. Tut left and disappeared for three days, during which time his only communication was a text message from the brig listing all the cultures besides Judaism that practiced circumcision.

There was more than one reason why Cohen would rather talk to me than to Tut.

"Youn Suu," the captain said, swiveling in his command chair to face the diplomats, "this is Commander Miriam Ubatu and Ambassador Li Chin Ho. Commander, Ambassador, this is Explorer Youn Suu. First in her class at the Academy." (Cohen always introduced me that way. I'd actually been second in my class, but every time I tried to correct the captain's claim, he chose not to hear.) "Youn Suu will know what's going on, you watch." He swiveled back to me. "Five minutes ago, we received a distress call from our embassy on Cashleen. There's been trouble."

"At the embassy?"

"No. In a Cashling city named Zoonau. The embassy sent us footage."

Cohen turned a dial on the arm of his chair. The bridge's main vidscreen changed from an unremarkable starscape to a picture of what must be Zoonau. It looked like a typical Cashling city—enclosed in a giant glass dome and devoted to one of the five "Worthy Themes" that fascinated the ancient city-builders: water, mirrors, shadow, illusion, and knots.

Zoonau was dedicated to knots. The buildings were made of dull gray concrete, bland and unpainted, which might have produced a drab panorama; but every skyscraper body turned in twists and bends, even full loops and elaborate braids, made possible by carefully placed antigrav fields, which prevented unbalanced weight distributions from causing structural collapse. No street ran straight—they all intertwined, circling, crossing, passing over or under each other. It was a profusely contorted labyrinth: like living in a mandala.

Fortunately, Cashling cities had computerized voice-guides built into every streetlamp, able to direct passersby toward any desired destination. And if you didn't like the roundabout nature of the streets, you could always get above the problem. Every twenty paces, knotted ropes rose from the ground, strung all the way to the dome. Cross-cords connected from rope to rope, along with the occasional solid rope bridge and macramé walkways that offered far more direct routes than the streets below. At one time, Cashlings must have been as nimble and strong as orangutans if they found such traverses practical.

But no longer. Even if Cashlings were physically able to clamber through rope jungles, they couldn't be bothered. In the footage of Zoonau displayed on the vidscreen, every single Cashling was down on the ground . . . and not doing much of anything.

Cashlings were roughly humanoid, with two legs, two arms, and one head; but they had almost no torso, so their gawky legs reached nearly to their armpits. Though none in the vidscreen picture wore clothes, they showed all the colors of the rainbow, plus quite a few shades no self-respecting rainbow would tolerate. Cashling skins were naturally adorned with vivid swirls, stripes, and spottles. Each individual had unique coloration, and most augmented their birth appearance by adding tattoos, slathering themselves with cosmetics, and randomly juggling their pigmentation genes.

But making themselves more eye-catching was the Cashlings' only field of expertise. Otherwise, they were laughingstocks: a race of lazy fools, practically incapable of taking care of themselves. Their species would have died out from sheer incompetence, except that less decadent ancestors had created cities like Zoonau: fully automated self-repairing havens that satisfied all the residents' needs. Cashling cities served as nannies to creatures who remained pompously infantile their whole lives.

As I watched, flecks of red began drifting from the top of Zoonau's dome. The flecks looked like blood-colored snow. Soft. Slightly fuzzy. Floating gently. Not real snow—more like airborne seeds. I'd seen pictures of Earth thistle fields lost in blizzards of their own thistledown . . . and numerous nonterrestrial plants also emitted clouds of offspring, sometimes so profusely they could smother unwary Explorers. I wasn't aware of such plants on Cashleen, but I'd never studied Cashling botany. Explorers cared more about the vegetation on uncharted planets than on worlds that were safely developed.

The red seed-fall started to settle: a dusting of crimson on the streets, soon thickening into solid mossy beds. The Cashlings themselves seemed untouched—not the tiniest speck on their colored hides. A few tried to catch seeds drifting past, but when they opened their hands, their palms were empty. The vidscreen showed one Cashling man bending to pick up a handful of the stuff . . . maybe thinking he could make a snowball. But as he reached down, the red particles fled: slipping just out of reach. When he withdrew his hand, the red seed-things flowed like water, back to where they'd been.

"So, Youn Suu," Cohen said. "Do you know what the red stuff is?"

I hesitated. Crimson particles. Able to move so they couldn't be grabbed. Forming into thick patches. Like moss . . .

The streets were now coated except for tiny clear patches around each Cashling's feet; and the blizzard was still falling. Getting thicker. The camera barely penetrated the cloud of red, but I could make out the wall of a building . . . and moss climbing that wall as fast as a human could walk . . . climbing the ropes too, spreading across the whole knotted network until every rope looked like cord covered with plush crimson velvet . . .

Red moss. That could move. That could see the Cashlings and get out of their way.

A chill went through me. I said, "It's the Balrog."

Balrog?" echoed Ambassador Li. "What's a Balrog?"

"A highly advanced creature," I said. "Much more intelligent than humans."

I looked at the picture again. The moss had begun to glow: shining dimly as the city grew darker. Mats of fuzzy red clotted on Zoonau's glass dome, cutting off sunlight from outside. Streetlamps flickered to life, but their bulbs were already covered with crimson fuzz. "The moss goes by many names," I continued, trying to keep my voice even, "but when interacting with *Homo sapiens*, it calls itself the Balrog. The name refers to a fictional monster from Earth folklore, originally appearing in J. R. R. Tolkien's—"

Li made a strangled sound and kneaded his temples as if I'd aggravated his hangover headache. Neither he nor Ubatu was seated—*Pistachio*'s small bridge had no guest chairs, and safety regulations forbade visitors from sitting at an active control station unless they were qualified to operate the station's equipment—so Li just tottered shakily from one foot to the other until he overcame whatever spasm had gripped him. "Explorer," he said in a forced voice, "we don't want your thoughts on literature. Stick to what's relevant."

"This *is* relevant," I replied. "When an intelligent alien adopts a name from human mythology, it's making a statement. If you met an extraterrestrial that introduced itself as Count Dracula, would you let it near your throat?"

"He would if it offered him trade concessions," Ubatu said.

"Now, now," murmured Captain Cohen, "no garbage talk on my bridge." He turned back to me. "Go on, Youn Suu. Tell us about Balrogs."

"It's not *Balrogs* plural." I gestured toward the screen as Zoonau continued to disappear under a blanket of red. "That's all one creature: *the* Balrog. It's a single consciousness, distributed over quadrillions of component units usually called spores. And the spores have been found on hundreds of worlds throughout the galaxy."

"So it's a hive mind?" Li muttered. "I hate those things."

"Yes, Ambassador," I said, "it's a hive mind. The spores stay in constant telepathic contact with each other, regardless of how far apart they are. *Instantaneous* contact, even when separated by thousands of light-years. The Balrog is like a single brain with lobes in different star systems, but still intellectually integrated. Some experts believe hive minds are the next evolutionary step above individual creatures like ourselves. We've certainly encountered lots of hive minds in our galaxy: not just the Balrog, but the Lucifer, the Myshilandra, possibly Las Fuentes—"

"Hold it," Li interrupted. He was massaging his temples again. "Let's get something clear. How smart is this Balrog?"

"Smarter than *Homo sapiens* and our usual alien trading partners," I said. "How much smarter, nobody knows. The Balrog is so far beyond humans, when we try to measure its intelligence, we're like two-year-olds trying to rank the IQs of Newton and Einstein."

Li curled his lip in disgust. "How typical. Explorers love saying that humans are idiots. You *enjoy* thinking you're at the bottom of the heap. That's where you're comfortable."

"Now, now," Captain Cohen murmured.

"No, really," Li said. "What makes her think this Balrog is smart? Better technology?" The ambassador waved his hand dismissively. "Better technology isn't a matter of intelligence; it's just how long you've been in the game. We have better machines today than the ancient Chou Dynasty, but we're not a milligram smarter."

"Oh God," Ubatu groaned. "He's going to quote Confucius again."

"Ambassador Li," I said (all the while watching the city of Zoonau being buried alive), "you don't grasp the nature of superior intelligence. Suppose you create a brand-new intelligence test. Give it to average humans, and they'd finish in, say, an hour, probably with a number of mistakes. Give it to the most intelligent people in the Technocracy, and they might finish in half the time, with almost no mistakes. But if you approach the Balrog with your test in hand, it'll say, 'What took you so long? I've been waiting for you to show up since last Saturday. I got so bored, I've already finished.' Then it will hand you a mistake-free copy of the test you just invented. The Balrog can foresee, hours or days or months in advance, exactly what questions a person like you would invent. It doesn't read your mind, it *knows* your mind. *That's* superior intelligence."

Li snorted in disbelief. I wondered why. Because he couldn't imagine a universe where he wasn't on the top rung? "Look," I said, "when we classify the Balrog as 'beyond human intelligence,' we don't mean it's faster or more accurate in mundane mental tasks. *We mean it can do things humans can't.* In particular, the Balrog displays an uncanny ability to intuit *Homo sapiens* thoughts and actions. Not just vague predictions but precise details of what we're going to do far into the future."

Li looked like he was going to interrupt. I went on before he could. "You may be thinking of quantum uncertainty and chaos theory: principles of human science that imply the future is inherently unpredictable. You're right, that's what human science says—which only proves the point. Humans are so stupid and self-centered, we think everything else in the universe has to be as limited as we are. But we're wrong. The Balrog has demonstrated repeatedly it can predict the actions of lesser creatures like us. If you don't believe that's possible . . . then you're a typical human, regarding yourself as the standard by which everything else should be measured."

"And what about you?" Li sneered. "Aren't you also hampered by human limitations? I suppose the less human you look—"

"Now, now," Cohen interrupted, waggling a scrawny finger at the ambassador. "Now, now."

"Explorers are just as limited as other humans," I said. "The difference is we recognize our limitations. Otherwise . . ." I took a breath to catch my temper. "Do you know how we first learned about the Balrog? I'll tell you. An Explorer took a single wrong step."

Ubatu looked up. "That sounds interesting. I don't know this part." As if she already possessed extensive familiarity with superior alien intelligence, so hadn't bothered to listen. Now, however, her nostrils flared as if she'd caught the smell of blood. I wondered if, like many of the most privileged in the pleasure palace, Ubatu had a ghoulish streak. Fascinated by tales of other people's suffering. She said, "I assume you have an amusing story to tell?"

"Not amusing but important," I said. "If you're ready to listen."

Li had gone back to rubbing his temples. He didn't speak—didn't even glance in my direction. I decided this was as attentive as he'd allow himself to be . . . so I began to tell the tale.

* * *

"You can see what the Balrog looks like." I nodded toward the vidscreen. The streets and buildings of Zoonau were completely lost under crimson fuzz. Cashlings, still untouched, either stood afraid to move or wandered in a daze. The Balrog slipped silently out from under the feet of the wanderers, then slid back after they'd passed, obliterating their footprints with spores of glowing red. The glow was brighter now, like the embers of a fire just before it's fanned into a blaze.

"When the Balrog isn't glowing or overwhelming a city," I said, "it looks like nothing special. A patch of colored moss. Most humans would pass it without thinking . . . which is what a woman named Kaisho Namida did. Thirty years ago, she was an Explorer on a survey of some unnamed planet, and she stepped on a bit of nondescript red moss. No human had ever encountered the Balrog before, so Kaisho didn't know what it was. She found out soon enough. The instant her foot came down, the Balrog ripped through Kaisho's boot like paper and injected spores into her flesh."

Cohen, Li, and Ubatu looked toward the vidscreen. In Zoonau, moss was still dodging out of the Cashlings' way. "As you can see," I said, "the Balrog is mobile. *Very* mobile. We think it can teleport across the galaxy in seconds. If it didn't want to be stepped on, it could easily have got out of Kaisho's way. But it didn't. It waited for her to step down, then it took her like lightning—sending spores through her bloodstream, her nervous system, every tissue in her body."

Ubatu's face was keen. "You say it *took* her. Like a parasitic infestation?"

"Yes. The spores invaded all her major organs."

"Did she die?"

"No. She felt almost nothing—just a pain in her foot where the spores had entered. Her partner rushed her to medical treatment, and that's when the doctors found bits of Balrog throughout her body. They considered chemotherapy to see if they could kill the spores without killing Kaisho . . . but before they could start treatment, the Balrog took possession of Kaisho's mouth and said the magic words."

"What magic words?" Li asked.

"*Greetings*," I recited, "*I am a sentient citizen of the League of Peoples. I beg your Hospitality.*"

Cohen gave a little chuckle. "This parasite waltzed into a woman's body like cancer, then asked to be treated nicely? That's chutzpah."

"True," I said. "But the Balrog had done nothing to violate League of Peoples' law. It hadn't killed anyone. Kaisho was still in excellent health. On the other hand, if the doctors tried to kill the spores inside her body, maybe the doctors would be guilty of killing sentient creatures."

"Why?" Li asked. "Killing a few spores in a hive mind doesn't hurt the organism as a whole. Last night I served champagne for dinner—killed a few cells in people's brains and livers—but the League didn't come after me for murder."

"The League cares a lot about motive," I said. "Presumably, you served that champagne to be hospitable—not to commit deliberate homicide on cells you thought were sentient beings. But if the doctors had injected Kaisho with chemicals intentionally designed to kill spores they knew to be sentient . . ." I shrugged. "You can never tell with the League. Common sense may say one thing, but you can't help wondering if the League thinks the opposite. And where will they draw the line? If a doctor is declared nonsentient for killing Balrog spores, will the League blame the hospital for not preventing the crime? Will they blame the navy for improper supervision of the hospital? Will they blame the entire Technocracy?"

"Oy," said Cohen. "These things always make my head hurt."

Li growled and continued to massage his temples.

"In the end," I said, "no one was willing to risk removing the Balrog—especially since Kaisho seemed unharmed. They sent her to a navy rehab center to monitor her condition, and nobody ever again suggested killing the spores."

"So that's it?" Ubatu asked. "Nothing happened?" She didn't bother to hide her disappointment.

Without answering, I walked to a tiny control console stuffed into the bridge's back corner. The console saw little use on *Pistachio*—it was the station from which we Explorers would operate reconnaissance probes if we ever got a planet-down mission. Once a week in the middle of the night, Tut and I used the station to run drills and diagnostics; otherwise, the equipment gathered dust.

I sat down to search through some files. When I found the photograph I wanted, I displayed it on the vidscreen, replacing the footage from Zoonau. "This," I said, "is Kaisho Namida today."

The picture showed a woman in a wheelchair. Her face was hidden behind long salt-and-pepper strands of hair; these days, she combed her hair forward to conceal her features. But I doubted if many people ever lifted their gaze as high as her head. They'd be too busy staring at the continuous bed of glowing red moss that reached from her toes, up her legs to her pelvis, and on as high as her navel.

Though it couldn't be seen in the photo, I knew the moss wasn't just an outer coating. Her legs had no flesh left, no blood, no bone—they were solid moss through and through, still shaped like the limbs they'd once been, but entirely nonhuman.

No one knew what remained of Kaisho's lower abdomen. Three years after her "accident," she'd checked out of rehab, got discharged from the navy, and refused further medical exams. Now, with the moss grown above her waist, did she still have intestines and reproductive organs somewhere beneath? Or was there just moss, a thick undifferentiated wad of it from belly to spine?

Ubatu and Li leaned forward. I'd finally caught their full attention.

"Is it *eating* her?" Li asked.

"Not precisely," I said. "The spores get most of their energy from photosynthesis, so they aren't consuming her for simple sustenance. They *are* breaking down her tissues and using the component chemicals to build new spores."

Li was now holding his stomach instead of his head. "Why the hell doesn't the League do something? This Balrog is devouring a sentient woman."

"But it's not *killing* her. Kaisho is still very much alive. And given the speed at which she's being consumed, she'll live a full human life span before the moss finishes her off. Possibly longer. The Balrog isn't just absorbing her, it's changing her. The spores keep her arteries free of plaque; and her heart is as strong as a teenager's, even though she's now . . ." I looked at a data display on my console. "She's now one hundred and sixteen years old."

"Oy." Captain Cohen was also leaning forward in his chair, staring at the moss-laden woman. "So what does poor Kaisho think about this? Me, I'd cut off my legs as soon as I saw moss growing."

"That wouldn't have helped," I said. "The moss had permeated her internal organs long before it showed outside. Amputate the visible spores, and there'd still be plenty in her heart, her lungs, her bloodstream—everywhere. As for Kaisho's opinion of what's happening to her . . ." I tried to speak without inflection. "She's thrilled to have been chosen as the Balrog's host. It's transforming her into something glorious. She admits that her primitive brain sometimes panics at the thought of being cannibalized, but her higher mental functions soon reassert themselves, and she recognizes the privilege she's been given. Kaisho is deeply, joyously, in awe of the Balrog and loves it without reserve."

"In other words," said Li, "she's been brainwashed."

"The spores," I said, "have suffused every part of Kaisho's nervous system, including the brain. When she speaks, we have to assume it's the Balrog talking, not whatever remains of the original woman."

"You think there's some Kaisho left?" Cohen asked.

"The Balrog can't entirely obliterate her human personality; that would upset the League. The spores must have preserved enough of Kaisho's psyche that she's still technically alive."

"Oh good," said Li. "So she's conscious enough to *know* she's being eaten, enslaved, and brainwashed."

Ubatu flinched. She mumbled something under her breath, then turned her back on both Li and the vidscreen.

"Forgive an old man his senility," Captain Cohen said, "but what is the Balrog's point? If it's so inhumanly smart, why's it doing this? Kaisho . . . Zoonau . . . what does it want?"

"I can't answer about Zoonau," I told him. "As for Kaisho, there are plenty of theories why the Balrog took her, but they're all just speculation. The only thing we can say for sure is that the Balrog's action was premeditated—it can predict human actions with a high degree of accuracy, so it must have known when and where Kaisho would be. It waited for her at the perfect spot for an ambush. Then it took her the moment she came within reach."

"Did it want this Kaisho in particular," Li asked, "or was she chosen at random?"

"Only the Balrog knows."

"Damn." The ambassador paced a few steps, then turned back to me. "Has it ever taken anyone else?"

I checked. "There's nothing in navy records."

"Has it ever done anything like it's doing to Zoonau?"

This time I knew the answer without doing a data search. "A few years ago, the Balrog attacked an orbital habitat belonging to the Fasskisters. It overgrew the entire place—coated every square millimeter."

"Ah!" Li said, rubbing his hands together. "Now we're getting a pattern. Did it leave the Fasskisters themselves untouched the way it's leaving the Cashlings?"

I shook my head. "You know that Fasskisters are puny little aliens who encase themselves in robot armor? Big powered suits that compensate for the Fasskisters' physical weakness? Well, the Balrog covered each Fasskister suit with a thick mass of spores that disrupted the mechanical control systems. The Fasskisters ended up imprisoned like knights in suits of rusted metal. Kaisho, speaking for the Balrog, said the Fasskisters would be kept immobilized for twenty years. Their life-support systems would stay operative, and they'd be supplied with whatever they needed to survive, but they wouldn't be allowed to move till the Balrog let them go."

"Did she say why the Balrog did it?" Cohen asked.

"As punishment. Apparently the Fasskisters had captured a few Balrog spores and locked them in containment bottles. Then they used the spores' long-range telepathy as a private communication system. The Balrog was furious at having bits of itself kidnapped to serve as someone else's intercom. It imprisoned the Fasskisters as vengeance."

"Vengeance." Li echoed the word as if he liked the sound. "Do you think that's the reason for Zoonau?"

I shrugged. "Cashlings aren't noted for prudence. They might have done something to make the Balrog angry."

Li nodded. "They annoy the crap out of me every time I meet them. And they're greedy too. I could easily picture them trying to exploit the Balrog and getting the damned moss mad."

"Do you think that's it?" Cohen asked me. "You know this Balrog better than we do."

I didn't answer—I just turned a dial on my console. The picture of Kaisho disappeared, and the screen returned to Zoonau. No significant change in the picture. A few Cashlings were talking into comm implants now, holding animated discussions. Knowing Cashlings, they probably weren't calling home to check on loved ones; they'd be contacting local news services, trying to sell their stories. TRAPPED BY A MOSS MONSTROSITY: MY TERRIFYING ORDEAL! Others were no doubt calling politicians, bureaucrats, anyone who'd answer. The people of Zoonau would howl to government officials, and those officials (eager to pass the buck) would call our Technocracy consulate for help . . . wailing, "Please, we can't handle this on our own."

Although our consuls were probably sick of Cashlings whining, this particular crisis would elicit a quick response . . . because people at our consulate knew that sooner or later, some Cashling in Zoonau would fight back.

Cashlings seldom turned nasty. They were usually too lazy, vain, and petulant to take forceful action against obstacles they met. When something went wrong, they'd complain, complain, complain to other species till somebody bailed them out.

But even a race of useless idlers had some few individuals with sparks of spirit. In Zoonau, some Cashling would eventually be pushed beyond its limits, becoming so angry or upset it would stir into action.

Like trying to set Balrog spores on fire.

Or dousing them with dangerous chemicals.

Or simply smashing them with a rock, over and over and over.

Which would be understandable . . . but we couldn't let it happen.

Not that I feared for the Balrog's health. If it didn't want to get burned, doused, or smashed, its spores would just avoid the attack. This was a creature that could teleport . . . and could foresee the actions of lesser beings far in advance. The Balrog wouldn't let itself get hit unless it wanted to.

But the Cashlings of Zoonau didn't know that. Cashlings were bottomless pits of ignorance when it came to most other species. And if some Cashling tried to pummel a clump of moss, the League would regard that action as attempted homicide: deliberately intending to kill sentient Balrog spores. The Cashling responsible would be considered a dangerous nonsentient. Furthermore, the Cashling government might be in trouble for not doing its utmost to avoid such violence; the Technocracy could be accused of negligence for not helping the Cashlings; and I myself might be considered callously indifferent if I saw this mess coming and did nothing to stop it.

"How old is this footage?" I asked. "When did the Balrog attack?"

"About an hour ago."

"Do we have anything more recent?"

Cohen shook his head. "The city's internal cameras aren't broadcasting anymore."

"Probably mossed over," said Li, stating the obvious.

So the Cashlings had been trapped for an hour. And the readouts on the console in front of me said it would take another hour for *Pistachio* to reach Cashleen. By which time, the people of Zoonau would be getting antsy.

"We have to go in as soon as we achieve orbit," I said. "Before one of those Cashlings does something we'll regret."

"Looks like it," the captain agreed. "We're the only non-Cashling ship in the star system."

"But suppose the Balrog is punishing the Cashlings," Ubatu said. She'd finally turned back to join our conversation. "Suppose the Balrog is punishing Zoonau like it punished those Fasskisters. If the Cashlings have done something to anger the Balrog, we have to think twice about coming in on the wrong side."

Li nodded. "We don't want to get caught in the middle. Otherwise, we might find our own cities covered in moss. This is just the sort of incident that could escalate—"

"Haven't you been listening?" I shouted. "Don't you understand?"

The bridge went silent. I could almost hear the echoes of my own voice ringing from the metal walls. Li looked shocked, like a man who'd never been yelled at before. Ubatu too—as if nineteen-year-olds in her world never felt the urge to scream. Cohen lifted his hand, about to pat my arm . . . which would only have made me more furious. But he must have realized this was not the time to play patronizing grandfather. He let his hand fall and said, "What?"

I took a shuddering breath. "Captain Cohen. Sir. The Balrog isn't going to misunderstand our presence. The Balrog timed its arrival exactly to catch *Pistachio* and reel us in. You yourself said we're the only non-Cashling ship in the star system."

I looked around. Nothing but blank faces. "The Balrog *wants* us to come," I said. "It's been waiting precisely for this moment. It could have hit Zoonau anytime, but it held off until we were near . . . because it knew the Cashlings would demand help, and we'd have no choice but to get involved."

"It wants *us*?" Ubatu whispered. "Why?"

"We'll have to go down and ask."

"What if it's . . . hungry?"

I looked her in the eye. "Just hope you're not the one it wants to eat."

3

Paticcasamupada [Pali]: Interconnectedness. The principle that nothing exists in isolation.

CASHLING authorities claimed the Zoonau dome was completely sealed off. They were wrong. Satellite photos showed that the Balrog had shut down Zoonau's transit ports—five conduit-sleeves connected to orbiting terminals, plus an iris-lens hole in the dome that let shuttlecraft enter and leave—but there was one access point the spores had left open: a door leading out of the city into the surrounding countryside.

I wasn't surprised the Balrog had left us an entry. It wanted us to come. It was waiting.

I also wasn't surprised the Cashlings had overlooked the open door. They simply wouldn't consider it a possible option. Cashlings never left their closed environments; if they wanted to travel from one city dome to another, they used shuttles, conduit-sleeves, or some other means of transport where they could shut themselves in metal cocoons. They *never* ventured outdoors . . . because the entire Cashling race had become agoraphobic: afraid of open spaces.

The ground entrance to Zoonau had been built centuries ago, likely as an emergency exit. True to form, the Cashlings had forgotten it was there. In a human community, such a casual attitude toward civic safety would be a crime. With Cashlings, it was probably better for them to stay inside the dome, even if the city was endangered by fire, flood, or some other disaster. If Zoonau's inhabitants fled to the wilds, they'd soon die from their own ineptitude.

Not that the wilds outside Zoonau were hostile. Satellite scans showed a temperate region of trees, meadows, and streams. Clear skies. Late spring. A few minutes after noon. You couldn't ask for a more pleasant landing. We didn't even have to worry about animal predators: according to navy records, all dangerous wildlife on Cashleen had been driven to extinction millennia ago. (Likely by accident. If the Cashlings had deliberately set out to exterminate unwanted species, they would have botched it the same way they botched everything else.)

So nothing prevented us from landing a negotiating team, flown down in Ambassador Li's luxury shuttle. The ambassador himself took the cockpit's command chair; he seemed more excited about the chance to play pilot than to talk to an alien superintelligence. As for Commander Ubatu, she arrived in the shuttle bay wearing her best dress uniform: form-fitting gold leaf, almost like a reverse of Tut (her face unadorned, but her body sheathed in shining metal). Li made some remark about the ridiculousness of formal navy garb, especially if Ubatu thought her wardrobe would impress a heap of alien moss. Ubatu replied she had to come along because she couldn't trust Li to handle the Balrog on his own.

Of course, Li *wasn't* on his own. Tut and I were there too. In the grand tradition of the Explorer Corps, we were required to thrust ourselves into the jaws of danger so that more valuable lives could remain safe. We'd been ordered to enter Zoonau, make first contact with the Balrog, and set up a comm relay for the diplomats outside. Li and Ubatu could then "engage the Balrog in frank freewheeling discussion" while Tut and I tried to keep the Cashlings from doing anything stupid.

Considering that Zoonau contained two hundred thousand people, Tut and I had no chance of controlling the city if things went sour. Our very arrival might set off a riot. I could imagine being mobbed by the first Cashlings who saw us. "Help, help, O how we've suffered!"

But if Tut and I were lucky, we could contact the Balrog without setting foot in Zoonau itself. What I've been calling a ground-level door was actually a type of airlock: a tube ten meters long passing through the dome, with one end connecting to the outside world and one to the streets of the city. If Balrog spores had spread into the tube, we could walk right up to them without being seen by Cashlings in the city proper. Even if the moss had stopped at the cityside door, we could get close but still stay in the tube, out of sight of Zoonau's residents.

At least that was the approach I suggested to Tut. He said, "Anything you want, Mom," as if he wasn't listening. When I asked if he had a better idea, he told me, "We'll see when we get there."

That set off warning signals in my head. I feared deranged notions had captured Tut's fancy, and he'd pull some stunt I'd regret. But he was my superior officer. I couldn't make him stay behind.

Despite his disdain for Ubatu's gold uniform, Li had dressed up too: donning a jade-and-purple outfit of silk, cut to make him look like a High-Confucian mandarin. Tut and I wore tightsuits of eye-watering brightness—his yellow, mine orange, to make it easier for us to keep visual contact with each other from a distance. I didn't plan on straying more than a step from Tut's side, but better safe than sorry.

The name "tightsuit" may suggest such suits cling tightly to one's flesh. Just the opposite. A tightsuit balloons at least a centimeter out from your body; it's "tight" because the interior is pressurized to make it bulge out taut, as if you're sealed inside an inflated tire. This is important on worlds with unknown microbes: if your suit gets a rip, the high internal pressure won't allow microorganisms to seep inside. It's only a temporary measure—if you're leaking, you'll soon deflate—but the pressure differential may last long enough for you to patch the hole.

That was the theory, anyway. The pressure hadn't protected Kaisho Namida from the Balrog . . . and I was more afraid of mossy red spores than the germs in Cashleen's atmosphere. I'd been inoculated against Cashling microbes—I'd been inoculated against all unsafe microbes on all developed planets—but there was no known medicine to hold the Balrog at bay.

Inside my suit, my feet itched . . . as if they could already feel themselves being pierced by spores.

Explorers seldom touched down lightly on alien planets. Our usual method of landing packed a much harder wallop than being flown in an ambassador's shuttle. Therefore, I'd scarcely realized we'd arrived before Tut bounded out to reconnoiter.

Li had set down on a small creek overgrown with Cashling soakgrass: a frost green reed that could grow profusely in shallow streams, forming deceptive "lawns" that hid the water beneath. A childish part of me wanted the diplomats to step out for a stroll in the "meadow." There was no real danger, since the stream was only knee deep, but I would have liked to see Li and Ubatu cursing at sloshy shoes. Instead, they both stayed in their plush swivel seats, not even glancing toward the door as I slipped out into the creek.

Water surged up my calves, but didn't penetrate the hermetically sealed fabric of my suit—not the tiniest sense of dampness. This particular suit could cope with temperatures from –100° to +100° Celsius, had a six-hour air supply, and was tough enough to withstand low-caliber gunfire. I felt foolish hiding inside such extreme protection when Li and Ubatu just wore conventional clothes. However, tightsuits were compulsory for Explorers in uncontrolled situations, and our foray into Zoonau definitely counted as uncontrolled. Besides, without the suit I wouldn't have had storage space for all the gear I wanted to carry. The suit's belt pouches and backpack let me bring every Exploration essential: my Bumbler, a first-aid kit, a few emergency supplies (light-wands, rope, food rations, a compass) . . . and my stun-pistol.

Many Explorers despised stun-pistols. The guns emitted hypersonic blasts, supposedly strong enough to knock out attacking predators on worlds where such predators lived; but the pistols often had no effect, since alien carnivores frequently didn't possess the sort of nervous system that could be frazzled by hypersonics. On the other hand, I didn't have to worry about dangerous animals on Cashleen. I *did* have to worry about Tut doing something irrational, and the gun would work fine on him. One shot, and he'd be unconscious for six hours.

By which time, the Balrog situation would be resolved, one way or another.

Tut did a few dozen stride-jumps on the riverbank. This was and wasn't a sign of derangement. Explorer policy strongly recommended loosening-up exercises at the start of mission: getting used to the feel of your tightsuit. However, stride-jumps weren't nearly as useful as slow stretches and rotating the joints (arm circles, hip circles, knee circles). Jumping around wildly just raised your body temperature and made your suit's air-conditioning work harder.

So I did some squats and extensions as I took stock of our situation. Zoonau's dome dominated the skyline fifty paces away. It rose more than a hundred stories high, a great glass hemisphere that sparkled in the midday sun. The sparkles were all blood red—the interior of the dome had clotted solid with spores, blocking any view of events inside.

The entry tube stood out from the rest of the dome, mostly because of its construction material: a gray pseudoconcrete that contrasted dully with the dome's glinting glass. I recognized the concrete look-alike as *chintah*—a Cashling word that meant "garden." Though it seemed like plain cement, *chintah* was a complex ecology of minerals, plants, and bacteria. Under normal conditions, *chintah*'s living components did little but hibernate, keeping themselves alive through photosynthesis or by eating dust from the air.

However, any damage to *chintah* set off a frenzied round of growth, like the scrub vegetation that rushes to fill gaps caused by forest fires. Within days, any gouges would be covered over with rapid response microorganisms. Then the microbes themselves would gradually be replaced by more solid growth, the way trees slowly reclaim land clogged with underbrush. *Chintah*'s complete healing process took a Cashling year . . . by which time all trace of the original damage would vanish.

So I wasn't surprised the *chintah* entry tube looked perfectly intact, despite centuries of wind, rain, and snow. What *did* surprise me was the door on the end: a flat slab of metal that should have rusted in place long ago. As I watched, the door swung open without a creak, exposing shadowy darkness beyond.

"Hey look, Mom!" Tut said. "Like a haunted house. Last one in is a zombie!"

He ran for the opening. I took a second too long debating whether to shoot him in the back with my stunner. By the time I unholstered my gun, Tut was out of range. Three seconds later, he reached the entry tube and disappeared inside.

I had no chance of catching him—I was a strong runner, but Tut was good too and his legs were longer than mine. When I reached the mouth of the tube, I found myself hoping he'd been stopped by a solid wall of moss closing off the tube's other end . . . but there were no spores in sight, and no Tut either. He must have sprinted straight through the passage, into the streets of Zoonau; and the Balrog had let him go.

Did that mean the Balrog approved of whatever scheme my crazy partner intended? Or was it possible the Balrog hadn't expected what Tut would do? The moss could predict the actions of *normal* humans; but what about the insane? Even the Balrog wasn't infallible—somehow, for example, those Fasskisters had caught the Balrog unawares, captured some spores, and used them in ways that made the Balrog furious. The Fasskisters had suffered for their presumption . . . but the incident showed the Balrog didn't anticipate *everything*. Sometimes lesser beings could still manage surprises.

"What are you up to, Tut?" I muttered.

As I entered the tube myself, I got out my Bumbler. It was a stocky cylindrical machine about the size of my head; in fact, two weeks earlier, Tut had painted eyes, nose, and mouth on both his Bumbler and mine. (I'd stopped him from smearing mayonnaise on the left sensor ports to simulate the goo on my cheek.) Naturally, Tut had used paint that withstood every solvent *Pistachio* kept in its storerooms . . . so Tut's portrait of my face stared back at me as I powered up the tracking unit.

The top surface of the Bumbler—the "scalp" area, if you're still picturing the machine as a head—was a flat vidscreen for displaying data. I keyed it to show where Tut was, as determined by a radio beacon I'd planted in his backpack when he wasn't looking. Generally, Explorers didn't use homing transmitters; they could be deadly on survey missions, especially if you were investigating a planet where carnivorous lifeforms could "hear" radio waves and use them to hunt prey. (Explorers found it unhealthy to be flashing a big loud "Come eat me" signal.) But that didn't matter on a tame planet like Cashleen . . . which is why I'd hidden a beeper in Tut's gear for exactly this kind of emergency.

A blip flashed on the Bumbler's screen: Tut, still running, heading deeper into the city. But the knotted nature of Zoonau's streets made it impossible to tell if he had a goal in mind or was just turning at random whenever he reached a corner. Either way, his path was a sequence of zigzags, loops, and switchbacks, reflected by the blip on my screen.

A voice yelled in my ear. "What's going on, Explorer?"

Ambassador Li. Who'd cranked up the volume on our shared comm link, either because he didn't know better or didn't care. I almost did the same with my own end of the link, but decided not to be petty.

"My partner," I said, "has proceeded ahead to reconnoiter. I'll be joining him in a moment."

"What's the Balrog doing?" That was Ubatu. Her voice sounded strangely eager . . . but I put that down to more ghoulish fascination with aliens that ate people.

"I don't have visual contact yet," I said. "Just a second."

I'd stopped halfway down the entry tube in order to use my Bumbler. Now I walked the rest of the way forward, feeling my heart thud in my chest. There were no Balrog spores directly in sight, but a dim ruby glow shone through the door in front of me, as if a bonfire burned just around the corner. I paused before the doorway, took a long slow breath, then peeked around the frame.

A glowing red face looked back at me. My own. Mouth open in shock. Which is surely how I looked myself.

I came perilously close to screaming, but reflexes kicked in and kept me from crying out. In fact, my reflexes kept me from doing *anything*.

As an ongoing experiment, the navy conditioned Explorers with one of three "instinctive" reactions to sudden shocks:

1. Dropping flat on the ground and staying down.
2. Diving, rolling, and ending up back on your feet in a fighting stance.
3. Freezing in place till you could think clearly again.

The goal was supposedly to see which response gave the best chance of surviving unexpected dangers . . . but most Explorers believed the Admiralty was just having fun at our expense. ("Let's make the freaks dance!")

I'd been assigned to the third group: I froze when something took me by surprise. After years of systematic programming—through classical stimulus-response, sleep induction, and "therapeutic sensory dep"—I could no more resist my conditioning than I could fly by flapping my arms. There in Zoonau, face-to-face with my glowing red look-alike, I stood paralyzed into impotent numbness.

Thought and motion returned simultaneously: I relaxed as I realized the face in front of me was only a sculpture—a topiary version of myself constructed from red moss. The Balrog had seen me coming . . . had known I'd stick my head around the doorframe . . . and had arranged a group of spores in my likeness to startle me.

You demon, I mouthed to the spores near my face. But I didn't say it aloud. Instead, I spoke the words that came almost as automatically to me as freezing in the face of danger. "Greetings," I told the statue. "I am a sentient citizen of the League of Peoples. I beg your Hospitality."

For a moment, nothing happened. Then the statue collapsed like a marionette with its strings cut. Slump, thud. The spores from the image quickly spread themselves out on the ground, joining the carpet of moss already there. A second later, all sign of my look-alike had vanished.

"Have you made contact with the Balrog?" Li asked over the comm link.

"Yes. But it didn't want to talk to me."

"Of course not. This is a job for diplomats. Set up the relay."

I refrained from mentioning that Explorers are trained in diplomacy, just as we're trained in planetary science, crisis management, and down-'n'-dirty survival. In fact, we received more formal training in diplomacy than the navy's Diplomatic Corps. It was an essential part of our jobs. After all, who got sent on First Contact missions? Who might encounter extraterrestrials at any time, and whose initial actions would set the course for future human–alien relations? The Explorer Corps. Diplomats didn't talk to anyone till Explorers broke the ice.

Which was what I was doing in Zoonau. Gauging the Balrog's mood. And since it didn't immediately want to eat me—nearby spores kept their distance from my feet—the situation seemed safe enough that I could turn the parlay over to Li and Ubatu.

As I worked to deploy the relay—just a small black box on a

chest-high tripod—I paused now and then to examine my surroundings. Moss covered everything like spray-foam insulation. Undifferentiated red coated every surface as far as the eye could see. Streets. Buildings. Rope walkways. Even the atmosphere was tinted red: the only light was the dusky crimson that filtered through the moss-clotted dome, plus the dim streetlamps just visible beneath masses of spores.

No Cashlings moved anywhere in sight. I assumed they'd run for cover into buildings. That raised the question of whether the Balrog would pursue them inside, or whether the moss would be content to remain in the street. If this attack on Zoonau was just a way to get *Pistachio*'s attention, the Balrog had already succeeded. Therefore, it had no need to bash its way into Cashling homes. On the other hand, the Balrog reportedly enjoyed terrifying lesser creatures . . . like putting that statue of me precisely where I'd be startled to maximum effect. If the Balrog liked such cheap scare tactics, it might invade Cashling homes just to hear them squeal.

You demon, I mouthed again.

Are you finished?" Li shouted in my ear.

"Yes, Ambassador." I turned the activation dial on the relay. Immediately, life-sized hologram images of Li and Ubatu appeared on either side of me, projected by the relay's black box. The images turned their heads back and forth, as if scanning the city . . . which is exactly what they were doing. Just as the relay projected images of the diplomats onto the streets of the city, it sent images of Zoonau back to Li and Ubatu—a two-way VR connection that would allow "face-to-face" negotiations while the diplomats remained safe in the shuttle.

"Good afternoon, Balrog," Li said, bowing toward the moss. The volume on his feed was now perfectly dulcet.

"Yes, good afternoon," said Ubatu. She knelt, head bowed, and pressed her palms together in front of her chest—much more obsequious behavior than I expected from a professional diplomat. The moss beneath her hologram knees made no effort to get out of the way. Spores avoided contact with real people, but apparently didn't bother to move for holos.

The diplomats began a prepackaged message of goodwill. While they talked, I looked down at my Bumbler. The blip showed that Tut was still running. Not as fast as before, but now he was traveling in a straight line. He must have clambered up into the network of ropes—they were the only straight thoroughfares in the city. It was perfectly possible Tut had hit the ropes just for the fun of swinging around like a monkey . . . but it was also possible he'd decided on a destination and was now taking the most direct route available.

That worried me.

Li and Ubatu were still talking. They'd got no response from the Balrog, but that didn't slow them down. ". . . pleased for the opportunity on this historic occasion . . ." I slipped away, my boots making no sound on Zoonau's pavement. When I looked down, I saw that my footfalls were being muffled by moss: the Balrog wasn't getting out of my way, but was helping keep my escape silent.

To the best of my knowledge, I was the first person to walk on the Balrog without getting bitten. Such an unprecedented distinction filled me with dread.

As soon as I rounded a corner, the spores pulled back from my feet; once again, I was on bare pavement. It seemed the Balrog didn't like being stepped on but had tolerated my boots in the interests of a quiet departure. I mouthed the question *Why?* but got no answer: just a mossy nudge against my leg, urging me forward.

I began running.

At the next intersection, I checked my Bumbler for which way to turn. Tut's blip was close to the heart of Zoonau. Since every knot city had the same general plan, I knew Tut must be approaching the central square, where the most prominent feature would be a ziggurat: a huge terraced pyramid with gardens at various levels, plenty of open areas for performances, and at the top, a raised pulpit where prophets could shout sermons to the populace. I could picture Tut jogging along the ropeways, heading for the pulpit where he'd . . . where he'd . . .

I couldn't guess what he'd do. And I couldn't get there in time to stop him. He was almost at his goal, while I was still blocks away.

But even as that thought sparked through my brain, a mass of spores rose before me, pushing up from the ground like a pantomime demon making its entrance through a trapdoor. The spores arranged themselves into a shapeless blob twice my height; then suddenly, the blob smoothed out into . . .

. . . a perfect moss-replica of my most recent egg sculpture. A tall slim egg with a single barred window, the bars wrapped with holy guardian snakes. One of the snakes lifted its head and winked at me; then the front of the egg swung open like a door, inviting me to step inside.

What's this? I mouthed. *A carriage?* Once again, no answer . . . but the Balrog's intent was obvious. It wanted me to climb into one of my Gotama prisons. Once I stepped inside, the door would lock behind me. Then I'd presumably be transported to Tut, carried into the city center fast enough to participate in whatever happened next. The Balrog was giving me a chance to make a difference in Zoonau's fate.

But I knew this was more than an offer of transit. I had to make a choice: I could join forces with the Balrog, volunteering to help in whatever the mossy alien was up to . . . or I could walk away and forever hold my peace.

My teachers at the Academy had warned about such situations—when a smarter-than-human alien asked you to buy in or opt out. There was only one reason you'd ever be given such a yes-or-no choice: because you risked getting killed if you did what the alien wanted.

Suppose the Balrog foresaw such a threat to me. Then the League of Peoples demanded I be offered the chance to say no. Otherwise—if the spores just grabbed me against my will—the Balrog would be guilty of dragging me into a lethal situation without option of escape. In other words, murder. The Balrog would catch trouble from the League unless I willingly stuck my head in the noose.

Which was where I was at that moment. If I stepped into that big mossy egg, I doubted I'd have another chance to back out. These things were almost always onetime offers. Like swallowing a porcupine—once you started, you had to keep going till you got it all down.

I hesitated. League law said the Balrog couldn't lure me into *certain* death—there had to be a chance I'd survive. Maybe a good chance. But there was also a chance I'd die. Too bad the Balrog wasn't obliged to explain what the percentages were.

Whatever the chances were, I knew what I was going to do—not what I *had* to do, but what I *would* do.

One step forward . . . and the Balrog closed around me.

I half expected to be teleported straight to some final destination. Navy records reported Kaisho Namida jumping instantaneously from star system to star system, sometimes hundreds of light-years in a single bound. But my mossy carriage simply lifted a centimeter off the pavement and accelerated at a couple of Gs, soon skimming along at a pace my Bumbler reported as a kilometer a minute.

This gave me time to take readings—in particular, to see where Zoonau's inhabitants had gone. I switched to an IR scan . . . and gasped as I saw a blaze of heat sources at the city center. A huge mob of Cashlings had gathered there. Thousands. Tens of thousands. The whole population of Zoonau? A moment later, data analysis gave me a tally: 91,734 Cashling heat signatures . . . and two humans.

Two humans? Tut and who else? The second human wasn't me—I hadn't reached the square yet, so I wasn't included in the count. Could there have been another human in Zoonau when the Balrog attacked?

Plenty of humans visited Cashleen, but almost all stayed in the planet's capital, thousands of kilometers away. The capital was home to our Technocracy embassy . . . and humans usually stuck close to the embassy. Whatever your purpose for coming to Cashleen, the embassy staff were far more likely to provide useful assistance than any Cashling you might find. So who would have reason for coming to a backwater like Zoonau?

I winced as an answer came to me: someone from the embassy staff.

Zoonau had been attacked two hours ago: plenty of time for somebody to fly in from the capital. No embassy personnel had been sent to Zoonau officially—the powers that be wanted *Pistachio* to handle everything—but I could easily imagine an ambitious vice consul buzzing off to Zoonau as soon as the news came in. He or she could have reached the city before our landing party, hoping to win a career boost by dealing with the Balrog single-handed. It was just the sort of grandstanding maneuver one expected from success-hungry bureaucrats . . . and just the sort of rashness that made Explorers grind their teeth.

Now I had to deal with a madman *and* an intrusive amateur.

I heard the people in the square before I saw them: thousands of gabbling voices, loud despite the muffling moss on every echoing surface. Then my transport egg rounded a corner, and the crowd was directly before me. No one had stayed down on street level; they were all packed onto the ziggurat, trampling flowers in the terrace gardens, clogging the open areas, milling on the stairs. I counted eight levels to the ziggurat, all of them spacious by normal standards . . . but with more than ninety thousand Cashlings crammed onto a single building, it looked like a dangerous squeeze.

Why had they come to this central area? Only one answer. The Balrog herded them here. It had used its spores to push or intimidate people through the streets until they reached the heart of the city.

The Balrog wanted an audience.

Once again, I tuned my Bumbler to Tut's homing beacon. He was on the top level now, heading for the pulpit in the center. The Bumbler could reconstruct what was happening up there, as if looking through a telescope. Dozens of Cashlings fought for the pulpit, either because they had some inspired message to proclaim or because they just wanted to seize the highest spot on the pyramid—an "I'm the king of the castle" impulse. When Tut shoved his way through the crowd, several people tried to grab him, hold back the human in their midst . . . but a few blasts from Tut's stun-pistol, and the opposition slumped to the roof tiles. The Cashlings edged back as Tut climbed to the pulpit's perch.

Meanwhile, my Balrog-built egg had reached the ziggurat and started ascending the stairs. The egg didn't fly, but surfed on a wave of spores that carried us smoothly upward. Cashlings ahead of us got brushed aside by a mossy wedge that preceded the egg, like the cowcatcher on an Old Earth locomotive. Anyone in our way was knocked left or right, their falls cushioned by beds of moss that sprang up to provide a safe landing. Other wads of moss performed crowd control—making sure no one accidentally got trampled.

Interesting. Navy files claimed the Balrog disliked contact with lesser beings . . . but the moss was taking a hands-on approach to keep the Cashlings safe.

Despite Balrog efforts to clear the way, our progress up the ziggurat was slow. Hundreds of people stood between us and the top. Many of them seemed eager to block us if they could, shouting curses and throwing themselves in our path. I don't know what they hoped to accomplish; they were just so angry at the Balrog, they must have decided that if it wanted to take me upward, they wanted to get in the way. In other words, the Cashlings were acting out of sheer rebelliousness: the sort of rebelliousness that could turn to violence, especially if Tut did something inflammatory.

"People of Zoonau!" Tut's voice boomed over the city. The pulpit obviously had a built-in sound system, and he'd patched his tightsuit radio into the feed. Giant hologram images materialized in the air, scores of them, all showing Tut's golden face five stories tall. The pulpit had holo-projectors too.

"My name is Tut," he said with a cheerful metallic smile. "I'm from the Technocracy's Outward Fleet—here to assess the situation and lend a hand." He paused, looked around. "Okay, here's my assessment. You're all really really pissed off. Right?"

A roar thundered from the crowd. The Balrog continued bearing me upward. Slowly. More people hurled themselves at our egg.

"You're pissed off," Tut said, his words ringing through the streets, "because this big bully Balrog is pushing you around, and you feel like there's nothing you can do. Am I right?"

The Cashlings roared again. I'd been hoping a lot of the crowd wouldn't understand English. But almost everyone in the Cashling Reach learned our language, purely so they could amuse themselves with human movies, virties, and other forms of entertainment. Cashlings wouldn't lift a finger to do productive work, but they'd spend long hours acquiring an alien tongue if that's what it took to get the jokes in a mindless sitcom.

"I know what it's like to feel helpless," Tut went on. "I'm an Explorer. I know what it's like to get reamed by fat-ass aliens. But guess what: I also know how to take back control. I can tell you how to beat this damned Balrog. Do you want to hear the secret?"

The crowd screamed yes. My egg finally topped the steps, onto the flat uppermost level. Just a short distance now to the pulpit.

"Here's what you do, Zoonau!" Tut shouted. He reached up to his chest and dug his thumbs under protective flaps on his suit's yellow breastplate. Everyone watching mimicked his action . . . everyone except me. I was too busy thinking, *Oh no. Oh no.*

Suddenly Tut threw his arms and legs wide, like a giant human X. Every Cashling did the same. I didn't. All I wanted to do was bury my face in my hands; but I held my head up, eyes open, to witness what happened next.

A tightsuit is usually an Explorer's best friend. It provides you with air and protects you from lethal environments. Once in a while, though, your tightsuit becomes a liability: if there's a life-threatening malfunction . . . if the suit's weight means the difference between sinking or swimming . . . if something small and toothy has got inside the suit with you. Therefore, the Outward Fleet equips each tightsuit with an emergency evac system, for occasions when you have to get your gear off in a hurry. You activate the system by pressing hidden buttons on your breastplate—just as Tut had done. Then you spread your arms and legs wide—just like Tut—and you wait for a very short countdown.

Three . . . two . . . one . . .

Tut's suit exploded from his body. Literally. Shaped demolition charges blew out the seams that held everything together. His helmet went straight up, disappearing from sight as it bulleted toward the dome overhead. Tut's sleeves shot off his outspread arms like jet-propelled bananas; the same with his pant legs, which flew apart in pieces and slapped into the upturned faces of nearby Cashling spectators. The breastplate cannonballed into the pulpit in front of him, knocking the lectern stand off its supports and toppling it onto the crowd. The backplate rocketed out and away over the edge of the ziggurat, probably falling on some unsuspecting Cashling several levels below. Other bits and pieces hurtled in random directions, belt pouches, shoulder pads, hunks of the crotch . . . until Tut was standing there, stark naked and hologrammatically enlarged, in front of all of Zoonau.

Huh. He'd been telling the truth. The gold *wasn't* just on his face.

My egg reached the pulpit (now just a bare platform) two seconds later. For a moment, nothing happened. Tut looked down at me, beaming a big bright smile. I stared back from my egglike prison, a Princess Gotama just before all hell breaks loose. The Balrog did nothing. The Cashlings did nothing. I thought about drawing my stun-pistol and shooting Tut before he caused further trouble . . . but that might send the crowd berserk.

Two heartbeats of silence.

Then the Balrog egg melted around me—all the spores slopping straight down. My helmet visor became flecked with red, and my suit felt heavy with dust. Most of the spores, however, just dropped to the roof tiles and pooled around my ankles. Several square meters of them. They glowed a soft red.

"Thanks, Mom," Tut murmured. "Knew I could count on you." Then he raised his voice and called to the Cashlings, "Here's how to show the bastards you don't care. Swan dive!" And he jumped from the pulpit, straight into the pile of spores that had just dripped off me. He was like a child leaping into a mound of autumn leaves. A moment later, Tut rolled happily naked on the red moss, laughing out loud and crooning, "Ooo, it's fuzzy!"

A murmur went through the Cashlings. A sigh. A cheer. Then they were running, sprinting at astonishing long-legged speed toward the patches of spores dabbed around the ziggurat. On the lower levels, people raced down to the city streets, crowds of them hitting the pavement and throwing themselves onto the first clumps of moss they found. If the Balrog had dodged, the Cashlings might have broken their bones as they struck cement-hard *chintah*; but the spores stayed in place, and the people plopped down on mattresses of soft moss. In seconds, 91,734 Cashlings were flipping and flopping deliriously, tossing handfuls of spores into the air, smearing red fuzz over their bodies.

Down by my feet, Tut grinned. "See, Mom? Problem solved. No one will go homicidal today—they're having too much fun."

He looked up at me with spores covering his face and body: even on the gold parts where you wouldn't think moss could stick. I smiled back vaguely, but only from reflex; inside, I was waiting for the other shoe to drop.

Why? Because I knew this was far from over. The Balrog wouldn't have caused such a fuss, only to let the uproar be defused by a lunatic doing a fast striptease and rolling in the red. As far as I could see, the Balrog hadn't accomplished anything yet. All this sound and fury had gone nowhere . . . which meant "Stage Two" of the plan was still waiting to unfold.

But I said nothing. The Balrog was famous for showmanship. It was the sort of monster that held off its attacks until someone said, "We'll be safe now," or "I think it's gone." Above all else, the Balrog loved dramatic timing.

"So," Tut said, "looks like we've got this bitch under control."

I had time to wince.

Zoonau erupted in geysers of red. Spores shot up from the ground. More gusted down off the dome. Trillions of red particles tore away from the buildings. A crimson dust storm battered my world, thudding against my helmet, buffeting my body hard enough to be felt despite the tightsuit's protection. Radio static roared in my ears. The heads-up display in my visor went black. A wind ripped the Bumbler from my hands, and a moment later, I felt the little machine's shoulder strap break. The Bumbler bounced away in the tempest, but I didn't see or hear it go—the only noise was static, and the only sight an impenetrable onslaught of spores.

Pouches tore off my belt. My backpack flew away. Even the weight of my stun-pistol, holstered at my hip, suddenly departed as the gun was snatched by the gale.

Then, abruptly, the fury ceased. Replaced by deep silence. The blinding red chaos was sucked away, leaving only a glimpse of the last spores sailing up out of sight into the sky.

Afternoon sun poured painfully bright through the dome. The glass was clear. The buildings had returned to their dull gray. The patches of moss where Cashlings had been rolling were gone, revealing nothing but bare *chintah*.

The Balrog had abandoned Zoonau. Just like that. Not a single spore left in sight.

"Uhh, Mom . . ."

Tut still lay on the roof tiles. I looked down. He pointed to my feet.

Both my boots were covered with spores, like fuzzy red slippers. I did nothing but stare at them dumbly—like a villain in a cheap action virtie, who looks down in surprise to see she's been shot through the heart.

"Oh," I said. "Oh."

My boots vanished like smoke. The rest of my tightsuit too—totally consumed as the spores chewed upward, faster than the speed of thought. Even my helmet didn't slow the spores down: they slashed past my eyes in a wash of crimson, leaving nothing behind but the touch of a light spring breeze blowing against my skin.

My suit was completely gone, eaten by the Balrog. Now all I wore was the thin, thigh-high chemise that most women put on under tightsuits for protection against chafing.

I looked at my feet again. The fuzzy red "slippers" were gone. Just two spores left, one on each foot, glowing in the center of each instep like Christian stigmata. I closed my eyes.

Two little kisses of pain, no worse than mosquito bites, piercing the flesh of my feet. When I opened my eyes again, I saw two pinpricks of blood, nothing more. They barely showed on my skin.

But now, the spores were inside me.

I felt nothing. Like Kaisho Namida, I couldn't sense the Balrog as it colonized my tissues. Still, I had no doubt I was rapidly becoming riddled with spores. My heart. My womb. My brain. Perhaps my nervous system was screaming in agony, but the spores invading my brain didn't let the pain register in my consciousness.

"Oh, Mom," said Tut. "You got bitten."

"I know."

"By the Balrog."

"I know."

"It's in your feet."

"I know."

"They gotta come off."

"What?"

Tut didn't answer. He scuttled across the roof tiles to a half-open equipment pouch that had fallen off my belt. My first-aid kit had slipped partway out of the pouch. Tut grabbed the kit, opened it, took out a scalpel.

"If those things spread, Mom, you're in trouble."

"They've already spread, Tut. They're deep inside me."

"You don't know that. They could just be nibbling your toes."

"Tut, when the Balrog attacked Kaisho Namida—"

"When the Balrog attacked Kaisho Namida," Tut interrupted, "her partner didn't do shit. Maybe he could have saved her."

"He didn't do anything because she was infested from head to toe in seconds."

"How did he know?"

"He scanned her with his Bumbler."

Tut shrugged. "We don't have a Bumbler."

It was true. His had disappeared during the emergency evac explosion; mine had been torn away during the Balrog's departure.

"Gotta cut off your feet," Tut said again.

I took a step back from him. "It won't help."

"It might. You never know."

I backed another step. "I'll bleed to death."

He gave me a withering look. "Think I don't know about tourniquets? And I ran past a hospital on my way in. Less than five minutes away. No problem."

"Then get me to the hospital, Tut." Another step back. "Don't cut off my feet right here."

"Time's a-wasting. And I gotta ask why you're fighting me on this. Maybe that Balrog is twisting your mind."

"If it's in my mind already, there's no point cutting off my feet."

"If it's in your mind already and it's so insistent on leaving your feet alone, amputation sounds like a *real* good idea. Anything the Balrog doesn't want, that's what I should be doing."

"Please, Tut." I felt tears in my eyes. "I won't be myself much longer. Don't take my feet. I'll lose them soon enough. Please, Tut. Let me stay me as long as I can."

He didn't answer—just rolled across the roof and grabbed another piece of equipment that had fallen from my suit. The holster holding my stun-pistol. I turned to run; the pistol whirred as he shot me in the back.

I dropped, with muscles like water. But I didn't black out—just went limp and powerless. *That shouldn't be*, I thought. Shot at close range with a stunner: I should have gone completely unconscious. How could I still be awake? Unless . . . oh.

The Balrog was inside me. And navy records said the Balrog was immune to stun-fire. The spores in my nervous system must have given me enough stun-resistance to stay conscious, but not enough to fight back as Tut scurried forward with the scalpel.

"Maybe I'd better take more than your feet," he said. "Cut you off at the knees. Or maybe the hip. Just to be safe." He patted my cheek. The bad one. The oozing one. Idly, he wiped his hand off on my chemise. "You'll look pretty with artificial legs, Mom. I bet you can get gold ones."

He lifted the hem of my chemise, spread my legs, and put the scalpel to my thigh. I thought of how I'd once been a dancer . . . how I hadn't been practicing enough recently . . . how I'd let the feel of movement slip away. Now I'd never get it back.

The blade was so sharp, I barely felt Tut slice in. What I did feel was the warm gush of blood running down my flesh.

Then something went WHIR. The sound of another stun-shot. And Tut toppled forward, landing unconscious on my blood-slick leg.

Still paralyzed, I couldn't turn my head to see what was happening. I could only watch as a human hand reached down and rolled Tut off me. A stun-pistol whirred again, making sure he was out cold.

More sounds of movement outside my line of sight. A fat white bandage appeared and pressed hard against the scalpel cut in my leg. "Not too bad," a woman's voice said. I could see her hand and her sleeve. She wore an Outward Fleet uniform. Admiral's gray.

Fingers on my chin turned my head toward her. She had a strong face, piercing green eyes, and a furious purple birthmark splashed across her right cheek. The dark of it against her light skin was like a photographic negative of my own white-on-dark disfiguration.

Ah, I thought. *The other human my Bumbler detected.* Not an ambitious bureaucrat from the embassy, but the most famous admiral in our navy. Festina Ramos.

I had a terrible suspicion the Balrog had done all this to bring the two of us together.

4

Karma [Sanskrit]: The consequences of one's previous actions.

RAMOS got surgical glue from the first-aid kit and carefully closed my wound. As she worked, I tried to guess what she was doing here. By "here," I didn't mean the top of the ziggurat—if Festina Ramos had been anywhere on Cashleen, she'd hurry to Zoonau as soon as she heard of the Balrog's attack. She would then search the city for the point of maximum chaos and inevitably find her way to Tut's pulpit. Lieutenant Admiral Festina Ramos was the navy's official troubleshooter-at-large. Her job and her instincts would have brought her unfailingly to the heart of the furor.

But what was she doing on Cashleen at all? What was important enough to bring her when she could have been the darling of New Earth?

Two years earlier, she'd driven the navy's High Council of Admirals into meltdown by presenting evidence of their massive corruption and wrongdoing. Felony charges against council members still had to work through the courts, but that was just a formality. The important trial had been held in the news media, and the verdict was unequivocal: guilty as charged.

The entire High Council had resigned in disgrace. Even rank-

and-file admirals who weren't on the council fell prey to suspicion . . . except, of course, Ramos herself. She became so popular, newswires willingly printed her picture—usually with the birthmark lightened to soft mauve, but sometimes (when an article wanted to depict her as an implacable force for justice) with the birthmark left dark and foreboding.

Ramos had dominated the news for a month. During that time, she met with almost every politician on New Earth, plus many more who flew in from other planets just to grab a photo op. Those of us at the Explorer Academy believed that Ramos would be named president of the new High Council; she was the only admiral who still held the public's confidence. Rumor said the civilian government wanted to announce a complete slate of High Admirals all at once, and needed time to make sure none of the new appointees had been involved in the old council's crimes . . . but as soon as the background checks were complete, Festina Ramos would surely become the navy's admiral-in-chief.

Then Ramos disappeared. No word where she was going—just a brief interview with a third-string reporter who happened to be hanging around New Earth's main spaceport. Ramos said duty called her elsewhere, and she might not be back for some time. "Best wishes to the new High Council, may they serve with honor, I trust they'll receive everyone's full support, gotta go now, bye." Or words to that effect.

With that, Festina Ramos swept off the public stage like a tired ballerina who wants to get away before someone calls, "Encore!"

Navy gossip occasionally reported Ramos sightings around the galaxy—a day on Troyen with Queen Innocence . . . four days on Celestia with Lord Protector York and his Mandasar wife . . . three weeks in seclusion on Demoth with some junior proctor of the Vigil . . . rumors of surprise visits to archaeological digs, disease research centers, and the YouthBoost vats on Sitz—but Ramos avoided the media, never gave public statements, and kept on the move. By the time word leaked out where she'd been, she was already someplace else.

Her behavior provoked countless theories. For example, some suggested that during her investigations into the High Council, she'd discovered something she hadn't made public: a threat much worse than the crimes she'd revealed, and now she was racing from planet to planet, trying to end the danger before disaster struck. A number of my fellow Explorers, however, were sure she was the victim of "pretty people politics"—the top echelons of the Technocracy couldn't stomach a disfigured purple-cheeked woman taking command of the fleet, so they sent her on meaningless errands to remove her from the spotlight. Personally, I wondered if she'd just got fed up with the politicians, the media, and all the other talk-talk-talk. If she'd really been offered the highest post in the navy, she might have turned it down as more trouble than it was worth. Then she'd happily fled the public eye and was now on extended vacation, going wherever she liked . . . perhaps helping out here and there, but certainly not battling galactic-scale dangers.

Still, I'd known better than to mention my suspicions to other Academy cadets. They'd worshiped Ramos as a hero. She'd been an Explorer herself before the Admiralty abruptly bumped her (at age twenty-six) to lieutenant admiral and made her the navy's problem-solver-without-portfolio. Nobody knew how she'd won such a promotion, though everyone suspected she'd caught the High Council in some mischief and blackmailed them into making concessions. Certainly, Ramos's first official act was to conduct a "policy review" of the Explorer Corps, leading to an overhaul of corps operations and substantial improvements in the treatment of Explorers by other branches of the service. That alone would have made her popular among us "expendable crew members" . . . but more important, she carried out her highly visible activities *while still looking like an Explorer*. As an admiral, Ramos could easily have obtained treatment to remove her florid birthmark; but she'd stayed the way she was, no matter how much it disconcerted "normal" people.

Was it any wonder Explorers loved her?

I'd admired her as much as anyone else had. But now, as she checked that my wound was closed, I felt a dawning resentment.

Ramos's history proved she was surrounded by extraordinary karma—which is not some mystical force but the everyday processes whereby seeds sown in the past bear fruit in the present. Karma simply means that the choices you made yesterday affect the options you have today. It's common sense. Nothing is inevitable or predetermined . . . yet your actions and the actions of others can sometimes produce a cumulative momentum almost impossible to resist. That's what karma is: the momentum of cause and effect that drives you forward, occasionally into bottlenecks or booby traps.

Some people have more momentum than others. Some are riding an avalanche. Festina Ramos was clearly one of those avalanche riders; her karma would sweep her from crisis to crisis until her luck or momentum ran out.

And people like me would be caught in the avalanche too.

Here's what I was thinking as I lay paralyzed, watching Ramos repack the first-aid kit. Why would the Balrog care about an Ugly Screaming Stink-Girl? It wouldn't. It *would* care about a high-ranking avalanche rider like Festina Ramos; she could be useful in the Balrog's plans, whatever they were. And if those plans required a pawn to serve as host for fuzzy red spores, the Balrog would find great amusement in choosing a host who looked like the admiral's dark twin.

In other words, I'd been picked because my appearance would get a rise out of Festina Ramos.

She and I were almost the same height. We were both strong, lean, and athletic. Her hair was cut much like mine: short and uncomplicated. Our faces weren't similar if you compared individual features—her green eyes, my brown, her finely cut nose, mine wider and flatter—but anyone looking at Ramos and me would ignore such minor differences. Observers would be transfixed by our disfigured cheeks. Nothing else would matter.

Even Ramos couldn't help staring. She checked that Tut was sleeping peacefully and shooed away some curious Cashlings by brandishing her pistol; then she came back and knelt by my side. For almost a minute, she did nothing but gaze at my face. If I'd been able to move, I would have told her to stop. It reminded me too much of my mother, who'd gaze at my cheek in sickened fascination when she thought I wouldn't notice. But at least there was no disgust in Ramos's expression—I was used to stares of disgust, and the admiral's eyes were blessedly free of such condemnation. Free of pity too. Whatever Ramos was thinking, she hid it well.

In time, she turned away from my face. That's when she saw the blood pricks on my feet. "Oh fuck," she said—not angrily, just a whisper. "Are those Balrog bites? Is that why your partner went after you with the knife?"

"Yes."

When the word came out of my mouth, I was just as surprised as Ramos. For a terrifying moment, I thought I was still paralyzed, and the Balrog was speaking through me as if I were a ventriloquist's dummy. But somehow I'd regained control of my muscles, with none of the staggering nausea that usually follows a stunner blast. I sat up . . . spent a moment straightening my chemise, until I was flooded with embarrassment by my ridiculous attempt at modesty . . . then scrambled to my knees in front of the kneeling Ramos and saluted. "Explorer Third Class Ma Youn Suu, Admiral."

We were almost nose to nose . . . like little girls kneeling together, getting ready to play some game. Ramos swallowed hard and edged away. She didn't return my salute. "You, uhh, you did get bitten, didn't you? That's why you got shot by . . . uhh . . ."

"He calls himself Tut."

"Appropriate name. Anyway, if you can shrug off a stun-charge that quickly, you're . . ."

"Infested. Yes, Admiral."

She looked at me. The uneasiness on her face slowly softened. "How do you feel?"

"I don't feel different, if that's what you're asking."

"That's not what I'm asking. How do you feel?"

I looked at her. She was an admiral, yes, but only a few years older than I. Not like a prying mother—just a concerned big sister. Or a friend. "I feel . . . I don't know . . ."

That was the moment it caught up with me. Everything. Not just being in my underwear at the top of a pyramid in the center of an alien city, with two bite marks on my feet and extraterrestrial parasites in my blood. Not just the prospect of becoming like Kaisho Namida, a cripple in a wheelchair, solid moss from the waist down, and a brain so overrun with spores that she spoke of the Balrog like a lover. Not just the realization that I would be changed against my will and could never again trust my own body, thoughts, emotions, perceptions, or desires.

What caught up with me was my life. The whole of it. The isolation of a childhood as Ugly Screaming Stink-Girl. The unfairness of being forced into the Explorer Corps. The loneliness of months on a starship with nothing but a lunatic partner, a collection of amateurish figurines, and a crew of thirty-five people who couldn't look me in the face but constantly stole sidelong glances.

I should have been somebody else. Not an Explorer, not a virgin, not an alien parasite's host. I was only nineteen. I should have had a future; I should have had a past; but I had neither.

So I sank to the ground and wept. In anger, sorrow, fear, regret, grief, self-pity, and loneliness.

After a while, I felt Festina Ramos gently stroking my hair. Some time later, she was holding me as I sobbed against her shirt. But when I'd cried myself out, she eased away. She put a handkerchief in my hand; then she stood up and turned her back while I wiped my eyes, blew my nose, mopped my cheek.

I was left holding the handkerchief, wondering if I should give it back to her. It was damp and filthy . . . but at least my cheek hadn't bled the way it often did when I fell to pieces.

"I'm sorry, Admiral," I mumbled.

"Call me Festina," she said. "I'm sick of formality . . . especially with fellow Explorers."

I didn't answer. I could easily get past the military convention of addressing people by rank . . . but I squirmed at the Western rudeness of using no titles at all. Why couldn't I call her Daw Festina? Or if our shared background as Explorers made us "sisters in arms," I could bring myself to call her Ma Festina. But just a plain unadorned Festina? It was like spitting in her face. Still, there was no point explaining proper etiquette to Caucasians. Even if they decided to respect my good manners, they always put an ironic tone in their voices as if they were humoring a simpleton.

I would just have to get used to calling her by name alone. Festina. At least it was pronounceable, unlike many Western names.

"So that's over," Admiral Ramos—Festina—said in a light voice. "Now we set emotion aside and get busy."

"Busy doing what?"

"Immediate practical things. When life goes to shit, do immediate practical things. Like head for a starbase hospital."

"They won't be able to help me."

She gazed down at me with her piercing green eyes. "You're right. But it doesn't matter, because I doubt we'll reach the hospital. You know why?"

I nodded. "Something will come up. The Balrog intends to use you somehow, and I'll have to come for the ride. I'm the carrying case for the spores."

Ramos . . . Festina . . . winced. "Yes. Sorry about that."

I shrugged. "If I really am just a carrying case, maybe when this is all over, the Balrog will let me go."

She gave me a look. "Do you really believe that?"

"No. But they still haven't answered the Alvarez question."

Festina allowed herself a little smile. The Alvarez question had arisen at the Explorer Academy decades ago, first asked by a professor named Ricardo Alvarez. The question was this: *Which is more deadly? Despair or false hope?* When, for example, you're possessed by alien spores, is it worse to give up immediately or to let yourself hope some miracle will save you? Both options were undesirable—or, as the Buddha would say, "unskillful." Alvarez had wanted some student to resolve the question through statistical research . . . but generations of Explorers had preferred to let the question go unanswered. Instead, they used it as a private shorthand for *I'm not dead yet; let's leave it at that.*

"When I was at the Academy," Festina said, "the Alvarez question *did* have an answer."

"It still does." We recited in unison, "Fuck off, Ricardo!"

The way past despair and false hope is just letting go. It doesn't improve your odds of survival, but it doesn't waste mental energy.

Festina grinned. I grinned. Our comm implants buzzed in unison, and we both stopped grinning immediately.

"Ready?" Festina asked.

I nodded. "Immortality awaits." Those were the last words an Explorer traditionally spoke before embarking on a mission. No one took the phrase seriously; but if you died, IMMORTALITY AWAITS almost always looked better on a memorial plaque than your real last words . . . which were far too often "Oh shit." ("Going Oh Shit" was an Explorer euphemism for death.)

Our comm implants buzzed again—a general hail on the standard Explorer Corps channel. Festina said, "I'll take it," and clicked her comm to answer.

I didn't hear much of the conversation. Festina had an old-style Explorer comm—the kind that was embedded in her throat with the audio feed snaking up under the skin to her jaw and making her whole skull resonate. It gave her a noticeable lump on the neck . . . which I thought would be uncomfortable, though I didn't know for sure. Thanks to Festina's changes in the Explorer Corps, my own comm unit was much less intrusive: subcutaneous audio wires in the pinna of each ear; a primary voice pickup that replaced the roof of my mouth; and a secondary subcutaneous pickup running the length of my sternum. (The secondary pickup could be activated remotely. If I ever got knocked out, *Pistachio* could turn on my chest mike from orbit and track me down by the sound of my heartbeat.)

The new systems were more reliable and practically unnoticeable once you got used to a slight taste of plastic in your soft palate. Festina, however, had never upgraded. Most old Explorers hadn't—diehard holdouts. I activated my comm with my tongue to see if I could pick up the admiral's conversation . . . but as soon as I did, my ears were blasted with a mechanical voice. "Explorer Youn Suu, come in. Explorer Youn Suu, come in. Explorer Youn Suu, come in . . ."

Pistachio's ship-soul on autorepeat. I stepped away from Festina and tongue-switched to transmit. "Youn Suu here," I said. "Go ahead."

There was a pause while the computer notified my caller that I'd finally responded. Five seconds later, Captain Cohen came on. "Glad you're there, Youn Suu. We were worried. Tut's suit sent a signal it was executing an emergency evac, then your suit sent an autodistress call half a second before going no-comm. Everything all right?"

"No, sir. But we don't need assistance."

"You're sure? I could contact the Cashling authorities . . ."

"They'd just get in the way. We can handle—"

Ambassador Li broke in. "Explorer, where the hell are you? Ubatu and I are ready to go."

"There've been some complications, Ambassador."

"What complications? I told that damned Balrog to leave, and it did. Just goes to show, aliens may act cocky, but they'll knuckle under if you take a hard line. That's what diplomacy *is*. Now I intend to use the same approach on the Cashling government—fly straight to their capital, point out how I saved their city, and demand some juicy trade concessions. If you aren't back to my shuttle in five minutes, you're on your own."

"You might as well leave now, Ambassador. I don't know where Admiral Ramos and I will go next, but it probably won't fit your schedule."

A silence. "Admiral Ramos? Admiral Festina Ramos?"

"Yes, Ambassador."

"She's here?"

"Right in front of me. She's taking a call that will probably lead to work for both of us."

"You and Festina Ramos?"

"Yes, Ambassador."

I could guess what Li was thinking. With Festina on the scene, no one would believe Li and Ubatu had any part in expelling the moss from Zoonau. People would assume Festina had been responsible . . . though, strange to say, it was actually Tut who'd done the most to make the spores leave.

But if Li had no chance of taking credit for the Balrog's departure, he could still boost his prestige by being seen with the admiral. Any photo op, any joint appearance in front of witnesses, and Li could capitalize on it for months. ("When Admiral Ramos and I were together on Cashleen . . . I happen to know Admiral Ramos believes . . . my good friend Festina wants me to say . . .")

So I wasn't surprised when Li told me, "We aren't in *that* much of a hurry, Explorer. If I or my shuttle can provide any assistance . . ."

I looked toward Festina. She was still talking, facing away from me. "Ambassador," I said, "Admiral Ramos can't be disturbed right now, but we might need a ride very soon. Probably back to *Pistachio*. Could you come and get us? We're on top of the central ziggurat. I don't know the nearest shuttle pad, but Zoonau's air traffic control can tell you where to land."

"To hell with air traffic control," Li said. "I'll pick you up where you are. Five minutes."

I winced as he cut the transmission. Thirty rope walkways ran at various levels over my head. I doubted Li had the piloting skill to weave his way through all the cat's cradles . . . and if he broke even a single rope, the Cashling government would howl themselves hoarse over "thoughtless human hooligans" laying waste to "irreplaceable urban transitways."

On the other hand, if Li wanted to create a diplomatic incident, that was his problem. Maybe he *liked* diplomatic incidents. They were his form of job security.

Festina continued to talk on her comm. I kept my distance so she wouldn't think I was eavesdropping. Once she turned in my direction and asked, "I assume you're here with a ship?"

"Yes, admiral. A Model D frigate named *Pistachio*."

"No Class One duties?"

"We're strictly Class Five."

"Not anymore."

She turned back to her conversation while I pondered her words. Class One duties were "crucial to the survival of the Technocracy and the Outward Fleet"—which generally meant missions required to placate the League of Peoples. A ship with Class One duties was sacrosanct; nobody could interfere with it until it finished its mission. Furthermore, Class One duties were so vital that the crew had to be informed of exactly what was going on. Less important missions might operate on a need-to-know basis; but with Class One, nobody was kept in the dark for fear that ignorance would lead to mistakes. I was therefore certain we had no Class One jobs in the offing . . . unless Festina was about to give us one.

Any admiral could commandeer navy ships to carry out Class One jobs at any time . . . after which, only the High Council could reverse the decision. Since the High Council wouldn't dare overrule the illustrious Festina Ramos, she'd have free rein to make *Pistachio* her own. (Most admirals commanded flagships already, but not Festina; she'd lost hers to a saboteur some years earlier and had never asked for a replacement. According to rumor, she preferred to travel incognito on civilian vessels—usually ones operated by aliens, who were less apt to recognize her famous face.)

Therefore, it came as no surprise when she waved me to her side a few minutes later. "Call your captain, please. Say I'm invoking my Powers of Emergency and making your ship my flag. Class One mission. Verify authorization through Starbase Trillium. Prepare to leave orbit as soon as we're on board."

"What destination, Admiral?"

"A planet called Muta."

I'd never heard of it. She gave me a set of coordinates. Only fifteen light-years from Cashleen, but in an unexpected direction. "Isn't that Greenstrider territory?" I asked.

"Used to be. The Greenstriders sold it to the Unity."

I stared at her. "The Greenstriders *sold* it?" Greenstriders were aliens with extreme territorial instincts—extreme to the point of lunacy. Once Greenstriders took mates, all they wanted was to claim a chunk of property and live there the rest of their lives. They wouldn't travel . . . not even to move to bigger, more prosperous holdings. Greenstriders bonded with their land for better or worse, and never willingly left their homesteads more than a few hours at a time. I said, "Greenstriders wouldn't sell a square millimeter of ground to their own grandmothers. They'd *never* sell an entire planet to outsiders. Unless the place is utterly uninhabitable . . ."

"No," Festina said, "Muta is apparently superb—9.7 on the Habitability Index. Perfect for colonization. Nevertheless, the Greenstriders sold it to the Unity ten years ago."

"And now?"

"Now the Unity has small settlements there. One of which just sent a distress call."

"What kind of distress call?"

"A nonspecific SOS. Someone just pressed a MAYDAY button, and now isn't answering the comm."

"So let me guess," I said. "The Unity tried to call everyone else on Muta to see if anybody knew the reason for the Mayday. None of the other settlers responded."

"Exactly. Muta's gone completely silent. We have to find out why . . . and try to save any survivors."

"Why us?" I asked. "Doesn't the Unity have ships in the area?"

"No. The Unity only has a dozen ships in their entire fleet—huge damned things called luna-ships because they're the size of small moons. Mostly, the lunas keep to the core of Unity space, making short trips between well-populated planets. Muta's a long way off from other Unity holdings—and it only has a few thousand colonists, so it's not worth visiting often. A luna-ship drops by two or three times a year. The rest of the time, Muta is on its own."

"What about the Greenstriders? Even if they sold the planet, it's still near their territory. Don't they have ships within a few light-years?"

Festina shook her head. "From what we can tell, the Greenstriders give Muta's system a wide berth . . . although they *do* have a number of unmanned observation posts nearby."

I rolled my eyes. "That says a lot, doesn't it?"

Festina nodded but didn't speak . . . like a professor at the Academy, waiting for me to explain, though she already knew what I meant.

"There's something bad on Muta," I said. "Bad enough to scare off the Greenstriders. Or more likely, the bad thing killed every Greenstrider colonist, since I can't imagine Greenstriders leaving their land, no matter how frightened they got. The Greenstrider government wrote off Muta as too dangerous for further settlement, so they sold the planet to the Unity. Even then, the Greenstriders didn't want to turn their backs on whatever had killed their people . . . so they built unmanned observation posts as an early-warning system in case the bad thing on Muta started to spread."

"My thoughts exactly," Festina said. "And the Unity?"

"Full of themselves, as usual. They only colonize high-quality planets, which are never easy to come by. So they bought Muta, even though they must have known the Greenstriders had run into trouble. The Unity is famous for believing it can succeed where others have failed. They founded some settlements on Muta, probably filled with elite survey teams on the lookout for danger . . . but obviously they weren't as good as they thought."

"That's the way I see it too," Festina agreed. "Lucky for us, we don't have to *live* on Muta. Just go in, rescue survivors, and get out."

I looked at her. "It won't be that easy."

She sighed. "I know. All this"—she waved her hand at the city around us—"the Balrog did this for a reason. It had advance knowledge that we'd be called to Muta, and it decided to come along."

"Inside me."

"Inside you."

"Why?"

"I don't know," Festina said. "Do you think the damned moss confides in me?" Her face remained hard for a moment, then softened. "Look. I won't say the Balrog is benevolent. It has its own agenda and gleefully manipulates people to achieve its ends. But at least the Balrog is sentient. It respects sentient life. And if there's something on Muta that's been killing settlers, the Balrog *can't* be on the killer's side. If anything, the Balrog might intend to eliminate the killer. Maybe the Balrog will score points with the League if it makes Muta safe."

"So why make the trip inside me?" I asked. "If the Balrog wants to play hero, why not teleport to Muta on its own? It could smother the killer with spores, the way it smothered Zoonau."

"Maybe the Balrog wouldn't win a direct confrontation. Maybe it needs to land on Muta incognito."

"And I'm the Trojan horse?"

"That's not necessarily . . ." But her words were drowned out by a thunderous crash over our heads. Li's shuttle had arrived.

The rope walkways of Zoonau had lasted for millennia. Like *chintah* concrete, they weren't nearly as simple as they looked—each rope was an amalgam of artificial fibers and microbes that could heal any fraying or decay. They could not, however, heal outright breakage . . . like the snapping and slicing caused by a several-ton shuttle coming straight down from the top of the dome.

The ropes weren't the only casualties. They were tied to numerous supports: to buildings, to stanchions, to the dome itself. If a rope happened to be stronger than its end attachments, the attachments gave way first. Screw bolts got wrenched from the walls of skyscrapers, spilling chunks of *chintah* into the streets below. Pylons buckled and bent, or broke clean off and plunged earthward like spears. The glass of the dome resonated with pops and bangs and clatter. Occasionally, some cat's cradle proved strong enough to hold the shuttle's weight, at least temporarily; but Li just applied more downthrust, pressing the craft into the web of ropes until they collapsed under the strain. Panicked Cashlings ran for cover, while the more courageous (or foolhardy) called the newswires again. Dust and debris showered around us as rope ends whizzed past at high speed, slashing like bullwhips. Festina threw herself on top of Tut to protect him. I could only flatten facedown on the roof and hope I didn't get slammed by some jagged piece of concrete.

My eyes were closed against flying dust. I covered my ears with my hands to block the roar of the shuttle's engines. Wind buffeted around me. Yet I was still *aware* of exactly where the shuttle was. Not through vision, hearing, or the feel of disturbance in the air, but through sheer mental comprehension.

I just *knew* the shuttle's position. Knew too where everything else was: Festina, Tut, nearby Cashlings, falling *chintah*. I didn't sense these things through the chaos. I just knew.

And I knew more about those people and things than just their position. I could sense . . . I had no simple word for what I was perceiving, but it seemed like some kind of life force. An aura. I sensed the ordered, monastic community of plants and microbes inside the *chintah*. The chaotic labyrinth of Tut's madness. The watery shallowness of the Cashlings. The avalanche karma of Festina Ramos, distorting the space around her like a black hole, so that the woman herself was almost invisible within.

I could sense the Balrog's life force too. Inside me. The alien was filled with a powerful karma like Festina Ramos . . . but not an avalanche, not a black hole. A peaceful placid presence, undemanding, unyielding, neither hot nor cold, neither light nor dark, just *there*: inhabiting every part of my body like a calm and calming mist.

Or so it seemed . . . if I could trust this revelation. This sixth sense.

My people have long believed there *are* six senses: the usual five recognized by Westerners, plus the Faculty of Mind. Whenever I had to explain this concept to non-Buddhists, I'd mumble about the Mind's "ability to extract meaning from raw perception." Putting things together. Making logical deductions. The Mind didn't gather input per se, but processed input from the other senses and was therefore part of the sensory system. Yes, it was a sixth sense . . . sort of.

But suppose—at least for higher beings—the Mind really *was* a sense organ. Suppose it didn't just process input, but could somehow accumulate input on its own. Unmediated perception. Could that have been why the ancients classified Mind as a sixth sense? And we moderns had invented weak arguments to explain away the old beliefs rather than admitting our blindness.

But now I could sense the world. I knew everything's place and its nature. I also knew how I'd acquired this new mode of perception.

"Balrog," I said under my breath. "Please stop."

The radarlike awareness vanished immediately . . . leaving me with nothing but dust, wind, and an emptiness where the comprehension had been. The emptiness wasn't painful—I didn't feel blind and bereft, as if some part of me had been gouged away. I felt no craving to have the uncanny perception back. I was just aware of the absence. Like when you cut your hair, and for a while you're cognizant of what's missing.

"Is that how you do it?" I whispered to the Balrog. "Is that how you seduced Kaisho? How you think you'll seduce me? You share a bit of your awareness . . . and then, like a perfect gentleman, you stop when you're asked. But you make sure I know the offer is still open. A sixth sense that's mine anytime I want, and all I have to say is please. Like a kiss hovering a millimeter from my lips—I just have to lean in and take it. Is that how you'll make me let down my guard?"

No answer. But I remembered the way my Mind's eye had perceived the Balrog's life force: calm, peaceful, wise . . . like a Buddha. *Exactly* like a Buddha. As if the Balrog had knowingly portrayed itself in the guise I'd find most trustworthy.

Another aspect of the seduction. I was supposed to conceive of the Balrog not as a parasite, but as a saintly creature of pure enlightenment.

"Suppose I were a Christian," I said to the Balrog. "When I looked at you, would I see Christ? If I were a Hindu, would I see Ganesha? Or Krishna? Or Kali? And when you showed me Festina and Tut, did I really sense their inner selves? Or were you just reflecting what I already knew about them, so I'd believe your mystic sixth sense could reveal hidden truths? Was it all just a trick to tempt me into inviting you back? To get me interested in taking another look?"

Still no answer. I didn't expect one.

"Never again," I said. "Don't do that to me, ever. I don't believe what your sixth sense shows me, and I definitely don't need it. Just leave me alone."

But I knew even then, I wouldn't hold out forever. Forever was too long not to give in eventually. To take just another tiny peek.

The shuttle settled on the ziggurat's roof. When I lifted my head, Festina was already standing, dusting *chintah* off her uniform. She looked down at me. "So. Did *you* arrange for the shuttle?"

"I said we might need immediate transport. I wanted to meet the shuttle at the nearest landing pad, but it's being flown by a diplomat who doesn't think other people's laws apply to him."

"Oh," Festina said. "A dipshit. I know the type." She sighed. "Who is it? Anyone I should know?"

I reported what I knew about Li and Ubatu. I couldn't recite their résumés, but I could sketch their personalities. (Inwardly, I wondered: *what would their life forces look like?*) After I'd finished, Festina asked for more details . . . and in the ensuing conversation, she invariably abbreviated "diplomats" to "dipshits." It proved she was an Explorer of the *old* school. For some reason, they all loved profanity and rough talk. Maybe to shock the more genteel navy personnel around them. I could never swear like that myself—I'd been raised with Bamar manners, which abhor harsh speech—but once I got used to it, Festina's crudeness made me smile. Weren't her words just another chant to scare away demons?

As I finished my précis on Li and Ubatu, the shuttle's access door opened. No one came out, but Li spoke over the shuttle's loudspeakers. "Admiral Ramos! It's an honor. Would you care to come aboard?"

Festina turned to me. "Are you ready?"

I looked around the rooftop. Pieces of equipment lay scattered around us, though a lot had blown away in the wind from the shuttle's descent. "Let's pick up the pistols and the first-aid kit. Otherwise, the Cashlings might hurt themselves."

"You do that," Festina said. "I'll get your partner."

I wanted to tell her *I'd* handle Tut. Being gene-spliced, I assumed I was stronger than she was, even though we were the same size . . . and a man Tut's height would be heavy, despite his beanpole frame. But before I could speak, Festina slung Tut over her shoulder in a firefighter's lift and began waddling with him toward the open hatch. I hurried about gathering the gear we didn't want to leave behind.

As I collected equipment, I surreptitiously tucked and tugged at my chemise in an effort to cover myself more decently. I didn't like the thought of Li and Ubatu leering at me on the trip back. However, I needn't have bothered. By the time I climbed inside, I had the entire passenger cabin to myself . . . except for the unconscious Tut, slumped in one of the chairs and belted securely with a crash harness. Festina and the diplomats were all in the cockpit, with Li occupying the pilot's seat, Festina the copilot's, and Ubatu a pull-out chair blocking the doorway. Ubatu called back over her shoulder, "Stay in the cabin, Explorer. Take care of your partner. Admiral Ramos wants to talk with us up here."

I had a split second's glimpse of Festina's face showing the plaintive look of a woman who definitely *didn't* want to talk with ambitious dipshits. Then the cockpit door shut, leaving me on my own.

Li took off at once. I almost lost my balance as the floor shifted beneath me, but I caught hold of a nearby seat and steadied myself. Grappling myself into place next to Tut, I got belted in and checked that he was all right. He'd remain unconscious for at least six hours, but he'd been buckled up snug and safe. All I could do was let him sleep it off.

Which left me at loose ends. Trying not to think. Staring at the bite wounds on my feet—so small they'd heal completely in a day or two. By the time we reached Muta, no one would be able to see where I'd been boarded by fuzzy red hijackers. I'd be the perfect Trojan horse.

But I didn't want to brood about the spores in my blood. Casting about for other subjects to occupy my mind, it occurred to me that Li had interrupted my last communication with Captain Cohen, long before I'd had a chance to make a full report. I tongued my transmitter, contacted *Pistachio*'s ship-soul, and was transferred to the captain.

"What's going on down there?" Cohen asked. "The mayor of Zoonau is up in arms. He wants to arrest the lot of you for wanton destruction and public endangerment. Did something go wrong with the Balrog?"

"No. Ambassador Li got carried away in his haste to meet Admiral Ramos."

"The Cashlings are furious, Youn Suu. They'll want someone's head for this." Cohen didn't have to add, *Your head goes first—you were the lowest-ranking person on the mission.* Everyone in the navy knew that shit flowed downhill.

"Captain," I said, "a court-martial is the least of my worries." I gave him a summary of what had happened, including the coordinates for Muta and the admiral's wish to set sail as soon as we reached *Pistachio*. Cohen reacted with gratifying horror when he heard I'd been infected with spores . . . but thirty seconds later, his tone brightened greatly as he learned he had a Class One mission. He raced me through the rest of my story, in a hurry to contact Starbase Trillium for confirmation of the assignment.

I didn't know why he was excited. For Cohen, the trip to Muta was no different from his usual duties. *Pistachio* would fly Festina where she needed to go, then wait in orbit till she decided to leave. Maybe there'd be survivors to evacuate, but so what? They were all just passengers. Transporting passengers was routine business for *Pistachio*.

Why did the captain welcome this trip when it was really the same old thing? Cohen would never set foot on Muta; he'd just watch from the high exosphere and listen to our reports. At most, he'd have the excitement of being a passive witness as we faced whatever had attacked the settlers . . .

Was that why Cohen sounded so eager? For the chance to observe a life-or-death mission from the safety of his command chair? Or was I simply in such a negative mood, I immediately thought the worst of everyone's motives?

Time to clear my head of unskillful thoughts.

One good thing about the ambassador's shuttle: it had remarkably wide seats. Wide enough that I could pull up my legs and assume full lotus while still wearing my seat belt. I settled in, let my breathing go quiet, and forced myself to meditate.

Westerners believe a lot of nonsense about meditation . . . especially that it's some kind of trance where you lose touch with reality. No. Just the opposite. Meditation aims at awareness of the here and now. You don't let your mind wander to the past or future, to the tug of memories or plans; but you also don't compel your thoughts to go somewhere you think they should. You don't strive for bliss or release from old regrets. Meditation is just being where you are.

Which is much much harder than it sounds.

When meditation works, nothing special happens. There's no mystic ecstasy—just a sense of truly being present. Sitting in the cabin of Li's shuttle, I simply perceived what was there. The plush seats. The dusty smell of upholstery. The motion of the shuttle. The sound of Tut's breathing. My own breathing. My own breath.

No fancy life force perception. Just being awake and aware. Calmer than I'd been in a long time. Certainly better meditation than I'd managed in many a month or year . . .

Suddenly furious, I jerked back to my normal clenched-up

ground-state: ambushed by the thought that the Balrog was behind my atypical meditation success. It was helping me—clearing my mind. Since becoming an Explorer (and long before that), I'd only managed fitful bits of quiet . . . a second here, a second there, interspersed with long bouts where my thoughts drifted off on a string of casual distractions. Sitting sessions still helped me relax, but they'd seldom delved anywhere deeper. Now, unexpectedly, with all the troubles on my mind, why could I immediately reach a crystal-clear dhyana state and hold it?

The Balrog was manipulating my mind: making meditation trivially easy.

You demon, I thought. *You've ruined this for me. You've cheapened the most valuable thing in my life.*

I could never meditate again. If I achieved any heightened awareness, I'd always fear it was the Balrog's doing. And if I didn't achieve any "skillful effect," what was the point of meditation?

"You utter bastard," I said in a low voice. "You've cut my lifeline."

No answer.

For the rest of the trip, I just stared out the window at the black airlessness of space.

5

Yana [Sanskrit]: Vehicle, conveyance. The different schools of Buddhism are often called "vehicles" since they are different ways of traveling toward the same goal: enlightenment. Hinayana (the small vehicle) centers around monastic life. Mahayana (the large vehicle) is more populist, teaching all people to strive for compassion. Vajrayana (the diamond vehicle) has a mystic bent; a number of Vajrayana sects practice esoteric rituals to gain spiritual purity. Tarayana (the starry vehicle) arose after humanity left Old Earth; it concentrates on the psychology of freeing one's mind from unskillful ways. While there are doctrinal variations among the schools, history has seen very little actual conflict (as opposed to, say, Protestants and Roman Catholics in Christianity, or Sunni and Shiite Muslims). Differences are more a matter of emphasis than of outright dispute.

WHEN we got back to *Pistachio*, my first priority was clothing. Luckily, I had a spare uniform in the Explorer equipment lockers, not far from the shuttle bay. I could get dressed without having to sneak half-naked through the ship to my cabin.

While I was in the equipment area, I found a Bumbler and checked myself for alien tissue. The scan was solid black: Balrog deposits from my head to my toes. If I slashed my wrists, I'd ooze spores instead of blood.

It was quiet in the equipment room. I sat on a bench for a while, wondering if I'd cry.

I didn't. Enough was enough.

By leaving to get a new uniform, I missed the uproar surrounding *Pistachio*'s exit from Cashleen vac-space. The Cashlings refused to give departure clearance until they received reparations for the damage done to Zoonau's ropeways. Our Technocracy embassy on Cashleen wanted Li to come back and make some token appeasement—not necessarily an apology, but at least a repentant gesture. Li wanted to gesture at the Cashlings, all right, but not in a contrite manner. Captain Cohen wanted Li and every other diplomat off his ship, to free up passenger space for Muta survivors. Festina just wanted to get under way as soon as possible . . . and since Class One missions took priority over other concerns, she had the clout to cut short the yammering.

In the end, Li and Ubatu ordered the rest of their delegation to go down to Cashleen, where the team of diplomats would smooth the ruffled feathers of the Cashling government. Li and Ubatu themselves remained on *Pistachio* . . . partly from a ghoulish desire to see what would happen on Muta, partly from an urge to keep riding Festina's coattails, and partly from the need to get out of the Cashleen system before the authorities pressed charges. Still, we divested the ship of ten unneeded diplomats, which gave Cohen more room in the passenger section and gave everyone else something to smile about . . . except possibly Tut. He was still unconscious, and would stay that way for five more hours. Festina suggested that Tut be taken to the infirmary, and Cohen said he'd "take appropriate measures."

Considering Cohen's feelings for Tut, that might have meant leaving Tut's body on the bare floor of the shuttle bay and letting him wake up on his own.

* * *

Pistachio pulled out of orbit and headed sunward to recharge the ship's energy envelope. The envelope was commonly called a Sperm-field: a milky sheath that formed a pocket universe around the ship and let us move at faster-than-light speeds through the universe outside. Charging the field in a star's chromosphere was a new procedure—until recently, the navy had believed Sperm-fields would be torn apart if a ship got too much solar radiation. Then between my junior and senior year at the Academy, all the textbooks suddenly changed to say that a solar bath made Sperm-fields *stronger* . . . and every ship in the navy abruptly became ten times faster.

Science marches on.

Anyway, the voyage to Muta would once have taken two weeks; now, we'd get there in a day and a half. We had precious little time for preparations.

The instant we left Cashleen, Festina called a meeting in *Pistachio*'s small conference room. Only Captain Cohen and I were invited . . . but Li and Ubatu showed up too and Festina let them stay. (She whispered to me, "They'll just cause trouble if I kick them out. They'll be nuisances here too, but at least I can keep an eye on them.")

When everyone was seated at the conference table, Festina convened the meeting. "All right. We have thirty-six hours to develop a plan for the landing. First step: reviewing available information about Muta. There's quite a lot—Starbase Trillium has forwarded files obtained from the Unity. Every bit of data they have on their settlements there."

Li gave a derisive snort. "Every bit of data? I doubt it. Those bastards hate sharing *anything* with the Technocracy."

"Admittedly, they seldom talk to us," Festina said. "In this case, however, they have no choice. Withholding information from a rescue mission would endanger our lives and the people we're trying to save. The Unity has to tell us everything they know, or they'll get in trouble with the League."

Ambassador Li looked dubious. Perhaps he had unhappy past dealings with the Unity. No surprise: the Unity and the Technocracy had been at odds for centuries, with plenty of resentment built up on both sides. This state of tension wasn't a war—not even a cold war. More like the huffiness between a divorced couple who want to conduct themselves with decorum but simply can't stop bickering.

The Unity had divorced itself from the Technocracy three hundred years ago: a mere century after our ancestors left Old Earth. The cause of the breakup was irreconcilable differences over the raising of children. Children like me. Bioengineered.

As I've said, gene-tinkering is illegal in the Technocracy (except to cure serious medical conditions and in a few other strictly regulated situations). Most artificial enhancements are also banned: amplification chips in the brain, subcutaneous armor, and similar augmentations. The laws aren't always obeyed—on every planet, there are people like my self-centered mother or Ubatu's haute couture parents who believe laws only apply to others—but in general, Technocracy citizens are pure *Homo sapiens* without too much embedded hardware or unnatural DNA.

The Unity, on the other hand, don't accept a priori limitations. Their ancestors questioned the ethics of remaining merely human. Why, for example, would you force people to make do with "natural" babies when science could produce children who were healthier, happier, and smarter? Wasn't it cruel to create inferior offspring when superior children were possible? How could you justify the continued production of weaklings and cripples when it was entirely unnecessary? It wasn't fair to the children, it wasn't fair to the parents, and it wasn't fair to society.

Similarly, why balk at modifying humans after birth? If, for example, people opted to live in a deep-sea colony, why not give them gills? It was a simple surgical procedure that solved a host of problems. Without it, one needed bulky and expensive machinery to survive (scuba tanks, air-pumping systems), and even then, there was always the risk of accidental failure. The Technocracy claimed that tampering with human essence was "immoral" . . . but how could it be immoral to protect people from drowning?

Those were the kinds of questions that started the schism. A group of humans who disagreed with the Technocracy's ban on augmentation quietly vanished from the neighborhood of New Earth. Fifty years later, the same people and their children resurfaced as the Unity: industrious, placid, and annoyingly sane.

Technocracy doomsayers might have expected the Unity to become hellish cyborgs: brain-linked mutants with robot arms, and wheels instead of feet. But our Unified cousins remained human in appearance . . . mostly. Those in specialized jobs modified themselves as needed and changed back when they were finished. If they had any qualms about getting fingers amputated and replaced with welding torches, they kept it to themselves. Probably, they took such changes in stride and wondered what the fuss was about—members of the Unity were irritatingly well adjusted. (They looked like they *never* screamed at their mothers.)

In a way, the Technocracy and the Unity acted like two halves of a broken family in a broadcast comedy. Our half was made up of ne'er-do-wells: the ones who fought and hollered, whose government was perennially corrupt and whose lives were an ongoing fiasco of greedy ineptitude. Their half consisted of the ever-polite gentry, unfailingly well behaved and earnest, but clueless about how to deal with their brash, obnoxious relatives. They were embarrassed by our crassness, while we were peeved at their wholesomeness. Both sides preferred to avoid each other . . . and when circumstances forced us together, we always began with "This time we'll make it work," but ended in our usual roles: the Technocracy as squabbling buffoons and the Unity as stuffed-shirt prigs. Like a divorced couple, we brought out the worst in each other.

But like a divorced couple, we weren't utterly blind to each other's strengths. Members of the Unity sometimes admitted they might be a little too obsessed with control; they planned and planned and planned, but if they encountered an unexpected obstacle, they knew they had trouble with spontaneous improvisation. Their process of reaching a careful consensus meant they seldom got caught by surprise . . . but if a surprise *did* come along, they were slow to react. They weren't stupid or uncreative; but centuries of genetic tinkering had bred out "lone wolf" impulsiveness, and that sometimes left them at a disadvantage.

On the other hand, I didn't like lone wolves myself. Explorers survived through teamwork and forethought, rather than going their own impetuous ways. No plan could anticipate every contingency, but thinking ahead was far better than leaving things to chance. One should never depend on luck.

So, unlike Li, I admired the Unity. In particular, I admired their survey teams—the only people in the galaxy who might equal our own Explorer Corps. Their equipment and training were just as good, their advance planning was better, and they actually had their people's support. Unity surveyors were treated like heroes: lauded by the public and held up as examples. Little girls and boys grew up *longing* to win a place on first-landing teams.

Contrast that with Explorers. I wondered if the Technocracy had staffed our corps with pariahs just to be different from the Unity. It wouldn't be the first time our government had been that petty.

But in the Unity, surveyors were the best of the best . . . and Muta had been settled by survey teams. Every last colonist was a trained surveyor: elite, bioengineered for genius, and augmented to the *n*th degree. If the entire populace had *still* been wiped out with only time for a single Mayday . . .

. . . how much better could Explorers do?

Each of us at the conference table had a vidscreen with access to all the files on Muta. My first action—and probably the first action of everyone else present—was to send my personal data agent tunneling through the files in search of "hot spots": juicy information it knew I would care about.

My agent was almost as old as me—software that had grown by my side, learning my likes and dislikes, developing algorithms to winnow fields of data down to the most meaningful grains of fact.

The program had changed a great deal over the years . . . especially when I entered the Academy and was forced to pay attention to information I'd never cared about before. The software and I had both endured a radical reeducation; but we'd got through together, and now my agent could zip through the files with a skilled Explorer's eye.

Ultimately, of course, I'd have to read everything in detail myself—nobody who understands computers trusts them completely. But I could rely on my software servant to provide me with a good first overview, and to highlight key words or phrases I'd found important in the past. Considering how little time we had before reaching Muta, such shortcuts were valuable.

So, an overview report, courtesy of my agent. The Unity had approached Muta with maximum caution. A single survey team had landed and stayed in one place for several months, carefully monitored by an orbiting luna-ship. Then another team put down on the other side of the planet, in a completely different type of ecosystem. Three more teams set up camp a month later, again in different terrains. All were watched closely for five full years, always with at least one luna-ship ready to evacuate everyone at the first sign of trouble. Finally, another four teams were assigned to "points of interest" from earlier observations, with another full year of monitoring. Only then did the last luna-ship depart, leaving the Mutan teams to continue gathering information. If all went well, the Unity had planned to start full colonization in another ten years.

Not bad, I thought. More patience and caution than the Technocracy would have shown. Of course, the Unity knew something had scared off or killed the Greenstriders. Moving in too many people too quickly was an unacceptable risk. The longer they held off on full settlement, the more chance the survey teams would find whatever threat lurked on Muta.

But so far, the teams had turned up nothing . . . or at least nothing my data agent noticed. The agent's report had a few lines at the bottom summarizing geological, hydrological, meteorological, and other findings, but they simply confirmed what I'd already been told—Muta was a first-rate planet for colonization. It was highly Earth-like, but too young to have evolved intelligent life. More precisely, it had reached its mid-Triassic period, with abundant land vertebrates and lots of ferns. Flowering plants weren't due to arrive for another fifty million years; but the Greenstriders had thrown everything off schedule by bringing in their favorite crops, a supply of pollinating insects, and various other lifeforms they liked to have around. (Pets. Farm animals. Ornamental shrubs. The Greenstriders always surrounded themselves with the comforts of home, and to hell with the indigenous ecology.)

I clicked my vidscreen's controls and proceeded to the next section of the agent's report: key words and phrases. The top word on the list was naturally "death"—always an Explorer's number one concern. But the word only appeared in innocuous contexts ("Average death rates of microorganisms . . ." "Protomammals dissected after death . . .") so I scanned down the other entries for anything noteworthy. Some of the words were simple (danger, threat, risk), while others were technical terms I'd never heard of till I reached third-year planetology. None of the references rang any warning bells . . . until I reached a phrase that always caught an Explorer's attention: *Capsicillium croceum.*

It was a species of tree noted chiefly for fruit shaped like small yellow chili peppers. Definitely not native to Muta—it was too biologically sophisticated compared to Muta's fernlike flora, and besides, *Capsicillium croceum* had been recorded on more than ninety other planets. In fact, there'd been plenty of these "minichili" trees on my homeworld, Anicca . . .

I found myself remembering a morning when I was twelve: the first clear day after months of monsoon rains, and everyone wanted out into the sunshine. Even my mother deigned to leave the house; by that time, I did most of the shopping so Mother didn't have to be seen by others with her bare thanaka-free face, but she could still bear a little public scrutiny under congenial circumstances. I wanted to go to the market where we might see pretty things . . . including a certain boy who'd watched most keenly when I danced at a recent street masque. But Mother wanted to visit a temple—and after her usual maddening hour of vacillation, she chose the Ghost Fountain Pagoda on the edge of town. (She thought it would be less crowded than places in the city center. I told her *every* temple would be crowded in such lovely weather, probably more crowded than the market, and couldn't we go shopping instead? But with the sky so clear and the temperature perfect, I was in too good a mood to start a major fight. Besides, I could prowl the market later by myself, once my mother got her fill of fresh air.)

Like most temples on Anicca, the Ghost Fountain Pagoda was ecumenical—open to Buddhists of every denomination, and anyone else who might drop by. We therefore shared the walkways with saffron-robed Theravada monks and nuns, their heads shaved and their begging bowls full of donations from sun-happy passersby . . . with hawkers selling favorite Mahayana icons—prints and holos and statuettes of the saintly Bodhisattvas who symbolize various virtues . . . with Vajrayana mystics engaged in their perennial rituals, spinning prayer wheels, banging drums, chalking impromptu mandalas on the pavement . . . and with those of my own school, Tarayana, "the starry vehicle," not monastic, populist, or mystic, but more oriented toward psychology. We Tarayana adherents were respectful but dubious about showy religious practices, and therefore kept a restrained distance from the temple's more exuberant devotees. My mother (convinced as always that she was somehow exceptional, a jewel apart from the common crowd) disdained the "superstitious breast-beating and mumbo jumbo" of the older sects in favor of the "pure scientific spirituality" of our own. Sometimes I secretly felt the same, wondering what the no-nonsense Buddha would have thought of PARINIRVANA BRAND INCENSE-STICKS™ or the man and woman practicing Neo-Tantric sex in the middle of an open sunny glade; but I refused to admit I agreed with my mother on anything. I put money into every begging bowl we passed and bought a bag of pricey red sand to sprinkle ostentatiously on patches of gravel I pretended were especially holy.

The pagoda lay in the middle of the Arboretum of Heroes: a park with concentric rings of trees and statues. The statues (bronze, stone, plastic, ceramic) depicted noble figures from myth or history—great warriors, enlightened sages, and tragic martyrs. Many individuals had been all three; there's nothing dearer to my people's hearts than an admired soldier who refuses to break some minor Buddhist precept and, therefore, dies horribly. The more pain and mutilation, the better. In Eastern legends, death is *always* part of the story. Even if a hero dies peacefully at a ripe old age, you have to include that death as part of the hero's tale. Many Western champions just vanish into the sunset or "live happily ever after," as if death passes them by . . . but in the stories I heard growing up, the time and manner of a hero's death were never glossed over. Often, they were the whole point.

Which is why the trees surrounding the statues were *Capsicillium croceum*. The trees' yellow chili-fruit contained a protein that acted as deadly nerve poison to most Terran creatures. You could always see animal corpses rotting in the shady groves—squirrels and sparrows, bees and butterflies, who'd nibbled on minichilis and died within seconds. Their decomposing bodies were left where they fell, as object lessons for people walking past: "One day, this will happen to you too." The trees bore death in small fruit clusters, just as the statues carried reminders of death in the stories they evoked.

In fact, the entire temple grounds whispered of things long departed. Millennia before humans colonized the planet, Anicca had housed an alien race whom archeologists called Las Fuentes. The temple had been built on the same land as a Fuentes town . . . yet little remained of Las Fuentes now but the minichili trees they planted wherever they settled. They'd inhabited more than ninety planets in this part of the galaxy—planets now belonging to the Technocracy, the Unity, and several other intelligent species—but Las Fuentes had ceased to be, some sixty-five hundred years ago.

They hadn't eradicated themselves by the usual means: war, plague, or nanite disaster. They'd gone much more quietly and deliberately than that. Before they went, Las Fuentes had cleaned up almost all trace of their presence—their cities, their farms, even their garbage dumps and cemeteries, all reduced to a fine sandlike powder. The thoroughness of this erasure drove modern-day archeologists wild with frustration; Las Fuentes had left virtually nothing our scientists could study for clues to the past. Ninety planets empty except for a few bits of bric-a-brac, one or two broken pieces of furniture . . . and *Capsicillium croceum*. The trees the aliens had planted everywhere.

Las Fuentes left one other set of mementos. On each of their planets they'd built hundreds of simple stone fountains, plus a network of roads joining every fountain to its neighbors. The fountains and roads were left intact when Las Fuentes eradicated the rest of their civilization. Most experts thought the fountains had religious significance—so sacred they couldn't be destroyed, even when Las Fuentes divested themselves of everything else. I had my doubts about that; I disliked how xenoanthropologists used "religious significance" to label every alien practice they didn't understand. But many human worshipers thought the fountains had religious significance too. Elsewhere in the Technocracy, Christians had constructed churches at fountain sites, Hindus had set up shrines to Vishnu or Ganesha, and Santeria worshipers conducted midnight ceremonies beside fountains in the depths of jungles. On Anicca, almost every Fuentes fountain had an associated temple or lamasery . . . including the Ghost Fountain Pagoda, where the pagoda was built around such a fountain, and the "ghosts" were Las Fuentes themselves.

Not that Las Fuentes were extinct . . . at least not in the usual sense. As Mother and I entered the pagoda (where a giant golden Buddha with lotus-petal hair and clothes of saffron spider-silk smiled in the fountain's bowl), we passed holo images of Las Fuentes as they are today: blobs of purple jelly that shone with UV-indigo light.

Sixty-five hundred years ago, Las Fuentes hadn't died; they'd leapt up the evolutionary ladder to transcend normal flesh and blood. They'd become purple jelly-things that could teleport at will, foresee the future, manipulate objects through force of mind, and violate most of the laws of physics.

Were powers like that sufficient compensation for becoming grape jam? Looking at the blobby jelly holos in the pagoda, I wasn't sure if the transformation had been a fair trade-off. But then, nobody was sure of *anything* when it came to Las Fuentes. For example, no one knew how they'd managed their ascension. Juggling their DNA? Downloading their consciousness into nanite subsystems? Impressing their intellects onto the universal background radiation? Technocracy scientists would dearly love to replicate the Fuentes uplift procedure . . . but because Las Fuentes had erased their culture so effectively, our experts had nothing to go on when trying to reproduce the technology.

The new jelly-form Fuentes refused to explain what they'd done. They seldom interacted with humans; they maintained an embassy on New Earth, but the doors were usually locked. Once in a while, a mound of shimmering purple would materialize in someone's home, make a pronouncement, then disappear again . . . but the jelly-things never stayed long enough to be analyzed, and they *definitely* didn't answer questions from "lower beings."

Rather like gods.

That's one reason why Aniccans built a temple around a Fuentes fountain, and why we put purple jelly holos under the same roof as the Buddha himself. Powerful beings deserved acknowledgment. We didn't *worship* Las Fuentes any more than we worshiped Buddha, but we liked having their images around for inspiration. Even my mother gave a little bow and chanted something softly as she passed the purple holos. A moment later, she said, "You pray too, Ma Youn. Maybe the spirits will heal your cheek."

"They aren't spirits, Mother. They're aliens."

"They're smart aliens with advanced technology. That makes them *better* than spirits. Show them respect, and maybe they'll help you."

"These are just holos, Mother. The Fuentes aren't really here."

"You never know, they could be listening. Maybe standing right beside you, but invisible."

"The Fuentes have better ways to pass the time than lurking in one of our temples. They're higher beings, Mother. They must . . ."

I stopped—because the holo in front of us had become tangible. Not just a lighting effect, but an actual mound of jelly: shining UV/purple. It slid a short distance toward me and raised a pseudopod to my face . . . but before it made contact with my skin, the creature suddenly lurched backward with a sharp feline hiss. Like a Western vampire reeling away from a crucifix. The jelly bolted for the pagoda's exit; and without thinking I ran after it, a twelve-year-old girl eager to follow anything strange. I got to the door and scanned the grounds, trying to see where the jelly had fled . . .

. . . and every statue in sight had changed. All the bronze warriors, the marble sages, the martyrs in terra-cotta—they were now possessed by aliens. The purple jelly had climbed up a chiseled image of the Holy Madman of Pegu, while beside it, the noble features of King Thagya Min were obscured by smears of what looked like crawling black sand. A granite rendering of Buddha's lovable but dim-witted disciple Ananda was surrounded by a whirling cloud of dust; Hui-Neng, the Sixth Chinese Patriarch and founder of Zen, had scarlet lava dripping down the right half of his body, while the left had turned to glass. Through all the Arboretum of Heroes, not a single statue remained untouched: flames enveloped one, blue-leafed vines another, cottage-cheese goo a third.

I turned back to my mother, abandoning my usual hostility and just wanting to say, "Hey, Mom, come see this!" But the words were never spoken. My eye was caught by the Buddha in the fountain, entirely coated with glowing red moss . . .

In the conference room of *Pistachio*, I almost jerked out of my chair with a scream. Almost. But my "freeze-in-place" reflex had kicked in, and I made no sound, no movement. No physical reaction at all; but inside, my thoughts were racing.

Had any of that truly happened? Had my mother and I gone to the Ghost Fountain Pagoda on a clear sunny day? *Was* there actually something called the Ghost Fountain Pagoda on the outskirts of our town? Had I seen a purple-jelly Fuentes, had it recoiled from me, had the Buddha been covered with Balrog spores? The memories seemed so real—one hundred percent genuine. Yet they were also far-fetched: the Fuentes, the Balrog, all those other transcendent aliens casually manifesting themselves for no reason. And if something so strange had truly happened to me, why hadn't the memory of the moss-covered Buddha leapt to mind as soon as I saw the pictures of moss-covered Zoonau? Why was I only remembering it now?

Sometimes, in the middle of the night, I've awakened from a dream unable to draw the line between dream and reality. I may dream I signed up for some computer-run training course and come morning I have to take the exam, even though I haven't done any of the lessons. For minutes after I wake, I lie trickling with sweat, trying to decide if I really did enroll in such a course or if it was just a figment of my sleeping imagination. Did I or didn't I? Such dreams could be so convincing, I honestly couldn't sort out the truth.

This felt like the same thing. Did I really go to that temple and see what I saw? Or was it just a false memory?

A false memory planted by the Balrog.

You demon! I wanted to scream. *You demon, you demon, you demon!* The demon's spores were inside my head, and I couldn't even trust my own memories. I truly didn't know if those things at the pagoda had happened. The recollections seemed so real, but . . .

"Something wrong, Youn Suu?" Festina asked.

I must have made some noise that caught her attention. My body had finally unfrozen and given away my inner turmoil.

Now Festina was looking at me. Her expression wary. Regarding me as a spore-infected security risk. Her mistrust was entirely justified—my inability to judge memories true or false proved that. If I'd had any sense of responsibility, I should have declared myself unfit for duty and walked out of the room.

But I didn't. I didn't want to admit I was broken, and I didn't want to isolate myself from Festina. I didn't want to be alone.

So I mumbled, "I think I've found something," and looked at my data screen, hoping there'd be something I could pretend was noteworthy.

I read the words, EXTENSIVE WELL-PRESERVED RUINS.

EXTENSIVE WELL-PRESERVED RUINS OVERGROWN WITH *CAPSICILLIUM CROCEUM*.

EXTENSIVE WELL-PRESERVED RUINS OVERGROWN WITH *CAPSICILLIUM CROCEUM*, DATING BACK 6500 YEARS.

What?

Quickly, I opened the corresponding file. Festina's eyes still watched me. The computer displayed a survey conducted from orbit early in the Unity's investigation of the planet. They'd sent robot probes to check promising areas for settlement . . . particularly fertile plains with plenty of rivers to serve as water supplies. Unsurprisingly, they'd found evidence of recent Greenstrider habitation—Greenstriders always sought out good farmland—but the Unity also found *Capsicillium croceum*, and ruins much older than the Greenstrider colonies.

The ruins dated back to the days of Las Fuentes civilization. But Las Fuentes didn't *leave* ruins. On every other world they'd colonized, they'd erased all remains of their presence.

I keyed my data agent to do a cross-reference. Yes: several similar sites had been found in other regions of Muta: sixty-five-hundred-year-old ruins and *Capsicillium croceum*, all in the sort of areas where Las Fuentes usually lived. The Unity had even followed up their findings—the last four survey teams sent to Muta had all established camps near ancient ruin sites. They'd then proceeded to excavate the ruins . . . albeit with extreme caution.

The surveyors had found artifacts. *Lots* of artifacts. Anything from simple tools (hammers, saws, hand drills) to high-tech gadgets of unguessable intent. Most were in terrible condition—what could you expect after six and a half millennia?—but a modest amount of equipment had avoided the ravages of time inside weatherproof containers. Result: the Unity had stumbled across a treasure trove of technology from aliens who were more advanced than anyone we knew and who'd never left so much as a thumbtack anywhere else.

I lifted my head and looked Festina right in the eye. "I *have* found something," I said. "Something important."

"Like what?"

I told her.

I didn't get far into what I had to say—ruins, artifacts, Las Fuentes—when Li interrupted me. "Who are these Las Fuentes and why should we care?"

Festina didn't answer. She was keying her way through the files, looking for the records I'd found . . . and perhaps she also disdained any professional diplomat who wasn't familiar with a species that had an embassy on New Earth. I wondered about that myself; but there are hundreds of species, major and minor, with a presence on New Earth, and Li might not know them all. Especially not a race with a history of spurning all diplomatic overtures. I told Li, "Las Fuentes were an alien species who used to live in this part of the galaxy. Around 4000 B.C., the race transmuted itself up the evolutionary ladder. Now they look like heaps of purple jelly."

"Oh," said Li. "Those bastards. Useless."

He sat back in his chair as if he'd lost interest. I suppose from a diplomat's point of view, the modern Fuentes *were* useless. They refused to trade with humans, they wouldn't talk about science, and they seldom even shared tidbits of information about the galaxy and its inhabitants. "Las Fuentes may not interact much with humans," I said (trying to suppress my true/false memory of meeting a Fuentes at the temple), "but they're still important to the Technocracy. We know of many alien species beyond human level, but Las Fuentes are the only ones who ascended within reachable history. Not long ago, they were at the same evolutionary level we are now. Then they developed some process that let them become something superior."

Li rolled his eyes. "I don't consider purple jelly my superior."

Ubatu muttered, "I consider orange marmalade your superior."

"Now, now," Captain Cohen said.

"The point is," I said, "of all the races above us on the evolutionary ladder, Las Fuentes are the most recent to climb there. If you count 4000 B.C. as recent."

"Actually," Festina said, "the most recent Fuentes ascension was two years ago. I was there."

She'd spoken softly—a quiet statement that caught the rest of us off guard. I felt my automatic "freeze reflex" kick in again . . . just for an instant, then it was gone. Li opened his mouth, then shut it. Ubatu's mouth was open too; her hand came up to cover it.

"Admiral," Cohen said, "you'd better tell us about it."

I met some Fuentes," Festina said. "Possibly the only two left who hadn't ascended."

Li and Ubatu leaned forward eagerly, but Cohen and I eased back in our chairs as if we were about to hear bad news. I don't know why the difference. Maybe because diplomats treat secrets like currency—the more they have, the more they can spend at opportune moments—but captains and Explorers treat secrets like bombs to be disarmed: nobody tells us classified information until it's festered into a crisis we're expected to fix.

"When the majority of Fuentes transformed themselves," Festina said, "a few couldn't bring themselves to take the plunge. Too afraid of radical change. Personally, I don't blame them. Who wouldn't be horrified by the thought of becoming a mound of jelly? I'd consider it healthy to say, 'Fuck that,' and get on with your life.

"But those who refused to ascend," she said, "never forgot what they'd turned down. It must have preyed on their minds constantly; they just couldn't get past it. I suppose they might have been lonely—missing the world and the people they'd known. Perhaps they also suffered from survivor guilt . . . or shame. Anyway, the holdouts never made anything of themselves; they just wandered the galaxy in the last Fuentes starship, no purpose but listless survival.

The only work they could bring themselves to do was to sabotage up-and-coming races they thought might eventually become threats . . . but even for that, they couldn't muster much energy. As if they'd died when the rest of their kind ascended.

"So one by one, the remaining Fuentes gave in. They still had the means to transform themselves; and each year, a few of the hold-outs decided that risking change was better than centuries of going nowhere. By the time I found where they'd been hiding, there were only two left—two pathetic specimens. Physically, they were fine, even after six millennia. Las Fuentes must have had superb antiaging treatments. But mentally . . . what would you expect from creatures who'd lived a hundred lifetimes in fear of taking a leap of faith? I admire caution, but eventually one's spirit shrivels. The last two Fuentes were the most soul-shriveled beings I've ever encountered."

"But they eventually ascended?" Ubatu asked.

"Eventually." Festina spoke the word as if there was a great deal more to the story but she preferred not to go into details.

"How?" Li asked. "Did you see the process?"

Festina nodded. "You probably know Las Fuentes left thousands of fountains behind. Those fountains produced a fluid called blood honey. Bathing in the fluid brought on the transformation."

"They changed into purple jelly?"

"They changed into creatures who looked like jelly, given our limited vision." Festina shrugged. "I've met a number of elevated beings; none looked like much to human eyes. Does that mean ascended creatures aren't impressive? Or could it be that *Homo sapiens* aren't perceptive enough to see what's really there?"

Li made his usual face of disgust. He clearly hated any suggestion that humans weren't the crowning glory of the universe; but he was reluctant to contradict the celebrated Admiral Ramos. Instead, he changed the subject. "So these fountains," he said. "They're the key to the transformation. Have we studied them?"

Festina shook her head. "They've been dry for thousands of years. Nothing left to study . . . except for the one used by the Fuentes I met."

"And what about that fountain?"

"It's no longer available."

We waited for her to explain. She didn't. In the silence, a thought struck me; I did a quick search on our files. "There were no fountains on Muta," I said. "At least none found by the Unity."

"Interesting," Festina said. She sat back in her chair with a pensive look.

"These Fuentes," Cohen said. "We had a lot of their fountains on my home planet . . . but nothing else. Before they ascended, they cleaned up, right? Pulverized all traces of their civilization?"

Festina nodded.

"But Muta has ruins," Cohen continued, "as if the Fuentes didn't have time to clean up. They just left things as is."

"I see where you're heading," Ubatu said. "We know there's something dangerous on Muta—something that attacked the Greenstriders and the Unity. So maybe it attacked the Fuentes too. They might have started some settlements, built things up for a few years, then suddenly got taken by surprise."

"Right," Cohen said. "And this happened before the Fuentes began their process of ascension—before they built the fountains, which is why there aren't any fountains on Muta. Later, when the Fuentes were cleaning up in preparation for ascension, they couldn't erase their abandoned colony on Muta because they were too afraid of whatever was on the planet."

Ubatu nodded. "That's why there are Fuentes ruins on Muta, unlike everywhere else. They didn't dare go back to clean up."

"It's possible," Festina admitted. "But if so, I'm more worried than ever. Sixty-five hundred years ago, Las Fuentes were much more advanced than we are. The few Fuentes artifacts that survive are technologically superior to anything we have now. If Las Fuentes had such high tech and were still scared of whatever's on Muta, we're really going to have our hands full."

So what else is new? I thought.

* * *

We studied the files for several more hours but found no hints of what might lurk down on Muta. The Unity had been thorough in their investigations; they'd checked as many possibilities as time and personnel allowed, yet they'd turned up no unusual threats.

Of course, their knowledge had gaps. For one thing, the files contained almost nothing on activities in the past six months. That was how long it had been since the last luna-ship visited the planet and received downloads of survey team findings. It would have been nice to know what the teams were doing just before they went non-comm . . . but the Unity swore they didn't have that information.

Perhaps, as Li suspected, the Unity was hiding something from us. Or perhaps we'd received everything the Unity had, and it just wasn't as much as we hoped. A handful of survey teams can't possibly learn all about a planet in just a few years. For example, the Unity knew almost nothing about Muta's oceans: a serious problem, considering that three-quarters of the planet's surface was covered with salt water. I couldn't help remembering the Technocracy planet Triomphe, which once housed three hundred thousand human colonists . . . until an army of intelligent octopi had emerged from the deeps to exterminate every man, woman, and child.

On Muta, rampaging octopi wouldn't be an immediate problem; the Unity had located their settlements well away from ocean shores until they could explore the marine world in depth. But the seas weren't the only unexamined source of hazard. There were also vast numbers of unknown microbes living in the atmosphere, water, and soil. The teams had done their best with their limited time and resources—almost a third of the people on Muta were studying microscopic life-forms—but there was so much to learn, they could easily miss some microbial species that was lethal to human life.

On the other hand, microbial action was unlikely to silence everyone on every survey team simultaneously. The teams were spread all over the planet, in widely dissimilar ecosystems. Different microbes would be present in different proportions, growing at different speeds under different conditions in different individuals.

How could natural germ activity strike down everyone in the same instant?

And if not natural germ activity, what about unnatural? Deliberate bioweapons. That was also possible. At the Academy, we studied a recent bioengineered plague on the planet Demoth. The plague organisms had been created by nanotech "death factories" left over from a long-dead culture that had destroyed itself through germ warfare . . . and even though the aliens who made the factories had died millennia ago, the factories were still perfectly capable of analyzing *Homo sapiens* and producing a lethal disease precisely tailored to human metabolisms.

Thinking about that plague, I remembered something important about Demoth's epidemic. The source of the disease had been discovered by a karmic avalanche named Festina Ramos.

I glanced at her grim face. Was she tortured by the possibility that history was repeating itself?

On Demoth, the plague had claimed sixty million lives.

A lot of death. A lot of death.

At six o'clock ship's time, Captain Cohen was called away to talk with the Executive Officer—routine business about the next day's arrival at Muta. Festina took the interruption as an excuse to adjourn our "conference" . . . not that we'd been conferring much. We'd read the files in silence, Festina and I concentrating on planetological data while the others went through daily logs and personnel reports. Ubatu and Li got the occasional snicker from what the Unity chose to record ("Lieutenants Yardley and Juarez fined ten credits for disturbing the peace through contentious disputes on the taxonomy of slime molds"), but none of us found any glaring clues to Muta's hidden danger.

In retrospect, we shouldn't have expected obvious warning signs. Unity surveyors were smart and cautious. If they'd run into overt prospects of danger, they'd quickly evacuate their settlements. Even if they didn't have a luna-ship waiting to take them away, each team had an emergency escape shuttle that could blast off from the surface and go into stable orbit until help arrived. According to the files we'd received, all those shuttles were still on the ground. The teams had been completely blindsided—they hadn't seen what kind of trouble they were in, and, reading their records, neither could we.

So the meeting broke up. Li and Ubatu invited Festina to dinner in the VIP suite, but she said she wanted to inspect *Pistachio*'s landing equipment. When the diplomats had gone, however, she sat back down in her chair. "Youn Suu?"

"Yes?"

"How do you feel now?"

"No different than usual," I said. Which was true. Whatever the Balrog might be doing to me, I couldn't sense the changes . . . any more than I could tell if my "memories" of the aliens at the pagoda were real or artificially constructed.

"Have you checked yourself with a Bumbler?" Festina asked.

I nodded. "The Balrog has spread everywhere."

"If I were in your position," Festina said, "I'd be terrified. Probably screaming my lungs out."

"I doubt that."

"Oh, I wouldn't scream out loud. But inside my head . . ." Festina shrugged, then gave a bitter smile. "Inside my head, I'd beat myself up—saying a normal person would scream and what was wrong with me that I never had normal reactions? But I'd still feel like shit."

"I feel like shit too," I assured her.

"Good." She smiled. "That's a normal reaction." Then she said, "You know I can't trust you, right?"

I suppressed a shiver. "I don't trust myself."

"And that partner of yours . . ." Festina made a dismissive gesture. "When we get to Muta, I'm tempted to go down solo. I'm the only one I *do* trust."

My turn to make a dismissive gesture. "But you can't go solo because it violates regulations. No one can go into danger alone when other Explorers are available as backup."

"The precise words of the regulation are 'when other *competent* Explorers are available as backup.' Between myself, Captain Cohen, and *Pistachio*'s doctor, I'm sure we could find grounds to declare you and Tut unfit for duty."

"I don't doubt it." I looked at her. "But you aren't going to do that?"

She shook her head. "The Balrog clearly wants to take part in this mission. If I said no, it would find a way to tag along in spite of me—probably by taking over your body and doing something drastic."

A prickle of fear went through me. "That would be bad."

"I agree. So I'll let you come to Muta. I just won't trust you." She looked at me with sad eyes. "Which means I've already ordered the ship-soul not to let you near the Explorer equipment rooms unless I'm there to watch you. I can't take the chance that the Balrog will use you to sabotage our gear. I have previous experience with the goddamned moss. It likes to play games."

Festina waited for me to say something. I didn't. After a moment, she said, "If it's any consolation, I've told the ship-soul to keep Tut out too."

"Will you let him go with us to Muta?"

"I haven't decided. Do *you* want him along?"

"Yes. He's part of this too."

"Is that Youn Suu speaking or the Balrog?"

"I don't know." I took a breath. "From this point on, I'll never know who's speaking, will I?"

"No. You won't." Festina lowered her eyes in thought, drumming her fingers on the arm of her chair. "Okay," she finally said, "I'll give Tut the choice. This is a dangerous mission—possibly lethal. He can decide for himself whether he'll volunteer."

I thought about the Balrog giving me a similar choice down in Zoonau. If I'd known what it would entail . . . suddenly I was conscious of the tiny pain from the wounds on top of my feet.

Festina must have seen some change in my face because she asked, "Is there anything I can do?"

An idea popped into my mind: a way to check whether the

pagoda incident actually happened. "Arrange for me to call my mother," I said. "Tonight. A direct link as soon as possible."

"I can authorize that." The navy seldom allowed direct calls home, but the great Admiral Ramos could undoubtedly pull strings to circumvent the bureaucracy. "Anything else?" she asked.

"Yes. Kill me if I start talking like a brainwashed zombie in love with the damned moss."

"Do you think that might happen?"

"I have no idea what I think. I don't even know who's thinking." My eyes felt hot. Before I embarrassed myself by crying, I walked stiffly from the room.

6

Dharma [Sanskrit]: A word with many meanings, all related to "truth." In Gotama's time, any teaching was called a dharma—the teacher's view on what was and wasn't true. Subsequently, Dharma (often capitalized) came to mean the Buddha's teachings in particular. Dharma can also mean the whole of reality: the ultimate truth of the universe.

FROM habit, I returned to my cabin . . . but as soon as I got there, I knew I couldn't stand being cooped up in a tiny room. All my instincts said, "Go check your equipment. Make sure everything's perfect." But Festina had barred me from doing that. I felt like a mother cut off from her children.

For something to do, I went down to the mess. It had been hours since my last meal, and I knew I should eat, even though I had no appetite. (Why wasn't I hungry? Had the Balrog already replaced my digestive system? I imagined the moss photosynthesizing inside me, pumping unknown alien nutrients through my veins, mutating my internal organs. The idea was ridiculous—how could spores in my lungs or liver get enough light to photosynthesize? More likely, they were feeding off *me*. So why didn't I feel hungry?) Nevertheless, I forced down a few mouthfuls of the vegetarian dish of the day: a casserole whose components had surrendered their individual identities and blended morosely into a homogeneous mush.

At least the mess's dining area was empty. I'd come in after the normal supper hour . . . which was good because I didn't have to put up with regular crew members asking questions about Festina. ("What's she really like?") On the other hand, eating alone in the silent room got on my nerves. I felt an irrational urge to shout obscenities or throw my bowl of mush against the wall. If somebody caught me, so what? The Balrog infesting my flesh was worse than any punishment the navy could impose. Besides, I had a perfect defense: I could claim mental incompetence because of the spores. "They made me do it, your honor!" Like a free pass that let me flout petty regulations.

Only one thing stopped me from a heartfelt rampage. Suppose I tried to run amok, and the Balrog froze my muscles; suppose the spores didn't let me make a fool of myself. They wouldn't want me getting thrown in the brig—that would interfere with the Balrog's plan. So I might find myself incapable of causing any sort of ruckus.

I didn't want to put that to the test. I didn't want to lose control of my body even for an instant . . . because that would prove I was lost. Better to retain a false hope that the Balrog couldn't really make me dance to its tune.

Of course, if it could already plant false memories in my mind . . . but I still couldn't decide whether the temple scene was fact or fiction. *Pistachio*'s comm officer had begun setting up a call to my mother, but it would take at least another hour before I could be put through. Don't ask me why. Explorers weren't taught the principles of real-time FTL communication, except that it was fiendishly complex and energy-consuming. Even with approval from the illustrious Admiral Ramos, I had to wait my turn for an opening in the schedule. After all that, I wondered if my mother would answer. She'd be home, of course—she was always home—but sometimes when calls came in she'd just sit in mouselike fear, holding her breath till the caller gave up. It'd be just my luck if the one night I really needed to talk with my mother, she'd be having one of her "spells."

With such gloomy thoughts going through my mind, I stared at the casserole mush and tried to gather strength to eat another spoonful. "Damn, Mom," said a voice, "that looks like cat puke. Can I have some?"

I looked up. Tut stood there, wearing his usual cheerful expression. (The edges of his gold eyes were permanently sculpted into a friendly crinkle. The mouth moved a bit when he talked, but the corners were perpetually turned up in an amiable smile. Tut might be crazy, but he'd had the prescience to mold his metal face into unending good cheer.) I was so glad to see him, I almost wept. "Tut!" I cried. "You're awake!"

"Awake and feeling like I licked a dingo's anus. Man, am I starved!" He poked a finger into my food, scooped up a wad, and popped it into his mouth. Speaking while he chewed, he said, "I notice you've still got your legs."

"No thanks to you. I should belt you a good one for that."

"Aww, Mom, don't spank me. I was just trying to help." He looked down at my legs as if trying to see through my trousers and boots. "So, have you gone all red and fuzzy?"

"No." For some reason, I blushed.

"But you got moss all through you?"

"Yes."

"Checked out by the doctor?"

"Checked out by myself with a Bumbler."

His eyes narrowed beneath the gold—probably a dubious look, though it was never easy to tell with his face so hidden behind metal. Finally, he shrugged and sat down beside me. Plucking the spoon from my fingers, he started to eat my meal. "So what's it like, Mom?" he asked between mouthfuls. "Being all alien inside."

"So far, not much different."

"Kaisho Namida got all spooky. Do you think you will too?"

"What do you mean, spooky?"

"First thing I did when I woke up, I searched navy files for Balrog info. Know what stood out? People have tried to kill Kaisho more than a dozen times. She gives some folks acute xenophobia."

It didn't surprise me. Many humans are edgy around aliens, but a few suffer aversions so strong they lose control. One glimpse of a woman who's half red moss, and a severe xenophobe could collapse into moaning fits. The panic might even turn violent: attacking the source of terror to make it go away. A deranged hysteric lashing out is no laughing matter . . . especially if the crazed person finds a weapon. "So," I said, "these xenophobes came at Kaisho, and she did something spooky?"

Tut nodded. "She just sat there . . . but she always saw them coming, even if they ran up from behind. And when one of the wackos tried to hit her, she grabbed their hands faster than lightning and held on so hard they couldn't move."

"Impressive." Panicked people were noted for abnormal amounts of strength. I imagined Kaisho, sitting calmly in her wheelchair, snatching the wrists of a howling maniac and instantly clamping her attacker immobile.

"That's not the spooky part," Tut said. "As soon as she caught hold of somebody, she'd pull 'em down so she could look in their eyes. Wouldn't say a thing—she'd just stare. And five seconds later, they'd either faint dead away or go all calm like vanilla ice cream. They'd stay like that a few minutes, then get up and ask what all the fuss was about." He set down the spoon he'd been eating with, then turned and looked at me. "Can you do stuff like that, Mom?"

He waited . . . as if daring me to do something to his mind while our eyes were locked . . . or maybe he was *hoping* I'd affect him somehow. I held his stare for only a few heartbeats; then I dropped my gaze. "I can't do spooky stuff, Tut. And if I could, I wouldn't want to. Back in Zoonau, the Balrog gave me a vision—like it was letting me in on the way its spores perceived the world. Suddenly I had this sixth sense that could see the truth of people: their life force or karma or something. I put up with it for maybe three seconds. Then I yelled at the Balrog to take the visions away."

"Because the truth about people is scary? They're evil and ugly or something?"

"Nobody was evil or ugly. I just didn't want . . . it was like the

Balrog was offering me an incredible gift, and I didn't know what would happen if I accepted. I was afraid of what might be expected from me."

"Huh." He looked at me. "Am I sensing a sexual subtext here? Cuz I gotta tell you, Mom, you're talking like a virgin who's afraid she's going to like it."

"Go to hell." I pushed him away and got out of my chair. "That's the last time I confide in you."

"Oh, you were confiding? No wonder I didn't recognize it. Hey, where're you going?"

I was already halfway to the door. "I'm going to my cabin. You've eaten all my supper anyway."

"Okay. Do you want me to come with you?"

I stopped and stared at him. "What?"

"Should I go with you back to your cabin?"

"Why would I want that? I'm mad at you."

"Yeah, but . . . I got this message from Auntie Festina . . ."

"Auntie?"

He shrugged. "She's obviously your sister, Mom. Think I don't see the family resemblance?"

It was a waste of time trying to reason with Tut once he'd got an idea into his head. "Okay. You got a message from Auntie Festina. What did she say?"

"She asked if I wanted to go on some dangerous mission tomorrow. I said sure, why not? She started to give reasons, like maybe she hoped I'd back out, but I kept saying no, no, I'd come along. So finally, she told me okay, but it'd be a good idea if I got my affairs in order. Took me a while to figure out what she meant, but . . ."

I rolled my eyes. "You thought she was telling you to have an affair."

"Aww, come on, Mom—'putting your affairs in order' is a figure of speech."

He sounded like I'd hurt his feelings by thinking he was stupid. "Sorry," I said. "My mistake."

"Auntie Festina meant I should take care of stuff in case I die tomorrow. I tried to think of anything I should take care of . . . and eventually, I thought of you." He rolled his chair back from the table, then turned it in my direction and kept rolling till he'd come right up to me. He was still sitting down, but with his tallness and my shortness, we were almost eye to eye. "Anything I can do for you tonight, Youn Suu?"

I couldn't remember him ever calling me by name. It took my breath away. "What are you thinking of?" I asked.

"Anything you like. Want me to play harmonica? Read you your favorite stories? Fuck you till you turn to butter? Kill you in your sleep?"

"*Kill me in my sleep?*"

"Well, yeah. If you can't stand the thought of becoming moss, I could save you from a fate worse than death. I haven't figured out how to kill you without the League of Peoples killing me first, but if we both put our heads together . . ."

"No," I said, "you don't have to do that." I leaned forward and kissed him on the cheek. The gold was warm with Tut's body temperature . . . but it was just gold, and I wished it had been flesh instead. "It's sweet of you to offer, but I'm fine, really. Shiny-finey. Best thing for both of us is to get plenty of sleep. We want to be sharp for the landing."

"Okay, Mom. But the offer's still open. Not just killing you, but any of that other stuff too."

I smiled . . . and for a moment I imagined saying what the hell, why die a virgin? Why not have one night, even if it's Tut? It would be painfully awkward—before, during, and after—and I couldn't imagine drowsing languidly in his arms after he'd offered to kill me in my sleep—but if not Tut, who? And if not now, when?

Silence. Then a sigh. I couldn't do it. It was too much like the fantasy scenarios that girls discuss when they're thirteen: *suppose you've got this fatal disease and the only guy you can sleep with is someone who's okay, but you don't love him at all . . .*

I didn't feel like a bubbly girl. "Good night, Tut," I said. "See you in the morning."

He watched me all the way to the door. As I walked away down the hall, I heard him start wheeling around the mess hall on his chair, slamming into things hard.

Back in my cabin, the ship-soul informed me that the call to my mother would go through in twenty minutes. I passed the time writing a preliminary report of what happened in Zoonau—preliminary because it was just a list of point-form notes. Without too much trouble, I could have fleshed it out into a complete linear narrative, but I liked the abbreviated format better: the last, hurried testament of a tragic heroine, doomed to die on Muta or be consumed by parasitic spores. I imagined future Explorers reading my words and thinking, "How brave she was! To keep to her duty, writing reports, while staring death in the face."

(Now I think, "How childish I was! To put on a show for unknown readers in the hope of winning their pity." I certainly was my mother's daughter.)

I kept my eye on the clock as I wrote, hurrying so I'd be done in time. Exact to the second, the ship-soul announced that the call was going through . . . and almost immediately my mother answered.

"Raymond?" she said a bit breathlessly.

Her face on the vidscreen was made up Western style: lipstick, eyeliner, mascara. No thanaka. Though she was forty-five years old, YouthBoost treatments left her looking my age. I. In fact, she was almost my twin; the backstreet engineer had based me on Mother's DNA, so we looked very much like sisters. I'd been designed to be beautiful, so my version of her features was a little better in almost every respect—better skin, better bone structure, more lustrous hair, more luminous eyes—but she didn't have a leprous weeping cheek, which put her far ahead of me in the beauty contest. On the other hand, *my* face was washed and clean, not slathered with Caucasian makeup like a slut.

"It's me, Mother," I said . . . unnecessarily, because she could surely see my face on her own vidscreen. A moment later, I *knew* she could see me: her eager expression fell when she realized I wasn't the caller she hoped for.

"Who's Raymond?" I asked. I knew it didn't matter—his existence mattered, his actual identity didn't—but I couldn't help myself.

"He's just a friend," my mother said, confirming all my suspicions. "Where are you, Youn Suu?"

Not *Ma* Youn Suu. Mothers weren't required to address their daughters politely. Especially not when the daughter called with inconvenient timing. "I'm in space," I told her. "Light-years away. And I just have a single question."

"What?" Her voice went wary.

"When I was twelve, did we go to a temple together? The Ghost Fountain Pagoda. Is there really such a temple, and did anything strange happen there?"

She didn't answer immediately. Whatever question she might have expected, this wasn't it. (I wonder what she was afraid I'd ask. What secrets did my mother have that she feared I might uncover?) It took several seconds for her to switch mental tracks to what I'd actually said. "Of course there's a Ghost Fountain Pagoda," she finally replied. "We went there once or twice, but I didn't like it. Too many people. Too loud and crazy."

"Did anything unusual happen any of the times we went there?"

"How do I know what was unusual? I told you, we only went once or twice. Or three, four times, I don't remember. Not often enough to know what was usual."

"But did anything remarkable happen while we were there?" I tried not to shout. Though I hadn't talked to my mother in months, we'd fallen back into our old dysfunctional patterns: as soon as I asked a question, she instinctively tried not to answer it. But for once, I wanted to have a conversation with her that didn't end up screaming.

"What do you consider remarkable?" my mother asked, still evading the question. "People having sex out in the open?"

"No." We'd seen that at a lot of temples. The Neo-Tantric sect had a constitutional right to copulate in public, and they exercised that right whenever, wherever. "If you don't remember anything out of the ordinary, Mother, just say so."

"Why is this important?" she asked . . . yet again dodging the question. Despite my good intentions mere seconds before, I found myself losing my temper.

"It's important because I'm being eaten!" I snapped. "I'm infected by a parasite that may be driving me mad, and I don't know if I can trust my own memories. I thought, maybe, *maybe*, you'd help me decide if the spores were playing games with my mind. But of course I was wrong. You don't want to help me with anything, Mother. You just want me to shut up before your precious Raymond calls."

She stared at me a moment . . . then let out an Oh-I'm-a-martyr sigh. "Really, Youn Suu. You look perfectly fine. Nothing's eating you. Have you been taking drugs or something?"

"No. The parasite's inside me. It's an alien infestation that doesn't show up on the surface until it's too late."

"Then go see a doctor, you silly girl."

"Doctors can't help. And neither, apparently, can you. Sorry to disturb you, Mother. I won't do it again. I won't last long enough, will I?"

I almost punched the DISCONNECT button: an ingrained reflex to cut off conversation after I'd delivered a good parting shot. But I stopped myself in time. Did I want to squander my chance for truth out of sheer petty pique?

On the vidscreen, my mother looked like she knew exactly what thoughts were going through my head. She wore a "Well, are you going to do it?" expression . . . based, I guess, on all the times I *had* hung up on her, or stormed out of the room, or just covered my ears and screamed, "Shut up, shut up, shut up!"

Taking a breath, I said, "Look. Let's start over. Was there a day we went to that temple and something extraordinary happened?"

"Why do you want to know?" Again, answering my question with a question.

"Why don't you want to tell me?" I said, giving her another

question back. "You're being so evasive, it sounds like something *did* happen, and you're afraid to admit it."

I paused. Mother said nothing—looking somewhere off-screen. "Don't be shy," I said. "It's not like I'll think you've gone crazy. If there's one thing I've learned as an Explorer, it's that the universe is full of strangeness. I'll believe whatever you tell me."

Mother gave me a look. "If you've finally begun to believe what I say, the universe is getting strange indeed." She sighed. "We were in the pagoda, Youn Suu. You were watching a pair of Neo-Tantrics doing their usual in a corner. You were pretending to meditate, but you were twelve years old, fascinated by all kinds of sex and not good at hiding your interest. People were watching you more than the Neo-Tants; you were so obvious, the way you kept taking oh-so-casual peeks at the couple in the corner, and I suppose a lot of folks found that cute."

"Or they just couldn't take their eyes off my cheek."

"Maybe that too," Mother said. "You always drew attention. It was hard taking you out in public. I got so embarrassed . . ." She shook her head. "I guess that's what happened at the temple. I was embarrassed by everybody looking at you, so I thought I'd go outside for a few minutes. Get some air. Pretend you weren't with me. But when I got to the door . . ."

"*You* went to the door?"

"Yes. And outside, a bunch of statues were covered with stuff that hadn't been there when we came in. Purple jelly, black sand, lava . . . every statue had something crawling on it."

"*You* saw the statues?"

"That's what I'm saying. You were too busy staring at two not-very-attractive people having sex, but I saw what I saw."

"What about the Buddha statue? The one inside the pagoda, in the fountain."

"That was the strangest part," my mother said. "I came running back inside to get you—to drag you away someplace safe, in case the stuff on the statues was dangerous—and I glanced at the Buddha, just for half a second. In that instant, the statue was suddenly replaced with a woman in a wheelchair. She was moss from the waist down, Youn Suu: glowing red moss. And she was looking at you. You had your back to her, so you didn't see. But she smiled at you. Her eyes were hidden behind her hair, but I could see her mouth, and she smiled. She lifted her hands toward you in the Wisdom mudra . . . then she disappeared, and the Buddha was back to normal. When I got you outside, the other statues were back to normal too. I hustled you away before anything else happened and never told you what I'd seen. Never went back to that temple either." She gave me a probing look. "Well? Was that what you wanted to hear?"

I couldn't answer—once again frozen in surprise. Kaisho Namida, the mossy woman in the wheelchair . . . she'd shown up on Anicca? She'd been interested in me? And she'd made the Wisdom mudra: one of the many hand gestures used to symbolize virtues and principles of faith. Had she been suggesting I needed to strive for wisdom? Was she bestowing wisdom upon me?

If she *had* given me wisdom, it wasn't enough. I didn't understand any of this. My mother had just confirmed that the events of my "memory" had actually taken place . . . but *she* was the one who saw the aliens, while I missed everything. And her account differed from my memory in several respects. She'd seen Kaisho in the fountain; I'd seen the Buddha covered with moss.

One thing seemed certain: the Balrog *had* played with my mind. Sort of. The spores had given me a memory of things I would have seen for myself if I hadn't been a silly twelve-year-old distracted by sex. Thanks to that artificial memory, I'd contacted my mother to find out what really happened . . .

. . . and I'd learned that seven years ago, the Balrog was already interested in me. It had sent Kaisho to "bless" me—perhaps knowing that my attention would be elsewhere and that I'd only be told the truth when my mother saw fit to share what she'd seen. The Balrog had been watching me (stalking me?) back when I was twelve: long before I became an Explorer. Now it had given me a false memory, possibly to prod me into calling my mother in search of the real story.

It wanted me to know about the temple. The Balrog was sending me a message. I just didn't understand what the message was.

"Youn Suu," Mother said, "are you all right?"

"I'm fine," I said in reflex—automatically shutting my mother out, refusing to yield information about how I really was. I forced myself to say, "Actually, I don't know how I am. I feel okay, but like I told you, I've got alien spores in my guts. Who knows what they'll do to me?" I could have told her I might end up like the wheelchair-bound moss victim she'd seen in the temple, but why sensationalize? "How are you doing?" I asked to deflect the conversation. "Is, uhh . . . is this Raymond nice?"

Mother looked at me with suspicion—maybe worried I'd launch into a tirade. "I told you, Youn Suu, he's just a friend."

"I hope it works out for you, Mother. Really."

She stared at me a moment. "You're in bad trouble, aren't you."

"Yes. All kinds of it."

Silence. Then: "You're strong. I told the man at the birth clinic, 'Make her strong.' And he did. I did everything I could to make you strong. You'll be okay. Really."

Part of me wanted to say, *Don't be ridiculous, Mother, you didn't do everything you could. You paid a lot of money in the bioengineering phase, but once I was born, and you saw my face, you lost every drop of enthusiasm. After that, I was just a burden.* But I stifled the words. "I *am* strong," I said. "We'll see what happens next."

We both pressed our DISCONNECT buttons. Neither of us said good-bye.

Still too early for bed. I found I was surprisingly hungry, but couldn't go down to the mess hall again for fear that Tut was still there. (What was I afraid would happen? Don't ask. I refused to contemplate the possibilities.) With no other way to distract myself, I went back to my latest Princess Gotama statue. A few minutes later, when the door chirped to announce a visitor, I gratefully said, "Come in."

I thought it might be Festina, or perhaps Captain Cohen checking up on me in grandfatherly concern. To my surprise, it was Commander Miriam Ubatu of the Outward Fleet Diplomacy Corps . . . looking less like a VIP and more like an ordinary nineteen-year-old coming to visit someone her age. The diamond studs were gone from her nose (replaced by simple steel wire), and she'd changed from her gold uniform into unprepossessing civilian clothes: plain black T-shirt and plain black pants, with enough silver skin-embeds on her arms and bare midriff to soften the black-on-black "ninja Amazon" effect. Still, she was a superior officer; I scrambled to my feet and gave a salute, which she waved away without returning. "Forget the formalities, Youn Suu. This isn't a business visit."

"Was there something you needed?" I asked . . . thinking she might have run out of champagne or wanted her uniform pressed.

"No, I'm fine. I thought we could talk."

I almost said, *Talk about what?* But the words sounded rude in my head, as if I doubted Ubatu and I had any common ground for conversation. Instead, I went with simple politeness: "Would you like to sit down?"

She took the only chair—the one at my desk. I settled onto the bed . . . sitting perched on the edge rather than letting myself relax. Whatever Ubatu had come for, I doubted this would be a session of casual girl talk.

"So how are you feeling?" she asked—not meeting my eyes.

"You mean with the Balrog inside me?"

"Yes. Do you feel . . . different?"

"Not really. Whatever the spores are doing to my body, there's no noticeable sensation."

"I see." Ubatu glanced my way, then averted her eyes again. "Do you think the Balrog is affecting your mind?"

"Why do you ask?" My mother wasn't the only one who could answer a question with a question.

"I just wanted . . ." Ubatu paused and bit her lip, as if trying to decide whether to say something. Finally she took a deep breath. "Have you heard of Ifa-Vodun?"

"Is that a person?"

"No. Ifa-Vodun means Spirit of Prophecy. It's a movement."

"You mean a religion."

She shrugged. "I see it more as a sensible response to humanity's position in the cosmos."

"What position would that be?"

"The bottom of the heap, looking up. Above us are all kinds of aliens with varying degrees of power and knowledge . . . so it makes sense for us to reach out however we can. Contact some of those aliens and see what happens."

"Don't we do that already?" I asked. "You're in the Diplomacy Corps. Surely you know how hard the navy and Technocracy government keep working to establish relations with higher aliens."

Ubatu made a face. "Oh yes, they're constantly trying to 'establish relations' . . . old-fashioned diplomacy with official envoys, and embassies, and notes of accreditation. But our diplomatic protocols have always been geared for creatures on our own intellectual level, not for higher beings. In the four centuries since we left Old Earth, our diplomacy hasn't got anywhere with elevated lifeforms. Sometimes an advanced entity will speak to selected humans for its own purposes, but it doesn't work the other way. Standard diplomacy has failed to set up any back-and-forth dialogue."

"In the Explorer Academy," I said, "our teachers believed that higher lifeforms don't want back-and-forth dialogue . . . any more than we humans want dialogue with slugs and earthworms. As you said, higher lifeforms only interact with humans when it suits their own purposes. Otherwise, they have better things to do than chat with *Homo sapiens*."

"Exactly!" Ubatu smiled as if I'd just proved her point. "We've been trying to catch higher aliens' attention for four centuries. If they wanted to talk to us, they would have. So isn't it time to admit that conventional diplomacy doesn't work?"

I kept my face passive, but internally I winced. When people announce that diplomacy has failed, there's always a Plan B they're eager to try. History is littered with disastrous Plan Bs. "What's the alternative to diplomacy?" I asked.

"Other forms of approach," Ubatu said. "Other ways of soliciting attention."

"Such as?"

"Ifa-Vodun. Which means recognizing that higher lifeforms *are* higher lifeforms. We can't approach superior beings as if we're their equals. It's better to approach them as supplicants."

"Supplicants? Ah." I suddenly got the picture. "You're setting up a religion to worship advanced aliens."

"We don't put it like that. Ifa-Vodun adopts traditional methods of divine entreaty as an alternative to sterile diplomatic culture."

She's quoting some pamphlet, I thought. "So instead of writing communiqués, you get naked and chop off the head of a chicken?"

I meant it as a joke . . . but she nodded.

"Yes, we're experimenting with animal sacrifice. Blood rituals of all kinds. And, of course, chanting, dancing, sacramental copulation. Ifa-Vodun is a new movement—we're investigating a diversity of avenues to see what works."

"So . . . so . . ." I'd just realized the significance of *Vodun* in the name of Ubatu's "movement." "Are you seriously telling me that members of the Dip Corps are trying to catch aliens' attention through voodoo?"

"Don't be dismissive," she said. "Traditional Vodun is a respectable faith—nothing like the way it's portrayed in Devils 'n' Demolition VR. Besides, Ifa-Vodun doesn't ask you to believe Vodun theology. We're just seeing if Vodun forms can win perks from higher beings."

"So you don't even respect voodoo as a religion? It's just a means to an end?"

"We would never trivialize . . ." Ubatu stopped herself and took a breath. "Our movement respects Vodun enough to adopt its practices. Doesn't that speak for itself?"

Perhaps. I knew little about Voodoo/Vodun. Maybe sincere believers would take it as a compliment if navy diplomats co-opted

Vodun rites to suck up to aliens. Probably a number of those diplomats were believers themselves; there must be a reason why they chose Vodun over all the other human religions that have sought to win favor with powerful spirits. And maybe the Dip Corps was full of such "movements." Ifa-Vodun struck a chord with people of appropriate cultural background. Meanwhile, maybe diplomats of Bamar origin did homage to advanced lifeforms by burning PARINIRVANA BRAND INCENSE-STICKS™.

But there was still one important question. "Why are you telling me this?" I asked.

Ubatu turned away as if the answer embarrassed her. Finally she said, "Do you know what it means to be ridden by the loa?"

"No. What's a loa?"

"A Vodun spirit. There are lots of different loa, but most are benevolent, wise, and powerful. When a loa rides somebody, it means the spirit takes over the person's body. The loa speaks and acts through the person being ridden."

"In other words, the person is possessed by the loa spirit."

"More or less," Ubatu said. "It's a time when others can talk to the loa. You ask questions, and maybe the loa will answer."

"The loa become diplomatically approachable?"

"Exactly! Using Vodun rituals, you summon a loa to ride a chosen host so you can converse respectfully. Ifa-Vodun is *very* interested in loa possession . . . and in finding ways to entice the spirits to do it more often."

Ah. Finally, I made the connection—what this visit was about. I had spores inside me . . . or to use Ubatu's terminology, I was being ridden by the powerful alien loa that called itself the Balrog. By the precepts of Ifa-Vodun, I was therefore a prime diplomatic opportunity. Maybe the Balrog would speak through me, sharing valuable knowledge about the universe. Even if that didn't happen, Ubatu wanted to learn what I'd done to draw the spores into me: how I'd made myself a tempting vessel for loa/alien possession.

Thinking back on the past few hours, I realized Ubatu had displayed great interest in Balrog behavior. I'd interpreted that as ghoulish fascination at the thought of others being eaten . . . but I'd been wrong. This went deeper than casual curiosity. It was like some religious imperative, fostered by a secret society within the Diplomacy Corps and leading who knew where?

"You should go now," I told Ubatu. "I want you to go. Get out."

"All right," Ubatu said. "For now. You still have too much personal control to let the Balrog speak to me. But that will change, won't it? The Balrog will slowly edge you out. Then I'll find ways to win it over."

"Beheading a chicken and writing with its blood?"

"We'll see."

She stood abruptly, a tall woman looming above me . . . and suddenly her black-on-black outfit with abstract silver symbols embedded in the flesh of her arms and belly struck me as much more than they'd originally seemed. I'd thought it was all just fashionable streetwear; but really she'd traded her navy gold for another uniform. An Ifa-Vodun priestess? A priestess who hoped the Balrog would expunge my Youn Suu personality, thereby becoming pure loa?

"Leave," I said.

"I'm leaving. Good night."

She made an odd gesture as she went through the door. I didn't want to guess its significance.

7

Anatta [Sanskrit]: The precept that no one has a permanent self. Other religions may believe in an "immortal soul," but the Buddha rejected this idea. He contended we are all composite beings, made of flesh, thoughts, emotions, etc., and all these change over time. There is no component one can point to and say, "That is my unchanging core."

IN the next half hour, I wrote a BE ADVISED memo about Ifa-Vodun and put it in *Pistachio*'s dispatch queue for eventual delivery to Explorer Corps HQ. Explorers across the galaxy used such memos to warn each other of possible risks—not just physical threats but anything that might make the job more perverse. Soon, Explorers everywhere would be on the watch for Ifa-Vodun and similar activities. It wouldn't take long for our corps to gather a dossier of useful information . . . and for teachers at the Academy to begin brainstorming what they ought to tell cadets.

Happy that I'd accomplished something useful on an otherwise bad day, I went to bed. Where I couldn't sleep. So I lay on my back, staring up into blackness. A starship cabin with no lights on is as dark as the deepest cave.

The room began to feel close and airless, as if the ventilators had stopped working. I was wearing the light nightie I usually slept in, but after a while, I couldn't stand the straitjacket feel of it against me. I fought my way out of the nightie's clutch, almost tearing it in my haste; then I balled it up and threw it into the darkness. The cloth had been soaked with perspiration.

I lay back down, this time on top of the sheets and covers, sprawling wide to radiate the suffocating heat that seemed to pour off me. Burning up. Fever—I was dripping with fever. My ears began to ring. Something swam inside my head, but I didn't know what it was.

It occurred to me my immune system had finally realized I'd been invaded by foreign organisms. This fever was the result. Perhaps I should call for a doctor—just whispering "Help!" would tell the ship's computer to start emergency procedures. But I couldn't bear the thought of being found naked and slick with sweat. Drenched. Sodden. Festina would see me, and Tut would see me, and Ubatu might smear me with pig's blood . . .

The blackness was pierced by two spots of crimson. They shone from the tops of my feet—bright red spores glowing from where I'd been bitten.

Slowly, I sat up: propped damp pillows behind me so I could flop back against the bed's headboard with my legs spread in front of me. Sweat trickled and rolled down my flesh. My weeping cheek was so runny, fluid streamed down my jawline and dripped off my chin onto my breasts. The splashes felt simmering hot.

In a while, I thought, *I'll be delirious*. Things had already lost their sense of reality. I moved my feet, and the red dots moved too . . . like tiny spotlights, bright enough to show the outlines of my legs in the pitch-dark room. The sight was numbly mesmerizing. I moved my feet again, watching shadows shift across me. Reflections of the red dots glistened in the sweat on my thighs. I looked at the dots with befuddled wonderment, as if they were miraculous phenomena . . . but despite my growing dizziness, I knew why the dots had come.

No more strength in my limbs. Limp. Sinking into the bed. My eyes slumped shut, exhausted from the effort of staying open . . . but it seemed as if I could still see the two red dots glowing in an otherwise black universe.

"All right, Balrog," I mumbled. "Talk to me."

* * *

A vision. Bodyless, floating. Over an infinite row of Youn Suu's, each inside some prison. Prisons shaped like eggs with barred windows, or glass-walled coffins, or golden castles with jewel-speckled towers but not a single door.

Many of the Youn Suu's were dead. Some freshly dead and cooling. Some well into putrefaction. Some gone dry and withered. The ones in worst condition were children. Five-year-old Youn Suu's who hadn't looked both ways crossing the street . . . two-year-olds who'd put the wrong things in their mouths . . . eight-year-olds who didn't notice the infected mosquito land on their arms.

Corpses now. Small, shriveled corpses. In some, the skin was intact enough to show the blemished cheek; in others, decay or some ravaging cause of death had erased all sign of disfigurement.

Every cadaver had a shining crimson dot in the middle of each foot.

So did the living Youn Suu's. All nineteen years old. A few maimed or crippled from unknown accidents. A few showing signs of disease, from palsied tremors to leprous rot. Most, however, were intact—even healthy—inside their varied prisons.

Some clutched the steel bars that blocked their freedom; those girls howled obscenities to empty air. Some had their backs to the bars of their cage, sitting at food-heaped tables: eating, drinking, carousing. Some seemed engaged with invisible sex partners: lying, standing, kneeling.

Many were dancing. Elegant, frenzied, languid, lascivious. Masked for a festival or wearing full ballet garb, dressed down in rehearsal tights or even naked. Tightly contained steps, or wild leaps that caromed off the walls of their prisons.

Every dancing foot revealed a spot of crimson.

A million million possibilities. All the Youn Suu's there could be. All imprisoned; all claimed by the spores.

The vision floated on, past ever-stranger versions of the same girl. With the left half of her face metal instead of flesh. Plastic instead of metal. Glass instead of plastic. The entire face unblemished . . . or gold-plated like Tut . . . or entirely missing, no muscles or bone, leaving the brain behind open and exposed.

Versions with fur or reptilian scales. Multicolored versions with Cashling spottles. Versions with insectlike mandibles or protruding snouts.

On and on the vision moved . . . till it reached not the end but the middle. The line of Youn Suu's the vision had followed was a single spoke of a wheel that spread the breadth of a galaxy. More Youn Suu's dotted the wheel's other spokes: Youn Suu's from different cycles of time, when all that had been would recur. Her string of lives would be relived, again and again as time repeated—each cycle a perfect rerun of all those before, unless, like the Buddha, she burned her way out from the ever-returning trap. But no Youn Suu had managed such a feat of liberation; all were still imprisoned, whether the cages were cramped stone cubicles or opulent pleasure palaces with the jail bars swathed in silk.

Except . . .

At the center of the wheel—the hub where the vision led—were two Youn Suu's free of all confinement.

One lay unmoving on a sweat-soaked bed. She had no Balrog marks on her feet; no spores anywhere on her body. She wasn't breathing: dead but cleansed. No Balrog. No prison.

The second Youn Suu was half-eaten: moss from the waist down, just like Kaisho, but with the left leg severed short at the knee and an abundance of blood-raked scratches wherever human flesh remained. This one was alive. Her eyes were open. She smiled, as if pleased with her cannibalized state. Delighted to be the Balrog's banquet.

Were these the only alternatives? Or was there a final version of Youn Suu: one who'd escaped the cosmic wheel and so wasn't here on display. A Youn Suu beyond the wheel's grasp . . . beyond the endless repetitions . . . beyond the prisons, beyond the Balrog, beyond all chains and fetters.

Dead or alive, the only Youn Suu worth striving for.

A choice was made; and who knows what did the choosing? Certainly not a girl named Youn Suu. All possible versions of her were locked in prisons of the wheel . . . not standing outside, looking on, assessing options. There was no Youn Suu free to make a choice.

And yet, a choice was made.

I awoke shivering.

The bedclothes were clammy. The air smelled of vomit and urine. When I moved, I could feel crusty deposits flaking off from my chest and upper arms. The taste in my mouth was so vile I gagged; I might have thrown up again on the spot except there was nothing left in my stomach.

But I was alive.

The red dots had disappeared from my feet. Healed over. The cabin lay in total blackness. I thought of asking the room to turn on the lights, but decided I didn't want to see the mess I'd made. Instead, I walked lumpenly to the washroom and rinsed my mouth ten or twenty times.

"Balrog?" I said in the darkness. "Did I make another choice? Was that what the dream was about?"

No answer. Never an answer.

I washed myself off in the shower, scrubbing with all my strength. Then I went back to the bed, gathered up the sheets, and washed them in the shower too until the smell of soap overcame the reek of bodily fluids. As for the bed itself, I offered my thanks to whoever decreed that navy mattresses should be one hundred percent waterproof—able to be cleaned with a damp cloth. I wiped the mattress down, then sat at my desk to give everything a chance to dry.

Through all this, I hadn't turned on the lights. I didn't need to. Despite the utter darkness, I could make my way without stumbling. I knew the exact position of every object in the room. If I concentrated, I knew the location of individual dust motes in the air. I didn't sense them; I just knew. And this time, I didn't tell the Balrog to take away its gift of inhuman perception. Keeping the room pitch-black was comforting after I'd almost died.

"I *did* almost die," I said to the Balrog. "Right? And you let me decide . . . or did you? Was it just another trick to seduce me?"

The vision I'd had—an infinite wheel of Youn Suu lives from countless cycles of time—accorded exactly with the teachings I'd learned while growing up. *Exactly*. As if the Balrog plucked images from my mind and built a cosmic experience tailored to my expectations. And the decision I'd made (if I really did make a decision . . . and what had I decided?) . . . did the decision save my life? Or would the Balrog have kept me alive anyway? It controlled my body. It could suppress my deadly fever if it chose. The Balrog might have started the fever in the first place, so it could give me a taste of what I thought Ultimate Enlightenment would be like.

I couldn't trust anything I'd just been through. Wasn't this precisely the way nefarious cult leaders won converts? Wear down the target's physical resistance with fatigue, starvation, and fever. Orchestrate experiences that brought on heightened emotional states. Wait for the target to embrace offered truths and fall deliriously in love with the guru himself . . . or in this case, the guru *it*self. An alien known for playing games with lesser creatures.

"I'm tired," I told the Balrog. "If you're going to keep toying with me, save it till tomorrow."

Within minutes, I'd fallen asleep in the chair. No dreams. When I opened my eyes, it was morning.

8

Shunyata [Sanskrit]: The trait of being transitory and interconnected with other things. No thing is absolute or complete in itself. Where, for example, is a chair's chairness? Not in any of its parts: a chair leg is not a chair; a backrest is not a chair. But even a complete assemblage of chair parts is not enough for chairness. Chairs can be chairs only in appropriate environments—they need gravity, a species whose anatomy can fit into the chair, and various other external conditions. Chairness is therefore not a property of a particular object, but a set of relationships between the object and external factors. This quality is shunyata . . . often translated as "emptiness." In isolation, a chair may exist as an object but it's "empty." Chairness arises only when the object relates in a specific way to the rest of the world.

I ATE more that breakfast than at any other meal in my life. And I'd never been a hesitant eater: my high-powered gene-spliced metabolism always needed plenty of fuel. But that morning, I surpassed all previous records. I just couldn't stop shoveling in food.

The phrase "eating for two" kept echoing in my head. I pictured the Balrog siphoning off my intake, not letting a single mouthful reach my stomach . . . but even that image wasn't enough to slow me down. I remained so hungry I found myself casting ardent looks at the mess's meat section—bacon, sausage, kippers, and slabs of dead animal I couldn't even identify—to the point where I might have renounced my lifelong vegetarianism if Tut hadn't walked in the door.

He was looking surprisingly dapper, with his face burnished far beyond his usual shiny-finey standards. Gold glinted like pure rich honey under the mess's bright morning lights; either Tut had found some new metal polish or he'd spent untold hours buffing it to a perfect mirror surface.

"Hey, Mom," he said, "I've been looking for you. Were you messing with the door to the equipment room? It's locked, and it won't let me in."

"Festina did that. Admiral Ramos. She won't let us near the equipment, for fear we'd do something bad."

Tut made a noise like his feelings had been hurt. I told him, "Don't pout, it's mostly me she mistrusts. Or rather, the Balrog inside me."

"Huh." He looked down at the dishes all around my place at the table. There was nothing for him to steal this time—I'd eaten everything and practically licked the plates clean. "So when do we get to this planet?" he asked.

I tongued a control on the roof of my mouth. In the bottom corner of my right eye, a digital time readout appeared. "We'll be there in two hours," I told him. "Do you know what we're doing once we arrive?"

"Auntie gave me the basics last night. Mystery threat. Search for survivors. Save anyone we find. I'm also supposed to stun the knickers off you if the Balrog tries any tricks."

"Good luck. You'll need it."

My sixth sense was still in perfect working order; I hadn't asked the Balrog to turn it off after the previous night. Not only did I know the position of everything near me, including objects behind my back and out of sight around corners, but I'd begun perceiving life forces again. If Tut decided to shoot me, his intention would ring out loud and clear from his aura: enough warning to let me dodge, or even shoot him first.

It seemed unfair, in a way—having this extra edge over Tut's mere human perceptions. But if I asked the Balrog to turn the sixth sense off, what good would that do? The Balrog itself would still have its full mental awareness; Tut and everyone else would still be at a disadvantage relative to the spores. So why should I blind myself when it wouldn't help anyone? Staying augmented put me on a more even footing with the moss inside me. It might even give me the strength to resist any power plays the Balrog might attempt.

Yes. I'd keep the sixth sense for the time being.

As soon as I'd made that decision, my voracious hunger abated. It felt like a return to sanity.

A short time later, Festina called to say that Tut and I could check out the tightsuits we'd wear for the landing. She let us into the equipment area one at a time and kept close watch on everything we did.

I wasn't allowed to touch anything except my own suit. Festina said she'd checked the other equipment herself. I couldn't help asking a barrage of questions, mostly about how Festina had dealt with new gear and procedures—things that had changed since she'd been on active Explorer duty. But it turned out "Auntie" Festina had kept up with recent developments in the Explorer Corps: she'd done everything exactly the way I would have. She even let me look at the results of diagnostic tests she'd run earlier that morning. All equipment was working at optimal.

Once we'd finished with the tightsuits, Festina took Tut and me to the bridge, where she seated herself at the seldom-used Explorers' console. Sometime during the night, she'd programmed four probe missiles to perform initial reconnaissance on the site where we'd land. The missiles would be sent down as soon as *Pistachio* reached Muta orbit. Based on their data, we'd decide how to proceed.

"And what site are we going to?" I asked.

"The one that sent the Mayday."

Festina turned a dial on her console, and the bridge's vidscreen changed to show a satellite photo of Muta—one of hundreds included in the files we'd received from the Unity. A red dot glowed in the middle of a region that looked like a vast plain. "The Unity called this Camp Esteem." She made a face. "Typical Unity name. It happens to be the newest camp on the planet . . . so the survey team was fresher than any other team in residence. Maybe that's why they managed to get out a call for help when all the other teams went without a peep. Or not. It could just be coincidence."

"If that's the most recent site developed," I said, "it should be close to Fuentes ruins. The last four teams were all investigating Las Fuentes."

"I know. Team Esteem was poking through an abandoned Fuentes city they code-named Drill-Press." Festina made another face. I knew from the files I'd read that the Unity had named all of Muta's geography after wholesomely useful tools. (I was glad we weren't going anywhere near the Fuentes city called Reciprocating Saw.)

Festina went back to the satellite photo. "For the sake of caution, the Unity surveyors didn't pitch camp inside the city—they set up quarters a short distance away." She zoomed the view on the vidscreen. "That's the city, Drill-Press, in the lower half of the picture. You'll notice a good-sized river running through downtown. The river's called Grindstone. The Unity camp is here: fifteen minutes upstream from the city."

The original photo had shown a good chunk of the continent, so the zoom had disappointingly crude resolution—pixels the size of fingerprints, with a chunky lack of detail. Nevertheless, I could make out the features Festina had described. A good-sized river ran vertically down the center of the shot; it had a few gentle curves, but essentially flowed north to south (according to a legend in a corner of the picture). In the north, just west of the river, the Unity camp was highlighted with a digitally superimposed red circle. A cluster of prefab buildings lay within the circle: twelve small huts (living quarters for the survey team's dozen members) and four larger units . . . a mess hall, a lab, an equipment maintenance shop, and a general storage area.

To the south, near the bottom of the photograph, lay the Fuentes city. Drill-Press. Even after sixty-five hundred years, it was easy to identify. This was not some Old Earth archeological site where primitive peoples built houses from sticks; on Muta, the "ruins" had fifty-story skyscrapers made from high-tech construction materials . . . materials as good or better than the self-repairing *chintah* in Zoonau. Las Fuentes had been more advanced than the Cashlings, and this city must have been constructed near the height of Fuentes achievement. It was hard to see much on the poor-resolution aerial photo, but none of the buildings showed obvious damage. Most of the roofs had rectangular cross sections, and I noticed no irregularities that might indicate holes, or edges eroded away. All of Drill-Press seemed structurally intact; "ruins" in name only. At ground level, the city was likely a mess—in six and a half millennia, the river must have flooded its banks on numerous occasions, leaving silt and water damage on the buildings' bottom floor—but floodwaters wouldn't have climbed much higher. Damage on upper floors would come from other sources: insects and other local wildlife. Mold. Mildew. Microbial rot.

Anything subject to biodegradation would be long gone. On the other hand, anything of metal would still be intact, especially rust-proof alloys. Long-life materials like *chintah* would also survive, plus certain types of glass, plastics, stonework . . .

Looking over my shoulder, Tut said, "I'll bet there's all kinds of great shit down there."

"I'll bet," I agreed.

"Auntie," he said to Festina, "do you think these Fuentes had really good metal polishes?"

Li and Ubatu pushed their way onto the bridge in the final minutes of our approach to Muta. Captain Cohen immediately told them to be quiet . . . not rudely, but with a firm "Shut up, I'm driving" tone of voice. He wasn't driving directly—that job belonged to a Divian lieutenant who sat at the piloting console—and pulling into orbit was a routine maneuver that required no input from the captain and no special clampdown of silence. Still, we *were* coming up on a planet that housed unknown dangers. Cohen had every reason to be cautious, even if we suspected the dangers to restrict themselves to the ground rather than a thousand kilometers up in the exosphere.

The vidscreen showed a computer simulation of the planet before us: blue and beautiful, a perfect circle against the black background because we were coming in with the sun directly at our backs. (The sun was almost like Old Earth's Sol—yellow and well behaved, right in the middle of the primary sequence. The Unity had named it "Generosity of Light," which they abbreviated to "GoL." Festina said this proved everyone in the Unity had been engineered to unnatural levels of pain tolerance; a normal human couldn't say "Generosity of Light" or "GoL" without coming close to vomiting.)

But Muta itself was lovely. Drifting clouds, sparkling oceans, and continents teeming with life. I'd been taught to view such worlds with suspicion—better to land on some barren ice-planet, so cold it couldn't possibly house lifeforms that wanted to eat you—but my nineteen-year-old inexperience preferred a place that stirred the blood over one that was safely sterile.

Even now, I wouldn't say I was wrong.

One circuit around the planet—Festina wanted sensor readings for the dark side as well as the light—then *Pistachio* slid into high orbit as easily as a foot into a comfortable shoe. Our target, Camp Esteem, lay on the sunlit half of the globe, just outside the equatorial zone. It was currently experiencing a pleasant midautumn afternoon; initial scans showed intermittent clouds and a temperature of 17° Celsius. Shirtsleeve weather. A storm front was on its way up from the south and would reach the area in about six hours: lightning and thunder shortly after dark. But we planned to be gone by then.

Festina kept muttering we might not land at all. We hadn't come to assess the planet for colonization or to scavenge Fuentes artifacts. This was purely a rescue mission . . . and Festina wouldn't risk our lives unless we had someone to rescue. Therefore, before anybody left *Pistachio*, Festina intended to search the area with her remote reconnaissance probes. If the probes found survivors, we'd do our duty; otherwise, we'd stay safely in the ship.

The probes could search more effectively than a landing party on the ground. Probe missiles scanned more territory and were far better at finding survivor life signs: things like IR emissions, radio signals, and even (if we were lucky) the afterglow of human thoughts. The mental activity of *Homo sapiens* created faint electrical impulses; navy probes could detect those impulses provided there wasn't too much masking interference from the minds of local animal life. Considering that Muta was still in its Triassic period, none of the native fauna had brains much bigger than peanuts. A human should stand out like a searchlight in a nest of glowworms.

Speaking of lights, a soft green one warmed into life above the bridge's vidscreen. Only the captain could turn on that light; it indicated we were officially in stable planetary orbit. Readouts on the Explorers' console said we'd been in orbit for five full minutes . . . but Cohen was slow to acknowledge our arrival, fussing with by-the-book checklists, sensor confirmations, crew status call-ins, and other delaying tactics. Captains almost never turned on the green light, even when they were in orbit for days—"going green" had official legal connotations that captains preferred to avoid. Don't ask me to explain. It's just one of those mysteries of navy procedure that no one thinks to question. Cohen would never have turned on the light if there weren't an admiral on the bridge.

"Stable orbit achieved," he said stiffly.

Festina nodded. "Request permission to launch probes."

"Permission granted, Admiral."

She turned a dial. "Probes away."

The vidscreen showed four missiles spearing toward the planet. Each was surrounded by a milky sheath: bits of *Pistachio*'s Sperm-field pulled away when the missiles were launched. The sheaths dispersed as the probes entered thicker atmosphere, swirling away into eddies of unnatural energies. All four missiles disappeared soon after, becoming too small for the eye to track against the bright bluish background.

"How long will the probes take to get there?" Ubatu whispered in my ear.

"Three minutes," I said. Ubatu was so close, I had to make an effort not to lean away from her life force. With *Pistachio*'s bridge so tiny, I could sense everyone present—a constant 360-degree awareness—but Ubatu's aura was the only one that bothered me: intensely focused in my direction. Staring at me with the rapacity of a stalker. I could only read her general feelings, not her precise thoughts . . . but she seemed to be assessing my usability, how ripe I was for exploiting. I doubted that true Vodun was geared toward selfishly taking advantage of powerful loa; real religions frowned on egotistic playing with fire. Ifa-Vodun, however (especially Ubatu's version of it), was not a real religion. It was a cynical diplomatic tool, created by inbred dipshits who'd dreamed up the totally unfounded notion that high-level aliens might respond to voodoo.

At least I hoped the notion was totally unfounded. If a creature like the Balrog could actually be influenced by herbs gathered at midnight and black rooster sacrifice . . .

I shifted position to put more distance between me and Ubatu's aura.

"Probe data coming in," Festina said. "Nice clear visuals." She turned a knob . . . and Muta appeared on the screen.

The first thing that struck me was color: reds and blues and greens and purples. Every plant had staked out its own private chunk of the rainbow. Morphologically, all Muta's flora were ferns—wide multilobed fronds with single stems, whether they were tiny fiddleheads barely peeking out of the soil, midrange varieties reaching to knee height/hip height/head height, or broad-leafed giants stretching as tall as trees—but despite the plants' similarity of form, they showed no commonality in hue. As if each bit of vegetation had been colored by a child choosing crayons at random.

"What's wrong with the plants?" Ubatu whispered. "Some sort of disease?"

"No," I said. "They're just young. It's a young planet." When she continued to stare blankly, I elaborated. "This is common on early Mesozoic worlds. The plants are experimenting, trying to find an optimal color for photosynthesis. Each species has different pigments, with a slightly different biochemistry underlying the energy-gathering process. Some colors lead to better results than others . . . but at the moment, no single species is so superior it outcompetes the rest. They're all inefficient by mature Earth standards. Eventually, some chance mutation will lead to a significant improvement in energy production for some lucky plant; and that plant will set the standard all others have to meet."

"And everything will turn green?"

"There's no guarantee green will win. It depends on the composition of the sun, the atmosphere, the soil, and the usual random wiles of evolution. Maybe the plants will find some superefficient yellow pigment that's better than green chlorophyll. Or blue. Or brown. But eventually a shakedown will come, establishing more uniformity. Twenty million years should do the trick. Then homogeneity will last until some plant comes up with the idea of sprouting flowers to attract pollinators. Which will bring back colors again."

"Shush," said Festina. "There's the Unity camp."

While I was talking, the probe sending pictures had moved at high speed across Muta's terrain. Now the probe was traveling upstream along the Grindstone River. In the distance, we could see the huts and buildings of Camp Esteem.

No sign of movement. Not even insects or animals. I glanced at Festina's console—no IR readings that might indicate survivors. On the other hand, there were obvious heat sources all over: small ones in almost every hut, and larger ones in the big buildings. Festina zoomed the probe's camera to scan the building with the largest heat source. A plaque on the front displayed a pictogram knife, fork, and plate: the standard signage for mess halls. No doubt the members of Team Esteem could remember which building was their cookhouse even if it wasn't labeled . . . but the Unity was famous for flogging the obvious. They might paint DOG on a pet's forehead just to be thorough.

"If that's the mess hall," Tut said, "what do you bet the heat source inside is a stove somebody left on?"

"No bet," Festina replied.

"You could smash the probe through a window and see."

"Not just yet." Festina sent the probe on a looping circle of the whole camp. Still nothing unusual or out of place.

"I don't see corpses," Li said.

"Maybe they've all been eaten," Ubatu suggested. "I mean, by animals and insects."

"The Mayday was issued thirty-six hours ago," Festina said. "Local time, that was early yesterday morning. Pretty fast for scavengers to consume a body, bones and all."

"Unless," Cohen said, "the scavengers on Muta are more efficient than on other planets."

"It's possible," Festina told him. "Usually, though, native scavengers work quite slowly on human corpses. Earth flesh isn't their normal food. It can even be poison to alien predators. So on average, human meat doesn't get eaten very quickly on nonterrestrial worlds. Of course, Muta could be the exception."

A thought struck me. "You said the Mayday came yesterday morning. What time exactly?"

Festina checked a data display: "7:14 local."

"Then maybe we *should* crash the probe through a mess hall window. At 7:14, everyone on the team would be eating breakfast."

"True," Festina said. "Unity surveyors start breakfast precisely at 7:00 and end at 7:20."

"Goddamned robots," Li muttered.

"They prefer the term 'cyborg,' " Ubatu told him.

"I prefer the term 'morons.' "

"Now, now," Cohen said—more a reflex than a serious attempt to stop the bickering. Festina, however, was less inclined to put up with such nonsense. Her aura flared with annoyance.

"Enough!" she said. "Everybody shut up while I work. We've got four probes, so maybe it's worth sacrificing one to see inside the cookhouse."

Her life force hinted at words she didn't say: if the mess hall was filled with dead bodies, we'd be off the hook. For the sake of thoroughness, we'd have to check the other survey camps too; but if one team had been reduced to corpses, the rest would almost certainly be the same.

In that case, our mission was over. The Unity might want to retrieve the fallen and determine the cause of death . . . but that was their business, not ours. We were strictly here to save survivors. If we couldn't find anyone alive, we'd file a report and go home.

I knew it wouldn't be that simple. For Explorers, nothing is ever easy.

"All right," said Festina. "I'll send in a probe."

She manipulated the controls, not just setting up the first probe to bash its way into the mess hall, but bringing a second probe into position to get footage of the process. The picture on the vidscreen split down the middle: one half from the nose of the missile that would enter the mess, the other half from a more distant viewpoint that showed both the probe and the mess hall building. The probe was lean and black, hovering on antigrav right in front of the building's largest window. We could see nothing through the glass—the window had a reflective thermo-coat, designed to bounce off incoming light, so the interior would remain cool. Come winter, the coat would be changed to absorb light and collect heat . . . but at the moment, the windows were still on summer settings.

"Ready," Festina said. "In we go."

On the overview half of the vidscreen, the probe moved toward the window in slow motion; on the nose camera half, the window itself came closer and closer until it shattered under the probe missile's strength. We had time to see a large square table with twelve chairs around it, something cloudy in the air like smoke, the smoke rushing forward as if stirred by a breeze from the broken window . . . then the pictures on the vidscreen abruptly vanished into random digital snow.

Both halves of the screen.

God *damn*!" Festina said. "We got EMP'd."

"EMP'd?" Ubatu asked.

"An electromagnetic pulse," I told her. "It fried the probe's electrical circuits." I waved toward the screen, both sides showing nothing but static. "The EMP took out both probes. That's pretty powerful."

"You don't know the half of it," Festina said. "The pulse got my other two missiles too—the ones held back in reserve. Twenty kilometers away."

"Whoa." Tut gave a low whistle. "A pulse that big makes me think of a nuke."

"It wasn't a nuke," Cohen said. "Any significant explosion would show up on *Pistachio*'s sensors." He was looking at the console on his chair. "We got nothing."

"Did the sensors pick up the EMP?" Festina asked.

"No. And we should have, if it was large enough to damage probes at twenty kilometers. The pulse must have been directional, and so tightly focused there wasn't enough spillover for our sensors to pick up."

Tut frowned. "Can EMPs *be* tightly focused?"

"If they're properly generated," Cohen said. "A while back, the navy looked into EMP cannons. The Admiralty thought big EMP guns might be nice nonlethal weapons—one shot could melt an enemy ship's electronic circuits without hurting the people on board."

Festina looked sour. "Kill a starship's computer systems and the people inside won't stay healthy for long."

"True," Cohen admitted, "you couldn't go shooting indiscriminately. Still, an EMP weapon would be nice to have in the arsenal—to give more tactical options. Too bad the cannons weren't practical at normal space-engagement distance. We needed something with a range of one hundred thousand kilometers; EMP guns that big took way too much power. The idea's been shelved a few decades, till we get better energy-production technology."

"So maybe," Tut said, "the Fuentes had solved the technical problems in building EMP guns. Maybe they built an automated EMP defense system. And even though it's been sixty-five hundred years, maybe the systems still work. They could have been dormant, but somehow the Unity reactivated them. Next thing you know, zap: the survey teams are EMP'd to rat shit. Their equipment went into meltdown, but the people are all just fine."

Cohen turned toward him. "You think that's why they've gone incommunicado? Their communicators have just gone dead?"

"Could be."

"How'd they get out a Mayday?" Cohen asked.

"Someone might have cobbled together a distress signal from spare parts—bits and pieces untouched by the EMP. No weapon is one hundred percent effective, right? Especially if the EMP was tightly focused. And the newest camp would have the most spare parts on hand, so it makes sense they'd be the quickest to build a makeshift signal."

Tut had a point. I didn't honestly believe the threat on Muta was as simple as leftover EMP guns . . . but Tut's scenario *was* possible.

While I pondered the point, the vidscreen came back to life: a still shot of the mess hall interior. The table and empty chairs. Apparent smoke in the air. "All right," Festina said. "I've backtracked *Pistachio*'s record of the probe's data. This is the visual a moment before the probe went dead."

With the image frozen on the screen, we could notice more details. On the table, plates and bowls contained half-eaten portions of food: fruit, fiber-mush, and protein power-crunch. (The Unity loved to combine nutrients into artificial concoctions with the texture of gruel or hardtack.) A cup of juice had toppled over; after thirty-six hours on the tabletop, the spill looked dry enough to be sweet and sticky, but no insects were taking an interest. No insects on the food either. Why? Because the mess hall had been shut up tight and insectproof until our probe went through the window? Because Mutan insects didn't like the taste of Earthling food? Or because something had killed all the insects that should have been swarming over a meal left out for a day and a half?

One thing was sure: the picture showed no people. I looked at the empty chairs, half expecting to see little heaps of clothing—as if Team Esteem had been vaporized between one bite and the next. But no. The twelve chairs were pushed back from the table, the way they'd be if all the surveyors had run outside. Maybe the Unity folk had heard a noise; they'd thrown down their knives and forks, then raced to investigate.

At least, that's how it looked. Suppose that was how it happened. Then what? If the Unity teams just got EMP'd into radio silence, why did the mess hall still look like the *Mary Celeste*? If the people of Team Esteem had survived, wouldn't they come back to the mess hall eventually? Wouldn't they finish their breakfast, or at least clean their dirty dishes? Unity surveyors loved routine. If something unexpected happened, they'd deal with it as quickly as possible, then try to get back to their normal schedule. But it looked like they'd abandoned the mess hall the previous morning and hadn't been back since.

"What's the smoke?" Ubatu asked, looking at the picture. "Is something on fire?"

"Could be," Festina said. "The IR readings showed a large heat source in the mess hall. If someone left a stove burning in the kitchen—a gas stove, unaffected by EMPs—it could have been blazing away for thirty-six hours. Eventually, all that heat might have set fire to something. Hence the high IR readings. And the smoke."

But she didn't sound happy with the explanation. I didn't like it either—I didn't trust pat answers.

Li had said nothing through all this. His life force suggested he was trying to invent ways to turn this business to his advantage. "So what's the decision on this?" he asked. "Go for a landing? Send more probes?"

"Don't have more probes," Tut said. "*Pistachio* only stores four. We could manufacture new ones, but that'd take hours." He shook his head. "Can't waste that kind of time on a Class One rescue mission."

Festina gave him a look. "A few hours building new probes is nothing compared to the time we might waste searching blindly on the ground." She sighed. "But if we sent more probes, they'd probably just get EMP'd again without telling anything new."

"So you're landing?" Cohen asked.

Festina took a deep breath, then nodded. "I don't see any alternative. If the problem is just some automated EMP system left over from the Fuentes, there'll be survivors down there to be rescued. I doubt if it's that simple . . ." She glanced in my direction—maybe thinking about the Balrog and why it wanted to hitchhike inside me to Muta. ". . . but we have no excuse to give up the rescue, and no way to see what's going on without sending someone in the flesh."

"Once you're down there," Ubatu said, "how do you get back up? Won't your equipment get EMP'd too?"

"Presumably," Festina replied. "But we'll go down by Sperm-tail, and that can't be disrupted by EMPs. The Sperm-field is its own little universe, impervious to outside forces. Once it's in place, a nuke couldn't budge it."

Before Tut and I said anything, Festina gave us a warning look. What she'd told Ubatu was technically true—a Sperm-field like the one around *Pistachio* was indeed a pocket universe immune to electromagnetic pulses and most other natural energies. But Festina had skipped past an important step with the phrase "once it's in place."

Here's what she didn't say. The Sperm-field around *Pistachio* had a long flapping tail—a *very* long tail, stretching as much as ten thousand kilometers. *Pistachio* could plant that tail in the middle of Camp Esteem, like the bottom of a long thin tornado. We Explorers could ride down inside the tail, sliding safely through the funnel cloud all the way to the ground. Just one problem: we needed to plant the tail where we wanted to go. We had to anchor the lower end at our desired destination . . . and the only way to do that was with a small electronic "anchor" that grabbed the tail like a magnet and locked the Sperm-field in place. Once the tail latched onto the anchor, the anchor became part of the pocket universe and therefore safe from EMPs . . . but until that time, the anchor device could easily have its innards turned to slag by a single modest-sized pulse.

How could we send down an anchor when we'd lost our four probe missiles? Each of the probes had carried an anchor that could be deposited where we wanted to land; but with the probes knocked out, and their anchors probably ruined, what did Festina think she was going to do?

The look on her face said she had a plan. I tried to read her life force, but couldn't get anything definite. Either I didn't have enough experience interpreting auras, or Festina was better at hiding her thoughts than people like Ubatu.

"Captain," Festina said, shutting down the Explorer console, "it's time the landing party got suited up. Please prepare to drop the tail."

"And the anchor?" Cohen knew perfectly well there could be no landing till the tail was locked in place.

"I'll notify you when it's ready." Festina stood up. "Come on, Explorers. Let's get this done."

9

Dukkha [Pali]: Literally "out of kilter" like an unbalanced wheel, but used symbolically to describe "out of kilter" emotions: anything from acute suffering to persistent dissatisfaction to a vague but gnawing sense that things aren't right. The Buddha's first truth is that our lives are filled with dukkha. Even if we are sometimes happy, the state is only temporary—no one dodges dukkha forever.

I COULD say that getting into a tightsuit is a complicated process: the heavy fabric must be pulled into place, the seams must be sealed perfectly, the interior must be inflated to an exact pressure, seventeen tests must be performed on air supply, temperature regulation, comm units, heads-up displays . . .

Or I could say that getting into a tightsuit is a simple process: you stand on two raised foot blocks in a robing chamber while eight robotic limbs assemble the suit around you and perform diagnostics as they go along. Once that's finished (including triple checks on known points of vulnerability), you get bombarded with selected wavelengths of radiation aimed at exterminating all terrestrial microbes on the suit's exterior. This mass kill is important when visiting unexplored worlds, to avoid contaminating the biosphere with Earth-born bacteria. For landing on Muta, however, the sanitizing rad bath was superfluous—Unity humans had lived on the planet for years, and throughout that time they'd lived in direct contact with the environment. Muta was already irreparably tainted with whatever microorganisms the survey teams had carried on their skins, in their lungs, and along their digestive tracts.

So our suits would do nothing to keep Muta pristine—that was already a lost cause. The suits wouldn't help *us* much either . . . not if they got EMP'd. One good pulse, and the suits' electrical circuits would stop working. Would anything stay operational? Yes. The air tanks were purely mechanical, working with simple valves rather than sophisticated gadgetry; they'd be good for six hours, EMP or no EMP. All other systems depended on electronic controls. We might find ways to jury-rig workarounds, but that wasn't something to count on. We had to expect a completely unpowered mission.

Then again, if losing our electronics was the only thing that went wrong, we'd be getting off lucky.

Pistachio had only two robing chambers. Therefore, Festina and I got suited up first. When we emerged, Tut had stripped down to his underwear and was attempting to dress a chair in his uniform. He asked, "Do either of you carry matches?"

As a matter of fact I did—I'd stuffed my belt pouches with every emergency supply I could think of. But I just said, "Get suited up, Tut."

"Yes'm, Mom." He slid off his shorts, laid them carefully on the seat of the chair, and walked naked into the robing chamber.

Festina watched him go. After he disappeared, she murmured, "It's gold."

"Yes," I said. "I noticed in Zoonau."

"I made a point of not looking." Festina took a breath. "Gold is an excellent electrical conductor."

"True."

"If he goes down to Muta and gets hit with a big electromagnetic pulse . . . do you think . . ."

"Ooo. That's a thought I didn't need inside my head." For some reason I added, "I'm a virgin. I don't think about such things."

"Oh. Sorry." Festina's life force colored like a blush—the first time I'd seen anything in her aura except strength and composure. "Well, no point standing around. Let's get ready."

She left the room almost at a run.

Usually, sperm-tail landings start in a ship's rear transport bay. This time, however, Festina escorted me to the shuttle bay, where Li's shuttlecraft had been rolled into takeoff position. A crew member was putting away a power cord she must have used to top up the shuttle's batteries. "We're going down in this?" I asked Festina.

"That's the plan," she said.

"What happens if the shuttle gets EMP'd?"

"You mean *when* the shuttle gets EMP'd." She smiled. "Fortunately, Technocracy shuttles are flightworthy even without power—one of those safety features required by the League of Peoples. So no matter what our altitude when we get pulsed, we can glide the rest of the way. I've already plotted a course that takes us to Camp Esteem."

"Gliding is one thing," I said. "Landing is another. Without power, a shuttle can't VTOL. We'll need a landing strip—long, straight, and flat."

"Or else we'll need parachutes." Festina grinned. "We'll jump when we're over the camp. The shuttle will keep going at least another ten kilometers before it crashes." She patted the craft's hull affectionately. "It'll make one hell of an impact, but we don't have to worry about explosions. These things just crash without burning—another nice safety feature."

"Have you told Ambassador Li you're going to sacrifice his pride and joy?"

"I've informed him that pursuant to regulations covering Class One missions, I can commandeer any resources I consider essential for the mission's success . . . including civilian shuttlecraft."

"When he heard that, Li must have hemorrhaged."

"Actually, he took it pretty well. He just gaped for a second, then said, 'Very well, if you think it's necessary.'" Festina rolled her eyes. "When we get home, the greedy bastard will bill the navy twice what the shuttle's worth. Then the navy will charge the Unity three times more. Rescue missions for alien governments are big moneymakers for the fleet."

"I don't suppose we Explorers see any of that money."

Festina laid her hand on my arm. "Glad you're keeping your sense of humor. Let's go inside."

The shuttle's interior was still large and luxurious, with seating for twelve and what I assumed was a gourmet galley at the back (though the door to that area was closed). Each of the twelve seats now held a shimmering mirror-sphere the size of a soccer ball. I recognized the spheres as stasis fields: pocket universes like the Sperm-field surrounding the ship, except that the mirror-sphere universes only had three macrodimensions instead of four. Time didn't exist in a stasis field. The outer universe might age a billion years, but anything in stasis would remain as it was, caught in an instant that never advanced so much as a nanosecond.

Stasis fields couldn't take much physical damage; a strong sharp blow from the outside would pop them like a soap bubble. But they *were* immune to EMPs, which simply washed past the surface of the field without affecting the contents. Stasis was perfect for protecting equipment we didn't want to get zapped during our descent to Muta.

I picked up the mirror-sphere closest to me. If I'd done that with bare hands, I'd be risking serious frostbite—the outside of a stasis field is dangerously cold, though not as cold as the Absolute Zero inside—but with my tightsuit gloves, I was perfectly safe. Ice had begun to condense from the air near the sphere's reflective surface. If not kept clear, the surface would develop a solid frozen crust . . . which wasn't a bad thing, since the hardening frost would provide protection against accidental bumping.

"What's inside?" I asked Festina. "Sperm-tail anchors?"

She nodded. "An anchor in each. We'll have twelve chances to establish a Sperm-link . . . and I don't think an automated defense system will EMP us that often. EMPs take a lot of energy, especially when fired at range. An automated system isn't likely to keep pulsing targets it's already shot. So it EMPs us once, maybe twice; but we'll have plenty of reserve anchors left. Once we've anchored *Pistachio*'s tail, we don't have to worry anymore."

Her aura showed she wasn't as confident as she pretended—she knew there were never any guarantees. But with a supply of twelve anchors, each one protected from EMPs until we needed it, we really did have the odds on our side. "Anything else we should put in the spheres?" I asked. "Maybe a handheld comm or two?"

"Already done," Festina said. "Each stasis sphere has an anchor, a comm, a stunner, and a Bumbler. An extremely tight fit, but just barely possible."

"I didn't think *Pistachio* carried twelve Bumblers."

"It didn't. Last night I ordered the ship-soul to fabricate a bunch. You can never have too many Bumblers."

I agreed. Explorers could go through Bumblers as fast as eating peanuts. In Zoonau, we'd lost two on a mission that lasted only fifteen minutes. Usually, though, we didn't have the luxury of whipping up a dozen in advance. The navy labeled surplus production as "extravagant waste" rather than "sensible precaution." Apparently an admiral on a Class One mission could disregard standard fleet policies . . . and I got the impression Lieutenant Admiral Festina Ramos thumbed her nose at regulations whenever she had the chance.

Festina began familiarizing herself with the shuttle's controls. I was about to take an idle-curiosity tour of the craft when three ensigns arrived with our parachutes. Naturally, I had to make sure the chutes had been packed properly and were set for manual operation. (By default, parachutes were usually set for automatic deployment at an altitude considered optimal by the Engineering Corps . . . which was all very well if the chutes' laser altimeters were functional, but not so good if you expected every wire to be drips of molten copper.)

Tut arrived just as I was finishing with the chutes. We'd decided in advance we should wear our standard colors—Tut yellow and me orange, while Festina said she liked white—but when Tut appeared, he'd programmed his suit's skin to a lustrous metallic gold with all the markings of King Tutankhamen's ceremonial casket. Horizontal stripes of black and gold ran along the sides of his helmet and down the front of his chest; bits of lapis lazuli blue were layered down his front in a sort of striped bib that ended at a broad U-shaped collar halfway down his chest. Below that, the gold/black/blue stripes resumed and extended all the way to his boots. He looked like a bumblebee with a few sky-blue inlays.

"So what do you think, Mom?" He turned so I could see the back. More stripes. "Aren't I like the king's sarcophagus?"

"You are."

Festina came to the door of the cockpit and gave Tut a long cool look. "I like it," she said. "There's something refreshingly efficient about an Explorer already wearing a coffin."

We took off without ceremony—nothing but the usual "permission requesteds" and "permission granteds" that always mark a shuttle departure. No one came to watch us leave . . . not even Ubatu, who I thought might show up to give me some words of Ifa-Vodun wisdom. ("Don't endanger the spores. We haven't had a chance yet to kill something in their honor.") Festina noticed the absence of well-wishers too; just before takeoff, she murmured, "Li must have decided he couldn't bear to see his baby go."

I said, "He and Ubatu are probably up on the bridge getting in the captain's way."

"Probably," Festina agreed. "If the three of us don't come back, everybody will want to say they had a front-row seat when Festina Ramos met her doom."

"Fame's a bitch, isn't it?" Tut said. "Bugs the crap out of me."

We both looked at him, wondering what he thought he was famous for. I could have looked into his aura, but decided I didn't want to know.

Li might have been a bullying, self-absorbed man, but he had excellent taste in shuttles. He'd chosen a model whose cockpit was almost entirely transparent: a clear plastic bubble bulging from the front of the craft and providing a panoramic view of our surroundings. Overhead was *Pistachio*, a long white baton surrounded with its milky Sperm-field, set against deep starry black. Beneath us lay the sunlit blue of Muta, streaked with clouds and shining hospitably in the emptiness of space. Festina was in the pilot's seat, Tut in the copilot's, me in the pull-out chair behind . . . and the bubble around us was so close to invisible, I felt we were sitting on some outer-space patio, casually open to vacuum.

"Starting descent now," Festina said into her comm.

"Acknowledging your descent," Cohen answered. "Good luck, Admiral." His voice came through my tightsuit's radio as well as my comm implant; then it was replaced by a faint regular beep produced by *Pistachio*'s ship-soul. Festina had asked for the beep as a way of detecting EMPs: if the beep went silent, we'd know we'd been pulsed. Of course, we probably wouldn't need outside confirmation—when the shuttle's lights died and its steering yoke went sludgy, we'd have a good clue what had happened—but Festina liked redundant backups.

Beep. Beep. Beep.

As we angled down toward Muta, *Pistachio* began to turn from horizontal to vertical. Soon it would be straight up and down, nose toward the stars and stern pointing directly at Camp Esteem. The long swishing Sperm-tail would dangle like an unruly fishing line, down through the many layers of atmosphere until it reached the ground below. Once we landed, we'd catch that line with an anchor and secure an EMP-proof escape from Muta's dangers.

Or so we hoped.

* * *

Pistachio was soon out of sight: lost in the distant dark. Our descent path would circle Muta once, easing gently, down, down, down. None of us spoke as the sun (or should I say GoL?) disappeared behind the rounded edge of the planet. The dark half of the world, rolling far beneath us, showed no lights at all. In the age of Las Fuentes, that blackness must have been punctuated by the illumination of cities . . . but now there was only seamless night.

"What do you think is *really* down there?" Tut asked.

Festina said, "I'm afraid we'll soon find out."

Down and down. A digital display on the shuttle's console showed our altitude in kilometers: 900 . . . 850 . . . 800 . . . descending through the ionosphere, a constantly surging bath of electrically charged particles. Cumulatively, the electric fury outside had much more energy than the EMPs we worried about; but it was thinned over time and distance, rather than striking the shuttle in a single disruptive pulse. Our shielding could protect us without difficulty. I hoped.

500 . . . 450 . . . 400 . . . 350 . . .

We rounded back into sunlight and my helmet visor darkened to protect my eyes. I wanted to ask the others when they thought we'd get EMP'd, but they didn't know any more than I did; perhaps the Balrog had better information, but I avoided asking, for fear the spores might actually answer. As for my newly acquired sixth sense, its range was far too limited to tell me anything—it didn't even reach to the back of the shuttle's passenger cabin, let alone several hundred kilometers to the ground. My alien awareness could feel the hypersonic rush of thin atmosphere just outside the cockpit, but my perception stopped well short of the shuttle's own galley.

Beep. Beep. Beep. Our comms were still alive. Beep. Beep. The computerized signal was soft but unnerving in the otherwise silent cockpit. To break the tension, I opened my mouth to make some inane remark . . . but Festina must have heard me getting ready to speak because she quickly cut in. "Nobody say anything. Not a word."

Tut looked at her in surprise, obviously wondering what she was worried about. I had the advantage of being able to read her life force: Festina exuded a superstitious dread that if anyone said, "So far so good," the words themselves would make all hell break loose.

She was probably right.

Beep.

Beep.

Beep.

300 . . . 250 . . . 200 . . . things would get bumpy soon. The shuttle's wings were set to full extension; as the atmosphere thickened, they'd drag against the air, leading to random skips and flutters. Festina had said our course would pass directly over Camp Esteem, but that was only the computer's best-guess scenario. If we got EMP'd and lost control while bumping/jumping/thumping high in the atmosphere, we might veer hundreds of kilometers off course. The shuttle allowed for manual steering—wrestling the yoke without powered assistance—but it wouldn't be enough to get us back on track if we deviated too far too early.

Beep.

150 . . . 100 . . . 80 . . . then a Brahma-bull buck as we hit the mesopause, the line of demarcation between the outer atmosphere and the lower layers. Festina kept her grip on the yoke, pressing our nose into the dive. We could see nothing but planet now: a great wide plain filled our view, grasslands veined with wandering rivers that occasionally wandered too far and diffused into Mesozoic bogs. Those bogs would be full of reptiles and amphibians . . . not exactly like terrestrial species, but with points of similarity. Evolution was like weather—chaotic in specific details, but falling into large-scale patterns with a limited repertoire of effects. Muta's development would approximately echo Earth's. Its swamps would have quasi-crocodilian predators dining on quasi-frog amphibians and quasi-minnow fish . . .

Another bump—50 klicks on the altimeter. We'd entered the stratosphere. Within seconds, the cockpit bubble was surrounded by heat glow as we rammed into air particles and crushed them together. My sixth sense could feel the hull temperature soaring—still within safety limits, but higher than a normal entry. Festina had based our course on the possibility we'd get EMP'd much earlier than this; though the shuttle still had power, we were following the same path as if we'd been in an uncontrolled dive.

Fast and hot. Blazing through the sky.

Beep. Beep. Beep.

"You know," Tut said, "I thought—"

"Shut up!" Festina and I yelled in unison.

40 . . . 30 . . . going through Muta's ozone layer, and still no EMP. I was sure that's what Tut had intended to say: *I thought we'd be pulsed by now.* I'd thought the same. But EMPs take a lot of energy—especially at long range. It would be more efficient to shoot us close to the ground.

Twenty kilometers up. Festina turned from the controls. "It's time. Get ready to jump."

I got to my feet reluctantly. It seemed a pity to bail out of the shuttle while it was still working . . . but if we didn't jump when we were over Camp Esteem, the shuttle's momentum would take us far past our target. Then if we got EMP'd, we'd have a long walk back to where we wanted to go. Better to follow the original plan.

So I went back into the passenger cabin and strapped four iced-up mirror-spheres to my tightsuit, using specially padded carrying cases. Tut and Festina did the same. The cases hung from our necks like oversized pendants; I adjusted the straps until all four spheres rested evenly on my chest, then I secured them with a holding harness. The completed rig wasn't heavy . . . but with four soccer-ball-sized containers on my front and a full parachute on my back (over top of the tightsuit's backpack), I felt like a pagoda with legs. My only consolation was that Festina and Tut looked just as ridiculous.

"Skydiving like this should be fun," Tut said. "Is there anything else I can carry? Hey, I bet these seats detach! Ever seen someone parachute while holding a chair?"

The passenger seats *could* be detached by flipping release levers on each leg. Fortunately, Tut was too burdened with mirror-spheres to reach the levers. He was still trying to bend over as I went to the side hatch and grabbed the red door handle. "Everyone ready?" I asked.

Tut straightened up. "Sure," he said. "Immortality awaits."

Festina slapped him lightly on the arm. "Bastard. Don't you know the admiral gets to say that?"

"Grab something solid," I told them. Beep. Beep. Beep. I pulled the lever, and the door slid open.

Wind whipped through the cabin. If I hadn't been holding the lever, I might have been swept off my feet . . . but after a moment, the gale lessened as the pressure inside the shuttle equalized to the pressure outside. Neither pressure was high; fortunately, my tightsuit protected me against burst eardrums and subzero cold. Far below, the ground seemed to drift past slowly, though we were actually going faster than the speed of sound.

"Not long now," Festina said over her comm unit. We were using the Fuentes city as a landmark. When Drill-Press appeared beneath us, we'd hit the silk. Our momentum would carry us on toward Camp Esteem, and we could easily steer the chutes toward our destination. We'd already agreed on a rendezvous point just east of the huts.

Beep. Beep. Land slipped beneath us. The lower the shuttle dropped, the more our speed became apparent—racing through scattered clouds, rushing above small river valleys and copses where ferns rose as tall as trees. Beep. Beep. The broad river Grindstone appeared, a few low buildings, then suddenly the central skyscrapers of Drill-Press, towering like giants. The city streets were dirty but intact, and so were a score of bridges spanning the river, glimmering white in the sun. We waited till the last bridge was directly beneath us . . . but nobody had to say a word when the time came. Tut, Festina, and I threw ourselves forward, out the hatch, and into open air.

* * *

Skydiving in a tightsuit is different from being exposed to the elements. I'd practiced both ways at the Academy, and much preferred fully closed jumps. When you're not completely sealed in a suit, the wind burns unprotected skin. My cheek was too tender for that kind of buffeting: the gusts felt like daggers of ice stabbing through my face over and over. By the time I reached ground on an open dive, the entire left half of my head—my skin, my hair, my ear—would be streaked with wind-dried blood.

But inside a tightsuit was safe. No wind, no cold, no roaring in the ears. It was peaceful. Like floating in zero gee. That afternoon on Muta, the sun was shining, the view was superb, and for just a few seconds, I was empty. Free of the clamor of myself.

Falling in silence. Except for the beep . . . beep . . . beep . . .

Momentum and the angle of my dive carried me quickly past Drill-Press city. The heads-up display in my helmet said I was traveling due north. Not far in the distance, I could see Camp Esteem, built on a rise above the river valley. What looked like a cloud of smoke still drifted outside the cookhouse . . . until, as I watched, the cloud whirled away from the building and sped in our direction.

At first, I thought the cloud had been caught in a puff of wind; but no wind blew so direct and fast on such a mild day. The cloud shot straight for us, like steam propelled from a high-pressure hose. I didn't know what it was, but reflex kicked in immediately. "*Pistachio*," I said, "steamlike anomaly. A cloud of it coming in our direction. Its action seems purposeful . . ."

Tut and Festina were saying similar things, all of us speaking at the same time. With the three of us talking simultaneously, people on *Pistachio*'s bridge probably couldn't make out our words . . . but the main ship computer would be able to disentangle our voices. Eventually. But not before . . .

The cloud washed over me while I was still telling *Pistachio* what it looked like. A moment of mist and dizziness—the dizziness from a fierce eruption of my sixth sense, like a deafening blare of noise. The cloud was ablaze with ferocious emotion. Rage? Hate? Bewilderment? Passion so intense I couldn't identify its nature; just a howling unfocused adrenaline, vicious enough that my own emotions flared in sympathy, and for a moment I screamed without knowing why.

Then the feeling was gone. The cloud had moved past me, out of sight and out of my sixth sense's range, almost as if nothing had happened. I said, "*Pistachio*, the cloud has passed by and I am still . . ."

The sound of my voice was muffled—just me talking inside my suit, no echo from my radio receivers. I closed my mouth and listened . . . to *true* silence. Nothing but my own heartbeat. In particular, no beep beep beep from *Pistachio*.

So that was what it felt like to be EMP'd.

I thought back to what we'd seen as our probe jammed its nose into the cookhouse. The "smoke" had been drifting placidly through the mess hall . . . but as soon as the missile intruded, the cloud had shot forward, and the probe went dead.

Stupid, stupid, stupid—I wanted to smack my head with my hand. We'd all thought the smoke had been disturbed by breeze through the broken window . . . but the smoke was what carried the EMP. It might even be the ultimate danger that lurked on Muta: some airborne entity, perhaps a swarm of nanites left over from Las Fuentes . . . or a hive mind like the Balrog, but with spores as light as dust. The smoke might float its way around Muta, EMPing machines and . . . and . . .

But at least I was still alive.

My suit was defunct. The heads-up displays had vanished, and no other systems responded. My personal comm implant was also scrap—through my sixth sense I saw the fused subcutaneous circuits in my ears and soft palate, fine wires flash-melted by the energy surge. Good thing the navy's equipment designers had provided enough insulation to keep me safe when the implant got slagged; otherwise, it might have been unpleasant to have my sinuses full of molten electronics.

As it was, I felt no ill effects. I looked back at my fellow Explorers, and both seemed healthy too. They were out of range of my sixth sense, but they held their arms tight to their sides in a good airfoil position rather than just dangling limp. That meant they were still conscious, controlling their dives.

Looking up, I saw something else: the shuttle. Which should have been a long distance past us now. Its uncontrolled terminal velocity was much faster than three humans in tightsuits—we were lighter and dragged more on the air. The shuttle should have continued to spear forward at high speed, while we skydivers slowed down. But the shuttle had slowed down too. And although I was too far away to be sure, I thought the side hatch was now closed.

We'd left that side hatch open when we jumped.

At times, I regretted that swearing had never come naturally to me. I just yelled, "Li!" and left it at that.

He'd stowed away on the shuttle. I was sure of it. That's why he hadn't come to see us off; he was already on board. Ubatu was likely with him—following me to Muta on behalf of Ifa-Vodun. The two diplomats must have concealed themselves in the shuttlecraft's galley, and lucky for them, they'd been far enough back that my sixth sense didn't pick them up. Once we Explorers had jumped, the two diplomats came out of hiding, closed the side hatch, and took the controls. I had no idea why they'd do something so stupid . . . but as I watched, the shuttle began a slow turn toward the Fuentes city.

"Li!" I shouted again. "Li!"

I wasn't the only one to notice the shuttle's action. Festina had turned to watch them too. Without a working comm I couldn't hear her reaction; but she was probably swearing enough for both of us.

The smoke/steam/EMP-monster noticed the shuttle too. The cloud shot straight at the craft, a wispy misty stream as fast as a bullet. Moments later, the shuttle's engines went silent.

All this time, I'd been dropping in freefall. With tightsuits on, Explorers can jump from considerable altitude, and Festina had wanted us out of the shuttle as soon as practical—no sense hanging around a ship we knew was doomed to crash. (Would it still crash with Li at the controls? An unpowered "dead-stick" landing was a tricky exercise, even with a first-rate airstrip beneath you. Muta had no airstrips. Li's best chance was to aim for a long straight street back in Drill-Press and hope there was nothing dangerous in the middle of the pavement. If he hit a stone deposited by some recent river flood . . . or a basking crocodilian the size of a small dinosaur . . .)

But whatever problems Li might face, there was no way I could help him. Nothing to do now but open my parachute. One tug on the cord, and I was jolted as hard as smashing into a wall. The tightsuit helped cushion the shock, but the sudden snap still made something spurt from my cheek like slop from a wet sponge. By luck, the fluid didn't hit my helmet visor; otherwise, I'd have been forced to look at it until it dried and turned into a crusty spot on the otherwise clear plastic.

The chute splayed wide above me: a huge rectangular parasol against the afternoon sun. Its winglike shape made it easy to steer; I aimed in the direction of the rendezvous point, and floated serenely downward. No birds took notice as I fell—birds wouldn't evolve on Muta for another hundred million years. Even pterosaurs were far in the future. Only insects had mastered the mechanics of flight, and they stayed close to the ground, near their nests and food sources. I could hear their communal buzz in the last few seconds before landing, the sound so loud it pierced the muffling cavity of my helmet. Then I struck down, rolled (very awkwardly, given the mirrorspheres strapped to my suit), hit the chute release straps, and got to my feet on my first untamed planet.

Muta. Instinct made me stop . . . look around . . . take a deep breath. But the breath only gave me the smell of my own sweat. I'd have to get used to the scent—my tightsuit would soon become hot as an oven. A tightsuit is wonderfully comfortable as long as the temperature-control systems remain operational; now that they'd been EMP'd, however, I was walking around on a mild day in an airtight outfit insulated better than a goose-down parka. An hour or two, and I'd be risking heatstroke.

As for my surroundings, I couldn't see anything except a hodgepodge of multicolored ferns. My eyes weren't adept at extracting information from the motley chaos. I could hear the drone of insects and sense their exact locations with my mental awareness—a horde of them flying near the plants, crawling through the foliage, scuttling under the soil—but even knowing where to look, my sight was too dazzled by leafy reds, blues, yellows, greens, to make out slow-moving flies or beetles.

And most of the insects weren't small. Camp Esteem lay close to the tropics; according to my sixth sense, some of the bugs were as fat as my thumb and twice as long. But their coloration blended so well with the rainbow of plants, they were practically invisible.

It would be difficult not to tread on creepy-crawlies as I walked. I found that idea upsetting—not because I was squeamish about bugs, but because I'd been brought up in the tradition of *ahimsa*: avoidance of violence to all living creatures. Decent people watched where they stepped. Given so many other things to worry about, it may seem strange that my greatest conscious fear was accidentally tromping on a roach; but I'd been gripped by a sudden superstition that I had to keep my karma absolutely clean, or I'd never survive the mission.

I looked at the patch of flattened grass where I'd landed from the parachute drop. In the very first instant of my arrival, I'd squashed the local version of an anthill. Antlike corpses everywhere.

So much for clean karma.

I allowed myself a shudder. Then I shook off my misgivings and hurried to collect my parachute before it blew away in the breeze.

As I ran, I tried to ignore my sixth sense. It insisted on telling how many insects I crushed with every step.

10

Tanha [Pali]: Craving, in the sense of fixation. It's natural to want food when you're hungry, but it's unskillful to fixate on food. One can fixate on fears, hopes, ideas, etc., just as easily as one fixates on physical cravings. The Buddha's second truth is that fixation is the cause of all suffering.

FESTINA and Tut landed safely. Tut began gathering his parachute, but Festina just waved at me to take care of hers while she set up a Sperm-field anchor.

Captain Cohen would soon maneuver *Pistachio* to wag the ship's tail toward us. He'd been tracking us up to the point we got EMP'd, so he could approximate when we'd be in position for a lock attempt. Festina therefore unstrapped one of the carrying cases from her chest and drew the mirror-sphere from inside. All three of us looked for mist nearby . . . but the EMP cloud was nowhere in sight. Since its last target had been Li's shuttle, perhaps the cloud was staying with the craft. For some reason, I imagined the cloud hovering steamily just outside the cockpit, taking malicious delight in watching Li try to land without instruments or electricity.

Too bad for Li; but his troubles might make things easier for us. If Li and the shuttle kept the EMP cloud distracted, we could establish our lifeline back to *Pistachio* without interference. Festina set the mirror-sphere in the grass at her feet—the grass as yellow as saffron—then we waited for the Sperm-tail to arrive.

The waiting gave me time to look around again, not for hostile

EMP clouds but for a sense of where we were. The Grindstone was thirty paces to my right—a slow-moving river almost a kilometer wide, filled with coffee brown water and wads of foliage floating or caught on reeds near the shoreline. We stood on the western floodplain, and I do mean flood: the Grindstone's banks were so low, the area where I stood would be underwater almost every spring. Yellow grass grew at our feet, along with the sort of scrub brush that can sprout waist-high over a single summer; but nothing more permanent had seeded on these flats, because the yearly floods drowned any plants that tried to become perennial.

To my left, a hundred meters from the riverbank, rose a second bank that bounded the floodplain. This bank was two stories high, choked with multicolored vegetation but cut by a few scrabbly trails worn through the weeds—paths that animals had made when going to drink at the river.

On top of the higher bank, the Unity huts formed a single long line like a dozen river-watching sentinels. Some study had found that a survey team's productivity improved by 0.8 percent if every member's living quarters had a scenic view of water. Therefore, as per standing regulations, the huts lined across the top of the rise so that everyone could look out a window and see the river.

The huts themselves appeared primitive: wooden walls, thatched roofs. But the wood wasn't wood and the thatch wasn't thatch—both were flameproof, weatherproof synthetics with a high insulation factor and suffused with nontoxic repellents to discourage insects. Even so, the Unity did a superlative job of simulating natural materials. They even gave survey team huts a pleasant woody smell . . . because, of course, another study had found that performance improved by some fraction when team members could fill their nostrils with forestlike aromas. Everything inside the huts would be similarly optimized for efficiency, safety, and salutary psychological effect; but I had no more time for gawking around, because *Pistachio*'s Sperm-tail came sweeping across the valley.

Festina didn't hesitate. Usually you open a stasis field with a special needle-nosed tool that pops the outer shell like a soap bubble . . .

but Festina simply punched the silvery surface with her fist. The mirror-field burst with a gassy hiss, revealing its cache of contents: Bumbler, stun-pistol, comm unit, and anchor. The anchor was a small black box with four horseshoe-shaped gold inlays on its upper surface. Festina grabbed the anchor and moved it to a clear patch of grass. Then she pressed the ON switch.

The Sperm-tail reacted immediately. Up till now, it had simply been wagging at random, lazily swinging like a bell-ringer's rope . . . but as soon as the anchor was activated, the tail's behavior acquired a sense of purpose. It raced straight toward us, responding to the anchor device's invisible pull.

Sperm-tails always reminded me of long, thin tornadoes: the bottom tip kissing the ground . . . the funnel cloud creamy but sparkling with glints of green and blue . . . the whole thing stretching far up out of sight, past the clouds, past the ozone, all the way to where *Pistachio* waited.

And once we'd locked onto the Sperm-tail, it would provide a nearly instantaneous route from Muta's surface to our ship. For us as well as . . .

Uh-oh.

I closed my eyes, thinking, *Balrog, help me.* Then I did something I'd never done before: reached out with my sixth sense. Used it actively instead of passively receiving whatever came in. Spread my mind to the world, trying to listen rather than merely hear.

The busy life force of insects. The placid life force of plants. The ponderous life force of microorganisms, too simple to have any emotion—just the sense of presence, like the feel of stone when you're in the mountains. The complicated auras of Festina and Tut. And beyond those known entities, what else? I expanded my senses, sank into them as I'd sink into meditation, noted anything that seemed out of place . . .

. . . and there it was. A spark of eagerness, hidden in the background. Burning anticipation. The spark was so faint, it must be trying to conceal itself . . . but it was too excited, too *hungry*, to be perfectly restrained.

The EMP cloud was waiting for us to connect with *Pistachio*. It wasn't off chasing the shuttle; it had circled back in secret. And the Sperm-tail was now only meters away, speeding straight for the anchor.

Feeling sick at what I had to do, I lifted my heel and slammed it down on the little black box. The box's casing shattered; internal circuit boards snapped under my foot.

The Sperm-tail, our one route off Muta, danced away like a fishing line that's been deliberately cut.

Festina whirled toward me. Her life force erupted with fury, but with our comms dead, I couldn't hear the curses she must have been spewing my way.

Then suddenly, we were enveloped in fog. It came from everywhere: from the ground, from the river, oozing from pores in the scrub brush, vomiting from the mouths of insects, distilling from the very air. The cloud had even been hiding on our own tightsuits, nestled into tucks of the fabric, lurking in our belt pouches and backpacks. Now it emerged in a roar of anger, beating so hard on my mental awareness I almost passed out . . . until in a flash my sixth sense vanished—either burned out from overload or shut down by the Balrog to protect my vulnerable brain from the howling din.

Fog surged and roiled around me, as if clawing my suit with vaporous talons. I couldn't help thinking of *pretas*: the hungry ghosts of Bamar folktales, condemned to a realm near the lowest purgatory. They're spirits of humans who based their lives on greed. In the afterlife, *pretas* are always ravenous, with huge stomachs but throats so tiny they can never swallow enough food to sate their appetites. Hungry, hungry forever . . . or at least until they learn something from their punishment and are ready to be born anew.

The *pretas* of Muta—the smoky cloud—swarmed furiously, just outside my suit. I could imagine dozens of ghosts in that cloud pressing their gaunt, starved faces against my visor, frenzied to devour me. By reflex, I began a protective chant—one I'd used to ward off demons when I was Ugly Screaming Stink-Girl. But the fog-things, the *pretas*, whatever they were, refused to be dispelled. They continued to curl angrily around me, as if they would crush me to paste if only they had the strength.

Festina loomed out of the mist. She touched her helmet to mine so we could hear each other talk. Immediately I babbled excuses for what I'd done: "I realized the cloud—it was out there—it wanted to board *Pistachio*, I don't know why—but it was going to go right up the Sperm-tail and I—I'm sorry, but I had to . . ."

"Of course you did," Festina said. "I'm a fool not to think of it myself. I was just too busy trying to set up the link before we were EMP'd again. I never thought . . ." She turned her eyes skyward, though neither of us could see anything but fog. "This fucking cloud would have EMP'd the ship dead. Then . . . I don't know. Maybe the damned mist wants a way off planet. Maybe it could have taken over *Pistachio* and used the ship to spread to other systems." She turned her gaze back to me. "Glad one of us was thinking."

"But now we're marooned."

"Didn't you always assume that would happen?"

"Yes. Sooner or later."

"Then we're right where we expected," Festina said. "Mission unfolding according to plan: we land, we get screwed over, we try to survive." She gave a rueful smile. "The story of every Explorer's life."

"Did you see how the shuttle turned after we . . ."

"Yes. Li must have stowed away. Probably Ubatu too. And if they landed in one piece, they're now in Drill-Press. We'll have to go rescue them."

She looked at me—eye to eye, our visors touching. Her voice came softly through. "Didn't you expect that too, Youn Suu? Didn't you guess something would force us to visit the city? And we'll have to press on till we've solved this planet's problems. Isn't that what you expected?"

I thought about the avalanche of karma surrounding the woman in front of me. "Yes," I said. "I thought that's how it would go."

Festina flicked out her hand and slapped me on the side of the head—not hard, but not soft either. "Idiot!" she yelled, loud enough for me to hear, though the slap had knocked my helmet away from hers. She leaned in again. "You're an Explorer, for God's sake! Didn't the Academy teach you life is messy? You *don't* necessarily learn the answers. You *never* tie off all the loose ends. Damned near every time you walk away from a mission, you're thinking, *What the fuck did that mean? Why did it happen like that?* And you'll never know. You'll never even come close." She scowled at me through her visor. "How can you think this will work out neatly?"

"It won't work out neatly," I said. "Maybe it won't work out at all. But we *are* here to solve Muta's problems. That's why I got bitten by the Balrog. That's why you happened to be on Cashleen. That's why Li and Ubatu stowed away on the shuttle. And the Academy taught me exactly what it taught you: that an Explorer's life is messy *except* when your strings are being pulled by smart, powerful aliens. Then the going gets neat and tidy . . . doesn't it, Admiral?"

Festina glared for another moment; then she sighed. "Yes. When the Big Boys choose you as a pawn, they put you onto their chessboard and move you straight into trouble. But only up to a point. I don't know exactly how the League thinks, but in recent years, I've developed a hand-waving theory about the way they treat us lesser beings. They'll manipulate the shit out of us, without a shred of guilt, to bring us to a crossroads and a life-or-death decision. Then they let the chips fall where they may. The League won't save your ass if you choose wrong. And there's no guarantee you'll *like* your choices. You might find death the most attractive option. The League doesn't care much about human lives, but it cares a *lot* about human decisions. Sometimes I wonder if they deliberately arrange crises to test us. As if what we do in emergencies can answer some question they can't address on their own."

Silence. Then I rolled my eyes and groaned. "And people call Buddhists superstitious! If you actually believe that old wives' tale—that humans are needed by semidivine aliens to solve some grand problem that's too deep for anyone else—honestly, Festina, that's archaic! Haven't we outgrown such wishful thinking? 'Ooo, *Homo sapiens* may seem insignificant compared to higher species, but we're actually the only hope for the League's intellectual completion.' What's next, believing in fairies?"

Festina laughed and shoved me away. She made some retort, but the words were inaudible, muffled by her helmet. I found myself laughing too, not because anything was funny, but just from release of tension . . . and suddenly, the gloom around us was gone, literally as well as emotionally. The EMP cloud shot toward Drill-Press, and we were left blinking in bright afternoon sunshine.

I looked around for Tut. He wasn't immediately visible, but I finally caught sight of him lying on his back, half hidden by yellow grass. Not too surprisingly, he was naked again; though he'd (mostly) stayed in uniform while aboard *Pistachio*, Tut apparently had strong nudist leanings. This time, with his tightsuit dead, he hadn't had the luxury of instant undressing by emergency evac. Instead, he'd wrestled his suit off piece by piece—a strenuous process bare-handed, since disrobing was usually done by robots—then he'd piled component parts into a pillow for his head. When I walked up to him, he smiled and waved but remained where he was.

"Lot cooler like this, Mom. Want to join me?"

I shook my head. Explorers—*sane* Explorers—have a horror of exposing themselves to the microbes of an unknown planet. Eventually (as I'd already realized), my suit would have to come off. Its near-perfect insulation held in almost every microjoule of heat my body produced; without cooling systems, the interior was already reaching sauna temperature. Thanks to my Bamar genes, I could tolerate equatorial conditions for a while. But not forever. I was steeped in sweat like tea in a pot, all trickles and salt in my eyes.

Still, I could hold out till we got to the Unity camp. Then I'd rummage through the huts for clothing that fit me. Tut would have to do the same—nudist or not, he'd need clothes. It was autumn in this part of the world; come nightfall, the air would turn cool. And who knew how long we'd be here? In days or weeks, winter would come. Even though we were close to the tropics, there'd be frigid snaps that no one could survive naked.

Odd to think about freezing when I was verging on heatstroke. Welcome to the Explorer Corps.

When I turned back to look at Festina, she'd already removed her helmet. She hadn't taken it off purely because she was hot (though the hair framing her face was sodden with perspiration); she'd been forced to open up because she wanted to talk to *Pistachio*. In her hand was the comm from the first stasis field she'd cracked . . . but the unit had apparently been EMP'd by the fog. Festina poked the ON button a few times without any effect. Then she tossed the device aside and opened another mirror-sphere. Another anchor, stun-pistol, Bumbler, and comm. I looked, but didn't see the EMP cloud anywhere. Either it was truly gone, or it was playing possum in the hope we'd try to set up a Sperm-link again.

Festina turned on the new comm unit. It responded immediately: "Admiral Ramos, come in. Admiral Ramos, come in . . ." *Pistachio*'s ship-soul was once more on autorepeat.

"Ramos here," Festina said. Her voice barely reached my ears because of the muffling effect of my own helmet. I was annoyed to hear her so poorly . . . and annoyed that I immediately thought, *Oh, I'll take the helmet off*, when only a few seconds earlier, I'd told myself I'd keep my suit sealed despite the threat of heat prostration. What a vac-head I was! Stubborn in the face of possible death, but buckling immediately if it meant being left out of other people's conversation.

Still, I wanted to hear and to talk without my head trapped in a fishbowl. I flipped up the latches and unscrewed the helmet from its throat seal. The instant my suit was open, heat poured out through the neckhole, propelled by the high pressure that had inflated the suit's skin. The subsequent rush of coolness was bliss.

"Admiral!" Cohen's voice came through Festina's handheld

comm. Now I could hear it clearly. "What's your status, Admiral? We thought the tail had locked, but then—"

"There's an entity down here," Festina interrupted. "A cloud that can EMP things. Its behavior appears intelligent . . . or at least purposeful. Setting up a link would have given it a free ride to *Pistachio*."

"Oy. That would have been bad." The captain paused. "So what now?"

"We're close to Camp Esteem. We'll take a look around. But first, can you check the whereabouts of Li and Ubatu?"

A brief pause. Then: "The ship-soul says they aren't aboard."

"Damn." Festina made a face. "Anyone else missing?"

Another pause. "No, Admiral. Just those two."

"Then they're down here with us. Stowed away on the shuttle. Fuckwits. If they survived the landing, they're in Drill-Press; we'll have to go there after Camp Esteem." Festina took an angry breath. "While we're doing that, Captain, why don't you draw up a list of charges to put those shitheads in jail? It'll help pass the time."

"Anything else we can do, Admiral?"

"No. Do *not* under any circumstances send another rescue team. That's a Class One order. Stay in orbit and monitor the situation."

"I hate to ask this, Admiral, but how long do you want us to stay?"

"Last I heard, the Unity were sending one of their luna-ships. ETA three days. So stay till it gets here. After that, use your judgment; but given how little the Unity likes us, they'll probably order you out of the system once you've given them a report."

"So they order me," Cohen said. "Doesn't mean I have to go."

Festina suppressed a smile. "Captain, there's no need to set off a diplomatic incident. The Unity may be humorless, but they're not evil or incompetent. They'll do what they can to rescue everyone—us as well as their own people. And a luna-ship has a lot more resources than a small Technocracy frigate. If it's possible to get us back safely, the Unity will do it."

"And if it isn't possible?"

"That's what 'expendable' means, Captain. Ramos out."

* * *

The three of us started for the rise edging the floodplain. Tut took a few steps, then ouch-footed back to his pile of discarded suit parts. "Stepped on something," he said in a pained voice.

"An insect?" Festina asked. "A plant thorn? If it was something that might be poisonous to humans . . ."

"Nah, Auntie, it was just a sharp stone." Tut fished out his tightsuit's boots and put them on. They fit snugly, coming up to his knees. I made a mental note that when I abandoned my tightsuit, I too would keep the boots; they were tough, well cushioned, and precisely fitted to my feet. I'd never find shoes half so perfect in the Unity camp.

"Take your gloves too," Festina told Tut. "In case there's something you shouldn't touch with your bare hands."

Obligingly, Tut put on the gloves. With gold gloves and boots but nothing else, he looked like a dancer from the kind of establishment where good Bamar girls didn't go. In the past, I'd regretted not visiting such places—another sinful thrill I ought to have experienced. Now, looking at Tut, I decided I hadn't missed much.

Or maybe naked men looked better when there was music.

We started walking. My sixth sense was still shut down—deactivated since that moment I'd been surrounded by the cloud and felt its torment, like hungry ghosts. I considered asking the Balrog to activate the sense again . . . but as that thought went through my mind, something crunched underfoot. An insect? Or just a plant. Probably an insect. Since I didn't want to think of all the bugs I'd kill en route to the camp, I decided to hold off on life-force awareness for a while.

Besides, I had enough trouble concentrating on my own life force. Even with the helmet removed, my suit was torturously hot. I'd left my parachute where we'd landed, but I still carried a lot of gear, including the four stasis cases strapped to my chest. Back on

Pistachio, they hadn't seemed that heavy. Now . . . ugh. Maybe Muta's gravity was stronger than normal.

(Rookie that I was, I hadn't even *looked* at the planet's grav readings. I'd assumed if the Unity planned to settle here, the G-pull was close to Earth-standard. A stupid beginner's mistake. I'd have to get the numbers from Tut when Festina wasn't within earshot. Tut wouldn't chew me out for neglecting crucial data, but Festina would flay me alive.)

The climb up the rise wasn't difficult—just hot. And smelly. Every frond of Mutan vegetation had a mustardlike scent: sometimes sharp, sometimes subtle, but always there. These plants hadn't yet learned the trick of using perfumes to attract insect pollinators, so their odor was just an unintentional side effect of biochemistry. I assumed the mustard fragrance came from some chemical every plant shared, the way Earth plants all have a whiff of chlorophyll. The smell was so pervasive, the Unity survey teams surely must have investigated it and figured out what the chemical was . . . but I couldn't remember reading anything in the data they sent us. In fact, I couldn't remember a single thing about the ubiquitous mustard aroma.

Uh-oh.

Aloud, I said, "The Unity reports didn't mention the mustard smell."

Festina stopped dead in the middle of the trail. "You're right. Nothing about smell. Do you think those bastards edited their reports? Or held data back, even when they said they were sharing everything?"

Behind me, Tut laughed. "Don't get upset, Auntie. The Unity just can't smell."

Festina and I said in unison, "What?"

Tut laughed again. "They can't smell. Not a single one of them. Cut it right out of their genome."

"You're kidding," I said.

"Nope. Back in the early days, they decided maybe they should *heighten* their sense of smell—augment it the way they augmented their muscles and brainpower. They should have known better. A lot of them live in these luna-ships, right? Millions of people packed together. The smell's bad enough for normal senses, but augment everyone's nosepower a few hundred times, and it made for disaster. Not to mention they got a side effect: everyone's response to human pheromones shot sky-high. The anger pheromones, the sex pheromones . . ." Tut giggled. "Must have been fun. Anyway, the bigwigs admitted they'd screwed up . . . so you know the Unity, they overreacted the other way. Genetically altered all future generations to remove the nerves for both the olfactory cells and the VMO."

"Good thinking," I said. "That way when something catches fire, they can't smell the smoke."

"They have mechanical sensors for smoke," Tut replied. "Computerized sniffers, a thousand times more sensitive than normal noses. The Unity got good at artificial olfactory simulation."

"How do you know all this?" Festina asked. "I've never heard it before . . . and I thought I was well-informed on our ally races."

"The Unity are close-mouthed about certain things," Tut told her. "Things you only find out if you live with them."

"You lived with the Unity?"

He tapped his gold-plated face. "How do you think I got this? The Technocracy doesn't do face stuff, does it? Not for potential Explorers. If you got an Explorer face, no one in the Technocracy dares fix it." Tut shrugged. "So when I was sixteen, I ran off to the Unity. Got myself gilded, then spent three hundred and sixty-four days in a luna-ship before they kicked me out—some law against outsiders living with them a whole year. But I learned a lot of secrets. They confided in me. They liked me."

Festina looked as if she doubted that last statement. I, however, believed it. The Unity's overregimented goody-goodies might find Tut refreshing—like a court jester. He said things no one else would, but spontaneously, not just to be shocking. Tut was odd without being threatening. As a bonus, he was living proof of the Unity belief that Technocracy people were lunatics. I could see Unity folks being charmed by Tut the way rich urbanites might be charmed by country bumpkins. Sophisticates love artlessness.

"So what else do you know about the Unity?" I asked.

"Hard to make a list, Mom. But I'll tell you the most important: they stopped being human centuries ago. Don't even have the same number of chromosomes; they got twenty-four pairs now instead of our twenty-three. That extra chromosome contains a bunch of new features they wouldn't talk about, not even to me." He smiled a golden smile. "But hey, I was sixteen, and so busy getting laid, I didn't ask a lot of questions. They all wanted a night with me, Mom . . . partly because I *was* a different species, so no chance of them getting pregnant. And I was forbidden fruit, you know? Sex with me was exotic and perverse and—"

"We get the picture," Festina interrupted.

"Bet you don't. They're all augmented, right? So both the men and the women—"

"*We get the picture*," Festina repeated . . . which was half a lie, because I didn't get the picture at all. If we found any corpses at Camp Esteem, I intended to check their anatomies.

The camp lay before us as we topped the rise: huts lining the ridge, larger buildings a short distance beyond. "Check the huts first," Festina said. "Look for bodies or signs of disturbance. We'll be more thorough later, but right now we're just checking for survivors."

I headed for the closest hut, but Tut stayed where he was. "Hey!" he yelled. "Unity people! Anybody home?"

Festina turned to me. "You know, shouting never crossed my mind."

"Tut tends to be direct," I told her. "Also insane."

"Well . . . making noise shouldn't matter. That cloud thing already knows we're here."

I nodded, then called, "Come on, Tut. Let's check the huts."

He hollered once more, "Anybody hear me?" No response in

the camp, except from a small brown lizard that scurried away from the noise. "Okay, Mom," Tut said, "I'll help look around. But it sure seems like nobody's home."

Tut was right: nobody was home. He took the four huts in the middle of the line, Festina took the four on the north, and I took the four to the south. We found no survivors, and no corpses either—just empty living quarters, with no indication of trouble.

Each hut had a bed, a closet, and a desk, plus a utility table whose contents varied by team member. One person's table supported an electron microscope; another had a collection of soil samples; a third had a megarack of computer memory bubbles, while the last hut I looked in had dozens of small, mirrored stasis fields. (I cracked a sphere open. It held a partly dissected beetle.) The huts displayed military neatness, diminished only by a few last-moment touches of disarray from people hurrying to get to breakfast on time. A jacket tossed over the back of a chair. Wrinkles on the coverlet, where someone sat down after making the bed and didn't straighten the sheets after standing up. An orange fern leaf on the floor—maybe blown in by the wind, maybe tracked in on somebody's boot.

Apart from these lapses, the huts would easily pass the most stringent inspection. Clean, tidy, almost impersonal. On each desk sat a small holo globe showing a posed family scene—the number of parents varying from one to six, but the number of children always exactly the same: one son, one daughter, their ages two years apart—and every such globe was precisely the same size and placed in precisely the same position on the desk, as if the Unity had strict regulations for the proper display of one's family unit. Maybe they did. The Unity reputedly liked to regiment people's home lives as much as it regimented everything else.

But one area in each hut was *not* regulated: the mask shrine. The shrines hung on the wall immediately opposite the door, suspended at eye level beside the closet. Each shrine had a shelf, a backdrop, and a pedestal for the mask itself . . . but there the similarities ended. In the first hut I entered, the shelf, backdrop, and pedestal were all matte steel, and the mask a metallic thing of wire, gears, LEDs, and chrome; its eyeholes were covered with mirror glass, and its soul-gem, in the middle of the forehead, was a yellow industrial diamond. By contrast, the next hut's shrine was constructed entirely of organic things—a mahogany shelf upholstered with bird feathers, a backdrop of growing vines, and a pedestal made of bone, all supporting a mask of deerhide with a pearl soul-gem above its eyes. Next door had an outer-space motif, with a photographic starscape as background and star-shaped sequins everywhere else. The soul-gem had the pockmarked look of a stony meteorite. In the final hut I entered, the entire shrine was shrouded in lush black velvet, but the mask itself was pure white silk. The gem was a black opal: black on white on black.

I wasn't a stranger to extravagant shrines—every home on Anicca had at least one Buddha surrounded by small offerings and written vows to pursue enlightenment. But in the otherwise immaculate Camp Esteem huts, the mask shrines appeared too garish . . . as if the Unity members used the masks and the shrines as a way of venting all the emotion/anarchy/creative impulses they normally suppressed.

Of course, my reaction to the shrines was colored by what I knew. The straitlaced Unity, so restrained and socially delicate, had created a religion of total excess: primal, barbaric, orgiastic. Every night they donned masks . . . drugged or danced themselves into altered states of consciousness . . . then ended with ritual fights and copulation. If I'd been born in the Unity, I would have lost my virginity at my first sacred dance, around the age of twelve—but I would scarcely remember the experience or any other coupling thereafter, because all such sexual encounters took place in a trance-like delirium where normal mental processes were suppressed.

Copulation without conscience. Riot without responsibility. It was easy to see the attraction . . . and just like the Unity to cold-bloodedly design their religious practice as a psychological release valve rather than genuine spirituality.

Still . . . when I thought about the masks in the huts, I wondered what totem I might have chosen if I'd been a Unity child. What mask would I hide behind when I wanted to lose myself? Unbidden, a mental picture arose: a smooth woman's face sculpted in copper-brown leather, but with the left cheek gashed open by a knife.

Trying to force the image from my mind, I hurried to join the others.

We went to the mess hall next. It was just as the probe had shown—abandoned partway through breakfast, food on the table undisturbed by insects. I hadn't seen or heard any insects in the entire camp; the only living creature I'd spotted was that lizard who scuttled away when Tut yelled. I wondered if local fauna could have been "eaten" by the EMP cloud . . . but that didn't make sense. If nothing else, the cloud was mobile: it had, for example, enveloped us on the floodplain. But there'd been plenty of insects down on the flats. So even if the cloud was an insectivore, why would it devour all the bugs around camp but leave the floodplain swarms untouched?

Festina stuck her head out of the kitchen. "I found the source of the probe's IR reading. There's a gas stove still burning. Anybody want scrambled eggs that have gone all black and crispy?"

Tut immediately said, "I'll try some."

"Before you do," I said (knowing the only way to keep Tut from consuming burned eggs was to distract him till they vanished from his mind), "have you noticed there are no insects on the food? Don't you find that odd?"

"Nah," Tut said. "The Unity are great at insect repellants. It's one of the first things they do on a new planet—figure out what disgusts local insects, then gene-jiggle themselves to pump out the appropriate chemicals. Usually in their sweat. Remember, Mom, Unity folks have no sense of smell. They don't care if they stink to high heaven. Makes for some pretty exotic reeks in Unity cities, let me tell you."

Though I'd been breathing cookhouse air for at least a minute, I couldn't help sniffing in search of "exotic reeks." It didn't smell like much of anything—just a slight burned odor from the kitchen. The eggs had incinerated themselves more than thirty-six hours ago, so the worst of the char stench was gone. Tut also gave a sniff, then shrugged. "Mutan insects don't have Earthling noses. Maybe this place stinks of something we can't smell."

"Or maybe," I said, "the camp *did* stink while the Unity people were here—enough that insects cleared out and built their nests elsewhere. Now that Team Esteem is gone, the smell has faded too . . . but it's only been a day and a half, so the insects haven't found their way back yet."

"Hmph." That was Festina, returning from the kitchen. She went to the dining table and studied it. Tut and I did the same. Just like the recon photos—cutlery set down haphazardly, chairs pushed back . . . as if everybody had suddenly decided to rush outside and never returned.

But wait. Now that I looked, I saw not every place had been abandoned hurriedly. One chair on the far side of the table was tucked away tidily. The plate was clean except for a few crumbs, and the juice glass was empty. The cutlery had been neatly set aside. "See that?" I said. "One person had finished eating and left the table."

"Looks like it," Tut agreed. "But even in the Unity, there's always one person who eats faster than anyone else."

"Maybe," said Festina, "that person had reason to eat faster yesterday morning. Pressing work to be done. He or she ate quickly, then left the mess hall. Probably to get started on work."

"Then everyone else ran outside," I said. "Like maybe the person who left first called for help. Or there was some noise that made the rest of the team think the first person was in trouble."

Festina nodded. "It would have to be something like that—something that made everybody's reflexes kick in automatically. Unity survey teams are smart about survival. If they'd just heard a strange sound, they wouldn't let everybody investigate; they'd send two or three people to scout, keeping in constant contact by radio. The only time they'd respond to a threat en masse would be if one of their own was in danger right under their noses."

"True," Tut agreed. "Unity folk love following procedures. They'd only give in to impulse if, like, a friend was screaming, 'Help, help, help!'"

"So," Festina said, "this person X who left breakfast first must have got in trouble while crossing the compound. Except that we didn't see any bodies lying out in the dirt."

Tut said, "Maybe X got as far as one of the other buildings. Stepped inside, and bam, something happened."

"We've already checked the huts and this mess hall," Festina said. "Three other buildings to go."

As we walked across the compound, Festina reported our latest findings to Captain Cohen. We still had comm access to *Pistachio*: the EMP cloud hadn't zapped us since we'd opened our second stasis sphere. That meant we also had a working stun-pistol and Bumbler. Festina carried the stunner holstered at her hip—she wouldn't let Tut or me touch the weapon—but she made no protest as I took the Bumbler and strapped it around my neck.

I felt better having a Bumbler . . . not that its sensors revealed anything useful. The three remaining buildings gave off no special readings. In particular, there were no IR hot spots big enough to indicate human life—just a few patches of mild warmth, probably from the afternoon sun shining through windows and raising the temperature of objects that could absorb heat. The Bumbler showed no notable sources of other types of energy: no tachyons, no terahertz, no radio or microwaves. I'd seen more interesting readings from a patch of ragweed.

So it came as no surprise that we found nothing noteworthy in the first building we entered—the survey team's laboratory. It was a prefab design, with a single corridor down the center: two rooms to the left and two to the right, all four labs of equal size. One was devoted to plants, animals, and soil samples; another was obviously where team members studied microbes (with microscopes, petri dishes, and DNA sequencers); and the last two labs were both dedicated to technological artifacts that must have been retrieved from Drill-Press.

Most of the artifacts were typical products of high tech: nondescript boxes made of plastic and other artificial materials. Las Fuentes apparently liked their gear in earth-tone colors—every box was some shade of brown, from light biscuit to dark umber, sometimes in mottled combinations like desert camouflage—but apart from the color scheme, I drew no other conclusions. I certainly couldn't guess what the devices might do.

Perhaps the Unity had figured out the machinery's purpose, but there was no way to tell. A brief search showed the survey team had kept no notes on paper or in any other hard-copy form. That didn't surprise me—Unity people all had wireless computer links embedded in their brains. Why scribble notes in a journal when they could download their thoughts directly to a computer?

At least Team Esteem stored their data in bubble chips that used long-chain organic molecules to encode information. Such molecules weren't damaged by EMPs. Therefore, whatever the surveyors had learned about Fuentes technology could eventually be recovered.

But not by us. We couldn't read the bubble chips without a computer . . . and all the computers in Camp Esteem had been EMP'd into uselessness.

Quite possibly, the earth-toned Fuentes devices had also been killed by EMPs . . . if they hadn't already gone dead in the fall of Fuentes civilization, or in the millennia that followed. All these fancy machines were probably as defunct as my tightsuit.

But I didn't put that to the test by trying to turn them on.

* * *

The next building was a repair shop/garage: a single large space that housed the usual equipment required to maintain an installation like Camp Esteem, plus a pair of antigrav vehicles built for strength rather than speed. The AGVs probably couldn't go faster than 50 kph, but they looked powerful enough to lift twenty times their own mass. Good for making trips into Drill-Press and bringing back heavy artifacts. The artifacts I'd seen in the camp had all been small, light enough to be carried by hand. But the Unity always planned for contingencies, and if the survey team needed to drag a forty-ton hunk of Fuentes machinery back to camp, they had the horsepower to do it.

Too bad the AGVs had been EMP'd like everything else and were now just giant paperweights. We left them where they were and went on to the last building.

The sign on the building was a pictograph of stacked boxes, indicating general storage. The door was locked.

"The Unity is always so damned anal-retentive," Festina muttered. "Why the hell would they lock the door on a planet with no other intelligent beings? A simple doorknob would keep out animals. But no, they installed a big-ass lock."

I said, "Maybe some team members weren't allowed in here. Restricted access to prevent pilferage."

"Stupid," Festina grumbled. "They should trust their own people."

I raised an eyebrow. "The way you trusted Tut and me when you locked us out of the equipment room last night?"

"Oh. Yeah." She stared at the closed door in front of us. "Anyone good at picking locks?"

She was joking . . . trying to lighten the mood after her gaffe. It had been centuries since anyone manufactured locks that could be picked. Broadcast dramas still showed thieves opening doors with piano wire and crochet hooks, but no modern lock could be opened so simply. Lock-cracking these days required extremely sophisticated equipment—ultrasound projectors, nanite bafflers, protein synthesizers—and we'd brought nothing like that with us.

In search of another way in, we walked around the building. It had no windows; it had no second door. Tut tentatively kicked a wall, but his foot made no impression on the surface—the building was made from silver-gray plastic, probably tough enough to survive a hurricane and whatever other hazards Muta might dish out. Short of cannon fire, the walls were impregnable.

"This is annoying," Festina said as we finished back at the front door. "Doesn't it feel like the answer to our questions might be inside this building?" She paused. "Of course, if we *do* get the door open, we might regret it."

"Yeah," Tut agreed. "Like VR adventures where you bust your ass getting into a locked room, then find the room has a monster inside."

"Exactly. This is too tempting not to be dangerous." Festina stepped back and examined the building again. "Still, if there were a way in . . ."

"There may be," I said. "Why don't you puny humans step aside and let Balrog-girl show you some moss power."

In truth, I didn't know what moss power might do. Navy files said the Balrog had earthshaking telekinetic abilities, but I didn't know whether the spores would be willing to help smash a locked door. If I was the moss's Trojan horse—if it was hiding inside me so someone or something didn't know the Balrog was on Muta—then my alien hitchhiker would avoid revealing its presence with showoff tricks. The Balrog might also consider me presumptuous for acting as if I could command it to open doors. Still, this door had "Clue to the mystery" written all over it . . . and if the Balrog wanted our investigation to make progress, it would help us get inside.

Therefore, I closed my eyes and reached within myself as if lowering my body into dark water. *Balrog*, I thought, *can you do this? Can you help me do this?*

No answer. Not in words. But I got the impression I'd phrased my request incorrectly. A moment later, I realized what I had to say. I don't know if the answer came from my own intuition or if the knowledge had been planted in my mind; but I knew what the Balrog wanted to hear.

I took a deep breath . . . knowing I was moving another step down the path toward my own oblivion. *Balrog*, I said silently—feeling scared, feeling excited, feeling as if I'd once more been seduced into something against my better judgment but also feeling no desire to resist the heat of temptation—*Balrog, I will let you do this through me. I'll surrender to you that much.*

Seconds passed. I felt no change. I'd imagined I might be possessed, feel my body moving without my will. Possibly I'd hear triumphant laughter echoing through my brain, the demonic exaltation that always comes when the foolish maiden succumbs to the devil in some bad melodrama. I was even prepared to black out . . . then to wake up who knows where, who knows when . . . if I ever woke up at all.

But nothing like that happened. Nothing discernible changed . . . except that my sixth sense returned. Even that was no great transformation—more like opening my eyes after having them closed for a few minutes. I could be blasé about it: once again perceiving the auras of Festina and Tut, as well as the microbial world and a few pseudolizards hiding in nearby shadows. I couldn't perceive life signs inside the storage building, nor did I have any mystic "X-ray" intuition about the door lock. My sixth sense told me nothing I hadn't already seen with my eyes: the lock was metal; the door was the same tough silver-gray plastic as the rest of the building; the hinges were on the inside; there was no obvious point of vulnerability.

I reached into my mind once more, hoping the Balrog might hint what I should do next. No such hint came. I'd surrendered myself to the damned moss and got nothing in return. Blazing with anger, I yelled in my mind, *What am I supposed to do? Kick the door in?* I drew back my right foot and shot it out hard, aiming for the center of the door's blank rectangular face.

Just before my kick made contact, some unexpected strength added itself to my own muscle power. Extra mass. Extra acceleration. Extra force.

Slam!

The door split in two, straight down the middle. My foot almost did the same. The boot of my tightsuit absorbed some fraction of the impact, but not nearly enough. With my sixth sense I could see bones splintering from my heel to my toes. I perceived the massive fracturing process in a clear-minded thousandth of a second before the pain made its way up my nervous system and struck the "What the hell did you just do?" part of my brain. I even had time to think, "I'm really going to hate this." Then, agony exploded with a bloody red splash, and there was nothing in my skull but torment.

11

Niroda [Pali]: Cure; cessation of an illness. The Buddha's third truth is that suffering ceases when you let go of your fixations.

I DON'T think I passed out. If I did, it was only for a moment.

And I didn't fall down. Festina and Tut caught me, holding me upright till the pain subsided and let self-control reassert itself over sheer animal anguish. The pain didn't go away, but the shock did. In a few seconds, I could think again.

I said, "Ow."

"Yeah," Festina said, "I bet that sums it up."

"That was supreme, Mom!" Tut said. "You told me you were bioengineered, but I never guessed how much."

"Neither did I."

Despite my foot's agony, the Balrog's sixth sense hadn't deserted me. It calmly reported thirty-seven full or partial fractures in the bones of my right foot and lower leg. It also disclosed a flurry of alien activity: Balrog spores at work on the injuries. For a moment, I hoped they'd repair all the cracked and shattered bones . . . but no. The Balrog was no magic spirit who'd graciously make my injuries vanish. The Balrog didn't give miracles for free; it always exacted a price.

So the bones remained broken, but spores took their place,

cramming themselves together so tightly they assumed a solidity almost as strong as my original skeletal structure. Other spores sealed off the lacerated blood vessels sliced open by sharp bone fragments, while still more spores assembled themselves as surrogate tendons, ligaments, and cartilage. The result would be sturdy enough to walk on. It would *not*, however, be sturdy enough to kick through another door. Moss packed tightly is still just moss.

I thought of Kaisho Namida, her entire lower body turned to spores. Mentally, I asked the Balrog, *Did you eat her the same way? Did she trade herself for favors bit by bit? Did she accumulate injuries, accidentally or on purpose, and little by little she made deals to have you replace her original tissues?*

No answer, of course. Nothing but raging pain. The Balrog had supplanted my bones and stopped my bleeding, but it hadn't quieted the neurons that shrieked in outrage at so much physical trauma. *Oh for Buddha's sake*, I thought in exasperation, *just eat the nerves and get it over with.*

The pain stopped immediately. That's what happens when a bunch of neurons get devoured and replaced by spores.

Oddly enough, my sixth sense said the foot still looked normal . . . at least outwardly. The skin hadn't been broken. The displacement of the underlying bones had somehow been concealed—probably by spores eating away any outjuts and fragments that would have spoiled the foot's external appearance. All signs of damage had been forcibly eradicated.

But the foot was no longer mine. It had become alien territory.

I'm all right," I lied as I pushed myself away from Tut and Festina. I took an experimental step. There was no muscle feeling in my foot, but my extended mental awareness let me compensate. I wasn't receiving the usual body-position information along my foot's neural pathways, but my sixth sense provided a different sort of kinesthetic feedback that made up for the loss. When I set my foot on the ground, I didn't *feel* the foot touch down, I simply *knew* it.

That sounds as if I were experiencing things secondhand—watching my foot like a stranger's. Not so. I experienced the movement more directly: no longer distanced by my limited nervous system or the simplification of sensation and the lag time needed for neural impulses to spark up my leg to my brain. Now I perceived my foot without any neural mediation . . . as if I'd previously been living my life at some remove, but finally I was fully present in one part of my body.

Pity the foot *wasn't* part of my body anymore. This new mystic sense of immediacy, comprehending my foot as it really was rather than what my fallible neurons said secondhand . . . wasn't that just another Balrog deception? A trick to make me think I'd gained when I'd actually been diminished?

My foot was now alien tissue. It would never be *me* again. And for what? So I could kick in a door?

"There'd better be something damned interesting in there," I muttered. Walking on my nonfoot, I went inside.

At first glance, the storage building looked like any other: lots of small boxes on shelves, a few larger crates on the floor, and stasis-field mirror-spheres all over the place. Some of the spheres were as small as my fist, while others were big enough to come up to my chin as they sat on the ground. My sixth sense couldn't penetrate the spheres—their interiors were separate little universes, removed mathematically if not physically from our own—but I assumed they held food, pharmaceuticals, batteries, and all the other perishables Camp Esteem might need.

Bad assumption.

Festina crouched near one of the biggest spheres and pointed to marks on the ground. The floor itself was gray concrete; the marks were flakes of white, turning brown around the edges. They looked like bits of dry leaves strewed across the cement. "You've got the Bumbler," Festina said to me. "What's this?"

I glanced at the analyzer's readout. Did a double take and

checked again. Turned a few dials, then swallowed. "It's human skin," I said. "Sort of."

"What do you mean, sort of?"

"The cells have twenty-four chromosome pairs rather than twenty-three."

"So the skin came from a Unity member rather than plain old *Homo sapiens*."

"Also," I said, "the chromosome pairs aren't pairs. One chromosome in each pair is human. The other isn't."

"You mean the other chromosomes contain alien DNA?" Tut looked over my shoulder at the readouts. He was, after all, a microbi specialist . . . but I doubted even he could make sense of the Bumbler's finding.

"The other chromosomes aren't alien DNA," I told Festina. "They aren't even ordinary matter. It's like each human chromosome has acquired a shadow. The shadow has the same shape, size, and mass as the real chromosome, but it's something the Bumbler can't register. Like there's a normal chromosome, then beside it, there's a chromosome-shaped hole in reality."

Festina gave me a pained look. "A hole in reality? Bollocks. Couldn't it just be dark matter? Last I heard there were sixteen known dark particles and at least that many dark energy quanta."

"Why would human skin cells contain dark matter? And how could dark matter be assembled the way I'm seeing? I've never heard anyone suggest you could make dark molecules. Especially not complex biological modules like DNA. These are *chromosomes*, Festina. Chromosomes made of dark matter? How is that more rational than holes in reality?"

Instead of answering, Festina came to look at the Bumbler's scan. I'd magnified a single cell nucleus to fill the entire display screen. It was easy to see the chromosomes, each real one accompanied by a shadow: a cutout, an absence, unfilled by the nucleus's liquid interior. The pseudochromosomes drifted lazily across the screen, just like their real-matter counterparts. Finally, Festina said, "Okay, that's disturbing, no matter what the hell those things are."

She stepped away. "I can't help but notice the mutant skin flakes are all beside this one stasis sphere."

The sphere she indicated was the biggest in sight, almost as tall as me. The human/shadow hybrid cells were directly around its base. In fact, when I scanned with the Bumbler, I could find a line of such cells from the entrance door straight up to the sphere. The trail was too small to see with the naked eye, except for those marks near the sphere—as if someone had dribbled cells all across the floor, then stood long enough in one spot for the accumulation to become visible.

"Oh, Mom," said Tut, "I got a nasty idea what's in that sphere."

"We all have the same idea," Festina told him. She turned to me. "You like kicking things open, Youn Suu. You want to do the honors on this stasis field?"

"No thanks. My foot has had enough excitement for one day."

She raised an eyebrow. "Are you all right? You weren't limping."

"I'll be fine. But no more kicking for a while."

Festina held my gaze a moment longer. Then she shrugged and turned away. After a quick search of the room, she found a tool for popping stasis bubbles: a short wand with a barb on the end, like a miniharpoon. She fetched the wand and tapped it on the sphere's mirror surface.

<BINK>

The room filled with screaming—a scream begun the previous morning and now resumed as if no time had passed. On the floor, where the sphere had been, a man lay howling in agony. Flakes of whitish skin drifted off his body like snow.

The man's skin had not been white to begin with. His features and bone structure were clearly African, not so different from Ubatu; but his once-dark skin had lost its pigmentation, turning paper-pale and as fragile as ash. As for his life force . . . I didn't wholly trust my Balrog-given sense, but when it told me this man was dying, I had no reason for doubt. The man exuded an aura of contamination: a body at war with itself, literally ripping its tissues apart. Flecks of dry epidermis continued to shake off him onto the floor—falling from his face and hands, through the gaps between buttons on his shirt, and in powdery puffs out the bottom of his pant cuffs, as if both his legs had turned to talcum and were dispersing themselves across the concrete.

As for the man's clothes, they were cut in the style of Unity warm-weather uniforms, but their color was unique to Muta: a multihued motley of reds, blues, and oranges, matching the rainbow riot of local vegetation. It was obviously intended to provide camouflage when survey team members moved through the brush . . . but it made the man look like a clown.

A leprous clown close to death.

Tut stepped toward the man, but Festina pulled him back. "No! He might be contagious. Youn Suu, what's the Bumbler say?"

I looked at the Bumbler's display. "Shadow chromosomes in all his cells. Not just his skin. His hair, his nails, his eyes . . . the Bumbler can't find a single cell that's normal. And the cells are changing shape. The blood corpuscles are so deformed they're clogging his veins and arteries like logjams. His heart isn't strong enough to maintain circulation—it's barely beating."

The man screamed louder. I couldn't tell if he was reacting to my words or some new thrust of pain.

"If his blood vessels are obstructed," Festina said, "there's no point in CPR?"

"The best hospital in the galaxy couldn't save him. Every cell in his body is . . ."

I had no words to finish my sentence. Festina did. "Every cell in his body is fucked."

"That pretty much sums it up," I said.

Tut had slipped out of Festina's grip. Now he crouched near the moaning man—staying slightly beyond the man's reach, but directly in his sight line. If the man *had* a sight line. With the cells of his eyes and his optic nerves so dramatically mutated, who knew if the man could see?

"Hey," Tut murmured. "Hey." Then he spoke in a language I didn't recognize: a fluid language with no harsh consonants, like linguistic honey.

"Is that the Unity's secret tongue?" Festina asked. "I thought they didn't teach it to outsiders."

"I told you, Auntie, they liked me. Now shush."

Tut spoke again to the dying man. The language was soft and beautiful—purposely designed that way. Three centuries ago, the Unity's founders created a private language . . . partly to separate themselves from the Technocracy, partly as social engineering. The structures of language influence the structures of thought: not simplistically, but subtly. The way you're trained to speak predisposes you to patterns in the way you think. It isn't that you're incapable of thinking in other ways; it's just that you find some thoughts easier to articulate than others. Also, growing children hear more talk about easy-to-express topics than topics the language makes difficult. Inevitably, this affects their social and intellectual development—some thoughts are "normal" while others aren't. By constructing a new language with a certain philosophical slant, the Unity had tried to make it harder for people to be bad citizens.

Or so the rumor went. One should never entirely trust Technocracy gossip about the Unity . . . any more than one trusts divorced spouses talking about their exes.

Tut only spoke a sentence or two. The Unity man replied with a torrent of incomprehensible words. His life force contorted with the effort. He was using his dying energies to tell what had happened: a dedicated survey team member delivering his final report. Though I could see the emotions that drove him—relief at having survived long enough to tell his story, mingled with the pain of his incipient death—my sixth sense couldn't translate what he was saying. I could see his feelings but not his message.

Even Tut couldn't follow it all. Tut's aura showed him straining to understand. The dying man spoke quickly, gasping for breath, reciting details in a language Tut hadn't heard in years. Quite possibly, the man was also using sophisticated scientific terminology; he was an elite survey team member, giving his last technical report. Tut did his best to comprehend the words, nearly inaudible, in a language only half remembered from his youth . . . but I could see he was failing to catch what might be vital details. Frustration showed on Tut's face and deeper down in his heart.

Festina saw the frustration too (at least on Tut's face), but she did nothing. Asking questions would only make it harder for Tut to hear the mumbling man; and this was obviously our only chance to catch what the man had to say. A deathbed data dump. It would be a small miracle if this survivor of Team Esteem lived long enough to get it all out . . . but at last he fell silent, his aura showing triumph despite the torment of his flesh. He'd said everything he needed to. His head slumped back, his eyes drooped shut . . .

. . . and he turned to smoke.

It was sudden, but not violent. His skin had already been peeling away in flakes and powdery grains. Now his entire body fell in on itself with the sound of sifting sand. His tissues withered into leaf-thin fragments; the fragments broke down into pinpoint particles; and the particles rose in a cloud that wafted toward the storage building's roof. My sixth sense saw the cloud's life force, first rejoicing in release from the flesh, glorying in the departure of pain . . . then turning angry, furious at something, frustrated . . . outrage growing till it reached the level of madness, a fury that banished all rationality. The cloud whirled in frenzy, spinning more and more frantically until it was nothing but pure distilled wrath. It hurtled down upon us, wanting to hurt us, as if we were horrid abominations it hungered to kill; as if the cloud truly was a hungry ghost, a *preta*. But all the *preta* could do was swirl ineffectually, trying in vain to do us injury. When it saw its efforts were futile, its aura blazed with fresh anger at its failure. It left in a rage, sweeping out of the building, a mist-elemental searching for others of its kind.

"Whoa," Tut said. "What just happened?"

"We found out what happened to the survey team." Festina

glanced at the Bumbler, still strapped around my neck. "Surprise, surprise. The Bumbler's been EMP'd."

There was nothing left of the Unity man—not even the flakes and powder grains that had previously fallen off him. When I looked for the bits of skin on the floor, they were gone too . . . as if every part of the man had turned to smoke simultaneously, each component waiting till the whole was ready to go.

The man's clothes remained on the ground. Also an assortment of small electronic devices: the implants from inside the man's body. I recognized the cyberlink that would have connected his brain to Team Esteem's computers—it sat on the concrete, right where the man's head had been—but most of the other gadgets were unfamiliar to me. Perhaps if I'd had the time to examine them . . . but after ten seconds, the implants burst simultaneously into fizzing flame.

"Self-destruct mechanisms," Tut said as we all stepped back from the heat. "An automatic chemical reaction kicks in on exposure to open air. To prevent anyone from analyzing the gadgets."

"Personally," Festina said, "I'd be damned reluctant to have equipment planted in my body if the blasted stuff could explode."

"Think of the alternative," Tut said. "If the equipment *didn't* explode, we nasty Technocracy villains could dissect everything and figure out how to hack the systems. The Unity *really* doesn't want that. If we found a way to disrupt their brain-links . . . or the doodads that augment adrenaline flow . . . or any of the other implants they depend on . . . we could blackmail the crap out of the whole population."

"Still," Festina muttered, "I wouldn't—"

She was interrupted by a flash of flame as the man's uniform caught fire. It had been lying under the still-burning implants; probably the clothes had been treated with flame retardants, but the heat from the implants had reached some critical temperature the fabric couldn't withstand. In a few seconds, the uniform was nothing but flyaway cinders . . . and the implants were nearly the same. Nothing was left of the man and his effects but scorch marks on the floor and a burned metallic smell that made my eyes water.

"Huh," Festina said. "The Unity must really save money on gravediggers."

While I was still staring at the absence of remains, Festina opened another of the stasis fields strapped to her suit. She handed the anchor and Bumbler to me, but kept the stun-pistol and comm unit for herself. "See if there's anything left of the dead guy," she told me. "I'll call *Pistachio*. And you . . ." She pointed at Tut. "Get ready to report what the man said. You can tell Captain Cohen the same time you tell us."

Tut gave her a sheepish look. "I didn't follow a lot of it."

"You followed more than I did."

Festina hailed the ship. While she told the captain what had happened, I dumped my dead Bumbler on the floor and strapped the new one around my neck. The Bumbler confirmed what my sixth sense had already told me—the dying man was utterly gone, not a cell of him left. Not a hair, not a toenail, not a fleck of dandruff; the man had entirely disintegrated into mist/steam/*preta*. Even skin flakes separated from his body had joined in the transformation. As for his clothes and equipment, they were pretty much gone too. A few of his implants had left behind dollops of metal and melted plastic, but nothing bigger than a pebble. Mostly they'd turned to smoke and fumes, now wafting out the storage shed's door.

The rest of Team Esteem had probably vanished the same way: their bodies turned into hungry ghosts, their implants and clothing burned and dispersed on the breeze. A Bumbler scan of the camp might turn up little nuggets left behind by the implants, but to the naked eye, there'd be nothing to see. Even my sixth sense would detect nothing—the team members' life force had vanished.

Gone up in smoke. Smoke with shadowy chromosomes.

Which raised a discomfiting worry: whatever had done this to Team Esteem could already be working on Festina, Tut, and me.

We'd all been exposed to native atmosphere. If there was some kind of airborne agent . . . microbes, nanites, or chemicals . . .

I adjusted the Bumbler and took more readings.

So that's what we've found so far," Festina said into the comm. "Tut—time to report what the guy told you."

She handed the comm to Tut as he said, "I'll try." Speaking into the comm, he continued, "But I gotta say, a lot went over my head. These weren't good conditions for getting the guy's story."

"We know," Festina said. "Do your best."

"Okay. Sure. Okay." Tut took a deep breath. "The deceased was named Var-Lann. Team Esteem's chief microbiologist. That's why he survived longer than his fellow surveyors. Var-Lann's job was growing bacterial cultures, playing with viruses, stuff like that—so he was at special risk from germs. Before coming to Muta, he volunteered for some new experimental treatment, boosting his immune system a few hundred times."

Tut pointed at the scorch marks left behind when Var-Lann's implants had vaporized. "One of those gadgets produced special white blood cells. Super germ-killing leukocytes. That's why the man lived long enough to tell his story."

"What *was* his story?" Festina asked.

"I'm getting to that," Tut said. "The night before things went haywire, Var-Lann was working in his lab as usual. He happened to be studying live microbe cultures, trying to figure out the relationship between something and something else. I didn't understand the details; I hope it doesn't matter. But he was watching these little guys go about their business when suddenly a new set of microbes came barging in and ate everything in the test cultures. Really fast. Like within thirty seconds."

Festina's eyes narrowed. "What do you mean, barging in?"

"Var-Lann was growing the cultures in what he called Level Two containment—a closed environment supposed to keep out unwanted microbes. He thought he'd taken all the necessary precautions to avoid contaminating his samples, so he was mightily pissed when these new bugs showed up. Var-Lann checked where the new bugs came from and found they were everywhere. In the air, on every piece of equipment, all over his own skin . . . anyplace he looked, gathering by the trillions. Quadrillions. Quintillions."

Tut paused . . . maybe trying to think of what came after quintillions. Then he just shook his head. "Var-Lann had never seen this new microorganism before. Nothing even close. It certainly didn't match native Mutan life. This bug was one hundred percent alien."

Festina winced. "Why am I not surprised?"

"On this planet?" Tut said. "Of course, it's no surprise. The Fuentes and Greenstriders had colonies here. They tracked in microbes from their homeworlds—maybe from other worlds too. By now, Muta's biosphere has lots of bugs that aren't native. It wouldn't even be surprising if a bug became superaggressive. Organisms outside their native environment can develop all kinds of fluky behavior."

"Really?"

Tut gave Festina a look. "I specialized in micro, Auntie. Bugs released on other planets usually just die because they can't find the right food or living conditions. Once in a while, though, they multiply like a son of a bitch—either because they have no natural enemies or because they're just stronger and meaner than anything on the new world. Sometimes you get a die-off *and* a bloom. The bugs dwindle down near the point of extinction and limp along for years . . . then suddenly, pow! Some tiny mutation lets them adapt to their new world, and they grow like gangbusters." Tut shrugged. "Var-Lann knew all this. That's why he didn't issue a red alert the second he noticed the weird microbial buildup: what he was seeing might just be natural behavior.

"But," Tut continued, "Var-Lann realized these new germs might also be Muta's Big Bad Nasty Horror—the thing that wiped out the Greenstriders. He decided to be supercautious: he equipped himself with a hot-button gadget that would let him send a transgalactic Mayday within a heartbeat."

I looked down to where the man had been lying. No sign of any Mayday device. It must have self-destructed with everything else. Still, it didn't surprise me that Team Esteem had a few hair-trigger Maydays among their supplies . . . nor was I surprised that Var-Lann had only donned one when he thought he might be facing special danger. Years ago, our own fleet tried giving every Explorer an Instant Mayday signal. The experiment failed from too many false alarms. It was just too easy to hit the button by accident . . . but if you made the signal more difficult to trigger, the person in trouble was often killed or incapacitated before the button got pushed. Eventually the navy decided that hair-trigger Maydays were only appropriate to carry for short periods of time, and then only when an obvious, imminent danger threatened not just you but others as well. That way, even if you died a split second after pressing the button, your warning might save your companions.

Obviously, the Unity had come to the same conclusion as the Technocracy navy. Which is why Var-Lann didn't normally wear a Mayday but decided it was appropriate on this occasion.

I wondered how long the device had lasted before it got EMP'd.

"So Var-Lann strapped the Mayday gadget to his wrist," Tut continued, "then went back to studying the new microbe. Worked on it all night long, till one of his teammates dragged him off to breakfast. He ate as fast as possible so he could get back to the lab. He was just heading back again when the first spasm hit him."

"Ah." Festina only said the one word. Maybe she didn't even say it aloud—maybe I only perceived it through my sixth sense—but I could tell this was what she'd been waiting for. The moment when things went wrong.

"Yeah," Tut said. "Var-Lann had a major seizure. Like his whole body exploding. It happened so fast, he didn't even push the Mayday button. It must have bumped on something when he fell . . . or when he went into convulsions half a second later. All the time he was shaking, Var-Lann said he could hear the device's audio feedback: a loud, piercing screech, wailing away.

"He wasn't sure how long the seizure lasted—probably no more than ten seconds. By the time he stopped shaking, his teammates were crowded around him. Var-Lann had crashed just a few steps outside the mess hall, so the rest of the team jumped up from the table and came running. The camp's doctor began examining Var-Lann with everybody else there watching . . . and suddenly, they all turned into smoke."

"Var-Lann saw that?" Festina asked.

"With his own two eyes. His teammates vaporized simultaneously. Poof, up in smoke."

"Outside the mess hall?"

Tut nodded. "Their bodies just vanished. Clothes and implants self-destructed a few seconds later. Good thing the camp has gravel on the ground, or the implants might have started a fire."

"The gravel wouldn't show much sign of fire," Festina murmured. "That's why we didn't notice any evidence of burning. And the wind blew away any ash." She looked at Tut. "What happened next?"

"Var-Lann said the smoke from each team member swirled in place for a few seconds, then they all joined into a single cloud. The cloud closed tight around him . . . which is when his Mayday stopped screeching."

"The cloud EMP'd it," I said.

"Seems so," Tut agreed. "Var-Lann didn't know about the EMP, but he knew the Mayday had sounded long enough to be heard all the way back to the Unity homeworld. A rescue team would be on the way, and it was Var-Lann's job to live long enough to report what happened. Normally, he'd just upload his report via brain-link to the team's computers . . . but the link had stopped working."

"The cloud EMP'd the brain-link too," I said.

"Right. So Var-Lann realized he had to deliver his report in person. That meant he had to survive—hours or even days—and his best option was sealing himself in stasis. Otherwise, he knew damned well he'd become smoke himself. He could feel it coming on. Stasis was the only way to stave off the transformation."

"Good thinking on his part," Festina said. "You have to admire a man who did what he had to do."

"It wasn't easy," Tut told her. "Var-Lann got dropped by a few more seizures on his way to the storage building. And the EMP cloud stayed right on him—like it was trying to hold him back or fog him in so completely he'd lose his way. But he kept going till he reached the storage building's stasis generators and sealed himself in. By then, he was crumbling apart. He'd have turned to smoke like the others if not for his boosted immune system."

Festina looked pensive. "Var-Lann believed those microbes he'd seen were responsible for the transformation?"

"Absolutely. He'd had all night to study them, and . . ." Tut broke off. "You know how a virus reproduces?"

"The virus invades a cell," I said. "It hijacks the cell's protein-making facilities and creates copies of itself. Sometimes hundreds of copies, built with stolen materials from the cell. Once the cell is full of new viruses, its outer membrane ruptures, and the viruses scurry off to do the same thing in other cells."

Tut nodded. "That's the idea. Regular cells become Trojan horses, chock to the brim with freshly manufactured viruses. That's what Var-Lann saw: normal cells filled with alien stuff."

"When you say 'normal cells,' what do you mean?" Festina asked. "Normal Mutan bacteria?"

"Normal *Fuentes* bacteria. Team Esteem had found lots of Fuentes bugs in Drill-Press: microbes that weren't native to Muta, growing undisturbed since the Fuentes left. The new bacteria that Var-Lann found had similar DNA, the same sort of outer membrane, plenty of structures in common. However, Var-Lann's bugs also had stuff that normal Fuentes germs didn't have: human chromosomes floating inside."

"*Human* chromosomes?" Festina and I spoke in unison disbelief.

"Yes. Var-Lann's version of human—*Homo unitatis*. The Unity's twenty-four chromosomes rather than our twenty-three."

I said, "Let me get this straight. Var-Lann's working in his lab. Suddenly, he's surrounded by new bacteria he's never seen before. The bacteria look like Fuentes microbes, but they've got Unity chromosomes inside?"

"Exactly," Tut said. "The mystery bacteria contain hundreds of copies of each Unity chromosome. To Var-Lann, the germs looked like cells invaded by viruses and filled to bursting with viral copies . . . only in this case, the Fuentes cells were filled with human chromosomes."

"This does not sound good," Festina muttered. "This sounds very, very bad."

"Var-Lann thought so too," Tut replied. "He hypothesized the bugs were delivery systems for Trojan horse chromosomes. You know what I mean? These bugs would get inside human bodies, then break open and spill their chromosomes all over everywhere. The chromosomes would burrow into surrounding cells and . . . who knows? The new chromosomes would look like ones your cells already had. They'd be treated like members of the family. Next thing you know, the infiltrator chromosomes are screwing up the works somehow—making poisons, disrupting your metabolism . . . or turning you into smoke."

Festina made a face. "Don't tell me Var-Lann actually considered that possibility."

"Not till he saw it happen. Until Team Esteem vaporized, Var-Lann didn't know what the hell these chromosomes would do if they got inside a person's cells. That sort of thing takes months to figure out."

Tut looked down at the scorch marks on the floor. "He didn't have months, did he?"

Okay," Festina said, "let's go back a step. The night before things went bad, Var-Lann found Fuentes bacteria full of human chromosomes. But the flakes of skin we found—Var-Lann's skin—had human cells full of dark matter chromosomes . . . or if Youn Suu prefers, chromosome-shaped holes in reality."

She waited for me to comment. I didn't. "Anyway," Festina went on, "what the hell is going on? This shit doesn't happen by accident."

"Of course not," Tut answered. "Var-Lann had a theory about what was going on."

"Oh good. I'd be thrilled if anyone could make sense of this."

"Don't speak too soon," Tut said. "You won't be thrilled if Var-Lann is right. See, he believed the mystery bacteria were created by a Fuentes defense system. A weapon intended to attack invaders who dropped in uninvited. It's not a fast weapon, but it's thorough. Basically, the defense weapon analyzes invaders and creates biological agents tailored to their physiology."

"Booby-trapped chromosomes?" Festina asked.

"Exactly. Here's the scenario. Aliens land on Muta. The defense system activates. It gathers samples of the invaders' tissues—"

"How?" I interrupted.

"Probably with squads of nanites: microscopic robots. The nanites sneak into the invaders' bodies, grab some cells, and sneak away. They deliver the cells to a site where defense system computers do a complete analysis. It's not a quick process—the Unity have been on Muta for what, six years? That's how long it took the defense system to develop a bug that targets *Homo unitatis*. But once the defense system designed an attack agent, the bug was mass-produced and sent in swarms to every Unity camp. The germs surrounded each person and flooded everybody's metabolism; then the germs broke open and spread their nasty little chromosomes everywhere. Once the cells in every human body were infected, the defense system sent out a signal that set the bad chromosomes off. Result: everybody goes poof."

"Pretty elaborate for a weapon system," Festina grumbled. "If you wanted to defend your planet, wouldn't your priorities be simplicity and speed? Simplicity reduces the number of things that can go wrong. Speed means maybe you'll still be alive after the weapon has gone off. I mean, if hostile visitors show up on your doorstep, what good is a weapon that takes six years to mount a defense? By then, truly warlike invaders might have killed all the original population."

"But the invaders wouldn't be killers, would they?" I said. "The

League of Peoples won't let murderers travel from one star system to another. Aliens landing on Muta couldn't be totally homicidal."

"Hmm," said Festina, "you're right. People coming here *wouldn't* be stone-cold killers. They couldn't be. At worst, they'd be aggressive settlers . . . like the Europeans who came to the Americas after Columbus. Most Europeans weren't maniacs who got a kick out of massacring natives. They were just greedy and self-centered. They wanted the riches the natives had; they usually only murdered those who got in their way. If the same thing happened on Muta . . ."

"If aliens showed up," I said, "the Fuentes would do their best to keep things peaceful. Maybe they'd give the invaders gifts or negotiate treaties. They'd go along with practically anything, just to avoid confrontation for a few years . . . and they'd get away with it because the newcomers were guaranteed to be halfway reasonable people. The League automatically eliminates anyone who's totally ruthless."

"Right," Festina agreed. "So the Fuentes would give the newcomers whatever was necessary to keep the peace. Six years later, after the defense system has analyzed the invaders and developed attack germs . . . suddenly, all the invaders get vaporized simultaneously. Problem solved. And the bugs would remain in the atmosphere to wipe out any more of the same species who dropped by."

Tut nodded. "That's Var-Lann's theory."

Festina smiled grimly. "If he's right, it wasn't a bad defense strategy. Better than fighting the invaders directly—war makes such a mess. If the Fuentes acted conciliatory until their automatic defense system produced a means of genocide . . . lots fewer casualties and property damage. At least on the Fuentes' side."

"Of course," I said, "the League of Peoples would consider the entire Fuentes civilization nonsentient. A sentient civilization wouldn't callously slaughter visitors."

"Var-Lann talked about that too," Tut said. "He thought the Fuentes on Muta were a splinter group: a breakaway from mainstream Fuentes culture. They didn't behave like other Fuentes, did they? The other Fuentes cleaned up before they transcended the flesh . . . but the Mutan Fuentes didn't. Var-Lann believed the Mutan Fuentes had turned rabidly isolationist. They split from the rest of Fuentes society and built their defense system to keep other species out."

"So the Mutans didn't meet the League's definition of sentience," Festina said, "but it didn't matter. The League only kills nonsentients who try to leave their home star system. The Mutans were isolationist stay-at-homes who didn't want to leave anyway. They kept to this one planet, and the League never touched them."

I nodded to myself. It wasn't uncommon for planetary populations to turn isolationist—especially on beautiful worlds like Muta, with all the necessities of life. Even in the Technocracy, most planets had secessionist movements. The general public usually considered such movements to be crazy . . . but all a movement needed was a charismatic leader plus a few unpopular decisions by the central government, and soon breaking away became a serious topic of discussion.

During my lifetime, three star systems had cut ties with the Technocracy. One had since returned to the fold, but the other two continued to turn in on themselves, becoming steadily more xenophobic. Some experts thought it was only a matter of time before those two systems began shooting outsiders who came too close.

Was that what had happened to Muta? Had the people here split from the rest of Fuentes civilization, eventually building a draconian defense system to slaughter all visitors? Had that defense system built supergerms, killing the Unity survey teams and the Greenstriders that came before them?

No, I decided. It wasn't as simple as that. For one thing, Var-Lann and his teammates hadn't really been killed—they'd been turned into clouds that retained purpose and intelligence. And what about the shadow chromosomes in Var-Lann's cells? Where did that come in?

Festina was obviously having similar thoughts. "Tut, did Var-Lann say anything about dark matter?"

"Not a word," Tut answered. "At least nothing I understood.

There was a part where he completely lost me—almost a full minute. Sorry."

"Can't be helped," Festina told him. "We're lucky you understood anything." She looked around the room as if searching for hints of what to do next. Nothing presented itself. Finally, she turned back to Tut, and asked, "Is that it? Did Var-Lann say anything else?"

Tut paused, then said, "Yeah. He, uhh . . . he knew we were from the Outward Fleet. He recognized your tightsuits. And even though I spoke his language, he knew I was from the Technocracy too."

"Why?" Festina asked.

"Because I wasn't dead. Last time Var-Lann looked, there were still plenty of bugs in the air. If any of us had twenty-four Unity chromosomes, we'd be smoke by now. But . . ."

"But?"

"Var-Lann pointed out that *Homo sapiens* aren't much different from *Homo unitatis*. One chromosome, that's all: the Unity has that one extra chromosome. And as chromosomes go, it's pretty damned small—fewer than a hundred genes. Just a handful of things the Unity have added to themselves, and put onto a brand-new chromosome for fear of screwing up older DNA structures." Tut took a deep breath. "So if Var-Lann was right about this automatic defense system, he thought we were in big trouble."

"Because the system is already creating a defense against *us*," Festina said grimly.

"Right. And genetically, we're damned near identical to the Unity. All but that one chromosome. As soon as the system starts analyzing us, it'll see we're almost the same . . . so it'll be able to turn us to smoke with almost the same bugs. It sure as hell won't need six whole years to produce appropriate attack germs. Var-Lann thought the system might mount an assault within days. Or hours. He told us to get off Muta fast."

"We can't," Festina said. "The only way to leave is a Sperm-tail. If we try that, the EMP cloud will ride up the tail and zap *Pistachio*. We'll still be stuck, and the ship will be stuck with us." She shook her head. "No. Whatever trouble we're in ourselves, there's no point endangering *Pistachio* too."

Tut shrugged. "Then we'll all get smoked like Team Esteem."

"Not if I can help it." Festina turned to me. "You've got the Bumbler. Have you checked for the presence of Var-Lann's bugs?"

I nodded. "They're all around us. Inside us too. I don't know how long we've been breathing them—at least since we entered the camp. They're covering our bodies . . . creeping in through our ears, nose, and mouth . . . maybe penetrating our skin . . ."

Festina nodded. "Then we're completely infested. Just fucking wonderful. But we aren't dead yet . . . which gives us time to set things right."

"How?" Tut asked.

"By finding this damned defense system and smashing the shit out of it so nobody else dies."

"But Var-Lann might have been wrong," Tut protested. "He was just hypothesizing—halfway out of his head with pain. There might not *be* any system. And even if there is, it could be anywhere on the planet!"

"Then we'd better search fast. Let's go."

12

Magga [Pali]: Path. The Buddha's fourth truth is that the way to purge oneself of tanha (fixations) is to follow a program called the Eightfold Path: practices to lessen the grip of one's fixations and eventually achieve freedom.

NEXT stop: Drill-Press. The Fuentes city.

If there was any nearby information about Var-Lann's hypothetical defense system, it would lie among the mud-covered ruins. Not that the Fuentes would have left big signs pointing to secret alien-killing machinery . . . and not that we could read Fuentes writing, even if there were such signs . . . and not that the actual defense machinery was more likely to be in Drill-Press than anywhere else on the planet . . . but the city was still the first place to start looking. No other Fuentes settlement was close enough to reach on foot.

Besides, Li and Ubatu crash-landed in the ruins. Professional courtesy demanded we make a token effort to see what had happened to them.

First, though, we needed more practical clothing. I was soggy with sweat inside my overinsulated tightsuit; Festina was similarly steaming. Therefore, we scrounged through the Unity huts till we found clothes that would fit us. Not too surprisingly, we both obtained uniforms from the same woman: the only member of Team Esteem close to our size. Unity women tended toward Amazonian proportions—tall, broad-shouldered, long in the leg. Unity bioengineering policies decreed that females should average exactly the same height as males, and both should be built like demigods. Fortunately, Unity policies also decreed that each survey team should have one man and one woman substantially smaller than the norm, in case there was need to send someone into cramped spaces . . . exploring caves, for example, or picking through wreckage in a collapsed building. Festina and I searched till we found the hut of the mandatory short woman, then fought our way out of our tightsuits and into two of the woman's spare uniforms.

I let Festina have the official "dress" uniform. It was made from nanomesh fabric—an assemblage of nanites that adhered to the body as tight and thin as paint—but at least the nanocloth was a dignified black. (Black was the official color of both the Unity Survey Service and our own Explorer Corps. In the Academy, we'd often speculated if the Unity was imitating us, or vice versa. Historical records didn't help to determine who chose black first. Incredibly, the Technocracy had no records of when or how the Explorer Corps got started. No one knew if that omission was a deliberate snub, benign neglect, sheer incompetence, or something more sinister.)

As for me, I got stuck with a nanomesh uniform that clung just as revealingly—the Unity was the sort of culture that preached virtuous restraint while wearing clothes so snug and sheer that everyone could see your appendectomy scar—but besides being tight enough to show whether I was an inny or an outy, the uniform was one of those multicolored jester suits that passed for Mutan camouflage: yellow, blue, crimson, purple, orange, green, mauve, splashed in motley spottles and blotches all over the skintight cloth . . . as if I'd rolled in fruit salad. The moment I emerged from the hut, Tut yelled, "Hey, Mom, you look like spumoni."

Tut himself looked like a bear. While Festina and I had been dealing with clothes, he'd toured the other huts and collected all the sacred masks. Some of the masks were now slung on a belt at his waist, while others hung on a makeshift bandoleer draped from his shoulder to his hip . . . but he'd saved one mask to wear over his gold-plated face: a life-sized bear mask, complete with what looked to be genuine bear fur and teeth. In the middle of the bear's forehead was a blood-red ruby as big as my thumb.

The thought of Tut stealing the masks disturbed me; it was like looting relics from a temple. I had little respect for the Unity's mask religion—an outlet for the worst in human nature, not striving to achieve the best—but in the spirit-parched secular world of the Technocracy's mainstream, I felt kinship for *any* religious artifacts.

"Those don't belong to you," I told Tut. "If you take them, they'll get broken."

"But, Mom, they're shiny-finey!" He capered around me, making mock growls. "Grr-arrh! Grr-arrh! The bear says the masks want to dance!"

"Tut . . ."

"They've been stuck inside, grr-arrh! With no one to wear them, grr-arrh! Their owners have left, the masks are bereft, and they're looking for fun now, grr-arrh!"

He began making clawing gestures at me, still bouncing in circles and calling, "Grr-arrh! Grr-arrh!"

"Tut!" I said. "This isn't funny. It's disrespectful."

"Masks don't want respect, grr-arrh. They'd much rather play and pet, grr-arrh. They just want to dance, and to get in your pants. A mask is the best lay you'll get, grr-arrh!"

"Tut . . ." Then it struck me: this was a man who'd spent a year with the Unity. Living among them. Learning their language. Had he also taken part in their orgies? Did he get himself stoked up on ritual drugs or brain-feeds, then mask-dance himself into ecstasy? He'd been sixteen at the time; of *course* he'd attend an orgy if invited. Being Tut, he would have thrown himself into the experience with total abandon. If invited. Supposedly, the Unity didn't let you join their rites unless you had a spirit-mask of your own, but . . .

Wait. Tut *did* have a mask. The gold-plating on his face. When did he get that? During his time with the Unity. Had he been wearing a genuine Unity spirit-mask for as long as I'd known him?

No. Real spirit-masks had a soul-gem in the forehead. Tut's gold face didn't. But perhaps soul-gems were only for full-fledged members of the Unity. Outsiders like Tut might be allowed to have masks of their own but couldn't add a gem because they couldn't claim full Unity status.

That made sense. The Unity *did* accept converts to their religion; in some places, they'd angered the Technocracy by actively proselytizing. So it was entirely possible Tut's face *was* a mask and he was a practiced trance-dancer.

Which was bad news for us. The last thing we needed was Tut trying to relive his youth in a blur of unconstrained copulation.

Or was there more here at work than a simple yearning for the past? Something had happened to Tut's aura—something I couldn't define. It seemed more chaotic than before . . . not just Tut's usual insanity but a warring pandemonium of driving urges. Black anger. Crimson lust. White-hot hatred. Muddy grief. And some odd unnatural extra that fought all the rest: a slippery purple force I couldn't identify. The colors clashed against each other madly, like Muta's motley foliage. Their battle seemed strong enough to rip Tut's life force apart.

Unless I did something.

"Tut," I said in a quiet but firm voice. "It's broad daylight; the masks shouldn't be out. You know that. The masks might want to dance, but the sun hurts their eyes. Isn't that right? Isn't there a rule that says masks are only for after dark?"

I hoped I was right. One shouldn't trust Technocracy rumors about Unity beliefs . . . but in this case, I thought the rumors might be true. Mask dances were strictly regulated, like everything else in the Unity—Unity leaders didn't want people frolicking and fornicating when they should be doing productive work. I expected restrictions would have been built into the mask religion's dogma: dances could only take place at night, after a full day of contributing to the common good.

Besides, I thought, the masks would look more powerful after dark. In the bright afternoon light, they just looked shabby—the bear, for example, had a slightly asymmetric snout, possibly from getting banged around in wild dances and wilder couplings. Such small imperfections wouldn't be noticeable after dark, when the only light came from a bonfire . . . but now, under the glaring sun, the bear appeared soulless and silly. The masks on Tut's belt and bandoleer displayed similar weakness: bouncing haphazardly as he jumped around, flimsy constructions of glitter and plastic and feathers. Come sundown, they might become terrifying; for now, the only terror was Tut's losing what was left of his mind.

I wondered why we'd come to this planet in the company of a madman.

"Tut," I said. "The masks aren't supposed to come out in the sun—"

"I know!" he snapped. With an angry motion, he pulled the bear mask off his head. "You can be a real party pooper, Mom. Always so goody-goody. It's irritating."

"Sorry."

"Don't say you're sorry if you don't intend to change." Sulkily, he hooked the bear mask to his belt, where it hung like some flea-bitten hunting trophy. "We might turn to smoke any second. Isn't that enough to make you loosen up?"

I wondered what he meant by loosening up. Was this about sex? Or was it just that I disapproved of his fun, the dancing, the nudity, the pilfering of Team Esteem's sacred objects?

Looking at his life force, I couldn't tell. Tut's aura had returned to its usual jumbled confusion; the colors had faded, damped to a more manageable intensity. Emotions were swirling at random now—just bumping haphazardly against each other, not actively at war. Yet there was still a sort of after-haze of what I'd seen before: flashes of raw emotion, as pure and demanding as the overwhelming hunger of the *pretas*.

What was I seeing? Tut himself, or Tut infested with microbes that would soon make him into a frustrated ghost?

At that moment, Festina came out of the hut in her new Unity clothes. She looked good. I didn't know whether or not she'd been bioengineered, but few natural humans could meet the aesthetic demands of nanomesh: few natural bodies betrayed no sagging or fold-ing under the spray-on-thin layer of nanites. And the black color suited her perfectly—much better than admiral's gray. Her life force showed that she knew it; she seemed more vibrant, confident, and determined. When she saw Tut decked out with the masks, it didn't faze her. She just said, "You'll need more clothing. It'll get cold after dark."

"I picked up a uniform too. It's in my pack." Tut turned to show he wore a Unity backpack—just a small one, only reaching halfway down his spine, but with plenty of room for a change of clothes. I knew Tut might be lying, and the backpack contained something other than a Unity uniform . . . for example, the drugs Team Esteem would have kept on hand to help with their orgies. But Festina chose to believe Tut was telling the truth.

"All right," she said. "We're ready to go. Let's head south."

It should have been a pleasant walk. Bright afternoon. Riots of rainbow foliage. Protolizards sunning themselves on every rock. Our noses soon got used to the omnipresent odor of mustard, and we didn't have much gear to carry: Festina and I both lugged a single stasis-field container, but we'd left the rest at Camp Esteem. Besides the mirror-sphere, I'd filled a small Unity backpack with a water canteen, first-aid kit, and food rations; Festina had done the same. The supplies would let us last a few days in Drill-Press. If we needed more, we could always return to the Unity camp—assuming we hadn't turned to smoke in the meantime.

So a short, easy walk on a sunny fall day: it should have been pleasant. But my sixth sense wouldn't let me ignore the complications simmering around me. Tut and his chaotic life force . . . Festina and her avalanche karma . . . the insects who occasionally died under my feet . . . the gnawing sense of *pretas* never far away, ready to pounce if we tried to escape by Sperm-tail.

To distract myself, I took Bumbler readings of everything around me. We walked through a mass of invisible germs: Var-Lann's bugs, built to tear people apart. And they weren't just on the outside—when I turned the Bumbler on Festina, I could see the germs in her lungs, her stomach, her digestive tract, her bloodstream. Tut was the same . . . utterly infested. For a while, I avoided scanning myself because I didn't want to know the truth; but avoidance was unskillful behavior. At last I forced myself to use the Bumbler on my own body . . .

. . . and discovered I wasn't infected. Clean as autoclaved glass.

Yes, I inhaled Var-Lann's microbes with every breath. Yes, they congregated on my skin and were attempting to crawl in through my ears, the edges of my eye sockets, every possible orifice. But the moment they got inside—whether it was my bronchial tubes, my gut, or elsewhere—the germs were annihilated by tiny red spores.

I belonged to the Balrog. The moss wouldn't share me with interlopers.

The notion almost made me laugh: that I'd be saved from Muta's lethal defense system by the Balrog's prior claim. A slave protected by her master's possessiveness.

Dour thoughts made the walk hard to bear. Physically, however, it was no great effort. Team Esteem had made the trip hundreds of times, clearing a trail we had no trouble following. The route passed through varied stands of foliage: chest-high purple ferns . . . then knee-high rubbery red ferns . . . then yellow-orange giant ferns rising as tall as trees . . . yielding at last to *real* trees: *Capsicillium croceum*, the Fuentes' trademark groves.

This late in the growing season, the trees held none of their distinctive "minichili" fruit. The ground, however, was littered with fallen chilis: all of them bright yellow, the size of my little finger, and covered with crawling insects. Only one species of insect was actually eating the fruit—a bug like a small black ant, which by some fluke of evolution had found itself able to digest the minichili's alien sugars and proteins. The rest of the insects present were eating the little black ants, or eating the insects who ate the ants. Why didn't the ants run away? Likely because Muta's indigenous flora hadn't yet learned to produce fruit of their own. Minichilis were the only true fruit on the planet: a nutritional bonanza the ants just couldn't resist. Besides, there were so many ants chowing down on the fruit, the predators would never get them all. Plenty of well-fed ants would survive to breed . . . and next year the process would repeat itself.

The comforting cycle of life.

Above us, the *Capsicillium croceum* leaves were thick and green, even this close to winter. They wouldn't fall off till first frost . . . at which point they'd drop overnight, entire trees denuded. Until then, however, the dense foliage over our heads was enough to block our view of the city, right up to the moment when we emerged from the woods.

Suddenly, skyscrapers soared above us.

On aerial photos, the towers had seemed bland—we'd seen nothing but flat roofs with rectangular cross sections. From the ground, however, the blandness disappeared: each building was profusely decorated with mosaic tiles, some large, some small, some glossy, some matte, some forming abstract geometric designs, some coming together in pictures fifty stories tall.

For a moment we stood unmoving, enrapt by the giant pictures. Many showed furry bipeds, brown or black, with rabbitlike haunches and long tails that ended in a sharp-edged scoop like a garden spade. The creatures' heads were insectlike, with bulging faceted eyes and strong-looking mandibles: one mandible attachment on each side of the mouth, plus one on the top and one on the bottom, forming a diamond arrangement.

I wondered what the mandibles were for. Holding food? But the creatures had perfectly good arms—slightly shorter than human arms, but ending in well-proportioned hands with three fingers and an opposable thumb. You don't need mandibles when you have hands . . . unless the mandibles were for social display. Or for cracking some special kind of food. Or they played a role in mating, communication, perception, hunting, or some other aspect of life I couldn't imagine. Evolution doesn't create body parts for any particular purpose; the body parts always come first. If the parts prove useful to the creature that has them, both the parts and the creature survive. These creatures must have made the most of what they had, because they were probably the ones who'd built this city.

"Are those Fuentes?" I asked Festina.

She nodded. "Furry bad-tempered beetles. They may look ridiculous, but don't underestimate them—they're damned dangerous in a fight. Strong arms, stronger kicks, wicked bites from those mandibles, and they can swing their tails like maces. Not to mention they're immune to stun-pistols.."

"I thought there were no Fuentes left," Tut said.

"I thought the same till I met two. They told me they were the last, but I prefer to reserve judgment."

"So there might be fur beetles somewhere in Drill-Press?" Tut lifted the bear mask hanging on his belt. "I could put this on so they'd see me as a friend. You know . . . furry."

"No!" I told him. Sharply.

Festina looked at me with a raised eyebrow. Tut just let go of the mask. "Jeez, Mom, ease up, okay?"

"This is as eased as I get," I told him. "We're walking into a city of ghosts."

"You believe in ghosts?" Festina asked.

"Yes. Don't you?"

"No. But I'll give you this much," she said. "In a universe full of weird-shit aliens, there's always something to fill ghosts' ecological niche. Scary things that jump out and go 'Boo!' I can't tell you how often . . ." Her voice trailed off, apparently lost in memories of the past. After a moment, Festina said, "I take it back. There *are* ghosts. Problem is, we don't recognize them as such till we're in over our heads."

Without another word, she started into the city.

The streets were covered with silt, laid down whenever the river overflowed. When the Fuentes were here, they would have prevented such flooding by adjusting dams—the Unity files had noted a series of dams and sluices, starting hundreds of kilometers upstream and extending all the way to the sea. Once the Fuentes had gone, however, the system broke down; no one had lowered or raised the dams in millennia, so they'd become useless concrete waterfalls. The river had returned to its age-old pattern of rise and fall, occasionally swelling high enough to soak the city's feet.

At the moment, the water was low, and the dirt on the streets was dry. No plants grew in that soil; either the silt was too shallow to support plant roots, or the lack of vegetation had a more sinister cause. Some alien civilizations impregnated their paving materials with herbicides—a toxic way to prevent grass and weeds from sprouting. If the Fuentes had used the same trick six thousand years ago, the streets might still contain enough chemicals to discourage local plant life.

I didn't use the Bumbler to see if that was true. When you're walking on poison, sometimes you just don't want to know.

There's something eerie about uninhabited cities. Walking in the unnatural quiet. Drill-Press wasn't absolutely silent—insects buzzed, a soft breeze was blowing, and the river provided a constant babble—but without the noise of people or machines, the city seemed as hushed as a sickroom.

A thousand looming mosaics of furry beetles didn't help. Alien giants looked down on us, holding unknown objects (tools? toys? symbols of office?) or working at unknown tasks. I wondered if the pictures might be advertisements for consumer products or tributes to illustrious citizens. No way to tell. Each picture was probably rich with iconography . . . perhaps a particular position of the mandibles indicated a saint, or a gesture of the tail a sex-star . . . but that was a study for archeologists, if any ever visited this planet. Certainly, Team Esteem hadn't spent much time thinking about the pictures. In all the reports I'd read, the mosaics weren't even mentioned.

Then again, the reports said little about *anything* in the city. Team Esteem had been dropped on Muta by the last luna-ship to visit the system. Since then, whatever the team had learned was stored in computers at their camp—useless EMP'd computers, whose data had never been downloaded back to the Unity homeworld. Someday someone might manage to recover the data and read the surveyors' findings; but from our point of view, the only records Team Esteem had left were scuff marks in the soil.

Those scuff marks showed where the team usually went when they visited Drill-Press. Without a word of discussion, we followed the path most traveled. The Unity people had spent months searching this city for points of interest; gradually, however, they'd settled on a single trail to a single destination.

It would be useful to know what that destination was.

We walked down the street, our eyes and ears open. Tall buildings rose around us: nothing less than twenty stories. Obviously, the Fuentes hadn't believed in single-family dwellings, or little shops with a homey feel. They'd had plenty of room to expand the city—there'd been no other settlement within a thousand kilometers, and no geographical barriers to prevent them from spreading out as far as they liked. But the Fuentes had kept their city tightly compact. Either they preferred to squeeze together (some species instinctively liked to live in one another's laps) or they stuck to a crowded lifestyle established on planets where space was more limited.

My mental awareness penetrated a short distance into nearby buildings, but only showed mud-covered floors and water-damaged walls. No remains of furniture or other belongings. Floods had rotted or washed away the contents of all rooms at ground level, and my sixth sense didn't reach to higher floors.

So what had these places been? Homes? Stores? Amusement centers? How had the Fuentes lived? How had they filled their days? What did they consider important? Explorers seldom asked such questions—we were too busy assessing immediate threats to worry about more ephemeral concerns. We were scouts, not archeologists. But I found myself asking why the Fuentes had come here so long ago. Why journey tens or hundreds of light-years to a planet that would never feel like home? Why build a city in the middle of nowhere, not even close to other cities on the same planet? What would you do in such a place?

Aloud I said, "Do you think they were running from something?"

"What do you mean?" Festina asked.

"The Fuentes who lived here. Do you think they were running away? Maybe they followed an unorthodox religion, so they came to avoid persecution."

"It's possible," Festina said. "Why do you ask?"

"Because the cities are so far apart. Only two on this entire continent . . . and just four more Fuentes cities on the rest of the planet. Why space things out so much? Because the people wanted to avoid each other? Didn't want to be 'contaminated' by outsiders' beliefs?"

"Maybe they needed a lot of land," Festina suggested. "Maybe each family belonged to a separate clan, and they divided all of Muta between the clans. The Fuentes might have had the same sort of territorial instincts as Greenstriders."

"Or maybe," Tut said, "each city was doing dangerous shit, and they didn't want to blow each other up."

Festina and I looked at him. He shrugged. "You two come from civilized worlds. Farms, parks, gardens, all homey and domestic. Me, I was born on an ice moon where we kept blobs of liquid helium as pets. So why did my family live in a shithole whose temperature was damned near absolute zero? Because my old man was a nanotech guy, developing stuff so potentially lethal, one slipup could wipe out everything in sight. Gray goo meltdown. The only place he was allowed to work was that godforsaken moon, far from anything else."

I considered that a moment. "You think the Fuentes might have used Muta for risky research? And the cities were spaced far apart for safety?"

"We all have our own colored lenses, Mom. You see a city in the middle of nowhere, and you think it's because of religion. Auntie says maybe they were trying to grab the most land possible. I see the same setup and wonder if they were doing something so damned dangerous, they were sent to an isolated site on an isolated world to reduce casualties if someone dropped a test tube." He smiled a broad golden smile. "All a matter of perspective, isn't it?"

"True," Festina said. She looked around. "One more lethal possibility to worry about. Just bloody wonderful." She took a few steps, then turned back to Tut. "I understand now why you ran away from home as a teenager. Even the Unity must have looked better than an ice moon."

"Nah," he said. "I left home cuz my helium pets evaporated."

He started up the street . . . which is when I yelled, "Look out!" and grabbed for the pistol on Festina's belt.

My sixth sense had limited range: about ten meters. That's why I hadn't sensed Li and Ubatu stowed away in the shuttle, and why I didn't sense the ambush till almost too late. Fortunately, our attacker's life force was strong—a blazing ball of hatred that burned so fiercely, I knew it was trouble the instant it registered on my inner eye. Even so, I barely had time to shout my warning before Tut was under assault.

In loose zoological terms, the creature was a pouncer—a predator who lies in wait till prey walks by, then leaps from concealment and makes a fast kill. In comparative evolution terms, the beast was Muta's version of a pseudosuchian—a bipedal reptilelike land animal whose descendants would evolve into dinosaurs. In immediate life-or-death terms, what we saw was a mass of teeth and claws hurtling from a gap between buildings—the same height as Tut, but built along the lines of a slender *T. rex*. Big legs, small arms, strong tail, huge head, the whole of its body fast and light but as powerful as a striking hawk. Its scaly skin was leopard yellow with spots of red and brown: excellent camouflage for hiding in Muta's foliage, but also good when standing in shadows against a motley mosaic wall. Normal vision could easily miss it . . . until the moment it made its attack, hurtling toward Tut with its fangs poised for action.

At the last moment, it screamed—like an eagle's piercing cry, but as loud as a lion. No doubt the scream was intended to freeze the prey in terror; but Tut had started moving the instant I shouted my warning, and he didn't let the monster's caterwaul slow him down. Tut pivoted fast as soon as I yelled, looking for the source of danger. He spotted the attacking animal a split second after it started its charge . . . and instead of trying to dodge or escape, he ran toward the beast on a collision course. Just before impact, Tut angled off and threw out his arm in a classic "clothesline" maneuver. The animal (so primitive its species would need twenty million years just to become as smart as a *dinosaur*) didn't have the intelligence or reflexes to deal with a surprise tactic. The big reptile just continued its forward charge as Tut's arm caught it cleanly across the throat.

If Tut had hit *me* that way, I would have slammed to the ground hard on my back. Our pseudosuchian attacker was jerked off its feet and knocked backward, but was too lightweight to hit the street with much impact—the animal had more in common with birds than with massive reptiles like alligators. Furthermore, the beast's strong tail struck the street before its body, taking the brunt of the fall. Half a second later, uninjured by its plunge to the pavement, the creature whipped its tail furiously and used the momentum to spin to its feet. It screeched once more in rage, kicking up dust as it wheeled for another run at Tut. The screech died in the beast's throat as I fired the stun-pistol three times, as fast as I could pull the trigger. I would have kept shooting from sheer adrenaline . . . but the animal went limp with an annoyed-sounding gurgle, and Festina plucked the gun from my hand.

"You got it," she said quietly. Then her head snapped around as Tut stepped toward the beast. He reached out his bare foot to nudge the fallen animal and see if it was really unconscious. "Don't!" Festina cried. My mouth was open to yell the same thing, because everyone knows the monster always attacks one last time when you think it's down for good.

But Tut never had the sense to leave well enough alone. Despite Festina's warning, he prodded the predator lightly in its ribs. The animal's mouth yawned open . . . but instead of biting off Tut's foot, it gave a soft sigh. Steamlike vapors hissed from the beast's maw—a cloud whose life force roiled with fury. It wreathed once around Tut's body, possibly looking for something to EMP. I thought it would come for Festina and me next, shorting out another Bumbler, comm unit, and stun-pistol; but the cloud lingered with Tut, brushing (almost caressing) the masks he carried. I sensed the cloud's emotions shifting from hostility to unbearable sorrow. Then the cloud shot away, rocketing down the street faster than any pseudosuchian could run. In a moment, it had disappeared into the depths of the city.

The three of us watched it vanish. Then Tut said, "Umm . . . did we just find out the EMP clouds can possess Muta's minidinosaurs? Like, the clouds can make dinosaurs attack us?"

Festina and I nodded.

Tut beamed. "Cool!"

Using the Bumbler, I scanned for more predators. Nothing showed up on the readouts, but that didn't mean much. The nearby buildings blocked X rays, microwaves, terahertz radiation, and even radio—all the EM frequencies we used when looking for trouble. Fuentes construction materials seemed purposely designed to prevent the type of spying we wanted to do. It made sense that high-tech people would want their buildings opaque to prying eyes, but it put us at a disadvantage: more cloud-possessed carnivores might lurk down any side street, and the Bumbler wouldn't know till we were within ambush range.

When I reported this to Festina, she just shrugged. "I've been checking the dirt on the street," she said. "No tracks of big nasties except the one that just attacked. Large predators don't often come into this city."

"That makes sense," I replied. "Predators go where there's prey. Prey usually means herbivores, and Drill-Press has nothing to attract plant-eaters." I gestured toward the bare, weedless streets. "No vegetation anywhere."

"You think the baby *T. rex* wandered here by accident?" Tut asked. "Or did the cloud possess Rexy out in the countryside, then force him to come to the city?"

"Good question," Festina said. "I wish I knew the answer. It'd be nice to know if the cloud could really seize animal minds and compel them to do things against their instincts . . . or if the cloud only nudged a predator who was already close by."

"Either way," Tut said, "it's odd the cloud would be hostile . . . I mean, if it really is Var-Lann or one of the other Unity folks. Why would it make a Rexy attack us? Isn't it obvious we're here to help?"

"Who knows what's obvious to a cloud?" Festina asked. "The Unity and Technocracy have never been friends. Maybe Team Esteem thinks we're invading opportunists: trying to claim Muta now that it's unoccupied."

I shook my head—remembering how Var-Lann's life force had changed after he'd disintegrated. The man had showed no ill will toward us while he'd been alive. Once he became a cloud, however, his emotions changed as he grew frustrated at not being able to . . . to do something, I couldn't tell what. Frustration had turned to outrage, outrage to fury, and fury to a berserk need to lash out at anyone who wasn't suffering the same torment.

According to Aniccan lore, that sequence of emotions was the classic pattern for *pretas*. Ghosts might feel joy at the moment of death, either because they were released from the agony of dying or because they thought the afterlife would be some grand heaven that erased the discontent of living. Then they'd realize death *wasn't* an escape from their pasts—that the seeds of karma continued to grow, that one didn't achieve wisdom and tranquillity just because one stopped breathing. There's no free ride, not even in the afterlife. So the exhilaration of supposed freedom would turn to rage at continuing slavery . . . the ghosts' knowledge that they were still fettered by the decisions they'd made and the people they'd become as a consequence.

It took time for that rage to abate—time spent wandering through other realms of existence until the ghosts could stomach the notion of being reborn: until their anger burned out and they found themselves ready to take another try at life. That was the path the unenlightened dead always walked. So I wouldn't have been surprised if the ghosts of Team Esteem felt such an overpowering resentment, they'd want to make trouble for any living person who came within reach. However, I wasn't naive. Normal ghosts couldn't touch our physical realm; they didn't look like smoke, nor did they use dinosaurs to attack those whose hearts were still beating.

It was almost as if Var-Lann's hypothesized bacterial defense system killed people and turned them into ghosts, but left them trapped in this realm of existence. Even if they wanted to move on, they couldn't. They drifted as clouds of dissociated cells—cells with shadows in their chromosomes and murder in their hearts. The clouds carried enough electrical energy to short out machine circuits, and perhaps to goad primitive wildlife into fury; but they didn't have enough energy to . . . they didn't have the *power* to . . .

No. I still couldn't figure out what was happening. But I thought I was on the right track, if I could just fill in some blanks. Perhaps Festina was thinking along the same lines. As I came to an impasse in my own thoughts, Festina sighed, and said, "No sense brooding. Let's follow Team Esteem's tracks and see what they were working on. Maybe that will give some answers."

The path worn by Team Esteem led to the center of town. It wasn't a straight-line route—the streets never let you go farther than a block or two without running into a public square built around a statue or fountain or amphitheater, or maybe just a flat paved area closed in with ornate metalwork fencing—but the Unity team's tracks circled these obstacles and continued forward till they reached the city's core.

There, two bridges spanned the Grindstone a hundred meters apart . . . and built between the bridges, entirely above the water, was a graceful building radically different from the rest of the city's architecture. There were no brash mosaics on this building's walls, just an unadorned white surface that looked like polished alabaster but wasn't: any natural stone exposed to the weather for sixty-five centuries couldn't possibly retain such a mirror-smooth finish. The building was as glossy as a polished pearl. Unlike the squared-off high-rises elsewhere in the city, the river building's exterior had no sharp edges—just flowing curves that arced from one bridge to the other, like a third elegant bridge constructed between two less eye-catching cousins. If laid out flat on the ground, the building would only be a single story tall. As it was, however, its rainbowlike arch lifted much higher over the river . . . maybe a full six stories above the water at the center of its span.

"Pretty," said Festina, "but impractical. What are the floors like inside? Are they bowed like the building itself? You'd have to bolt down the furniture to keep it from sliding downhill."

"Forget the drawbacks, Auntie," Tut said. "Think about the possibilities. Get a chair on wheels, take it to the middle of the arch, then ride it down the central hallway as fast as you can go. Bet you'd get awesome speed by the time you hit the bottom."

"What if there is no central hallway?" I asked. "Maybe the architecture is designed to prevent people go-carting on office chairs."

"Come on, Mom, what's the point of building a place like that if you can't go cannonballing down the middle? That's just sick."

"Central hallway or not," Festina said, "this is obviously the heart of the city. Designed to catch attention." She glanced up and down the river. "It's visible quite a distance along both shores . . . and from the skyscrapers on either side."

"So what is it?" I asked. "A temple? A royal palace?"

"Go-cart track," Tut muttered.

"I don't know what it is," Festina replied. "But it appears to be where Team Esteem spent a lot of time." She gestured toward the trail we'd been following. It led up the nearest of the two cross-bridges, heading for the white building above the water. "Let's see what our friends in the Unity found."

She started forward again. Tut and I trailed silently behind her.

* * *

The path worn in the mud did indeed lead to the white, arched building. We followed the tracks to the middle of the nearest supporting bridge, then turned onto an access ramp that faded seamlessly from the bridge's gray stone into the pearl-like alabaster of the building before us. The doors to the place were made of the same material as the walls: so glossy I could see my face faintly reflected in the surface.

I looked scared.

Tut, however, showed no signs of fear. He went to the door, grabbed its oversized handle, and yanked the thing open. As he did, I noticed Festina's hand dart to the butt of her stun-pistol—but no EMP cloud or pseudosuchian hurtled out at us. The building's surprise was more subtle than direct attack. For a moment, I didn't even realize there was anything amiss . . . till it dawned on me the corridor beyond the entrance was perfectly, levelly flat.

A ridiculous instinct made me want to step back to see if the building still looked arched from the outside. I fought the urge; I didn't want to act like some bumpkin unable to believe her eyes. Besides, I could count on Tut to do the honors. As soon as he saw the flat corridor in front of us, he ran to the side of the access ramp where he could get a clear view of the building. "Looks all curved from here," he called. "Does it still look level to you?"

"As straight as a laser," Festina said. "Either it's a visual illusion, or the Fuentes had hellishly good spatial distortion technology. Looks like this building's interior is a pocket universe that can lie level inside an arched shell."

"Bastards," Tut muttered. "Now there's no point go-carting down the hall."

At that moment, the hall in question flickered—like a fluorescent light that's malfunctioning. In this case, however, it wasn't light that cut in and out; it was geometry. The flat floor jumped to the sort of curve one expected from an arched building . . . then back to a level surface . . . then bent, then flat again, fluttering rapidly back and forth till it settled down once more to a perfectly even keel.

Tut looked at Festina and me. "You saw that too, right?"

Festina nodded. "The building is losing its horizontal hold. Whatever technological trickery keeps the place level, it's not going to last much longer." Her eyes took on a distant look. "This isn't the first time I've come across Fuentes technology nearing the end of its life. Maybe their equipment uses some standard component, like a control chip or power supply . . . and that component has a working lifetime of six and a half millennia." She turned her head to the sky. "Maybe all over the galaxy, there are abandoned Fuentes settlements we haven't found; and in each one, lights are flickering, machines are stuttering, computers are crashing . . . because they all use the same crucial part, and that part is so old, it's become erratic."

The corridor flickered again. A single leap this time: like a skipping rope when someone snaps one end. The floor jerked precipitously, then dropped again to placid rest.

"If we were inside," I said, "would we have felt that? Like an earthquake tossing us around?"

"I doubt it," Festina replied. "If it had the force of an earthquake, it would have shaken the building apart. Even the few jumps we've seen should have caused major structural damage . . . and who knows how long the interruptions have been happening? Months? Years?" She shrugged. "Once we're inside, we likely won't notice the fluctuations. It's only while we're here, on the outside looking in, that we can tell weird shit is happening."

"What about when things finally die for good?" Tut asked. "Will *that* wreck the place?"

"Probably not," Festina said. "If flicking back and forth doesn't bounce everything to pieces, shutting off and staying off shouldn't either. But what do I know? This stuff goes way beyond anything I've learned about physics."

"I hope the place flies apart," Tut told her. "When the flatness finally goes, I hope the building can't stand its new shape and just goes kerflooey! Wouldn't that be great? Especially if you were inside and the floor under your feet just shot up, boom. Wouldn't that be *better* than riding office chairs down the halls?"

Festina stared at him a moment, then turned away. "Let's get in and out fast, shall we? Before anything dramatic happens. I'm allergic to excitement."

Once we'd stepped into the building's central corridor, we saw no more flickers in reality. We didn't hear or feel disturbances either—to our normal five senses, the building was as solid and unmoving as an ancient mountain.

But to my sixth sense, the place felt like a trampoline.

Every fluctuation sent my mental awareness skittering. It reminded me of age fourteen when I'd caught an inner-ear infection: the normally stable world seemed subject to swoops and staggers, movements made more disturbing because they didn't jibe with the rest of my senses. Being on a real trampoline wouldn't have been half so bad; at least then, all my senses would have agreed on what my body was experiencing. But having perceptions at odds with each other produced a sort of motion sickness—or nonmotion sickness—that left me dizzy with nausea after every bounce. I tried to hide my queasiness, but Festina noticed almost immediately.

"Are you all right?" she asked.

"Uhh, sure . . ."

"Don't lie to me, Explorer! Are you all right?"

"Uhh . . ." I tried to gather my thoughts. Fortunately, the fluctuations only lasted a few seconds, after which tranquillity returned. I'd never mentioned my sixth sense to Festina . . . and was afraid to do so now, for fear of the way she'd react if she learned I'd been keeping secrets from her. At the same time, I didn't want to tell an absolute lie. "It's the Balrog," I said, swallowing back my disorientation. "I think it can sense when the building bounces. It's . . . it's making me seasick."

Festina took the Bumbler and gave me a head-to-toe scan. "No obvious change in your infestation," she said. "No, wait. Your foot. The spores have spread."

"Which foot?" I asked. As if I didn't remember shattering the bones when I kicked down the door of the storage building.

"Your right," Festina said. She lifted her head from the Bumbler's display. "You don't feel any different?"

"In my foot? I don't feel much of anything."

"I imagine that's true." Festina stared thoughtfully at me. Her life force showed a growing mistrust—mistrust of *me*. Probably she was remembering how I'd smashed the door, then pretended to be all right. She realized now I must have been hiding what actually happened . . . and she had to be wondering what else I might have hidden.

The building flickered: a shudder so strong I almost threw up. *Turn the sixth sense off*, I thought fiercely to the Balrog. *I can't handle it here.*

"You'd better go back outside," Festina told me as my stomach heaved. Her aura showed concern for my health . . . but she was also glad for an excuse to send me away, at least till she decided how to handle an alien-infested stink-girl who'd obviously concealed important facts.

Balrog, I thought again. *She thinks I'm turning traitor. Shut off the sixth sense so she won't send me away. Please! I need to think clearly. Shut it off.*

And just like that, I became blind; the sixth sense vanished, and I was reduced to my five fleshly ones. I could no longer tell where I was or what was around me unless I actually looked. Tut and Festina had no auras: all surface, no interpretation. I saw them staring at me, but nothing told me what they were feeling.

It made me laugh—bitterly. How long had I had the sixth sense? Less than two days . . . but going without it now felt like losing a limb. In fact, I *had* lost a limb, my foot turned to moss; but that seemed like a minor inconvenience compared to the amputation of my mental awareness. In that moment, I mourned more for my lost alien perception than for my real flesh and blood.

Demon, I thought silently toward the red moss. *You got me addicted so easily. And if you're as prescient as everyone says, you probably saw this coming—that I'd set the sixth sense aside and realize how much I missed it. But I won't ask you to turn it back on. I won't.*

No response from the omnipresent spores . . . but I imagined them mocking me. The Balrog knew perfectly well I'd ask for the sixth sense back, probably the instant I left the building. I knew it too. I'd invent some rationalization for why it was necessary: it would be "in the best interests of the mission" to regain my heightened perception. As soon as I could, I'd ask the Balrog to reinstate my enhanced awareness. If the spores delayed even for a second, I'd be ready to beg.

Disgusting, disgusting addiction. Even worse, I didn't care how needy I might be, how much I'd have to grovel. I just wanted to see again. The only thing stopping me from pleading for the sixth sense back, right then and there, was the look on Festina's face.

"What's just happened?" she asked. I couldn't tell if her voice was sympathetic or dangerously restrained. "Something's changed, hasn't it? What happened, Youn Suu?"

"The Balrog . . . it's, uhh . . . it's *numbed* me. So I won't feel the fluctuations anymore."

"Did it tell you that?"

I shook my head. "It doesn't tell me anything—it never speaks. I just know I've been . . . numbed."

"I wish *I* could be numbed," Tut said. "Does it make you horny?"

"No." *It makes me sad.* "But I'm okay. I can go on now."

"Think again," Festina said. "You're going back outside—where you'll feel better, and we won't have to worry about the Balrog playing tricks."

I wanted to yell and argue; but if I did, she'd only mistrust me more. Luckily, Tut came to my rescue.

"Come on, Auntie," he told Festina, "we can't send Mom outside on her own. Not if she's sick. She might get eaten by a Rexy."

"You can stay outside with her. Keep her safe."

"No way," Tut said. "Then *you'd* be alone, Auntie . . . and who knows what dangerous shit might be in this building. Not to mention, if we're trying to find what the Unity was up to, three people can search a lot faster than one. There's a reason the Explorer Corps frowns on single-person operations."

I could have given Tut a big wet kiss for standing up to Festina . . . and standing up for me. But I merely held myself upright like a competent human being. I'd overcome my dizziness from the spatial fluctuations and hadn't yet begun to suffer serious withdrawal from losing my sixth sense. (I hoped there wouldn't *be* withdrawal symptoms; but I could feel some perverse urge trying to invent some. My ancestors would have blamed that urge on the demon-god Mara, who keeps people under his power by filling them with worldly cravings and delusions. I seldom believed in Mara, but I knew the ease with which my brain could create trouble for itself. It would rather be bleeding than quiet.)

Festina looked at Tut and me, then growled. "Three Explorers is a stupid size for a landing party. Not enough people to split up safely, but enough for the admiral to get outvoted." She glared. "Just remember, this *isn't* a democracy. I can and will pull rank if I think it's necessary. I'll do it the instant you *really* become a liability."

"I'm feeling better now," I said. "Honest."

"No, Youn Suu. The Balrog is letting you feel better. Or *making* you feel better. And that's assuming you *are* Youn Suu. For all I know, the real Youn Suu could have been silenced, and now the Balrog is speaking with her mouth."

I'm the real Youn Suu, I thought. But I didn't say it aloud—Festina wouldn't have believed it.

Even I had my doubts.

13

Bodhisattva [Sanskrit]: One who is close to becoming a Buddha; Prince Gotama was a Bodhisattva before his full enlightenment. In some schools of Buddhism, "Bodhisattva" also means a particular type of saint—people who are fully enlightened, but who hold themselves back from ultimate transcendence so they can remain in the world and help others achieve enlightenment too. (Such Bodhisattvas may be depicted as archetypal beings with divine powers. To the unsophisticated, they fill the role of gods and goddesses. On a higher theological level, they're metaphoric representations of spiritual virtues and right living.)

THE river building's central corridor only had a few doors leading off it—three to the left and two to the right. Apart from that, it was simply a dimly lit passage running more than two hundred meters, straight from the entrance to the exit on the other bridge. All five side doors were closed: blank expanses of the same pearly material as the exterior walls. Either the Fuentes didn't believe in signs on doors, or the labels had eroded over the centuries.

We examined the five doors before trying any of them. They had no distinguishing marks—no hint, for example, that Team Esteem had used one more than the others. There were bits of dried mud on the floor near the entrance, but the Unity people had politely wiped off their feet before venturing farther into the building, leaving us with no dirty tracks to follow. I found myself wishing I had my sixth sense back, just for a hint of what might lie behind the closed doors; but I thrust that thought aside before I started to dwell on it.

I dwelled on it anyway. Totally fixated. But I pretended otherwise.

With no reason to choose any particular door, we started with the one nearest the entrance. It had no lock, just a push bar. Tut and I stood against the walls on either side—out of the line of fire if something bad happened when the door opened—while Festina put her foot on the push bar and gave a heavy shove.

The door swung silently open. The room beyond was as dim as the corridor—lit by dirty skylights that created more shadows than illumination. The shadows were cast by boxy machines arranged in a five-by-five grid. Obviously, the room housed mainframe computers . . . and just as obviously (from the silence that hung in the air) the computers were no longer running. One near the door had been cracked open, probably by a member of Team Esteem; but even in the pallid light, it was easy to see that the machine's guts were a mess of fused metal and desiccated biologicals.

"EMP'd," Tut said, looking at the remains of the computer's innards.

"What a surprise," Festina muttered. She walked around the room anyway to make sure she didn't overlook subtle details, but the place was exactly as it seemed at first glance: a room full of big, dead computers. Perhaps an army of experts could learn something about Fuentes technology from the ruined remains, but Team Esteem hadn't spent much effort on the task. They must have busied themselves elsewhere.

On to the room next door. It was trashed. At one point, it would have been a lab; but now, glassware was smashed, microscopes had been battered to mangled metal, and delicate machines were reduced to wreckage. I could still recognize the sturdier pieces of equipment—a freezer, a fridge, an autoclave—but even those had been fiercely attacked . . . kicked and dented and bitten.

No mystery who the attacker had been. Sprawled across the debris was a dead pseudosuchian, a human-sized protodinosaur much like the one that tried to kill Tut. It had withered to nothing but skin over skeleton . . . and the skin was so thin, we could see where the underlying bones were fractured—its jaw, its feet, its tail.

"Poor guy," Tut said, patting the carcass. He stroked its shriveled flank. "What do you think?" he asked Festina and me. "The EMP clouds forced Rexy to come here, then drove him crazy enough to demolish the place?"

"Probably," Festina replied. "Looks like the animal was so berserk it kept bashing away, even though it was damaging itself as much as the lab. Eventually, it rolled over and died from its injuries."

"One problem with that theory," I said. While they'd been talking, I'd scanned the creature's corpse with my Bumbler. "Carbon-dating says this animal has been dead more than six thousand years."

"What?" Festina hurried to look at the readout. "Anything dead that long should be dust."

"Not necessarily," I said. "There's no weather inside this building. No insects either. And almost no microbes. Just the germs we're carrying with us, on our skin and in our guts."

"How can that be?" Festina asked. She took the Bumbler and twisted a few dials. The data remained the same.

"Maybe it's spatial distortion," Tut suggested. "This building is a pocket universe, right? Doing weird shit to everything inside. Maybe it kills microorganisms."

"It kills microorganisms but not the cells in our bodies? How is that possible?" Festina glowered at the Bumbler's display. "But this place *is* devoid of microbes. Truly mind-bogglingly clean." She looked back at the dead protodinosaur. "Which is why there's so little decay: no germs or bugs to break down the corpse."

"The corpse dates back to Fuentes times," I said. "If that's the case—and if we think the EMP clouds made the animal bust this place up . . ."

"That's what *I* think," Tut put in.

"Then where did EMP clouds come from so long ago? The ones we've seen so far are from Team Esteem. Aren't they?"

"Gotta be," Tut said. "Var-Lann turned into one. And he saw his fellow team members go the same way."

"If that was the work of a Fuentes defense system," Festina said, "other invaders probably turned into clouds too. The Greenstriders, for example. And any other race that tried to settle on Muta in the past sixty-five hundred years."

"And maybe the Fuentes themselves," I suggested.

"What do you mean?"

"Live by the sword, die by the sword. It's basic karma. Build a defense system that turns invaders into angry clouds of smoke, and it's only a matter of time before the same thing happens to you."

"Mom has a point," Tut said. "I've played a million VR sims where folks build a doomsday device, then some technical glitch sets it off . . . or saboteurs make the superweapon backfire . . ."

Festina grimaced. "Here's where I smack you on the head and say this is real life, not VR . . . except that my natural cynicism agrees with you. Building a superweapon *is* asking for trouble—especially an automated one that works in secret till the moment it lowers the boom. A design error or sabotage might well have turned the damned defense system against the Fuentes themselves. Next thing you know, all the people turn to smog, leaving cities like Drill-Press abandoned. The smog has nothing to do but drift, angry as a son of a bitch . . . occasionally venting hostility by driving local wildlife mad and sending poor Rexies to destroy random property."

"You think this attack was random?" I asked. "This room isn't closest to the entrance. The Rexy passed by the computer room—nothing in there had been touched. But the animal came here and stayed in the room, smashing equipment till it died."

"Yeah, Auntie," Tut said, "this looks premeditated. I mean, some clot of smog must have driven Rexy all the way from the countryside, into the city, onto the bridge, up an entrance ramp, down a dark corridor, past the first available door, and into a room in the middle of a long dark hall. Then the smog kept Rexy here breaking his own bones but still flailing about until he keeled over. If you ask me, that's not random. Some cloud had a major hate for this room."

"Fair enough," Festina said. "So why this room? What's here?"

"Look around, Auntie. Glass dishes. Microscopes. Autoclave. Doesn't that sound like a microbi lab? Where you might develop weird-shit germs as the basis for a defense system?"

Ouch, I thought. But Tut was right. If the Fuentes had developed a bacterial defense system, part of the work would be done in a lab exactly like this. Equipped with a big bank of computers like the ones next door. And possibly, the other rooms in this building would be development labs for other parts of the system . . . like whatever mechanisms delivered bacteria to places where invaders had landed.

Had we stumbled across the birthplace of the Fuentes' superweapon? And if so, was that just lucky accident? No, not an accident. The Unity had been on Muta for years. They'd explored other Fuentes cities. They'd gathered plenty of data—data that led them to send their final survey team to Drill-Press. Team Esteem had, in turn, searched Drill-Press till they discovered this lab. No one in the Unity suspected the true nature of what the lab had created; if they'd known it was a weapon to turn people into smoke, they would have evacuated the planet. But perhaps survey teams at other Fuentes sites had picked up hints about "important research" or "advanced weapons development" being conducted in this location. Team Esteem had been sent to investigate. Unfortunately, they didn't have enough time to analyze what superweapon this lab had produced. Only at the last had Var-Lann put together the pieces and come to a hypothesis about what was really going on.

I glanced at Festina and Tut. Both appeared thoughtful—possibly going through the same chain of reasoning I had. For a moment, I felt another pang of loss, wishing I could reactivate my sixth sense to see what was going on inside them. I wouldn't be able to read their thoughts, but if I saw their auras, their emotions, I could tell . . . *no, stop, stop. Stop thinking about it; stop wanting it.*

"Come on," I said abruptly. "Let's check the other rooms." Without waiting for them, I hurried back out to the corridor.

* * *

Two of the other rooms had also been attacked by pseudosuchians. (Tut said, "Aww, Rexy, are you in here too?" As if they were all the same animal—one who died tragically, over and over again, like some contaminated being who needed many protodinosaur rebirths to purge a karmic debt.) The devastated rooms were probably other laboratories, though their fields of research were unclear; they'd contained machines of various shapes and sizes, now smashed beyond recognition.

I probably wouldn't have known what the equipment was, even if it had been intact. How was I supposed to understand gadgets whose innards looked like dried green seaweed, or nests of thin blue tubes arranged like the back of a pipe organ? I imagined Team Esteem had prodded these remnants for hours, trying to discern their purpose. If the team had reached any conclusions, no record remained.

One door was left to open. We went through the usual routine—Festina insisting she be in the line of fire while Tut and I stood safely aside—and we let her have her moment of potential martyrdom. As with the other rooms, no threat pounced out when she kicked the door open . . . but this time we saw more than the remains of dinosaur vandalism. No Rexy had visited this room; but Team Esteem must have come here often.

It was a morgue. Or an anatomy lab. Or a torture chamber.

Fuentes corpses were laid out in a variety of positions: some flat on waist-high examination tables; some clamped to vertical slabs; some in huge glass jars; some inside shimmering silver balls of light, much like Technocracy stasis fields but transparent enough to show bodies within. Cadavers exposed to the air had dried and shriveled but not decayed, just like the Rexy carcasses in the other rooms. Cadavers sealed under glass or in stasis looked even better preserved.

All the dead belonged to the species shown on mosaic murals throughout the city—rabbit haunches, spade tails, insect eyes, and mandibles—but when I looked more closely, each specimen deviated from the norm. One's head was bloated and misshapen. Another had no skin covering its chest . . . not from dissection, but as if the creature had been born with bare ribs open to the world. A third had no arms, while a fourth displayed mandibles twice as big as normal protruding grotesquely from its face. All told, there were more than twenty deceased Fuentes on display in the room, each drastically maimed or disfigured.

"Hey look!" said Tut. "The Fuentes Explorer Corps."

Festina made a strangled noise. I'm not sure if it was a growl or a laugh.

Team Esteem had set up equipment around the room: scanners, data analyzers, and probes. The team had been examining the bodies—collecting DNA samples, taking X rays/MRIs/CTs/ PPETs/JJEs, and all the other usual peekaboos—and they were also three-quarters through a complete dissection of one cadaver, who'd been conveniently lying on an operating table.

While the team's medical and bio experts plied their trades, the hard-engineering types had busied themselves with dissections of their own: taking apart Fuentes gadgets that also occupied the room. I assumed the gadgets had been the usual things one finds in autopsy labs, like devices for testing the chemistry of body fluids or for checking the state of specific internal organs. Now that the Fuentes species had vanished, the machines weren't useful in themselves, but analyzing their components might reveal important information about Fuentes technology. Team Esteem must have hoped they'd find logic systems more advanced than anything known, or cute little black boxes that could violate the rules of physics. Carefully, cautiously, warily, they'd begun to dismantle every mechanical object in the room. The resulting bits and pieces were arranged in trays awaiting analysis.

Since Tut and Festina immediately went to examine the corpses, I turned my attention toward the disassembled machinery. I had no special expertise in electronics, positronics, or neutrionics, but I decided to give everything a once-over with the Bumbler just to see if anything noteworthy stood out. It did. I turned to my companions. "These parts," I said. "They haven't been EMP'd."

Festina raised her eyebrows. "Are you sure?"

"No signs of EMP damage. Even nano-scale circuits are intact."

"Hmm," Festina said. "So in sixty-five hundred years, no EMP cloud has come in here . . . even though the door was unlocked, there's no security system, and we think the clouds were responsible for Rexy rampages just down the hall."

"Jeez," said Tut, "sounds like the clouds were afraid of this room. Like maybe there's some kind of monster . . ."

"Shut up!" Festina snapped. "Not another word!"

For several heartbeats, all three of us stood in silence. No monster attacked. I reached out with my mind as if I still had a sixth sense, but I perceived nothing beyond what was already apparent—the corpses and dismantled machinery. At last, Festina let out her breath; she didn't speak or drop her guard, but she joined me and checked the Bumbler's data.

"You're right," she said. "No EMP damage. Strange."

"The clouds *have* avoided this room," I told her in a low voice.

"I know."

"For six and a half thousand years."

"I *know*." She looked around once more. "Either something here keeps them away—*not* a monster," she added, glaring at Tut, "but perhaps some device that causes them pain . . . or else the clouds stay away because there's some piece of equipment they don't want to EMP."

"Like what?" Tut asked. "What kind of equipment?"

"I don't know. Something the clouds like—something that makes them feel good."

"Or perhaps," Tut said, "something that would be dangerous if it got short-circuited."

"Don't you know when to be quiet?" Festina asked. "Don't you know not to tempt fate?"

"I'm just saying it's possible," Tut replied.

"Fine, it's possible. But not likely. Not when you realize that *every* EMP cloud has left this room alone. The Fuentes. The Unity. The Greenstriders. Who knows how many others. Every race that's come to Muta in the past six millennia has probably been turned to smoke by the damned defense system. How do they *all* know there's something in here they should leave alone? Do you think Team Esteem understood these machines? I doubt it. From the look of things, they were still trying to figure out what was what. Even more important, they were carefully tearing everything apart. So why when they turned to smoke would they suddenly say, 'Oh, we'd better leave that stuff alone'?"

"Maybe when they're smoke, they can see things we can't. Or maybe old Fuentes smoke can talk to new Unity smoke and explain what shouldn't be done."

Festina looked like she wanted to argue . . . then she just sighed. "Too many maybes, not enough facts. And I doubt if we'll find any great revelations. Team Esteem was here for months; does it look like they stumbled across important secrets?"

"Nah," Tut replied. "But that's how it is with the Unity: they're so damned careful, it takes them years to do anything. Look at this."

He went to one of the semitransparent balls of silver—a Fuentes stasis field. Inside was a body tucked into fetal position: arms squeezing knees, head down, tail wrapped tightly around the waist. Unlike other Fuentes in the room, the creature in the stasis sphere was entirely hairless, with bloated skin that bulged as if it were air-inflated. It reminded me of a soccer ball that'd been pumped up too much. Ready to pop its valve any second.

"See?" Tut asked. "How long has Mr. Puffy been inside this field? Since the old days, right? Since the Fuentes were still alive. But Team Esteem hasn't even opened the sphere. They saw all this stuff; and their first instinct was to draw up some long-term timetable for when they'd do what. Everything planned in cold blood. Heaven forbid they try anything on impulse . . . like this."

He pulled back his foot and kicked. It was not a particularly skilled move; Tut wasn't a dancer like me, nor had he done any more martial arts than the six-month course required at the Explorer Academy. Still, he had long, strong legs and plenty of time to deliver the strike: neither Festina nor I were close enough to stop him. I didn't even bother to try—a sharp impact might pop Technocracy stasis spheres, but who knew if the same was true for advanced Fuentes fields? Maybe they could withstand a hit . . . including the toe of Tut's boot driven full strength into the shimmering silver surface.

I was wrong. Fuentes stasis fields turned out to be just as flimsy as the Technocracy type.

The field dissipated with a hiss of released air, and Mr. Puffy tumbled onto the floor. A moment later, his spade tail whipped in a slashing circle, providing enough momentum to propel him to his feet. The alien stood there, tail writhing, mandibles weaving like daggers in front of his mouth . . . with Tut less than an arm's length away.

"Hey," said Tut, turning to Festina and me. "I found the monster that scared off the clouds."

The bald Fuentes stank—a stench like ancient urine, piercing and vile. I wondered if that was the natural odor of his species, or if this particular specimen, with his lack of hair and engorged flesh, was unique among his kind.

Of course, he's unique, I told myself. *After six and a half thousand years, he's still alive.*

I felt stupid for thinking "Mr. Puffy" had been dead—he was, after all, locked in stasis, where not a single microsecond had passed over the centuries. Since the room's other Fuentes were cadavers, I'd assumed the ones in stasis would be too. Team Esteem must have jumped to the same conclusion . . . which shows the stupidity of taking anything for granted when exploring alien planets.

But Mr. Puffy was alive. His breath rasped in and out, his tail and mandibles twitched. He looked like an angry animal in search of a target to bite. Perhaps the only thing holding him back was the strangeness of his situation. When he was first put in stasis, the room must have been full of his fellow Fuentes, plus working machinery and full-strength lights. Now the only Fuentes in the place were corpses, the machinery was half disassembled, the lights were dim as dusk, and he faced a trio of unfamiliar aliens. However upset Mr. Puffy might be, he had the sense to restrain himself till he figured out what was going on.

Tut, of course, showed no concern standing nose to nose with a newly exhumed mutant alien. "Greetings!" he said, holding out his hand. "I'm a sentient citizen of the League of Peoples. How's about some Hospitality?"

The Fuentes stared at him a moment with mandibles knitting themselves together in a complex pattern. Tut lifted his own hands to his mouth and twiddled his fingers in response. I made a soft, choking sound—when confronted with an infuriated alien, Explorers should *not* try to imitate the alien's actions. But Mr. Puffy ignored Tut's response. Instead, he turned to me. He gazed in my direction for a heartbeat . . . then suddenly, he charged.

Off to my right, something whirred: Festina firing her stun-pistol. She must have drawn her gun the instant Mr. Puffy came out of stasis, but she'd held off shooting till the Fuentes showed hostile intent. Not that it made any difference. Mr. Puffy wasn't fazed by the pistol blast; he didn't even slow as Festina pulled the trigger several times in succession.

As for me, I was frozen. Once again, I'd fallen victim to the reflexive paralysis programmed into me by the Outward Fleet: when taken by surprise, every muscle in my body went rigid. I had time to think, *Why now?* Why freeze in front of this alien and not when the Rexy pounced on Tut? But I knew the answer: I'd never expected the Fuentes to attack the instant he caught sight of me. Why would he? What had I done to provoke him? And if he was just attacking from undirected rage or confusion, why would he cross the room for me when Tut was right beside him?

So I froze. And Festina fired. And Tut said, "Hey, what'cha doin'?" None of which slowed Mr. Puffy as he leapt across the room, landed in front of me, and shoved his bloated hand into my mouth.

His urine stink had been bad before. This close up, it would have made me gag—if I hadn't already been gagging from his fat foul fingers sticking down my throat. The taste of his flesh was putrid beyond description; even now, just remembering, I feel my mouth pucker. Vomitous. I would have thrown up then and there, but the moment my stomach began its first flip-flop, some powerful force suppressed it. Like a plunger pushing down the bile, preventing the puke from rising. For a second, I had the crazed idea Mr. Puffy had extended his hand all the way down my esophagus and was physically doing something to stop my stomach from erupting. Then a more rational explanation struck me: the Balrog had taken control of my body to forestall unwanted regurgitation. Perhaps that was another reason why I'd gone frozen—the Balrog *wanted* me to let Mr. Puffy's fingers tickle my tonsils.

Even as that thought crossed my mind, I felt my teeth bite down. The action wasn't my own—if there could be anything more nauseating than the taste of urine-flesh stuffed into my mouth, it was the thought of biting that flesh and breaking the skin: spilling unknown body fluids across my tongue. But my jaw clenched anyway, without my volition; I bit full force, as if I wanted to chew off the alien's hand and swallow it.

The puffed-up flesh split in several places. Juices gushed out, squirting. Some ran down my chin; some dribbled into my throat. The alien's blood added a sulphurous taste to the repugnant flavors already in my mouth. Once more my stomach tried to vomit . . . and once more something cut short the process, paralyzing the muscles needed to spew my most recent meal.

The next moment brought a new horror: a flood of something pouring from the roof of my mouth. I could feel it streaming around the edges of the comm unit that had replaced my soft palate—as if the contents of my sinuses were suddenly spraying down at high pressure, forcing fluids past my implant to top up the goo already in my mouth. What could the fluids be? Blood? Mucus? Gray matter squeezed from my brain?

Then my teeth eased open. The Fuentes withdrew his hand . . . and just for a moment, in the bleeding bite marks made by my own incisors, small red dots glowed against the lab's faint light. Their glimmer faded instantly as the crimson specks swam deeper into the bloated flesh, entering Mr. Puffy's bloodstream.

Suddenly, the paralysis holding me rigid slumped away like a pregnant woman's water breaking. Splash. I doubled over and threw up gratefully. The taste of vomit was clean and pure compared to everything else I'd just ingested.

Then a hand touched my shoulder, and someone asked, "Are you all right?"

The words were spoken in Bamar, my first language. When I looked up, it was Mr. Puffy.

I gaped. How could a creature sixty-five hundred years old know my mother tongue? The Bamar language hadn't existed when Mr. Puffy went into stasis—in those days, my ancestors spoke some Indo-European dialect far removed from anything my modern ear would recognize. Besides, even if the Fuentes had visited Earth in the ancient past, and even if Mr. Puffy had learned the language of a minuscule tribe in the Irrawaddy river valley, how would he know to address me in that tongue? Telepathy? Could he pluck my background from my mind? Could he even learn my first language by drawing it from the whorls of my brain?

Then I remembered the red dots in Mr. Puffy's bite wounds and the fluids that had poured from my sinuses.

Spores. Balrog spores.

I almost threw up again. The whole thing, with the hand in my mouth and my involuntary chomping down, had been a data transfer. Mr. Puffy had taken one look at me and had seen the Balrog inside. He'd shoved his hand between my teeth and I'd helplessly *injected* him with spores—as if I were some rabid animal frothing crimson at the mouth. Moss had skittered into the Fuentes' wounds, then headed for his alien brain.

Now Mr. Puffy had a link to any data the Balrog chose to share. That included the Bamar language, which the Balrog had taken from my own memories. *Demon!* I thought. *Demon, demon, demon.*

I straightened up. Wiped vomit off my face with my bare hand, then cleaned my fingers by rubbing them on a nearby tabletop. Checked my clothes, and thanked whatever reflex had helped me throw up without getting puke on my borrowed Unity uniform. Taking a deep breath, I told Mr. Puffy, "Use English. Explain what's going on."

In a soft voice, speaking English with an accent identical to my own, he said, "What do you want to know?"

This time, it was Tut and Festina who reacted in shock. I enjoyed the looks on their faces.

Festina recovered first. "Who are you?" she asked.

"Ohpa," the alien said. Its mandibles twitched. "Does that irrelevant fact enlighten you?"

Festina gave a humorless chuckle. "Fair enough. I'll ask something more meaningful. How can you speak English?"

Ohpa waved his hand. "Also irrelevant." He didn't look in my direction. I wondered if he was keeping the Balrog's data transfer a secret for my sake, or if there was some other reason not to speak of it.

"All right," Festina said. "Relevant questions. What is this place and what were you doing here?"

"This place is a playroom of reductionism and control. What you would call a laboratory." Ohpa shook himself and hopped toward a cadaver on a nearby table. Under his breath he muttered something in a language I didn't know, then extended his hand in a gesture of blessing. He turned back and told Festina, "I'm here because I succumbed to hope and ambition. I volunteered to be a test subject." He spread his arms to display his hairless body; his tail gave a spasmodic jerk. "As you can see, the experiment was unsuccessful."

"What was the experiment supposed to do?"

"Make me Tathagata."

I gasped. Festina looked my way, then asked the Fuentes, "What's Tathagata?"

Ohpa waved as if I should answer—a movement so human, he must have learned my body language from the Balrog as well as spoken words. I told Festina, "Tathagata means 'the one who has come at this time.' It was an honorific for Prince Gotama, the Buddha . . . to distinguish him from other Buddhas who'd lived in earlier times or might come in the future."

Festina turned back to Ohpa in surprise. "The experiment was supposed to make you a Buddha?"

"Tathagata."

"A *living* Buddha," I said. "One who's enlightened *right now* . . . as opposed to someone who might become a Buddha in a million more lives. Theoretically, we're *all* Buddhas—we all have the potential and will get there eventually—but a Tathagata has Awakened in the current lifetime."

Festina made a face. "I'm not thrilled when an alien claims to be a figure from Earth religion. It's way too convenient."

"Ease up, Auntie," Tut said. "Ohpa likely peeked into our heads with X-ray vision, and Youn Suu's brain happened to have an approximation for what he *really* is." Tut turned to the alien. "You aren't really Tatha-whosit, right? That's just the closest equivalent you could find in our minds."

"I'm not Tathagata at all," Ohpa replied. "The experiment was supposed to make me so, but it failed."

"How did it fail?" Festina asked.

"The actual cause you would find uninteresting." Ohpa gave a sudden leap with his rabbitlike haunches, landing several paces away and pointing to a thigh-high gray box whose contents had been partly dissected by Team Esteem. "If I told you this machine had a flaw, would you be any wiser? If I said there was an unforeseen feedback loop between my DNA and the molecular logic circuits herein, would you hear more than empty words? Do you understand the complexities of dark matter and transdimensional biology, or would it be futile to explain?"

"Transdimensional biology?" Festina said. "You're just making that up."

"If I were, you wouldn't know, would you?" Ohpa made a rasping sound in his throat—perhaps the Fuentes version of a laugh. "Suffice it to say, the procedure I underwent had errors. Instead of becoming Success Number One, I became Failure Number Thirty-six. Instead of becoming Tathagata, I became a travesty."

I asked, "What did you think it meant, becoming Tathagata? A mental transformation? A process to remove fixations from your brain?"

Ohpa swished his tail, then drove the sharp spade tip into the computer-like box beside him. Fragments of broken metal and plastic spilled onto the floor. "A mental transformation?" he said. "Removing fixations? You give my people too much credit. We had no thought of changing our psyches; we didn't think we needed it. My people dreamed of becoming gods—increasing our intelligence a thousandfold, abandoning our physical bodies and becoming pure energy—yet we imagined we'd retain our original personalities. We'd be vastly more powerful, but the same people, with the same prejudices, conceits, fears, hatreds, blind spots, envies, distorted priorities, unexamined desires, irrational goals, unconfronted denials . . . ah, such fools. Believing we could don transcendence as easily as a new coat. So sure of our unquestioned values. So ready for a fall."

"What kind of fall?" Festina asked. "What happened to you? To this planet? *What's going on?*"

"Karma," Ohpa replied. "A harvest of suffering, grown from the seeds of arrogance. Trying to seize heaven by force. Taking the easy way again and again, rather than daring the hard way once."

Festina rolled her eyes. "Why do I always end up listening to gobbledygook from godlike aliens? And why can they never give a straight answer?"

"Here's a thought," Tut said. "Ohpa buddy, with your not-quite-Tathagata wisdom, why don't you just tell what we need to know? And please, your Buddhousness, give it in a form we're likely to follow. Okay?"

Ohpa's mandibles relaxed; I could almost believe he was smiling, if his complex alien mouth was capable of such a thing. Tut had done what every disciple must do: submit to the teacher's agenda rather than demanding the teacher submit to yours.

"Very well," Ohpa said. "I'll tell you a tale of hubris."

And he did.

There came a time [Ohpa said] when Fuentes scientists realized the body was not the self.

[He looked at me. He was quoting Buddhist doctrine. *One's body is not one's self. Neither are one's emotions, perceptions, desires, or even one's consciousness.* All those things are partial aspects, not one's absolute essence. We *have* no absolute essence. We're ever-changing aggregates of components that constantly come and go.]

If the body is not the self [Ohpa continued], perhaps the self could be divorced from the body—made manifest in some other medium besides flesh. Flesh is weak and short-lived. Would it not be better to place the self in a stronger vessel? One that did not age. One immune to sickness. One that could not die.

Many believed this goal might be achieved by becoming simulations within a computer; but that proved unsatisfactory. Computers could simulate a single person's intellect, and they could simulate small environments, but no computer has the capacity to simulate an entire planet, let alone the galaxy or the universe. Computerized personalities soon felt they were prisoners in tiny, predictable worlds.

But scientists determined there were other media to which an individual's consciousness could be uploaded. In particular, personalities might be impressed upon constructions of normal and dark matter. This may sound like nonsense, but your scientific knowledge is too primitive to allow for more detailed explanation. How would you describe a silicon-chip computer to preindustrial peoples? Would you tell them you'd combined sand and lightning to make a box that could think? They'd think you were mad. Some concepts can't be conveyed to those without the background to understand. You must simply accept that consciousness can be transferred from flesh into something more Celestial.

Or so our scientists believed. They still had to overcome technical difficulties.

A world was set aside for research. This world. Every person in every city was either a scientist or a support worker. If the project was successful, our entire species would use the resulting process to become higher lifeforms. To ascend. To become *transcendent.*

The research was divided into smaller subprojects. Experiments were conducted around the planet, but this building was one of two centers where everything came together. Scientists assembled subcomponents to create test processes, and to try those processes on volunteers who were willing to risk everything for the chance to become Tathagata.

[Ohpa waved his hand at the cadavers in the room.] Here lie the volunteers. Failures all. After their deaths, they were analyzed to see what had gone wrong. Errors were corrected, and the researchers would try again.

Compared to the dead, I might be considered fortunate. I survived; I even attained a partially heightened consciousness. I can perceive more than I once did—things that are hidden from mortal eyes.

[He glanced at me; I assumed he was looking at the Balrog under my skin. To Ohpa's expanded senses, the Balrog's life force might have shone like a mossy red beacon. Perhaps Ohpa and the Balrog could even read each other's thoughts to a small extent. That's how

Ohpa had known he needed to get bitten in order to acquire a load of spores and establish a full-bandwidth mental connection.]

But though I am more than I was [Ohpa said], I am not Tathagata. I am sufficiently Aware to know how Unaware I am—like someone blind from birth miraculously granted dark and blurry vision, allowing him to understand how much he still can't see. You who are still blind can't understand the torture. You have no hint of the glory beyond.

[Once again, he glanced in my direction. This time, he was looking at *me*—me, whose blindness had been lifted briefly, but who was now back in the dark. Did he mean I was a fool for rejecting the sixth sense? Or was he sharing a moment of sympathy with someone else who knew sensory loss?]

Despite such failures [he said], the experiments continued. With my spirit partly elevated, I became useful to the project. I was not wise, but I was wiser than the researchers. They sought my advice on particular efforts. They never really learned from my words, but they always found a way to twist what I said into confirmation of what they already intended to do. If I had truly become Tathagata, perhaps I would have had more effect. . . . No. Now I am merely voicing self-pity. And pity for those who suffered what finally happened.

Through trial and error—many trials, many errors—our researchers developed a successful transformation process. It worked in two stages: first, breaking down the physical body; second, reconstituting the consciousness in a higher vessel. The process worked well in small trials. Individuals truly became Tathagata . . . whereupon they departed to other realms of existence, without a single word to those who remained behind. Buoyed by success, the project leaders decided to uplift everyone on the planet, all at once. The same process would then be implemented on every world inhabited by our species.

Stage One was controlled from this very center. A global transformation system was engineered. The system created biological agents that diffused across the entire planet: clouds of them targeting each individual. Every person's DNA was automatically analyzed and duplicated by the microbial agents. Once the process was complete, the microbes infested the target's body and channeled dark matter into each individual cell. As a result, the host bodies discorporated—became nothing but clouds of particles, still partly conjoined and imbued with the original person's consciousness, but not yet transcendent.

[*Oh shit*, said Festina. *Oh shit*.

Not quite, Ohpa told her, *but close*.]

At that point [Ohpa continued], Stage Two would activate. The discorporate gas clouds, already half dark matter, would be imbued with more transformative energy, projected from facilities distributed around the world. The population would ascend as one . . . or so it was planned.

The plan failed. I don't know why; I spent my time here, in the center that implemented Stage One. The center for Stage Two lies on a different continent . . . and the people there were distant from the people here, socially as well as geographically. A childish rivalry—mostly in jest, but the two teams viewed each other more as competitors than colleagues. They did not share confidences.

So I can't tell why Stage Two failed. Stage One succeeded completely—every person on the planet was rendered into smoke. Except, of course, me. I am no longer normal; the experiment I underwent mutated my cells too little and too much. I did not become Tathagata . . . but my DNA became twisted and partly imbued with dark matter, to the point where the process that worked on everyone else cannot work on me. I was sent down a dead end. I cannot be pushed forward or brought back.

The people around me turned into smoke, then failed to proceed to full transcendence. Stage Two never activated. Those trapped in Stage One—deprived of physical bodies but denied a new state of being—soon went mad with frustration. *Literally* mad. People were never intended to remain in Stage One more than a few seconds; it's not a condition where one can remain mentally stable. The tiniest emotion flies to extremes. Impatience becomes fury. Frustration becomes homicidal rage.

I watched it happen. I watched everyone in this center driven insane by their inability to move on. My eyes find it easy to see the wrath, even in placid-seeming smoke.

For some reason, the clouds feared me. Perhaps the dark matter in my body exerts a force on their own dark matter that they interpret as pain. Or perhaps they cannot stand my very aura. Though I am not Tathagata, I do possess a grain of enlightenment; perhaps that makes my presence intolerable to them. They cannot face what they themselves are denied. Whatever the reason, they keep their distance.

[Festina said, *That explains why the clouds vandalized other rooms in this building but not this one. They hated what this place had done to them, and wanted to destroy it . . . but they couldn't bear entering the room that contained Ohpa. Even if he was locked in stasis. Speaking of which*, she said, turning to Ohpa, *how did you come to be in the stasis sphere?*]

I stopped time for myself [Ohpa said] because I had no other way to survive. My body is far from normal; it requires special food that combines dark matter with conventional nutrients. This center was the only place such food could be manufactured . . . but the clouds destroyed the machinery for doing so. I would starve if I did not take measures to preserve myself.

Since I am not Tathagata, a part of me still feared death. Besides, wisdom dictated I must not die until I had told my tale. My species still survived on other planets; they would come to investigate what had happened here. This was, after all, a project of great importance—its existence hadn't been revealed to the general public, but the government kept close watch on everything we did. Government scientists monitored everything from offplanet via observation posts and broadcast relays. They would know that something had gone wrong. Help would arrive as soon as it could be arranged; I felt I had to survive to speak with those who came.

So I put myself into stasis. And waited.

I have waited a long time.

* * *

There was silence when Ohpa finished speaking. We all must have been sorting through the ramifications of what we'd heard.

Var-Lann's theory about a defense system had been utterly wrong, yet not so far from the truth. The supposed "planetary defense system" hadn't been intended to destroy invaders; it was built to elevate the Fuentes. However, the effects were the same: the Fuentes turned to smoke, and so did every other race to colonize Muta. Stage One of the system continued to analyze newcomers' DNA and create microbial agents to convert everybody into angry clouds. Each time new settlers arrived on Muta, the system stirred into action . . . and a few years later, the settlers would be vaporized, set drifting on the wind and waiting for a Stage Two that never came.

As for what happened to Stage Two—who knew? Perhaps the researchers had made a simple but fatal mistake: they'd overlooked the EMP factor. Every Fuentes on the planet turned to smoke simultaneously. That must have caused a tremendous pulse, ripping wildly through every city. The researchers may have anticipated a radical surge of energy . . . but what if they'd underestimated its power? What if the machines controlling Stage Two weren't sufficiently shielded? If the worldwide EMP caused a breakdown in a single critical logic circuit, a power generator, or enough electrical switches to prevent Stage Two from initiating . . .

. . . everyone would be trapped in Stage One forever. Including Team Esteem. Plus Festina and Tut as soon as the Stage One system devised a way to rip them into smoke.

The same must have happened sixty-five hundred years ago. As Ohpa had said, the Fuentes offplanet would surely send teams to see what went wrong. Unfortunately, Muta's atmosphere was still chock-full of Stage One biological agents primed to work on Fuentes cells. Any team landing without protective equipment would turn to smoke immediately. Teams *with* protective equipment would get EMP'd and marooned, just like our own party. Soon, they'd be forced to take off their suits, whereupon they'd fall victim to the Stage One microbes.

How many teams had the Fuentes lost before they wrote Muta

off? Possibly the government continued to formulate plans for reclaiming the planet—with suits better shielded from EMPs, or perhaps by releasing counteragents into the atmosphere, designed to destroy the Stage One microbes. But it had never happened. Circumstances must have prevented it. If, for example, the Fuentes had a shifty government like the Technocracy's, a new party might have got voted into power, and the old government decided to destroy all records of Muta rather than taking blame for the disaster. On the other hand, maybe some new set of researchers had developed a different, more reliable process for ascending the evolutionary ladder. The Fuentes would then have no reason to return to Muta; they'd changed en masse into psionic purple jelly, conveniently forgetting the Fuentes on Muta still trapped as Stage One clouds.

They'd also ignored all future starfarers who might visit Muta and suffer the same fate. Muta was a death trap; how could a supposedly sentient race leave it like this, ready to disintegrate all visitors who dropped by? One could argue the original Fuentes researchers had been volunteers, aware their work was risky. But what about the Unity, the Greenstriders, and us? At the very least, why didn't the Fuentes build a warning beacon, telling passersby the planet was dangerous?

Perhaps they did. I could imagine other races ignoring such a beacon and landing anyway. Muta was so desirable, colonists might choose to take their chances, especially if they didn't know the exact nature of the problem. They might even dismantle the beacon to avoid attracting the attention of other races. The more I thought about it, the more likely that sounded. The recklessly territorial Greenstriders would immediately destroy any "keep out" beacon, if the beacon hadn't already been obliterated by species of similar temperament thousands of years earlier.

The Fuentes should have anticipated that . . . and in their elevated purple-jelly form, they should have taken steps to deal with the problem. If they now had godlike powers, why couldn't they just teleport inside any ship approaching the Muta system and telepathically explain why the planet was dangerous? Wasn't that basic courtesy? More important, wasn't that what the League of Peoples might demand? Surely the Fuentes were required to stop people dying from the effects of the Stage One microbes.

Unless . . .

"Ohpa," I said, "how long can people survive in Stage One? Do the clouds eventually dissipate?"

"No," the alien said. "They absorb energy from light and nutrients from the atmosphere. I don't know their maximum life span, but they can certainly remain alive for millions of years."

"*Millions?*"

"Till the sun begins to fail and renders this planet uninhabitable." Ohpa's mandibles bent in a way that might have been a smile. "In cloud form, my people are quite resilient. So are the others who've undergone Stage One. They may be insane, but they are definitely alive."

"Bloody hell," Festina murmured.

"Not bloody," Ohpa replied, "but most assuredly hell. Even with my meager awareness, I hear their screams of agony. To those with greater perception, the shrieks must be shrill indeed. But the enlightened beings of this galaxy must be inured to the sounds of suffering—they hear so much of it."

Ohpa's words left the rest of us silent . . . but the silence seemed to howl.

It was Tut who finally spoke. "Okay," he said to Ohpa, "how do we set things right?"

The Fuentes shrugged. The movement didn't suit his alien musculature, but his Balrog-inspired knowledge of human body language seemed to think it was necessary. "I don't know what you can do. I wasn't a scientist—merely a test subject. I have no idea how to reverse the effects of Stage One."

"We don't want to *reverse* Stage One," said Festina. "That might get us in trouble with the League of Peoples." She rolled her eyes. "I hate trying to guess how the League thinks . . . but if we take a bunch of smoke clouds with the potential for living millions of years, and we force them back into short-lived bodies, the League might consider that the moral equivalent of murder. Doesn't matter if the clouds are in never-ending torment; we can't cut their lives short without their prior approval. On the other hand"—she looked at Ohpa—"if we could stop Stage One before *we* get turned to smoke . . ."

Ohpa shook his head. "The Stage One microbes are autonomous. There's no switch to turn them off. In a way, the microbes form their own crude hive mind—not sentient or even very intelligent, but fully capable of carrying out their purpose without outside direction."

"Crap," Festina growled. "What kind of idiot builds an uncontrollable rip-you-to-shit system? Haven't they heard of fail-safes?"

"The project leaders feared someone might tamper with the process," Ohpa said. "They devoted much effort to making it unstoppable."

"And since you're only slightly wise, you didn't tell them they were imbeciles?"

"I told them not to mistake paranoia for prudence. But when you tell paranoids to be more prudent, they believe you are counseling them to be more paranoid."

"You didn't spell it out for them in words of one syllable? Make . . . a . . . way . . . to . . . shut . . . it . . . off."

Ohpa replied with something in a language I didn't recognize—presumably the Fuentes' ancient tongue. His intonation was the same as Festina's: short single syllables with brief spaces between. Then he switched back to English. "I told them exactly that. But they refused to listen. 'The fool knows not the wisdom he hears, as the spoon knows not the taste of the soup.' "

I glared at him. His words came from the *Dharmapada*, an important Buddhist scripture. Ohpa could only have learned that passage by plucking it from my brain . . . and it irritated me how easily my thoughts could be plundered. "So that's it?" I asked. "You've waited sixty-five hundred years to tell us there's nothing we can do?"

"Mom," Tut said, "there's *gotta* be something. We wouldn't have picked up your fuzzy red hitchhiker if our chances were nil. The Balrog must think there's some way we can shake up the status quo."

"We can change the status quo just by telling the outside world what's going on. We've got a working comm; we've got Ohpa's explanation. Maybe that's all the Balrog intended—we come and find out what's what. Now we tell *Pistachio*, and they pass word to the rest of the galaxy why Muta's so lethal."

"At which point," Festina said, "every treasure hunter in the universe rushes here to grab Fuentes tech. Then they *all* turn into pissed-off ghosts."

"What else can we do?" I asked.

"Simple," Festina answered. "Figure out a way to kick-start Stage Two."

Tut turned to Ohpa. "Is that possible?"

"I don't know," the alien replied. "I don't know why Stage Two failed." His mandibles worked briefly—maybe a mannerism to show he was thinking. "It might be something simple, like a burned-out fuse. Perhaps Stage Two is ready to go, and you just need to fix some tiny thing. But the malfunction could be more serious. Perhaps it can only be repaired by persons with special expertise. And that assumes it can be repaired at all. I've been in stasis a long, long time. By now, the Stage Two equipment may have degraded too much to salvage."

"Those are all possibilities," Festina admitted, "but unless someone has a better idea, I don't see we have much choice. We can't leave Muta by Sperm-tail for fear the EMP clouds will attack *Pista-*

chio. But if we activate Stage Two, the clouds will go transcendental, after which they'll likely leave us alone. Then we can go back to the ship and get decontaminated before we turn smoky." She looked at Tut and me. "Is that a plan?"

"I'm all for starting Stage Two," Tut said, "but why leave afterward? If Stage Two works, we can stay on Muta and turn into demigods, right?"

"Not quite," Festina told him. "If you stay on Muta, eventually you'll undergo a process created by alien scientists with a proven record of fuck-ups: a process that might work on Fuentes but was never intended for *Homo sapiens*. Sounds more like a recipe for disaster than a golden invitation to climb Mount Olympus."

"Auntie, you're such a spoilsport. Isn't becoming godlike worth a little risk?"

"I've met godlike beings. As far as I can tell, they do nothing with their lives . . . except occasionally manipulate mine."

"That doesn't mean *you'd* have to act that way. You could do good things for people who need it."

"I can do that now," Festina said. "Aren't I a fabulous hero of the Technocracy?"

"Seriously," Tut said. "Seriously, Auntie. What's wrong with being a god?"

"Seriously?" Festina sighed. "Deep in my bones, something cries out that gods are something you defy, not something you become. Humans should be standing on mountaintops, screaming challenges at the divine rather than coveting divinity ourselves. We should admire Prometheus, not Zeus . . . Job, not Jehovah. Becoming a god, or a godlike being, is selling out to the enemy. From the Greeks to the Norse to the Garden of Eden, gods are capricious assholes with impulse control problems. Joining their ranks would be a step down."

"Jeez, Auntie!" Tut made a disgusted sound, then turned to me. "What about you, Mom? You believe in gods and stuff. Wouldn't you like to be one?"

"I'm with Festina on this. Godhood is a phase of existence for those who aren't mature enough to be born human. Buddhists would never hurl defiance at the gods—that's just rude—but we don't envy the divine condition. The gods are stuck in celestial kindergarten: flashy powers, fancy toys, people prostrating themselves before your altar . . . it's just childish wish fulfillment. Hardly a situation that encourages enlightenment. If your karma condemns you to birth as a god, the best you can do is resist the urge to throw thunderbolts and hope that in the next life you'll get to be human."

"Oh come on!" He turned to Ohpa. "What about you? You're enlightened. Don't you want to be elevated beyond what you are now?"

Ohpa gave a small bow. "I yearn to be Tathagata . . . but will the process developed on this planet truly achieve that goal? My meager wisdom makes me mistrust easy solutions. Can genuine enlightenment be imposed by external forces? Can a normal being, full of conflicts and confusion, suddenly have every mental twist made straight? If so, is the resulting entity really the original person? Or is it some alien thing constructed from the original's raw components, like a worm fed on a corpse's flesh?"

Tut threw up his hands. "You're all hopeless! You've got a chance to go cosmic, but all you do is nitpick. Can't you think big?"

"Tut," I said, "suppose this process made you wise: honest-to-goodness wise. And suddenly, you weren't interested in shining your face, or wearing masks, or pulling down Captain Cohen's pants. All you wanted to do was help people transcend frivolous impulses, and recognize the emptiness of their fixations. Suppose that happened to you all at once, not gradually learning from experience, but flash, boom, like lightning. Doesn't that sound like brainwashing? Or even getting lobotomized? Not deliberately refining yourself step by step, but having a new personality ruthlessly imposed on you."

"I see what you're getting at, Mom . . . but suppose honest-to-goodness wisdom turns out to *be* shining your face, wearing masks, and pulling down Captain Cohen's pants. How do you know it isn't? Wisdom could be dancing and humping, not sitting in stodgy old lotus position."

Festina chuckled. "The Taoist rebuttal to Buddhism. But we don't have time for religious debate. We've got to start Stage Two." She turned to Ohpa. "Any ideas how we do that?"

Ohpa thought for a moment. "Stage Two involved a network of projection stations all around the planet—to bathe Stage One clouds with energy to complete the transformation. The closest such station is on this river, some distance downstream: a day's journey by foot, if your species' walking pace is close to ours. It's a large building beside a dam."

"A hydroelectric dam?" Festina asked. "I hope not. If the station depends on the dam for power, we're screwed. After sixty-five hundred years with no one looking after the place, the generators will be rusted solid and clogged with silt."

Ohpa gave his tail a noncommittal flick. "I don't know how the station obtains its power. I know almost nothing about it—as I said, the Stage Two workers kept aloof from those working on Stage One."

"Then come with us to the station. However little you know, it's more than we do."

Ohpa shook his head. "I've told you what I can; have faith it's what you need. If you yourselves don't lay my people's ghosts to rest, at least you'll pass on my words, and the news will spread. Eventually, someone will bring this to an end. But I won't live to see it—my part is over."

"What do you mean?" I asked.

He turned my way. His faceted eyes showed no emotion a human could recognize, yet I felt compassion flood from him—deep pity for my ignorance. "I told you, my body needs special food. I will die without it: very soon. I avoided putting myself into stasis as long as I could, in hopes that a landing party from my own people would find me. I only entered the stasis sphere when I was on the verge of collapse."

"We have rations," Festina said, reaching into her pocket. She pulled out a standard protein bar. "Maybe this can tide you over until . . ."

"No. My body needs more than nutrition; it needs stabilization."

Ohpa held out his hand. The tips of his claws were smoking. Evaporating, like dry ice steaming into the air. His hand didn't shake as the claws slowly vanished, and his fingers began to disintegrate.

"Stop," said Festina. "Don't you dare do this. There are still things we need to know."

"You've heard everything necessary," Ohpa told her. "And I couldn't stop this, even if I wished to. I stayed out of stasis as long as I could—until the time remaining to this body was just sufficient to do what was needed. To speak with you."

"You couldn't know that," Festina said. "You had no idea how much time you'd need. You didn't know who'd free you from stasis, you didn't know if you'd speak our language, you didn't know if we'd sit still and listen, you didn't know if we'd care what you had to say, you didn't even know if we'd be smart enough to follow your explanations. If we'd been a party of Cashlings, you'd have spent your last minutes listening to them complain how Muta had no good restaurants."

"But you aren't Cashlings, are you? You're members of the human Explorer Corps. With a mysterious knack for turning up where you're required." Ohpa's mandibles twitched. I could almost believe he was laughing at us. "Really, Admiral Ramos . . . I might not be Tathagata, but give me a little credit. My timing has been impecca—"

With a rush, the rest of his arm turned to smoke, followed an instant later by his entire body. The particles hung in the air a moment, still retaining the shape of what Ohpa had been; then the cloud dispersed, thinning out, spreading in all directions until there was nothing to see.

"Huh," Tut said. "He called you 'Admiral Ramos.' I wonder how he knew. None of us ever called you that."

Festina gestured irritably. "I've met enough higher beings to know their tricks. They're all incorrigible show-offs, they love getting a rise out of lesser mortals, and *they all know my goddamned name.*" She sighed. "They're also fond of dramatic exits. Speaking of which, we should get going ourselves."

"Downstream to the Stage Two station?"

"Where else?" She muttered something about "jumping through goddamned hoops for alien puppet-masters," then headed out the door.

14

Maitri [Sanskrit]: Loving kindness for all living creatures.

OUTSIDE the building we stopped so Festina could speak with *Pistachio*. She summarized what we'd learned, then asked Captain Cohen to do some eye-in-the-sky scouting for us. He soon reported a Fuentes building beside a dam thirty kilometers to the south. The dam had become a waterfall—silt must have closed the sluices, leaving the river with nowhere to go but over the top. Years of rushing water had mildly eroded the dam's upper ramparts, but there'd been no major collapse; the dam still held back a reservoir of cold autumnal water. The accompanying building lay on the east bank of the reservoir . . . which told us which side of the Grindstone we should be on for the trek downstream.

Pistachio's cameras didn't have enough resolution to see much detail—not from such high orbit. However, Captain Cohen had begun to build new reconnaissance probes as soon as we'd left the ship, and there'd be one ready within five hours: just enough time, he said, to gather advance data, since we'd need six hours to walk to the dam. (When Cohen said that, I thought, *Six hours?* We'd take six hours to walk thirty kilometers on clear flat roads. Traveling through brush, up hills and down ravines, following the shore of a meandering river and perhaps dodging the occasional Rexy, we'd take much longer . . . and that was ignoring nightfall, now only three hours off, plus the storm we'd seen heading our way. When Festina asked Cohen how the storm looked, he admitted, "Oy, it's a doozy.")

I wondered if Festina would decide it was safer to spend the night in the city, where we had shelter from lightning and pseudosuchians. There was also the question of Li and Ubatu; we hadn't seen any sign of the shuttle, but odds were they'd tried to land in the city, where straight, paved streets would make good emergency airstrips. I found it difficult to believe Li was such an expert pilot that he'd managed a dead-stick landing without smashing to smithereens . . . but if the diplomats hadn't died in a pancake collision, they might be lying injured, in need of medical help. With the three hours of daylight we had left, decency demanded we search for our fallen "comrades" in case we could save their annoying lives.

Then again, searching Drill-Press on foot would take considerably longer than three hours. We'd save time if we could get to one of the tallest skyscraper roofs for an aerial view of the streets. However, it seemed unlikely that elevators would still work after sixty-five centuries, and I didn't want to climb eighty stories only to find the doors to the roof locked or rusted shut. Perhaps *Pistachio*'s cameras could pick out the crash site, especially if the shuttle had blasted a significant crater in the heart of the city . . . but there might be an easier way to search: with a bit of higher help.

I settled against the side of the bridge, my elbows propped on the rail, my eyes gazing out over the river as if scanning for trouble. I paid no attention to what was actually before me; instead, I withdrew into my mind and murmured, *Balrog . . . I admit it, I can't stand being blind. How far do your senses go?*

As usual, the answer didn't come in words. A point of perception opened within me: a single point, not in my brain, but in my abdomen, my *dantien*, my womb. Though I sensed that point by means of the Balrog, this tiny part of my body seemed free of alien presence; it felt like an untainted refuge, a virgin core the spores had chivalrously refrained from violating. Knee-jerk cynicism said I shouldn't be so gullible—why should I believe anything the Balrog showed me, let alone a comforting fiction that some crucial portion of my being remained unraped?—but it felt so real, I had trouble doubting it. The point I sensed was *me*: me here and now, at this moment, complete . . . no more permanent than a sigh, no more real than any other temporary assemblage of atoms en route to elsewhere, but still, in that instant, *me*.

Then the point began to expand.

Expanding beyond tissues infested with spores, glowing red in the dark of my belly . . .

Beyond the boundaries of my skin, sweeping over the bridge's pavement where EMP clouds lurked in the cracks . . .

Up to Tut and Festina, their auras tainted with Stage One microbes . . .

Moving farther out, reaching down to the river beneath the bridge, where primitive fish darted after food or drifted with minds empty, occasionally flicking their tails to change course when the current took them near small obstructions . . .

Still growing outward, exceeding the former limits of my perception, edging up to and into skyscrapers abandoned for millennia, room after fetid room where furniture decayed under beds of mold, where strains of bacteria had evolved to thrive on Fuentes upholstery, where lice had colonized carpets and mites crawled busily through fungus-covered electronics . . .

Farther and farther, past blooms of vegetation where the city's artificial herbicides had been leached away by time, and multicolored ferns from the countryside had seeded themselves, creating little Edens for insects, maybe even for a small protolizard or toad, in areas as small as my cabin on *Pistachio* . . .

Continuing beyond, as my brain became dizzy, unable to handle so much detail—not like an aerial photograph that loses resolution as the scale increases, but retaining everything, perceiving multiple city blocks, the towers, the air, the soil, all down to a microscopic level filled with life, lifeforms, life forces, quadrillions of data elements flooding my mind, and still the view expanded, more buildings, more biosphere, every millimeter unique, all of it blazing/roaring/shuddering with energy, and somewhere in the middle, a woman whose brain couldn't take the barrage beginning to go into seizure as sensations sparked through her neurons. Too much input, too much knowledge, electrical impulses ramming down wearied axons to release volleys of chemical transmitters, her skull full of lightning and bioconductors, overload, grand mal, electroshock, white light breakdown, brain cells rupturing by the thousand in fierce flares of overexertion . . . and all observed from that point in my abdomen, like an impartial witness at my own beheading.

I can't say how long the blitzkrieg lasted—it was one of those imminent-disaster experiences that take place in slow motion, simultaneously drawn-out and fleeting—but before I could react, a dismaying percentage of my brain had been damaged irreparably. Neurons collapsed from the strain. Long-established pathways of thought got chopped into disjoint pieces. Where once my consciousness had lived, there was only a soup of demolished gray matter.

Yet I still could think. I still had the sense I was me. My heart still beat, and my lungs still breathed, because wherever my neurons burst under the rush of sensation, the Balrog instantly filled in the gaps. I could see spores annexing my brain like an invader's army: all the key connection hubs under the Balrog's control, and millions of other spores scattered like garrison soldiers at strategically located stations.

Before, I'd simply been conquered; now I was thoroughly digested. The very thoughts I was thinking had to pass through Balrog spores: like a computer network where every transmission was compelled to run along channels controlled by the enemy. I didn't truly believe my "self" was that point in my abdomen—whatever significance that point might hold, my intestines/uterus didn't have the capacity for thought. Thoughts could only be supported by the brain . . . and my brain was utterly compromised. Not just the higher centers, but the more ancient sections that controlled essential processes. My heartbeat. My breathing. My digestion. I could see spores completely integrated into my brain stem, and my own cells destroyed by the overload. Quietly, the spores lapped up the proteins and sugars released when my brain cells cracked open. Soon the Balrog would use my own biochemicals to build new spores.

I was irredeemably lost . . . and the Balrog had let me see it happen: to *know* I was watching my demise.

All this time, some part of me had nursed a delusion that the Balrog would let me go. Once I'd served my purpose (whatever that purpose was), how could I remain of interest to a higher lifeform? I was nobody special: just an ugly screaming stink-girl. I had nothing the Balrog could find desirable in the long term. Couldn't I eventually go free?

But now there was no going back. When the Balrog consumed my foot, I could have limped away, crippled yet alive. Now I couldn't survive without the spores. Vital brain cells were gone, destroyed. If the Balrog withdrew, my remaining gray matter couldn't sustain life. I was now more than a slave—I was *dependent.*

Why? Because again, I'd asked the Balrog for a favor. I'd wanted the moss to grant me a gift, and it honored my request in abundance. The flood of sensation must have been deliberately intended to cause mental overload, delivered in a way that didn't just target my perceptions but other parts of my mind as well. Why should a gush of awareness kill cells in my brain stem? But it had done so, because I'd foolishly given the Balrog carte blanche.

Stupid. Very stupid. And now my human life was over.

Unable to do anything else, I found myself laughing.

"What is it?" Festina asked, looking around as if my laughter heralded some threat.

She looked so humanly naive.

"It's nothing," I said. "Just some nonsense that got into my head." I laughed again. "By the way . . . I know where Li and Ubatu are."

Of course I knew where the diplomats were. The mind-crushing overload was past, but in its wake my awareness extended much farther than before. I didn't attempt to test the sixth sense's range—that might cause more meltdown—but what I wanted to see, I saw. As simple as that. With a brain that was now half-Balrog, my mental processes (perception, filtering, interpretation) took place on a higher level. If I chose to examine the bacteria in an aphid's gut two kilometers away, the data was instantly there: not just peeking into a place where normal sight couldn't operate, but hearing the impossibly faint sounds of microbes splashing through stomach fluids, feeling the brush of their cilia rowing them forward, tasting the tang of the chemicals they absorbed. All was within my grasp, just for the asking . . . so of course I knew where our missing diplomats were. The answer came as soon as I asked the question.

They'd landed east of the city, on a highway that continued several kilometers into the countryside. (The road led to a limestone quarry that must have supplied raw materials for the city's skyscrapers.) The highway made a good airstrip: it was one of the few paved roads that wasn't lined by tall buildings, so there was little danger of the shuttle hitting anything on its way in. Crash-landing had rendered the shuttle unrecognizable as an aircraft . . . but that just meant the craft's crumple zones had done their job, absorbing the crash's impact to protect the cockpit and passenger cabin. Other safety features had done their job too, including automatic airbags and flame-retardant materials that prevented fires after the crash—all measures that worked despite the electrical systems being EMP'd out of commission. Therefore, Li and Ubatu had come through unscathed, give or take a few bruises. Enough pain to prove they'd faced danger, but without causing real inconvenience. The sort of injuries they'd talk about endlessly at cocktail parties.

Getting out of the ruined shuttle was more of a challenge. Since all exterior hatches were part of crumple zones, the usual exit doors had been crushed. That wouldn't have mattered if the crash took place in a populated area, where rescue crews could rush to the scene and extricate survivors with laser cutters. The shuttle's designers, however, had allowed for crashes on planets where no outside help would appear. A number of hand tools were cached in the passenger cabin: drills and saws and long-handled metal snips that could (with diligence and strength) be used to mangle one's way to freedom. Neither diplomat had much knack for manual labor, but Commander Ubatu was an überchild with bioengineered muscles, dexterity, and stamina; she'd found the tools and begun cutting. Whenever she started to slow—and as a pampered daughter of the Diplomatic Corps, she had little experience with physical exertion that lasted longer than an aerobics class—Ambassador Li made snide remarks till Ubatu got back to work. Escape was therefore a team effort: brawn and bad temper. By the time we reached the crash site, they were minutes away from success.

It hadn't been hard to persuade Tut and Festina to follow me to the site. I'd told a version of the truth—that the Balrog had given me a "vision" of where the diplomats were. Festina grumbled about "the damned moss telling us where to go" but didn't otherwise question my story. She fully expected the Balrog to force images into my mind if it wanted to compel us down a particular path; that was just the sort of high-handed manipulation one received from alien parasites. It didn't hurt that *Pistachio*'s cameras could get blurry photos of the shuttle exactly where I said it was. Festina still suspected the Balrog of playing games, but since the "vision" had saved us time searching, she let me lead the way.

As we walked, she continued her report to Captain Cohen. Tut spent his time watching for Rexies, though my sixth sense reported none in the vicinity. I divided my attention between spying long-distance on Li and Ubatu and eyeing Stage One EMP clouds hiding all around us.

The clouds lay invisible to normal vision, spread microscopically thin along the pavement or compressed into cracks in mosaic murals. The cloud particles blazed with impatience: a hunger to see us removed. We were constant reminders of what they had once been. We had intelligence and physicality; we could affect the world directly with our hands. Threads of malice in the clouds' auras hinted that the *pretas* wanted to see us brought low like them—disintegrated into nearly impotent Stage One smoke.

But with my expanded perception, I saw that blazing anger was only part of the *pretas*' story. Beneath the fury, subtler feelings quivered: grief, regret, yearning, bewilderment. The clouds, after all, had been everyday people—not abnormally evil, even if they were now subject to extremes of emotion. Their desire to see us vaporized was more pique than true malevolence.

Mostly, the clouds just wanted us gone. The sight of us made them think and remember. Once we were removed, the *pretas* could go back to a neutral existence: drifting, purposeless, hopeless, hollow, neither asleep nor awake, letting the centuries plod numbly past but at least not tormented by reminders of what they had lost.

Seeing us caused them sharp regrets. They preferred the long, dull ache.

None of this was an individual decision—the clouds were a hive of hives. Each cloud was a composite being made of individual particles, but the clouds as a whole formed a loose gestalt: a collective emotional consciousness. They couldn't combine their brainpower, but they helplessly shared each other's feelings. Their auras showed that a tiny change in the mood of one cloud spread almost instantly to every other within range of my perceptions . . . even to clouds kilometers away. Conceivably, a single pang of torment might spread to *pretas* all around the planet.

So our presence caused global pain. The ghosts couldn't escape suffering just by keeping their distance from us. As long as we were on Muta, they'd feel us and burn.

Was it any wonder that the clouds wanted us gone, even if that meant sending Rexies to kill us?

One other thing I sensed from the smoke: the *pretas* didn't know about the Balrog. The moss had stayed concealed inside me; the one time it acted overtly was transferring spores to Ohpa, and that was done quickly in a room the clouds avoided because Ohpa caused them discomfort. Tut, Festina, and I had mentioned the Balrog in conversation, but Fuentes clouds wouldn't understand English, and the *pretas* of Team Esteem probably couldn't either—the Unity disdained all languages but their own. Only official Unity translators ever learned other tongues.

So the clouds didn't know what we were saying . . . and they didn't know the Balrog had hitched a ride in my body. A good thing they couldn't read auras—I could see the Balrog bright within me, shining like a forest fire. Ohpa, with his limited wisdom, had also seen the glow immediately; but the clouds were blind to the Balrog's brilliance.

If the *pretas* had known, perhaps a whole stampede of Rexies would be heading our way.

As we approached the shuttle, we could hear loud noises inside: not just the clatter of cutting tools, but Ubatu shouting and Li yelling back. Ubatu had reverted to some unfamiliar language, but I didn't need a translation—curses sound the same in any tongue. Li, on the other hand, opted for intelligibility in his outbursts. He spoke full English sentences devoid of actual profanity but loaded with the sort of insinuations that cause duels, bar brawls, and major diplomatic incidents. I could hear him accusing Ubatu of incompetence on the job, ignorance of every worthwhile achievement of human culture, and such a shameful degree of cowardice that Ubatu probably demanded general anesthetic when she got her scalp tattooed.

Listening to this, Festina rolled her eyes. "If we walk away now, will they end up killing each other or sleeping together?"

"Why not both?" Tut replied.

Festina sighed. "At least they're alive. And they sound healthy. Or rather, uninjured. So there's no need for us to stick around. We'll just leave some supplies and head for the Stage Two station."

"You think that's a good idea?" Tut asked.

"It'll be all right," Festina answered. "They're smart enough to wait someplace safe till we come back . . ." Her voice faltered. "They'll get into trouble, won't they?"

"Eaten by Rexies for sure," Tut said.

"Yeah." Festina sighed again. "We'll have to set them up somewhere warm and secure. But they're not coming south with us; they'd get in the way and slow us down. So neither of you say a word about where we're going. We'll put them in a Fuentes building, high enough up to be out of harm's way. We'll give them food and water, then get out fast before they can follow. Pretend we're going back to Camp Esteem for more supplies. With luck they'll stay put a few hours . . . by which time the storm will arrive and discourage them from going anywhere."

"You want to travel through the storm?" I asked.

"Yes," Festina said, "we can't waste time. The Stage One microbes are working on us. Who knows how long before they pull us to pieces? And who knows how long we'll need to start the Stage Two process?"

"How do you know we *can* start it?"

"I'm crossing my fingers the Balrog wouldn't be here unless there was a way to set things right. That seems to mean activating Stage Two. Maybe the Balrog will help us . . . though it's been remarkably useless so far."

I made a noncommittal shrug. The Balrog had actually helped us reach Var-Lann (by augmenting my kick on the storehouse door), talk to Ohpa (by passing on the ability to speak English), and find our missing diplomats (by locating the shuttle via sixth sense). The important question wasn't if the Balrog would *start* helping us, but if it would *stop*.

"Not to be a pessimist," Tut told Festina, "but you realize the Balrog doesn't need us? 'Us' meaning you and me, Auntie. Mom's got spores in her pores, and the Bumbler says she's immune to Stage One. So whatever needs to be done on Muta, maybe the Balrog doesn't care if you and I turn misty—Mom will survive to save the day."

"Then you should be happy, Tut," Festina said. "If you turn to smoke and Youn Suu activates Stage Two, you'll become a demigod. Wasn't that what you wanted?"

"If I become a *cool* demigod. Like a ninja Hercules, or a cross between Sherlock Holmes and Godzilla." He looked at Festina. "What about that, Auntie? Wouldn't you want to become hemi-demi-semidivine if you could be, like, a combination of Kali, Helen of Troy, and Picasso?"

"No," Festina answered.

"Cleopatra, Peter Pan, and a monkey?"

"I already said no, Tut. I respect humans more than gods or superheroes. Besides, surpassing mere humanity always has a price. Doesn't it, Youn Suu?"

"Yes. You pay and pay and pay." I tried to keep bitterness out of my voice.

"See, Tut?" Festina said. "Better to stick with humanity. It's what I'm good at. Being human."

"What if you don't have a choice?" Tut asked. "What if your only options are godhood or a billion years as a cloud?'

Festina didn't answer. None of us spoke.

We listened to Li and Ubatu snap at each other till they'd cut through the shuttle's hull.

As soon as the diplomats had a modest-sized hole in the fuselage, they pushed out the cutting tools and demanded we finish freeing them. I doubt I was the only one who considered throwing the tools in the river and leaving the stowaways in the shuttle—they'd be safe inside, since the hole was too small for a Rexy—but the opening they'd already made was big enough for the diplomats to squeeze out if they really pushed, and even if it wasn't, Ubatu's bioengineered muscles could widen the hole eventually. Then the two would head into Drill-Press, both too disgruntled for cautious behavior and guaranteed to get into trouble.

Grudgingly, we began hacking at the hull. For once, Festina didn't shoulder the hardest work; instead she sat sentry, watching for Rexies while Tut and I handled the manual labor. (I could have told her there were no Rexies within three kilometers . . . but then she'd ask questions about my newfound gift of perception. I preferred to avoid that subject, at least till I dreamed up an excuse why I hadn't mentioned the sixth sense earlier.)

Using the big metal cutters, I took a "slow and steady" approach to the job. Tut, however, threw himself into the work with vigor. He picked up a crowbar and used it to pry/smash/hammer the ship's battered hull. Soon, I heard him muttering. "The shuttle will buckle, grr-arrh. And then I will chuckle, grr-arrh. I'll rip up the tin, then the fun will begin. We'll shuck and we'll suck and we'll fuckle, grr-arrh."

"Tut," I said. "Stop that."

He didn't seem to hear. "We'll all soon be smoky, grr-arrh. But that's okey-dokey, grr-arrh. In the meantime we'll dance, and we'll rip off our pants, we'll pump and we'll prod and we'll poke-y, grr-arrh."

"That's enough, Tut," I said. But even his aura showed no response. It had taken a flat, damped-down appearance, like a gas fire on its lowest setting . . . and it had gone that way so quickly I'd been slow to notice.

"There's company coming, grr-arrh. They'll have us all humming, grr-arrh. We'll all become gods, and we'll all shoot our wads . . ."

"Enough!" I dropped my metal cutters and grabbed him by the shoulders. The instant I touched him, his aura flared with anger . . . and the same anger burst in every direction, echoed by hundreds of hidden EMP clouds watching from cover. For a moment, I thought I was seeing something new: *pretas* reflecting a human's emotions. They'd never before been affected by what we were feeling—for example, when Li and Ubatu were getting on each other's nerves inside the shuttle, the *pretas* hadn't reacted. But the second Tut got angry, the clouds responded as if he was one of their own . . .

Then the truth struck me. Tut's own aura was still flat and withdrawn; the anger that poured off him didn't belong to Tut himself but to EMP particles inside his body. I hadn't noticed them till they flared with emotion . . . and now that they were blazing, I could barely detect Tut's dull life force amidst their fierce glow.

An army of *pretas* had invaded Tut. Trying to possess him . . . just like they'd possessed the Rexy who attacked us. Maybe Tut's insanity made him vulnerable—his inability to resist any impulse that crossed his mind—or maybe the clouds simply targeted him at random. One way or another, they'd entered him so smoothly my sixth sense hadn't noticed.

Tut wasn't entirely under *preta* control—not yet. Otherwise, he'd be doing something far more drastic than chanting doggerel. But if I couldn't help him fight the clouds' mental influence, how long before he succumbed completely?

"Tut!" I said, shaking him. "Snap out of it!"

"What's wrong?" Li called from inside the ship. He and Ubatu had been watching our progress through the small opening in the hull.

"Tut!" I slapped his face, denting the thin gold surface with my blow.

"Youn Suu! Leave him alone." That was Festina, somewhere behind me. I ignored her and hit Tut again, denting his mask some more.

"Stop, Youn Suu, or I'll shoot." Festina had drawn her pistol. If she fired, I wondered if it would have much effect. When Tut shot me on Cashleen, I'd only gone down for a few minutes . . . and that was when the Balrog was new to my body. Now that I'd been more thoroughly assimilated, I suspected the stunner would barely slow me down.

"Wake up, Tut!" I yelled. One more slap to his face. Festina began to pull the trigger . . . but in that instant, Tut's aura flicked back to life. Immediately, clouds streamed out of him: erupting from his mouth, his nose, his ears, pouring like steam off his skin, surrounding both of us with fury-filled fog before it gusted away beyond normal sight. My sixth sense followed it a few seconds longer; then I turned my attention back to closer surroundings.

Festina still had the gun pointing at me, but her aura showed no intention to shoot. In the shock of seeing clouds gush from Tut, she'd simply forgotten to holster her weapon. Li and Ubatu hadn't had a clear view through the hole in the fuselage, and they knew nothing about *pretas*, so they were babbling questions that I didn't bother answering.

Tut himself was dazed, either as an aftereffect of being occupied by aliens or because I'd hit him hard several times. I eased him down to the ground. As I did, I couldn't help notice what I'd done to his gold-plated face: three strong slaps with my right hand had caved in his golden left cheek, opening a rip halfway between nose and ear. Blood trickled out of the jagged slit; when the metal buckled under my blows, a sharp edge must have gashed the flesh beneath.

Hey, Tut, I thought, *I've given you an oozing left cheek.* It seemed so ridiculous, I didn't know why I started to cry.

15

Samsara [Pali]: The ordinary world. Also, the ordinary condition of human life, filled with fixations and dissatisfaction. Samsara is the opposite of nirvana . . . but they aren't different places, they're different ways of experiencing the same place. Samsara is the sense of being messed up; nirvana is being free of clutter.

FESTINA nudged me aside and took care of Tut. All she did was dribble disinfectant into the golden crack—the wound underneath was only a nick. Then she used a scalpel from the first-aid kit as a delicate pry bar, lifting the jagged edges of gold and bending them away from Tut's face so they wouldn't cut him again. Meanwhile, she gave Li and Ubatu a minimal rundown of what we'd found out so the two diplomats would stop plaguing us with questions. Festina told how the Fuentes had botched their ascension and turned themselves into EMPing creatures of smoke . . . but she failed to mention the same would happen to anyone who stayed on Muta too long.

All the time she was speaking, I sobbed: quietly, trying to make no noise. Crying as much for myself as for what I'd done to Tut. Crying because I'd reached the limit of what I could repress. It wasn't so much emotion as a physical need—something my body had to do. I couldn't stop it any more than I could stop my heart beating. But I felt detached from my wet cheeks and runny nose; as I fought to silence my snuffles, my mental awareness continued to view the world more clearly than my teardrop-blurred eyes.

So I saw Ubatu take back the tools and finish widening the hole in the ship's hull. I saw Li clamber out into the late-afternoon sunshine. I saw Ubatu climb out too, her eyes on me as if appraising whether I was now ripe for attention from Ifa-Vodun. I saw the two diplomats lean over Festina's shoulder for a few moments before they lost interest in Tut and his injuries. I saw them gaze for a moment at their surroundings, then begin ambling toward the city. I heard Festina yell at them to stay put, and I saw both their auras flash with annoyance as they slowed but didn't stop their casual walk along the highway. They went another ten paces, just to show they didn't have to do what Festina told them. Then they turned around and came back.

By then, I'd got myself under control. Tut was coming around. "Whoa!" he said. "Whatever I drank, I want more."

"The cloud-things got inside you," Festina replied, still kneeling beside him. "Do you remember?"

"Nope. But I forget lots of stuff . . . which works out pretty well, cuz the memory gaps let me stretch my imagination."

I gave my nose a final wipe as Festina turned toward me. "What about you? What tipped you off something was wrong?"

"He was chanting," I said. "Bad poetry. He did the same at Camp Esteem while he was wearing a bear mask. I thought he'd fallen into a trance . . . like in a Unity mask ritual. Did you ever go to a mirror dance, Tut?"

"Hundreds," he said. "Now *there's* where you don't remember stuff."

Festina frowned. "And you're good at going into trances?"

"I'm a natural-born expert."

"Lovely." She rocked back off her knees and onto her feet. "I have no idea if you were really possessed, but I don't want a repeat performance. Who knows what you'd do?"

"Aww, come on, Auntie, I wouldn't hurt a gnat."

"Some things I prefer not to test."

She raised her gaze to the sky. Clouds had begun to build above the southern horizon. They weren't active storm clouds, but they were the leading edge of the front that carried the storm with it. We had maybe two hours left before bad weather hit.

"Let's find a place for the night," Festina said, raising her voice so Li and Ubatu could hear. "Somewhere we won't get drenched in the downpour. Come morning, we'll see what we can do about getting off this planet."

"I'm not staying in that Unity camp," Li told her. "They impregnate their quarters with all kinds of chemicals."

He was partly correct—we'd detected insect repellents, flame retardants, wood-smell perfume, etc., in the Unity huts—but I knew Li wasn't talking about conventional additives. Urban myths about the Unity ran rampant in the Technocracy; one rumor said Unity people filled their homes with mutagens in the hope that random jolts to their DNA would accelerate their evolution.

Of course, that was nonsense. Unity folk tampered with their genomes incessantly, but never by happenstance. The Unity mistrusted spontaneity.

"If you don't like the Unity camp," Festina told Li, "we'll search for quarters in Drill-Press. There must be something appropriate. Clean and dry and safe."

"I don't know, Auntie," Tut said. "How will we find anywhere good when Bumblers can't scan the buildings? And how will we get inside? The places are probably locked."

Festina picked up the nearby metal cutters and crowbar. "I don't know how we'll find a place, but getting past locks won't be a problem."

Festina had said we wanted somewhere "clean and dry and safe." Not so easy to locate. We'd thought, for example, that anything above the ground floor would be safe from Rexies, since pseudosuchians weren't built for climbing stairs. Unfortunately, neither were the Fuentes—with their rabbitlike haunches, they'd come from burrowing ancestors very different from our own tree-climbing forebears. Instead of stairs, Drill-Press's buildings had wide welcoming ramps, providing straightforward access for Rexies as well as Fuentes.

Similarly, the city was short on "clean and dry." As my sixth sense had already noticed, most available rooms were coated with mold and fungi. "Dry" was out of the question—humidity had penetrated everywhere, rising off the river, spread by spring floods, never going away. Even some distance from the river, Drill-Press simmered in moist boggy air. When the Fuentes lived here, every building must have bristled with dehumidifiers. Six and a half millennia later, all such gadgets were out of commission, and the skyscrapers had devolved into permanent rising damp.

As for "clean" . . . there, we got lucky. Most housing had been swallowed by beds of swampy fuzz, but a few buildings were so larded with chemical fungicides and brews of biological toxins that local bacilli and thallophytes had never established a foothold. Such places were probably built for people with extreme allergies or germ phobias; every city in the Technocracy had a few "ultrahygienic" residences for those with health problems (real or imagined), so why shouldn't the Fuentes have some too? Long-term exposure to alien bactericides struck me as a really bad idea, but one night wouldn't be too risky. I hoped. So when my sixth sense detected a building so chock-full of germ killers, weed killers, bug killers, and other poisons that it had stayed unbesmirched for sixty-five hundred years, I surreptitiously steered our party in that direction. ("Let's try down *this* block." After we'd passed four buildings whose lobbies were puffy with mushrooms, the one with no obvious overgrowth struck everyone as a likely candidate.)

Soon we'd claimed suites on the fourth floor, one apartment for each of us. Festina, scanning the rooms with our Bumbler, knew exactly why the place was mold-free . . . but she decided not to tell Li his quarters were "impregnated with all kinds of chemicals."

The apartments left much to be desired: ominously low ceilings and no couches or chairs, just thin cushions flat on the floor. At least the rooms were warm, thanks to superb insulation and a passive solar heating system still functional after sixty-five centuries.

But I wouldn't spend the night indoors. The pretense of claiming apartments was just to fool Li and Ubatu—to deposit them someplace safe while Tut, Festina, and I trekked south. Therefore, I kept a sixth-sense eye on Festina to know when she was ready to go . . . and it was a good thing I did, because three minutes after claiming a suite, she tried to sneak off on her own.

I caught up with her on the rampway down to the ground floor. "Leaving?" I asked.

"Going to Camp Esteem for more food."

"Wasn't that the lie we intended to tell the diplomats?"

"As it happens, this is the truth."

"No it isn't." That would have been obvious, even to someone who couldn't read auras. "You're heading for the Stage Two station by yourself. You think Tut and I are dangerous."

"You are," she said. At least she had the grace not to deny it. "He's vulnerable to possession. And you're already possessed."

"By the Balrog, not the clouds."

"I don't consider that a plus."

"The Balrog is sentient," I said. "It has its own agenda, but it won't try to kill you. It's even obliged to save your life if there's a foreseeable threat."

"I agree the Balrog is sentient," Festina replied. "That doesn't mean it's benevolent. Suppose it foresaw I would end up on Muta—me personally, not humans in general. Suppose there's a chance I might activate Stage Two and send the cloud people up the evolutionary ladder. What if the Balrog wants to stop that? What if it doesn't want competition from a lot of new Tathagatas? What if it plans to screw me up?"

"So it wants to prevent you from starting Stage Two?"

"Maybe. It wouldn't have to kill me; just slow me down. Then I'd turn into a Stage One cloud and cease to be a problem. Best of all, I wouldn't actually be dead—I'd be disembodied and damned near powerless, but my consciousness would still be alive. Therefore, the

League wouldn't consider the Balrog a murderer for letting me turn into smoke. The League might even pat the Balrog on the back for finding a nonlethal way to prevent the ascension of a planetful of undesirables. Muta returns to the status quo . . . till the next time someone threatens to start Stage Two, and the Balrog picks a new puppet to stop it."

I shook my head. What she said was possible, but didn't add up. "The Balrog has already had plenty of chances to stop you. As soon as we landed, I could have popped one of the stasis spheres, grabbed a stun-pistol, and shot you. I could have shot Tut too. It would have been easy . . . especially since I'm resistant to stunner fire myself."

"True," Festina said. "But the Balrog doesn't work that way. It's a tease; it times its shenanigans for maximum effect. Betrayal right when you think you've won." She looked at me sadly. "Youn Suu, at this moment I think I'm speaking to the real you, not the Balrog in Youn Suu disguise. Right now you're mostly in control. But when the crucial time comes—when I'm about to flick an activation switch or patch some broken machinery—you can't know whether the Balrog will seize your body and use you to interfere. You can't be sure you're safe. And *I* can't be sure you're safe. The Balrog is too fond of playing Ambush. You're a time bomb, Youn Suu, and I can't afford to have you near me."

"So you're going off alone. Never mind the Rexies."

"I can shoot Rexies."

"If you see them coming. And if they only attack one at a time. Suppose the clouds muster a dozen simultaneously?"

"I'll take my chances."

"What if the clouds possess *you*?" I asked. "How do you know they can't grab you as easily as they grabbed Tut?"

"They never grabbed Team Esteem," she said. "In all the years Unity teams were on Muta, there were no possession attempts. That's the sort of thing they'd have told us about—if one of their members went mad and attacked others. But their records had nothing like that. Tut's mental imbalance must make him vulnerable to the clouds. Sane people are immune."

"That's just an assumption."

Festina sighed. "Past a point, everything is an assumption. I have to make the best guess I can. Right now, that guess says I'm better off alone."

"If I follow, how would you stop me?"

She drew herself up. "Youn Suu, this is a direct order from an admiral of the Outward Fleet. Stay in this building. Do not leave for the next twenty-four hours. That's an order." A moment later, she relaxed and smiled ruefully. "As if Explorers pay attention to orders. But I'm asking you, please, stay here. If you don't, the next time I see you I'll be forced to assume you're being controlled by the Balrog. I'll stun you till your eyebrows melt, and if that doesn't work, I'll break your knees. Literally. I will punch and kick you till I've fractured enough bones to keep you from getting in my way. I'll do it on sight, without compunction. And I happen to know from Kaisho Namida, the Balrog does a lousy job of mending skeletal components. The spores will keep you alive no matter how much I beat you, but soft moss doesn't make a good substitute for hard bone. If I cripple you, you'll stay crippled for life."

She meant it. I could see no bluff in her life force. She'd hate to do it, and she'd feel sickeningly guilty afterward, but she wouldn't hesitate to put me in a wheelchair for the rest of my days—just like Kaisho Namida. Festina would damage my legs so thoroughly, the Balrog would have to replace my bones with spores . . . at which point, I'd become paraplegic. Moss from the hips down.

Suddenly, I wondered how Kaisho got the same way. Had there come a time when Festina decided Kaisho couldn't be trusted?

Festina gave my shoulder a gingerly pat. "Sorry it has to be this way. Under other circumstances, I'd love to have an Explorer like you watching my back. But I'm leaving now, and I don't want to see you again till this is over."

She turned and walked down the ramp. Around a corner and out of sight. With my sixth sense I watched as she left through the front doors . . . whereupon she ran to the side of the building, drew her stun-pistol, and waited. I'd never have seen her there with normal vision—she'd have shot me the moment I came out. But given my mental awareness, Festina had no chance of catching me in such a simple ambush.

I stayed where I was and waited. Ten minutes later, Festina decided I wasn't going to follow . . . so she set a brisk pace heading south. I waited a few more minutes, still watching by remote perception in case she set another ambush. Then I went down the ramp and took the same route south along the Grindstone.

According to navy regs, members of the Outward Fleet can legally disobey orders if there's no other way to save a sentient being's life. Sticklers for military discipline growl at the thought, but the League of Peoples cares more about lives than the chain of command.

So did I. Or at least that's what I told myself. I tried to believe I was acting out of concern for Festina's welfare and not because the Balrog was imperceptibly steering my thoughts in the direction it wanted me to go.

A sixth sense can come in handy. It let me keep an eye on Festina while I hung back out of sight. It also let me watch the rest of our party, still inside the chemical-laden apartment building. I could see as Tut walked into my assigned rooms (without knocking, of course), whereupon he discovered I was no longer there. He rushed to Festina's apartment and found she was gone too. Without hesitation, he ran after us—he guessed that we'd left to activate Stage Two, and he knew where we'd be heading.

Tut didn't try to be quiet: muttering indignantly as he raced in pursuit of Festina and me. Li and Ubatu heard him as he sprinted past their doors. Ubatu, ever the athletic Amazon, gave chase and caught Tut soon after he reached the street. She made short work of wrestling him to the ground—she must have trained in jujitsu or some other grappling art—and with the help of a vicious punishment hold, she forced Tut to tell her what was happening. By then Li had joined them, puffing from the chase but still with plenty of lung power to howl in outrage at being left behind. The diplomats informed Tut he would escort them downriver . . . and Ubatu crushed Tut's body into the pavement until he said yes.

Sorry, Tut, I thought as I eyed the mess of scrapes on his flesh and his golden mask. If not for me, Ubatu wouldn't have been so ruthless . . . but as long as my body contained a "loa" of prime interest to Ifa-Vodun, Ubatu would do almost anything not to lose touch. She'd already defied navy law to follow me to Muta. How much further would she go?

So Ubatu forced Tut to set out immediately, with an irritable Li tagging along. They didn't return to their apartments for food, foul-weather gear, or even a compass. They had no Bumbler, no comm, no stun-pistol. Tut surely realized they'd be in trouble once the storm arrived, but maybe he was hoping to escape during the downpour. Till then, he had no chance of outrunning or outfighting the pitiless Ubatu.

Besides, after the way she'd roughed him up, he might have relished the thought of leading her and Li into the countryside, then giving them the slip during a monsoon. Tut wasn't vindictive by nature, but he had his limits.

So there we were: a parade, with Festina in front, me in the middle, and Tut, Li, and Ubatu bringing up the rear. As Festina might have said, "just fucking wonderful."

My perception kept track of the entire group, though we started more than two kilometers apart. Once Festina left the developed area of the city, she was forced to slow down—following game trails rather than paved roads. I too went slower when I reached the brush, though I had the advantage of automatically knowing which routes were best (shortest, fastest, least obstructed by undergrowth). If I'd wanted, I could have beaten Festina to our destination by taking shortcuts she didn't know existed . . . but my goal was not to get there first, it was to protect the others along the way. I simply kept pace with Festina and watched the world for danger.

Tut and the diplomats closed some of the gap between us while they were still in the city and Festina and I had to fight our way through ferns. Once they ran out of road, however, they fell to the same speed as the rest of us. I thought they might slow even further; but Tut had been trained to find routes through thick forest, and Ubatu could clear paths quickly by muscling foliage aside. With such a combination of brain and brawn, they kept making reasonable progress.

Meanwhile, the sky darkened with dusk and clouds: clouds more purple and bruised than any I'd seen before. Just a quirk of Muta's atmosphere—on alien planets, skies that look like home in sunshine can assume unearthly tints come twilight—but I couldn't help wonder which clouds were simple water vapor and which were Stage One *pretas*, riding the storm like dragons.

Certainly, my mental awareness detected *pretas* within the looming thunderheads. I could sense their fury, frustration, and longing amidst the burgeoning gale, but I didn't have the delicacy of perception to distinguish one ghost from another. Were there only a few, their particles spread thinly through the mass of cumulonimbus? Or were there hundreds of the ghosts? Thousands? Millions? I could almost believe every tormented spirit on Muta—Fuentes, Greenstriders, Unity, and any others who might have visited over the centuries, only to become trapped in Stage One's hell—had gathered into a single sky-raging host, stampeding their war chariots overhead.

Tonight a great battle would be fought: a great, ridiculous battle, for we were all on the same side, wanting to end Muta's pain. But history is full of senseless wars based on out-of-control emotions rather than rational decisions.

Several kilometers to the south, lightning flashed. After a long time, the sound of its thunder rumbled up the river valley . . . but between the flash and the rumble, rain had begun to fall.

The tree-height ferns did little to shut out rain. Most had vertical fronds, running directly up from the ground like festooned flagpoles. Flagpoles don't make adequate umbrellas. A few ferns had long stems that curved into horizontal fronds resembling roofs over my head . . . but either the fronds were made up of many thin leaves and therefore leaked prodigiously, or they were solid enough to act as drainpipes, funneling every drop of rain toward some central point, then dumping it straight down the back of my neck.

The Unity uniform I wore was only partly waterproof, in that maddening way of all nanomesh. The nanites in the fabric were supposed to keep rain out while simultaneously drawing off sweat from my skin so I wouldn't stew in my own juices. (Pushing through untamed wilderness is hard hot work.) Most nanomeshes keep you comfortably dry for fifteen minutes of downpour, after which the mathematics of chaos begins to take its toll. Some random excess of moisture accumulates in the crook of your elbow, or your armpit, or under your breasts, surpassing manageable tolerances. You feel a brief hot wetness, disturbingly reminiscent of bleeding; then the fabric dispatches reinforcement nanites to correct the problem, and the wetness goes away. (Just as disturbingly.) But shifting nanites to the trouble spot thins out nanite concentrations everywhere else . . . so soon there's another ooze of moisture in some other area where rain and sweat abound. More nanite emergency crews are dispatched; more thinning occurs elsewhere; and the vicious circle spirals upward. Soon, transient seepage ambushes you every few steps, always somewhere new and unexpected; most of the time with the warmth of sweat but occasionally with the unkindly chill of a late-autumn torrent . . . and all the erratic "now you're wet/now you're not" water torture would be enough to drive you frantic if not for a more overwhelming concern: the uniform doesn't cover your head, leaving your hair, face, and neck so utterly soaked that gushes of dampness elsewhere seem like trivial annoyances.

The other people in our spread-out expedition were all similarly drenched. Festina ignored the wetness, plowing doggedly forward, her aura ablaze with determination. Tut, still clad only in masks, danced and sang whatever songs came into his head . . . a medley of smutty folk ditties, gospel spirituals, and Myriapod throat chants (the kind fashionably used for background music in VR shoot-'em-ups). Li, wet and sulking, occasionally yelled at Ubatu to make Tut keep quiet. Ubatu pretended not to hear Li over the rush of the rain and secretly hummed along with Tut on many of the tunes. Especially the dirty ones.

Over and over, lightning lit the sky, and thunder banged in answer. An extraordinary amount of lightning activity. Perhaps this was simply normal weather on Muta . . . but I wondered if the *pretas*, creatures capable of electrical pulses, might somehow be spurring the storm to loose bolts down on our heads. If so, the ghosts couldn't aim the attacks or overcome the basic laws of physics. Since we traveled low on the Grindstone's floodplain, none of the lightning strikes came close to us. Either they connected with buildings in the city (and passed harmlessly through lightning rods) or they blasted unfortunate ferns on the heights of land bordering the Grindstone valley.

If the lightning made me uneasy, it downright terrified the local wildlife. As I pushed my way forward, I felt nearby insects and lizards cringe every time thunder cracked in the heavens. Most animals had found shelter from the rain and hunkered down to wait out the weather: some grudgingly so (especially nocturnal creatures who'd woken up hungry at sunset and wanted to forage for food), others miserable at being cold and wet, still others simply putting their tiny brains on idle as they numbly endured whatever came their way . . . but all of them jumped or shivered at every flash-crash from on high.

A few animals stayed on the move: fish, of course, and aquatic amphibians . . . insects too stupid to realize it was raining . . . and six Rexies coming toward us at top speed.

Three of the Rexies approached from the south. They'd reach Festina first; and because each was traveling from a different distance, they'd arrive one by one. If she saw them coming, she could knock them out harmlessly with her stun-pistol . . . and she *would* see them coming because she'd programmed her Bumbler's proximity alarms to tell her when Rexies got close. Overall, she didn't seem in danger.

Tut, Li, and Ubatu, however, would meet the other three Rexies en masse in about half an hour.

Tut's party had no stun-pistol. Nor did they have a Bumbler to warn them of attack. Worst of all, my sixth sense told me at least two of the Rexies would reach them simultaneously . . . possibly all three. In this storm, Rexies moved much faster than humans—the *pretas* pushed the animals mercilessly, driving them to thrash through jungle vegetation without regard to safety. Their scaly skins showed numerous gashes, cut by encounters with thorns and sharp stones. Occasionally, the animals tripped on vines or slipped on slicks of wet mud, falling heavily enough to knock out teeth or fracture ribs and the delicate bones in their spindly arms. But the clouds in the Rexies' skulls didn't care about such minor injuries. All they wanted was the kill; and the sooner the better.

Thus the ruinous speed. By contrast, Tut and company moved with much more caution, plus the slowdown that always accompanies dampened spirits. There was no chance they'd outrun the predators heading for them.

As time went on, I saw one more thing: the Rexies adjusted their routes to set up a pincer operation. Two aimed for a position ahead of Tut et al.; the third would come in behind. I expected the two in front, bred by evolution to be pouncers rather than chasers, would find a place to lie in wait while the one at the rear drove the humans into the trap. On Earth, packs of wolves used the same tactic, but I doubted the Rexies had enough brains to devise such a plan. The *pretas* were the guiding intelligence, coordinating efforts over a distance of several kilometers as they brought the Rexies converging on their intended victims. Obviously, the EMP clouds could communicate with each other as well as share emotions. The ones riding the storm overhead might be acting as high observers, conveying directions to the clouds who'd got inside the Rexies' heads.

Considering the *pretas*' coordinated assault, I wondered why they'd never attacked the Unity in the same way. Team Esteem had recorded no unusual EMPs, no pseudosuchian ambushes, no odd clouds of smoke hovering in the distance. Why not? Why had the Unity been left alone for years, while our own rescue party was EMP'd before we landed and harried ever since?

Perhaps it could be explained by the knee-jerk enmity between the Unity and the Technocracy . . . and by the raw pain Team Esteem must have felt in their newly disembodied condition. The Fuentes clouds had suffered in Stage One for thousands of years; when the Unity survey teams landed, the clouds knew that the newcomers would soon turn to harmless smoke. Even as *pretas*, the Fuentes had learned some patience and restraint.

But the Unity *pretas* had no such control. When we sent reconnaissance probes into their camp, Team Esteem's ghosts must have whipped themselves into fury at the thought of hated Technocracy rivals "invading" Unity territory. The smoky Team Esteem had EMP'd our probe in outrage. When we showed up in person, they'd EMP'd us again . . . and even if the Fuentes *pretas* might have preferred to avoid direct action—or if the newly transformed Var-Lann told the others we were a rescue party, not opportunistic usurpers—hostilities had already commenced.

It didn't help that we'd talked to Ohpa (whom the *pretas* hated or feared) and that we were now marching toward the Stage Two station. Perhaps the ghosts thought we intended to destroy the station, thereby destroying their only remaining hope for release. However the *pretas* usually handled visitors, this time they'd decided we couldn't be left to be pulled apart by microbes. We had to be eliminated: the sooner the better.

Hence the Rexies. And hence, I had to do something. Which would have been easier if *I'd* had a stun-pistol, a Bumbler, or a comm. But I was just as ill equipped as Tut's group . . . nor was I enough of a fighter to take on three homicidal protodinosaurs.

The Rexies would kill Tut. They would kill Li. They would kill Ubatu. If I was there, they'd kill me too . . . unless the Balrog played deus ex machina to save me, probably consuming more of my body in the process. Either way—whether I got eaten by an alien dinosaur or an alien clump of moss—it seemed so unreal, I couldn't work up much concern over either prospect. As for the others, I disliked Li, I feared Ubatu, and Tut might become as dangerous as the Rexies if the *pretas* possessed him again. Letting them all die would solve a lot of problems.

But it wouldn't solve my biggest problem: remaining human.

I didn't want to become a thing who calmly let others be killed. I didn't want to descend into what I imagined was the Balrog's attitude: unconcerned with the fate of lesser beings. The thought of Li and Ubatu dying didn't fill me with much emotion, but the thought of me casually letting it happen—*watching* them die with my sixth sense, seeing their life forces ripped from their bodies and cast off to dwindle into the ether—that made me shudder. I was absolutely terrified of changing into an inhuman entity devoid of compassion.

So I had to save them. I *had* to. Which meant I had to do the only thing that might rescue them in time.

I had to get Festina.

If I traveled fast, taking shortcuts, I'd have just enough time to catch up with Festina and bring her back to save the others. Persuading her to help wouldn't be easy. First, I had to get close enough that she could hear me over the storm. (Briefly, I wondered whether the Balrog could amplify my voice . . . but every time I asked the moss for a favor, I lost more of myself. No.) I had to get near enough to be heard, which was also near enough for Festina to break my legs. She'd unhesitatingly carry out that threat unless I found the perfect words to stop her. Assuming words would stop her at all; quite possibly she'd ignore talk completely, thinking it was just a Balrog ploy to slow her down.

Nor would it be easy explaining how I knew the locations of six widely separated Rexies. Even the nearest was more than a kilometer away, hidden by night, rain, and shrubbery. But perhaps that problem would solve itself—by my estimate, I'd reach Festina about the same time as the first Rexy coming her way. A big toothy predator howling for blood would help make my point that our friends were in similar trouble.

But only if Festina gave me a chance to speak.

As I hurried forward through soaking wet ferns, I tried to devise a persuasive approach. No inspiration presented itself. Anyway, "persuasive" was exactly what she'd expect if the Balrog were speaking through my mouth . . . unless the moss decided to go for "fumbling and artless" in an attempt to seem more genuine. The more I thought about it, if I chose *any* effective approach, its very effectiveness would make it suspect. If I prostrated myself on the ground submissively . . . if I saved Festina's life from a Rexy . . . if I got in front of her and built one of those noose snares so popular in VR adventures, where the victims are suddenly lassoed by the ankles and yanked off their feet to dangle upside down, helpless to do anything except hear you out . . .

I couldn't believe those traps actually worked. In real life, they'd probably break your neck through sheer force of whiplash.

Broken bones were very much on my mind as I hurried through the rain.

I thought of no brilliant solution to my problem. No clever phrases to win Festina over. No inspired truths or lies to smooth everything out.

My Bamar heritage left me ill equipped for subtle-tongued persuasion. I don't claim my ancestors were scrupulously honest, but they'd never revered slick speech as an art form. Other cultures have trickster folk-heroes who can wheedle their way out of anything . . . but the heroes in Bamar folktales are either Buddhist saints who never tell lies, or else noble warriors who get betrayed (by treacherous friends, two-faced lovers, deceitful relatives) and die in elaborately gruesome ways. The greatest heroes are combinations—warriors who achieve saintly enlightenment just before being killed. Such people may become semidivine after death: *nat*-spirits chosen to serve Buddha himself as deputies and emissaries.

Perhaps I should have prayed to the *nats*; they occasionally granted supernatural protection to those deemed worthy. I even considered asking the Balrog for help—surrendering more of my body in exchange for a way to save the others' lives. But I had other options of surrender open . . . and by the time I caught up with Festina, I'd made my choice.

Festina and I met in a meadow of blue ferns: none more than knee height, most much shorter. Nothing else grew in the area but that one fern species. My mental awareness said the ferns poisoned the soil with a toxin exuded from their roots, a weak acid they could tolerate but other plants couldn't. It wasn't a unique survival strategy—terrestrial oaks do something similar—but it seemed ominously symbolic.

I'd taken shortcuts to get ahead of Festina. The path she was following led straight through the meadow, so I settled among the ferns, sitting in lotus position, waiting for her to reach me. I'd arrived before the approaching Rexy by a slight margin; Festina would have time to deal with me before she had to take on the predator.

My sixth sense watched her draw near . . . but the first my normal senses could discern was a sharp beeping sound that cut through the drone of the rain as she reached the meadow's edge. The beeping was the Bumbler's proximity alarm, warning her of danger: me. She'd programmed it to consider me a threat—no better than a Rexy.

I sat where I was and waited.

In my mind's eye, I saw Festina turn the Bumbler toward me: scanning, getting a positive ID. The expression on her face didn't change. Her life force flickered briefly with anger, sorrow . . . then she tightened the Bumbler's shoulder strap so it wouldn't bounce and strode purposefully forward.

I wondered if she'd try shooting me first. It might have had some anesthetic effect. But Explorer training taught her not to waste a stun-pistol's batteries when it wouldn't do the job.

Her first kick came down hard on my left calf. I was, as I've said, in lotus position: sitting cross-legged, with my feet lifted up on opposite knees. The position had already put stress on my tibia and fibula; Festina's kick snapped both bones at my ankle, the sound nothing more than a dull pop surrounded by meat. I'd promised myself I wouldn't react. I still couldn't help a gasp. The pain centered on the point of impact—the stamped flesh, not the broken bones. But my perception let me see the damage under the skin, the jagged bone ends slicing into muscle and tendon, the irrevocable shattering of my ability to dance.

I'd always been a dancer. I'd always been able to use that as a means of freedom. Now, my dancing was done.

Of course I felt the other kicks. The one that broke the bones in my other ankle. The ones that turned my knees to useless gumbo. The ones that pummeled my femurs, but were unable to break such big strong bones against ground that was soft with rain. I felt Festina's bootheel slam into me again and again; I felt it every time. But those kicks were only restatements of a truth I'd learned with the very first impact:

While I'd been able to dance, I wasn't quite a complete Ugly Screaming Stink-Girl. Though I never realized it, I'd been someone who could escape into blissful motion . . . and while I was moving, I could be radiant.

Now that was over. Lost. Squandered. As usual, I hadn't realized what I was giving up until it was too late.

When Festina finally stopped crippling me, she stood motionless for a moment. She seemed so tall. I'd been the same height once.

Then she turned away and vomited into the ferns.

Seconds later, the Bumbler's proximity alarm began to beep again: the Rexy, rushing toward us from the far side of the meadow. In Festina's aura, I saw an impulse to let it come: she considered waiting there in quiet submission like I had. Quitting and letting it all be over. No more pursuit of duty. The pain of the Rexy's claws and teeth, then nothing.

But the avalanche of karma propelled her onward. Wearily, she pulled her stun-pistol, steadied her aim, and waited for the Rexy's charge. She fired three times as it hurtled down on her, then stepped aside as the predator's body continued forward, unconscious, sliding through the wet ferns like a sled on ice.

Carefully, Festina picked up the Bumbler and scanned the great lizard to make sure it was unconscious. Then she forced herself to scan me too, to check her own handiwork.

When she set down the Bumbler the dampness on her face was more than rain.

"All right," she said in a too-harsh voice. "You wouldn't be here if you didn't want something. What is it?"

I told her. Nothing about my sixth sense—just that Rexies were converging on the others, and they needed her help. When I was done, she closed her eyes: squeezed them shut as if they stung. She laughed without humor. "Yes. Yes. Of course, I'll save them. What choice do I have? Gotta do the right thing, don't I? The right fucking thing."

She sat down beside me on the rain-soaked ferns. Drizzle pattered around us. Finally, she asked, "What do you think, Youn Suu? Did the Balrog foresee even this?"

"I don't know."

"But you knew what I'd do, didn't you."

"Yes."

"And you did it anyway. To save people's lives."

"Not really."

She looked at me. "No?"

"Saving lives sounds too heroic. Just that . . . if I didn't do it . . ."

I didn't know how to finish the sentence. We both sat in silence for a few heartbeats. Slowly, Festina got to her feet, as if fighting a fierce arthritis. "Does it hurt?" she asked.

"Yes."

"Will it hurt more if I carry you?"

"Probably not."

She tried to smile. "Not much left to injure. If I take you with me, can I still make it back to the others before the Rexies?"

"I think so."

"On Cashleen, I had to carry Tut. Now I have to carry you." Her smile became a bit more real. "Damned rookie Explorers, always getting themselves . . ."

Abruptly, she turned away. I wished my sixth sense would stop showing me the pain that threatened to crush her.

With a lurch, she picked me up. She must have thought if she held me so tight I couldn't see her face, she could hide what she was going through.

16

Arhat [Pali]: One who has achieved total enlightenment by heeding the words of the Buddha. Arhats are as completely transcendent as Gotama Buddha himself. The only difference is that Gotama perceived the truth on his own, without a teacher, while arhats needed assistance from the Buddha's words.

FESTINA carried me in a firefighter's lift, just as she'd carried Tut. I weighed considerably less than he did, so she managed to move at good speed: ten seconds jogging, ten seconds walking, over and over again. The jogging hurt as I bounced on her shoulder—hurt both of us, I could tell—but we pretended we couldn't hear each other's gasps over the rain.

Overhead the lightning had eased off, though another active storm cell would arrive soon. We were left with cool drizzle on mud. Puddles splashed under Festina's boots, and her jogging feet kicked dirty spatters so high they sometimes struck my face. Within seconds, the rain would wash me clean again. Our nanomesh uniforms had long ago lost the fight to stay waterproof; Festina and I were soaked to the bone.

Soaked to what few bones I had left.

Outwardly, my legs looked intact—the Balrog continued to hide its presence from spying eyes (from *pretas* or anything else watching). Inwardly, however, my legs were a mossy mess.

The bones were mostly gone: their remnants broken down by the Balrog into basic elements, to be used as raw materials for constructing new spores. The spores had then moved on to dismantle adjacent tissues—the muscles, tendons and ligaments damaged in Festina's attack. A number of important blood vessels had been severed by sharp bone fragments; if not for the Balrog, I might have bled to death through gashed arteries. But the spores had stopped the hemorrhaging . . . they'd reinforced my skin so no bone shards sliced into open air . . . and they'd restored blood flow to whatever parts of my legs remained human.

All this I saw through my mental perception: how little of me was left from hips to toes. And the Balrog hadn't finished. It was still mainly occupied with emergency repairs to keep my condition stable. Once it stanched my wounds, I had no doubt it would annex whatever flesh remained healthy—cleaning up unfinished business, but always invisible from the outside.

At least the pain was gone. The nerves at my injury sites had been cannibalized to make spores, so my brain could no longer receive neural messages of agony. No sensation at all below the pelvis. But my brain was not the only player in the game of "Who Is Youn Suu." There was also that sentient point in my abdomen (my womb, my *dantien*) which served as the seat of higher perceptions. The Point of *Me*. It watched with perfect clarity as my legs became alien territory. When I finally tried to move them—when I summoned the courage to try—nothing happened. The legs (no longer *my* legs) remained as limp as death.

I found myself speaking aloud: "Consider this body! A painted puppet with carpentered limbs, sometimes injured or diseased, full of delusions, never permanent, always changing."

"Is that a quote?" Festina asked, grunting under my weight.

"From the *Dharmapada*," I told her. "Look at these brittle white bones," I went on, "like empty husks of fruit left to rot at the end of summer. Who could take joy in seeing them?"

"Buddhism is such a cheery religion," Festina muttered. "Then again, my nana used to recite similar lines from Ecclesiastes."

"This body is only a house of bones," I quoted, "and I have searched many cycles of lives to find the house-builder. Who would construct such an edifice of grief? But now I have seen it was always my own hands wielding the tools . . . and knowing that, I shall not build this house again. I shall let the rafters fall. I shall let the bones break. I shall let in the sunlight of wisdom, so that when death comes I shall not be condemned to another prison of bones."

Festina suddenly broke into a true run—not just the jog she'd been using. Her aura showed some thought had upset her. I asked, "What is it? What's wrong?"

She ran for a few more seconds, then sighed and slowed to a walk. "You said 'when death comes' . . . how do you know it will?"

"Everyone dies, Festina."

"Every human does. But you aren't human anymore." She paused. "How much do you know about Kaisho Namida?"

"I've read *Pistachio*'s files." I gave a weak laugh. "Since the Balrog first bit me, I've read them at least ten times."

"Navy files are incomplete," Festina said. "The Admiralty lost touch with Kaisho as soon as she left the rehab center. I was the only one she kept in contact with. For a while, I . . . never mind. But know one thing, Youn Suu. Kaisho was middle-aged when she got bitten by the Balrog; now she's a hundred and sixteen, but physically, she's younger than me. The Balrog has rejuvenated her tissues."

"The few tissues she has left."

"The Balrog will never consume her entirely. That would be a nonsentient act. As long as the Balrog's alive, Kaisho will be too. I'm not sure Kaisho will ever die."

"Even the Balrog has to die eventually," I said. "If nothing else, it can't survive the end of our universe."

"Can't it?" Festina began jogging again. "These creatures . . . the ones way up the evolutionary ladder . . . they come and go from our universe . . . at least we think they do . . ." She slowed, out of breath. Not even Festina Ramos could jog, talk, and carry a full-grown woman without getting winded. "I was on Cashleen when the Balrog appeared," she said. "Spores literally came from nowhere. The

Cashlings got it on camera: one moment there was nothing, then there were spores."

"We know the Balrog can teleport," I said.

"But there was no trace of incoming matter or energy. It didn't look like the Balrog was traveling in some other form through our universe, then reconstituted itself into spores. There was no discernible transmission. The spores just showed up. From elsewhere. From outside." Festina jogged a few more steps. "Other species do the same—the purple-jelly Fuentes, for instance. Researchers think these creatures spend most of their time outside the normal universe . . . whatever the hell that means. Anyway, the end of our universe may not guarantee the end of the Balrog. It may have someplace else to run."

"Nothing lasts forever," I said. "Nothing is permanent. Even if the Balrog doesn't die a conventional death, it can't just go on and on. It *can't*. Over time it'll change into something different, the way rocks break down into soil. Then the soil is used by plants, the plants are eaten by animals, and everything keeps changing forever. If the Balrog lives in some universe where entropy doesn't apply, there'll be something else that makes things change. Impermanence is an inescapable fact."

I could sense Festina smiling, though I wasn't looking at her face. "That's the voice of your upbringing," Festina said. "If my nana were here, she'd lecture you on *her* inescapable facts: everlasting heaven, everlasting hell, everlasting souls, everlasting everything else . . . except, of course, for the physical universe, which she discounts as fleetingly insignificant. Nana sees immortality everywhere." Festina chuckled. "If it's any consolation, Kaisho Namida is on your side. She believes devoutly in change and impermanence."

A chill went through me. "Is Kaisho Buddhist?"

Festina nodded. "Zen meditation every day . . . at least until the Balrog took her."

"You mean the Balrog has only claimed two human beings in all history, and *both* have been Buddhist women? Female Buddhist Explorers?"

"Ooo." Festina's aura flickered. "Ouch. When you put it that way, it's an odd coincidence. I *hate* odd coincidences." She walked a few steps. "How many practicing Buddhists do you think we have in the Explorer Corps?"

"I'm the first Explorer ever from Anicca—I checked the records once, out of idle curiosity. And Anicca's the primary center for all Buddhist traditions. There are small retreats and communities on a lot of Technocracy worlds, but the only other planet with a sizable Buddhist population is Shin'nihon."

"Which was Kaisho's homeworld," Festina said. "I remember her once telling me . . . fuck."

"What?"

"Five years ago—after she'd been infected by the Balrog. Kaisho and I were talking about something else, when all of a sudden she told me she was the only Explorer ever to come from her world. She mentioned it completely out of the blue. When I asked why she'd brought it up, she said I'd figure it out someday." Pause. "By which she must have meant today. Damn, I hate precognitive aliens!"

"So Kaisho's the only Explorer from Shin'nihon, and I'm the only Explorer from Anicca. The odds are good we're the only Buddhists ever to join the corps."

Festina nodded. "There've only been a few thousand Explorers since the corps began . . . and most were drawn from the core worlds, where it's hard to find *any* religion beyond the usual vague sentiments."

She broke into another jog, while I returned to thoughts of Kaisho. If she and I were the only two Buddhists who'd ever become Explorers . . . and both of us had been taken by the Balrog . . . what did that mean? That Buddhists were better suited to the experience? That we could handle it better because of our mental discipline? That we were easier to invade because we were more open?

Or maybe just that our flesh tasted sweet from being lifelong vegetarians.

Of course, Kaisho followed Zen—a different tradition from my own Tarayana. But the two traditions had much in common. Zen had been a significant influence in the early days of Tarayana . . . and since that time, there'd been cordial relations between the two, allowing for a degree of intermingling and convergence. Different roots but not so different in modern practice.

Zen and Tarayana. Kaisho and me. Avatars of the Balrog. Why?

"It has to mean something," Festina said. "Five years ago, Kaisho made sure I knew. Unless the Balrog was just playing games: trying to make us think there's significance when there isn't. Taking another Buddhist woman to fool us into believing there's a pattern."

I opened my mouth to say I didn't like being consumed, physically and mentally, just so the Balrog could create a false mystique about its actions. But even as that thought glowered in my mind, a different one arose: *So what?*

So what?

So what?

A thing had happened. I wouldn't have chosen this fate if I'd been given the option, but so what? Life was full of unasked-for results. Sometimes you got sick; sometimes you got hurt; sometimes you got a windfall success from pure unadulterated luck. Or from karma. Karma was something we all had to live with: a web of cause and effect so vast that no one could fathom it.

So what?

So what?

So what?

So what if my life had irreparably changed . . . for an important reason, a trivial reason, or no reason at all? Change happened to everybody, all the time—sometimes devastating change through no fault of your own. Sixty-five hundred years ago, a Fuentes scientist had made a mistake (possibly major, possibly minor) and ever since, millions of beings had been unjustly condemned to endure a *preta* purgatory. Maybe our party would join them; maybe we'd somehow save them. Rescuing people was better than getting trapped ourselves . . . but there'd always be more trouble, new trouble, one thing after another, and no one could dodge every bullet.

So what? What to do? What could *anyone* do?

Simple. You did what you could, in the here and now. Nothing else was possible.

The past was past. Remember, but let it go.

The future was not yet with us. Wise people planned and prepared, but didn't obsess.

All anyone has is the present. Live there.

It sounds so trite when put into words. Stock phrases everyone has heard a thousand times. But in those few moments, as I bounced along on Festina's shoulder, the words fell away like shabby clothing to reveal pure nonverbal reality. As if words were like a boat that had helped me across some river. Now I was on the other side, and could proceed forward without assistance. No words, no platitudes, just inexpressible realization: unvarnished unspeakable truth.

A path you can identify as a path isn't The Path. A truth you can put into words isn't true enough.

Thus I experienced a wordless release while Festina carted me down a game trail in the middle of a rainstorm.

So what? Why fixate? Be free.

Don't ask why it happened then; how can such a thing be explained? And I realized this brief flash of freedom might be the Balrog's work. Regions of the brain's temporal lobe can be stimulated to create artificial feelings of spiritual awe. The spores in my head could have granted me a bloom of the numinous to distract me from other trains of thought, to keep me quiet, or simply to toy with me . . . the way you scratch a dog's belly and laugh at how much the dog likes it.

But I accepted that. I could live with it, as I could live with all the universe's other ambiguities. Would getting upset solve anything? Would it improve my life or anyone else's? No. So let it go.

Let it go.

Let everything go.

* * *

I told Festina about my sixth sense. How it let me perceive at a distance: the *pretas*, the Rexies, Tut and the diplomats. How I could sense a person's life force, including hidden emotions. How, back in Drill-Press, I'd overextended my brain and ended up with spores replacing much of my gray matter.

In other words, I told the truth. Up till then, I'd clutched my secrets as if they were rubies everyone else wanted to steal . . . but that furtive privacy had just been ego. The terror of being vulnerable. A desire to keep an ace up my sleeve. The dread of being chided for withholding important facts.

Disclosing the truth didn't hurt me. Why should I have thought otherwise? And Festina didn't react badly. She'd stopped trusting me long ago, and she knew the Balrog had senses beyond the human norm. I was telling her nothing she hadn't already considered. Her aura showed no self-consciousness at my ability to see beneath her defenses. Instead of getting flustered, she shifted into a virtually emotionless state, thinking through possibilities. I couldn't read her mind, but I believed she was debating how to use me: like a new kind of Bumbler, capable of scanning uncharted spectra.

If nothing else, she let me guide her on the shortest route back to Tut. The trip took slightly longer than expected, because Tut's group had stopped moving forward—they'd reached a clear area on the Grindstone's bank and had stopped while Li fussed about something. I could have eavesdropped to determine the exact nature of his complaint, but his aura revealed that the specifics didn't matter. Ambassador Li was cold, wet, and angry. He felt useless as Tut found trails and Ubatu ripped through foliage, so he latched onto some flimsy pretext to raise a fuss. Just to get attention.

Li couldn't stand being ignored. I saw that he bullied people out of loneliness . . . and how could I not sympathize? Hadn't I done ridiculous things for the same reason? Still, it didn't make his behavior any less obnoxious; and in this case, Li's grandstanding might have disastrous results. I'd calculated our travel times based on the assumption that Tut and the diplomats would keep trekking ahead.

Unfortunately, they'd remained on that riverbank five whole minutes while Li cursed and stomped about. It would therefore take Festina and me five extra minutes to reach them . . . which meant the Rexies might get there first.

I would have told Festina to drop me and go on alone, but that wouldn't help. My weight slowed her down, but my sixth sense compensated by showing the fastest routes. We were already going as fast as we could.

So were the Rexies.

The bank where Li was having his tantrum rose three meters above the water below: a low weedy cliff overlooking the river. The top of the bank was mostly chalk-white grass growing ankle high . . . but here and there, slightly taller red ferns had put down roots, where they stood out like blood drops on snow. Not that a normal human eye could discern the color—it was full night now, and with rain clouds blocking the stars, the darkness hung as thick as a velvet blindfold. Only my sixth sense let me perceive more than shades of gray in the ponderous black. (Festina carried a chemical glow-tube, tied in a loop round her belt. Tut and the others, however, had no light at all: one of the many things Li was railing at. "Stumbling blind through this stinking bush. I *hate* the smell of mustard!")

The darkness must have impeded the Rexies too—they were built for daytime hunting, so their eyes were relatively small, not the bulging orbs needed for regular nocturnal prowls. Still, the killer-beasts were driven by *pretas* who seemed unhindered by lack of light. Whatever senses the EMP clouds possessed, they could keep the Rexies on track despite the night and the rain. Perhaps the *pretas* had some limited form of the Balrog's mental awareness; that might have been a "gift" they'd received from their incomplete ascension. But whatever their abilities, the clouds were nowhere near the Balrog's omniscience. They couldn't, for example, perceive the spores inside me . . . which is why the Rexies were going after Tut instead of straight for me.

Three Rexies: two in front, one behind. As I've said, the *pretas* planned to catch Tut and the diplomats using pincer tactics, with the rear Rexy driving the prey into ambush by the two others. The two at the front had taken good pouncing positions a short distance up the trail, in a region of bush where tall ferns provided more cover than the low foliage on the bank. But as Festina and I approached, the *pretas* must have realized they wouldn't be able to spring their trap—our route would bring us to the two lurking Rexies before the third Rexy was in position. Festina would have time to stun the two predators, leaving only one Rexy to attack.

Furthermore, the remaining Rexy couldn't rely on surprise. It would have to charge across the open area of the bank, letting Tut and the others see it coming. At that point, the odds would be three humans to one pseudosuchian in a straight-up, in-the-clear fight. Human blood would surely be spilled, but the Rexy just wasn't big enough or strong enough to guarantee total victory. Tut was the same size as the predator, and Ubatu was slightly taller. Together, they might batter the Rexy into unconsciousness before it ripped out their throats.

Which meant if the *pretas* wanted surefire kills, they needed a new plan. They opted for simplicity: a massed assault. The Rexies in front broke away from their ambush positions and raced toward the bank, as the one at the rear did the same.

"Drop me," I told Festina. "Now you have to run."

Ubatu heard them first, thanks to her bioengineered hearing. But the Rexies made no effort to be silent, and within seconds even Li picked up the sounds of human-sized dinosaurs crashing through the foliage. The diplomats stared blindly into the dark, straining for a glimpse of their attackers . . . but Tut, with a grin on his face, didn't bother to look. Instead, he pulled on the bear mask and flexed his fingers like claws. Softly he whispered, "Grr-arrh."

Meanwhile, Festina sprinted toward the scene. The light on her belt let her see well enough to set a fast pace, and the trail she was following led straight to the open riverbank. She wouldn't get there before the Rexies; but if Tut and the diplomats could withstand the first assault—even if they just dodged or ran for cover—Festina would do the rest.

Provided she didn't get killed in the process. Her stun-pistol could fell a Rexy with only a few shots, but it wouldn't handle three at once.

I myself was out of the picture. Festina had set me down on the trail, and I sat there, seeing everything, doing nothing. Not yet. There would come a moment when I'd have to . . . no, I dismissed the thought. The future had not yet arrived; all I had was the present.

A present in which people were fighting for their lives.

All three Rexies screeched simultaneously: their piercing eaglelike cry. Tut screeched back, imitating the sound; a moment later, Ubatu did too. Her aura flickered with fearful hope she might frighten the animals off . . . but Tut was just shrieking for the fun of it.

The Rexies were not intimidated. As they reached the open bank, they screeched once again in unison; then they charged.

Tut went for the one in the rear. I thought he might try the clothesline maneuver again, since it worked so well in Drill-Press . . . but Tut never used the same trick twice. Instead, as he and the Rexy converged, he suddenly dropped to the dripping-wet grass and slid forward on his butt, easily passing under the snapping bite aimed at his face. If the Rexy had reacted quickly, it might have jumped on top of Tut with its great clawed feet, gouging his entrails with a few brisk swipes; but neither the dim-witted dinosaur nor the EMP clouds possessing it had been prepared for Tut's move. He slid on by, then spun to his feet with a helicopter swing of his legs. Half a second later, he'd jumped on the Rexy's back: one arm around its throat, the other pushing its head forward to expose its spine.

Then he slammed the bear mask's muzzle against the back of the Rexy's neck.

For a moment, I didn't understand what he was doing. Then I realized he thought he could bite through the dinosaur's vertebrae . . . as if he really *was* the mask he wore, able to snap with the sharp white fangs like a genuine bear. He'd have done more damage if he used his own teeth—the mask's jaw was locked in place so it couldn't open or close. When Tut smashed it up against the Rexy, all he did was dent the mask's nose.

But.

The Rexy wasn't built to carry a man-sized weight on its back . . . especially not on slippery wet grass while homicidal clouds interfered with its normal mental functions. The animal lost its footing and went down with a wailing cry. The cry ended when something went pop: the deceptively soft sound of bones breaking. Tut's bite had done nothing effective, but with his right arm around the Rexy's throat and his left still exerting forward pressure, the extra momentum of the fall had snapped the beast's neck.

For a moment, the Rexy's life force was nothing but anger: an outraged fire, furious for Tut's blood. Then the aura changed to confusion and fear; the panic of an animal discovering it can no longer move its limbs or tell its lungs to breathe. Perhaps outwardly, the Rexy looked dead—motionless, heart stopped—but inwardly, its brain would take minutes to die with the blood in its skull growing stale. Smoke leaked from the creature's mouth as the *pretas* who'd driven the animal to its fate now fled. The Rexy would die alone . . . bewildered by what was happening, frightened of being powerless, eventually slipping into stoic numbness as it waited for the end.

Tut stood and gave the Rexy a kick. Then he threw back his head and roared in triumph. Two seconds later he raced into the bush, making bearlike growls . . . as if he'd forgotten his companions. He never even looked back.

Meanwhile, Li and Ubatu had to deal with the other two Rexies. Li (true to form, but with indisputable common sense) ran away as best he could. Since running forward or back would take him too close to murderous Rexies, Li went the only way left: toward the river. Despite the darkness, he found the edge of the bank and eased himself over. Weeds grew on the low, muddy cliff above the water; Li got a stranglehold on some well-rooted ferns and dug his feet into the mud, plastering his body against the cliff side. His clothes, his hands, his face, were instantly covered with muck . . . but his grip was secure and his position safe—below the bank's lip so the Rexies couldn't see him, but above the torrents of the rain-swollen river.

Ubatu, however, didn't run. She thought she was a fighter; and the way she'd wrestled Tut into submission proved she knew some martial arts. Unfortunately, practicing in a gym or scuffling with an unaggressive man like Tut wasn't the same as dealing with two reptilian killing machines. If Ubatu had tried surprise tactics, she might have come through unscathed—we'd already seen that a Rexy's minuscule brain couldn't deal with the unexpected. But Ubatu chose to confront the pseudosuchians as if they were honorable opponents facing her in a dojo. I think she even bowed to them . . . though perhaps she was just assuming some preparatory jujitsu stance I didn't recognize.

It didn't help that her form of combat was based on grapples and throws. Rather than delivering strikes from a distance, she obviously intended to close with the animals—grabbing them, forcing them to the ground, maybe trying a chokehold to make them surrender. As if they were likely to moan, "I give up," and congratulate Ubatu on a well-fought match.

But that's just my uninformed guess. I don't know what Ubatu really planned; she never got a chance to explain.

One Rexy reached her a fraction of a second before the other. She grabbed the first by its small weak arms and began rolling back as if she were going to pull the animal with her, probably tossing it over her head.

Imagine her surprise when a spindly limb broke off in her hand. Snapped away clean at the elbow.

The arm had been flimsy to begin with . . . and the Rexy's *preta*-driven rush through the jungle had caused several damaging falls:

falls that fractured the arm with numerous cracks, to the point where Ubatu's bioengineered strength could finish the job of impromptu amputation. She continued rolling backward—couldn't stop her momentum—but now she was desperately off-balance, only gripping the Rexy by one of its arms while still holding the detached limb in her other hand like some blood-gushing back scratcher.

Ubatu hit the ground awkwardly: far from the smooth roll she must have intended. The Rexy came with her but slowly, not jerked off its feet the way a human might have been. (Jujitsu throws are designed for tossing *Homo sapiens*, not pseudosuchians with a completely different musculature and weight distribution.) Instead of sailing cleanly over Ubatu's head and smacking into the ground, the Rexy landed on top of her—screeching like a demon and snapping its jaws in an effort to bite anything within reach. Ubatu clubbed its snout with the severed arm she held, gashing the Rexy with its own claws; but the animal scrabbled wildly with its legs, trying to get away and stand up. Its great taloned feet raked Ubatu's own legs, shredding her trousers and gouging the skin beneath. She was lucky the claws hit no major blood vessels . . . lucky too that the Rexy just wanted to right itself rather than use its claws to cripple her. Even so, one talon pierced her left thigh, punching deep into the meat before the Rexy stumbled away. With an injury like that, I didn't know if she'd be able to stand, let alone maneuver and fight.

Then the second Rexy stepped in and sank its teeth into her face.

It was probably aiming for her throat—instinct would dictate attacking the quickest-kill target—but in the dark and confusion the Rexy missed its mark. The animal's huge mouth nearly engulfed the front half of Ubatu's head, jaws on either side of her face. Not quite enough strength to crush her skull, but the teeth punctured both her cheeks and scraped against bone at her temples. For a moment, the Rexy *chewed*; then Ubatu got her hands up and pushed the beast away. Its teeth minced her face some more as they dragged free. Ubatu tried to club the Rexy's snout with her fist, but it moved back too quickly, out of reach. Preparing for another attack? No. It turned its head aside and spat out its mouthful of cheek flesh and blood.

The Rexy didn't like the taste of Earthling meat. The animal spat again in disgust. Bits of Ubatu's face spattered down on top of her.

Festina ran into the open area, stun-pistol ready in hand. Neither Rexy noticed her; they were both too busy fighting the *pretas* inside their heads. My sixth sense told me the *pretas* wanted the animals to finish off Ubatu: she was down, with one leg injured and her eyes blinded by her own blood. But one Rexy—the one whose arm had been torn off—was afraid to close in on the woman who'd done it, while the other was still too revolted by the flavor of human flesh to take another bite. In the long run, the *pretas* would conquer the beasts' resistance by sheer force of will . . . but in the short term, the Rexies had managed a standoff by brute stubbornness.

Which meant Festina got off her first shot while the Rexies stood doing nothing.

The pistol's hypersonics focused on the nearest animal—the one still bleeding from the stump of its pulled-off arm. It staggered, head drooping: it was already woozy from loss of blood. Festina steadied the gun to fire again . . . but before she could pull the trigger, furious smoke rose up and surrounded the weapon. My sixth sense felt the resulting EMP: a surge of energy slagging the wires that connected the gun's battery to the hypersonic projectors. Festina's trigger finger finished its squeeze, but nothing happened. No whir to show that the pistol had fired. No reaction from the Rexy in response to the shot.

Festina had one last stasis sphere, containing one last weapon. She didn't even try to open it. Instead she switched her grip on the gun she already held, taking it by the barrel so she could pistol-whip the first Rexy to come within reach.

The Rexies charged in unison—spurred partly by the *pretas* and partly by a knee-jerk instinct to attack moving prey. (The one so sickened by the taste of Ubatu was too stupid to realize Festina would taste the same.) Festina lunged to the left, making it impossible for both animals to reach her simultaneously. In fact, the beast on the right tried to redirect its rush and only succeeded in jostling its companion so that neither could make a clean lunge. Festina had no such problem. Her hand lashed out, and the butt of her pistol caught the closest Rexy in the throat. It happened to be the one-armed animal who had already been shot once; that particular Rexy was moving more slowly, less quick to react . . . which was how Festina landed a clean solid hit on the creature's windpipe.

The Rexy tried to screech, but no sound came. My sixth sense saw that the beast's esophagus was crushed. In a moment the Rexy collapsed, sucking for breath that wouldn't come. Its heart pounded fast from fear and exertion; but without oxygen, the pounding pulse would stop soon enough.

Another feast for scavengers when the rain let up.

But there was one more corpse yet to come—either Festina or the last remaining Rexy. The Rexy screeched a challenge; Festina only shook her head sadly. "Greetings," she said. "I'm a sentient citizen of the League of Peoples. I beg your Hospitality." A brief silence. "But I'm not going to get it, am I?"

The Rexy screeched again and charged.

The fight was over in seconds. Most fights are.

Under other circumstances, the Rexy might have employed a variety of instinctive tactics . . . but the *pretas* had no such instincts, so they forced the animal to stick with a single form of attack: charging directly at Festina and trying to bite her somewhere vital. Festina didn't stay still long enough to make that possible. Furthermore, during her "sentient citizen" speech she'd surreptitiously untied the glow-tube from her belt. She held it in her left hand, the pistol in her right; whenever the Rexy charged she used the light for distraction, thrusting it out one way as she dodged the opposite direction, or ramming it suddenly toward the Rexy's eyes, blinding the animal for a moment while she kicked at its knees or punched the pistol's muzzle into the Rexy's ribs.

Neither combatant moved at peak efficiency. Like the Rexy who'd lost an arm, the one still on its feet had suffered numerous injuries on its run through the jungle; it was bleeding, battered, bruised. Festina wasn't damaged, but she was noticeably tired—fatigued from jogging so far with my body weighing her down. Perhaps that's why on one of her feints, she didn't move the glow-tube fast enough: the Rexy, pushing itself hard (or perhaps being pushed by the *pretas*), lurched forward quicker than expected. It caught the light in its teeth and bit down hard, spraying luminescent chemicals in all directions.

Including into its own mouth.

The Rexy gagged and squealed. The chemicals inside the glow-tube weren't aggressively toxic—at least not to terrestrial life—but the taste was engineered to be as vile as possible, to discourage children drinking the fluid if some accidentally spilled. (A typical safety precaution to placate the League of Peoples.) It seemed the Rexy's taste buds had the same reaction as *Homo sap* infants: the animal was so appalled by the chemical flavor that for a few seconds, all it could do was retch. The *pretas* tried to overcome the Rexy's reaction, but the animal's instinct to spit out the glowing chemicals was so basic, so visceral, that even the clouds couldn't stop the Rexy from wasting precious seconds on the urge to vomit.

Festina used those seconds. She too had luminescent chemicals sprayed across her—glowing/flowing down her arm, spatters splashed across her shoulders and the side of her face—but she ignored the shining polka dots as she clubbed the pistol hard against the Rexy's skull. The animal half turned toward her, fluorescent vomit spilling from its mouth. She clubbed it again in exactly the same place . . . and this time the skull broke open, disgorging blood and what little brains the Rexy possessed. Smoke poured out too, wreathing around Festina for a moment as if trying to asphyxiate her. Then the *preta* clouds flowed into the night, vanishing almost immediately from normal vision.

To my sixth sense, however, the clouds remained as visible as a forest fire—ablaze with irrepressible fury.

The chemicals from the glow-tube burned out quickly in the open air. Their shine lasted just long enough for Festina to check that all three Rexies were dead. Over their corpses, Festina murmured, "That's what 'expendable' means": a time-honored Explorer Corps phrase used when confronting the death of almost any living thing. Then she went to examine Ubatu, who wasn't dead or even unconscious.

Just bloodied and disfigured.

Both her cheeks were in tatters: fatty flaps of tissue were almost cut loose from her face. Her temples were also in bad shape—punctured, gore-smeared, oozing. My paramedics professor liked to say, "Head wounds always seem worse than they are" . . . but in this case, I thought Ubatu's injuries were just as bad as they looked.

As Festina bent over her, Ubatu tried to speak. The resulting slur of sound wasn't words. Her jaw couldn't move—the muscles to do that had been butchered by Rexy teeth. Anyway, what could Ubatu say? "I'm hurt," maybe? (As if that weren't obvious.) Or perhaps "Do I look hideous?"

As if that weren't obvious too.

But at least Festina could stop the bleeding. She got out her first-aid kit.

Some time later, from the bank of the river, Li uttered a weak "Help!" He'd held his tongue in fear, unable to see what had happened with the Rexies and afraid the big predators had slain his companions. I could see he was worried that if he made a sound, killer pseudosuchians would come for him . . . but as silence drew out after the fight, his nerves grew too frayed to keep quiet. He'd tried a few preliminary whimpers, then managed a more audible cry.

Not that Li really needed help. He could easily climb back to level ground on his own. His aura showed he just wanted to dramatize his situation, make it look like a fearsome predicament. He was dirty and wet, and in shock at *being* dirty and wet; he didn't know that Festina was more so, covered with chemicals, dinosaur puke, and Ubatu's blood. Li probably wouldn't have cared if he *did* know. He just wanted attention. "Help!" he called again when no Rexies came to attack. "Help! Help! Help!"

Festina was just about finished with first aid: Ubatu's bleeding was controlled, and her face had been swathed in bandages, leaving only her eyes exposed. The eyes had suffered no damage—the only part of her face that could make that claim. Festina murmured, "I'll be right back," to Ubatu, then shouted, "Hold your horses, Ambassador! I'm on my way." Moments later, she dragged Li back to the top of the bank, then listened to him babble about how he'd almost been killed. Meanwhile, she scooped water from a puddle and washed off the various residues smeared on her uniform.

When she was clean, she stood up and interrupted Li's tirade. "Did you see where Tut went?"

"How could I possibly keep track of . . ."

"Tut!" she called, ignoring the rest of Li's sentence. "Tut! You can come out now. The Rexies are dead."

No answer. Tut was already out of earshot, moving south through the bush. He still wore the mask . . . and occasionally, he went down on all fours and growled, "Grr-arrh! Grr-arrh!" *Pretas* hovered around him. I couldn't tell if they were trying to possess him or simply marveling at the sight, wondering what in the world he was doing. But whether by plan or by accident, he was heading south—toward the Stage Two station.

Festina, Li, and Ubatu would soon turn that way too: the two diplomats couldn't be left on their own in the jungle, and they refused to go back to Drill-Press. Ubatu could walk—slowly, with a limp, muttering inarticulately thanks to her slack jaw—so proceeding forward was the best of a bunch of bad possibilities. Anyway,

Festina wanted to get back to where she'd left me, to make sure I was safe. Who knew how many more Rexies might lurk in the darkness?

I knew. Two more Rexies were approaching fast from the south. They'd been coming this way all the time, following Festina and me as we'd gone back to help the others.

The Rexies would reach me long before Festina would—with her glow-tube destroyed she'd have to stumble through near-total blackness, while the Rexies came on, unerringly guided by *pretas*. I could even tell I'd been singled out as the animals' target; I was helpless, and they were zeroing in on me, timing their pace to arrive simultaneously.

Aloud I said, "The next few minutes are going to be tricky." Then I began pulling myself along the ground, heading for the river.

It was hard going. My legs were useless, nothing but deadweight. I could pull myself forward with my arms, but when the foliage was low it was slippery under my hands, and when it was high I had to bulldoze my way past countless stalks and tangles. The mustard smell of Muta's ferns was thick and pungent this close to the ground, made stronger as plants in my wake were crushed to pulp beneath me. I didn't have far to crawl to the river—only forty meters from where Festina left me—but getting there took the effort of a marathon.

Even as I crawled, I scouted ahead mentally. The bank itself was much like the one where Festina had just finished her own battle—a low, sandy cliff, slightly less than a story high and overgrown with a breed of tall, thin ferns that unfortunately had evolved primitive thorns. The area between me and the bank was slathered with the same sort of weed, mercilessly scratching my face and hands. (The rest of my body suffered no harm, thanks to the Team Esteem uniform. Nanomesh can't withstand rain, kicks, or Rexy bites, but at least it's resilient enough to shrug off a few plant prickers.)

I had one great advantage in the coming confrontation: my total mental awareness. I knew exactly where the Rexies were; I knew where to find a fist-sized rock that could be pried loose from the wet mud; I knew which sections of the bank were solid and which were ready to crumble if you put too much weight on them; I even knew how much weight was too much. I thought to myself as I crawled along, *I'm living a Bamar folktale*—one of those stories where a saint is threatened by ravenous beasts and wins out by the power of enlightenment.

Of course, in my ancestors' folklore, "winning out" didn't always mean surviving. Sometimes the beasts still got you, but you earned a really good rebirth.

I reached the lip of the bank mere seconds ahead of the Rexies . . . but along the way, I'd dug up the rock I needed. I held the stone tight as I waited on the edge of the drop-off.

The Rexies appeared moments later—the first time I'd seen them with my real eyes. They both looked tall and imposing (at least to a crippled woman sitting on the ground). I knew they'd screech before they attacked; all the other Rexies had done the same. Perhaps it was a standard tactic to freeze their prey with panic . . . or perhaps the Rexies were crying in agony as the *pretas* in their skulls jolted their brains into action. Either way, their auras gave away the exact instant when they began to open their mouths. I threw my rock at the closest and scored a perfect hit: straight to the back of the throat.

The Rexy blinked in surprise. It tried to shriek, but only managed a wheeze. Then it coughed, trying to dislodge the blockage in its windpipe. The animal wasn't completely choked up—the rock I'd chosen wasn't a perfect fit. Still, the Rexy could barely draw air around the edges of the rock, and its instincts would force it to hack and wheeze until it gagged up the obstruction.

One Rexy neutralized, at least temporarily. One more to go. It charged . . . not a smart thing to do when the target is right on the edge of a cliff.

I rolled aside at the last split second. The Rexy still got a chunk of me; though my upper body evaded fast enough, my legs straggled limply behind and my right calf got gouged by the Rexy's claws. Since my right calf no longer belonged to me—it was now strictly Balrog territory—I didn't feel pain. I simply saw the claw stab in . . . and I couldn't help laughing as Balrog spores under the skin beat a hasty retreat to avoid being seen at the edges of the wound. A moment later, the nanomesh uniform (briefly torn by the incoming talon) sealed itself back up, hiding the spores beneath.

As for the Rexy, it kept going, unable to stop its momentum after trampling me. Right over the lip of the bank, belly-flopping into the water below.

The Rexy could swim—not well, just the usual frantic paddle of land animals that find themselves in deep water—but I trusted the beast wouldn't drown. Not even in the fast-flowing flood from the rain. It was, after all, far lighter than a mammal of comparable size: almost as light as a bird. The Rexy would ride the torrent, head above water, till the current washed it ashore . . . and if we were all lucky, the shore where it landed would be the far side of the river. Ending up over there, the Rexy would lose its usefulness to the *pretas*. There was no easy way to get the animal to our side of the river again, since it couldn't swim against the Grindstone's heavy current, and the only bridges were back in Drill-Press. Therefore, if the Rexy washed up on the opposite shore, the clouds would have no further reason to keep it enslaved. They'd release their hold on its brain and let the animal return to its normal life.

At least, that's what I hoped. I had no wish for the Rexy to die. I had no wish for *anything* to die . . . including the Rexy who remained in front of me, still trying to clear its throat.

I wondered if there was any way a woman paralyzed from the waist down could administer the Heimlich maneuver to a dinosaur.

But that proved unnecessary. With a heave of its lungs, the Rexy finally coughed the stone onto the ground. It turned its head toward me, eyes bleary; it held my gaze for a moment, as if saying, "To hell with the *pretas*. Now this is personal." Then it screeched and came for me.

* * *

It didn't make the mistake of charging. Even if the Rexy itself wasn't bright enough to learn from what happened to its companion, the *pretas* realized another precipitous rush would only end up in the river. So the Rexy advanced with slow deliberation. I waited, equally stolid—I was sitting up now on the edge of the bank, legs slack in front of me but with my fists raised in what I hoped was a convincing ready-to-fight stance. If the predator tried to chomp my upper body, I'd fend it off as best I could.

But the Rexy (or the *pretas*) went for the easiest target: my legs. They were the closest body parts the Rexy could reach—limp and unmoving flesh, beyond the swing of my fists. Apparently helpless.

So my would-be killer took the bait.

The Rexy firmly, deliberately, clamped its teeth into my left leg, right at the knee. Blood squirted; incisors scraped bone. The bite was so crushing, one of the Rexy's teeth broke off from the force—deep, deep, the animal getting an unbreakable grip in preparation for shaking its head and ripping the leg clean off. I waited till the bite was irrevocably committed . . . then I pushed myself backward and off the cliff.

I don't know if the Rexy was capable of letting go; its teeth were so solidly embedded in my flesh, it might not have been able to release me even if it wanted to. But it didn't want to—its aura showed nothing but determination to hold on, no matter what. Which is why, when I started to fall over the edge of the cliff, the Rexy came with me all the way. Its birdlike weight was far too light to hold me back, and its feet had no purchase on the slick muddy ground. Together, the Rexy and I tumbled over the bank. After a deceptively quiet moment of free fall, we smacked down into the flood.

Deep water, deeply chilled. The momentum of my backward cannonball dive plunged me more than a meter below the surface . . . but the featherweight Rexy, still fastened to my leg, had the buoyancy of a life preserver. He rose fast and pulled me with him, the two of us bobbing into rainy air that was almost as cold and wet as the river.

I expected the Rexy to splutter with panic at its sudden immersion. It didn't. Maybe the *pretas* suppressed all fear reactions. More likely the animal was so focused on taking a chunk out of me, it didn't have the brainpower to think about anything else. It bit down; it shook its head hard, as violently as the water allowed; and after a moment of thrashing, my leg came off at the knee, as easily as pulling the plug in a bathtub.

Immediately, the Rexy and my detached limb began to drift away in the torrent. I swam a few strokes to increase the distance between us. The animal continued to chew on the bloody stump as it disappeared into darkness; my sixth sense told me the Rexy avoided swallowing my putrid-tasting meat, but gnawed and gnawed and gnawed until the bones were ground into mash.

Through all this, I felt no pain. Nanomesh fabric closed seamlessly around the jagged remains of my knee. Then the Balrog, concealed by the uniform, closed off my spurting blood vessels, tidied up the bone ends, and pulled the remaining flaps of my skin to make a smooth outer seal—better than the work of any Technocracy surgeon.

I'd expected no less. The spores had proved they could repair other kinds of damage to my anatomy; why shouldn't they handle an amputation? And I trusted them to save me from other threats too . . . like hypothermia, now that I was drifting helplessly in heart-chilling water, with no more protection than a sodden skintight uniform. Perhaps the Balrog wasn't legally *compelled* to help me survive; I'd thrown myself into the river of my own free will, knowing quite well that humans often died of exposure under similar conditions. If the Balrog let me freeze to death, the League of Peoples wouldn't object. Superior lifeforms can't be held responsible if a lesser being takes suicidal risks.

But the Balrog would save me anyway. Not to preserve its good standing with the League of Peoples. Not because I might still be necessary to its plans. It would save me because it was not a callous creature.

I saw that now. The Balrog was no villain. In fact, it was deeply compassionate . . . in its inhuman way.

Everything the Balrog had done to me—*for* me—had been a gift . . . at least from the moss's alien viewpoint. It believed it was improving me: making me less human and more like a "civilized" species. If the process scared and dismayed me, that might be cause for pity but not for backing off. When you take a beloved cat to the veterinarian, the animal may struggle and yowl; but you know you're acting in the cat's best interests, so you don't let yourself give in.

"This is for your own good, Fluffy."

This is for your own good, Youn Suu.

The Balrog believed it was doing me a favor: infesting my body, infiltrating my mind. If I didn't appreciate the favor . . . well, every pet owner has to deal with that look of accusation when Fluffy thinks she's been betrayed. Lesser creatures can't always understand when they should show gratitude.

Did *I* feel gratitude? No. But I felt acceptance. I put myself at the Balrog's mercy, letting it do whatever it saw fit.

Perhaps I'd be saved from hypothermia by having all my skin replaced with moss: an insulating layer of fuzz that would hold in my body heat, but make me look like landscaping. Was that so bad? With my cheek, I'd never looked entirely human. Wasn't I used to that by now? Why should I be dismayed by a new outward appearance?

I didn't regret what I'd done, no matter the price I paid. I'd removed the final two Rexies from the picture; I'd even done it humanely, so they'd both survive. My long-distance perceptions showed no other Rexies near enough to cause trouble. Festina could reach the Stage Two station without further risk.

She wouldn't press on immediately. With Li and Ubatu in tow, she'd return to the spot where she'd left me; she'd find my dragging trail through the thorns and follow it to the river; she'd see Rexy tracks in the mud and the spot where the bank crumbled when the Rexy and I went over the edge. Festina's Bumbler would pick up traces of my spilled blood . . . but by the time she used the machine to scan the water I'd be far downstream, out of the Bumbler's viewing range.

Eventually, she'd realize there was nothing she could do. She'd set off toward the station, probably sticking close to the river and using the Bumbler from time to time to see if I'd washed up onshore.

Tut would head in the same direction—hunched over like a bear, stopping occasionally to dance, roll in the mud, or kill some poor lizard and eat it raw—but he'd make his way to the station too. He had nowhere else to go. He certainly wouldn't go back to Drill-Press: there was nothing to interest him there. And if he just wanted to wander through the wilderness, curiosity would turn his steps toward the station; even if Tut had gone feral, he wouldn't find much entertainment in a wasteland of ferns. The station was the only nearby location where something extraordinary might happen.

Pretas continued to drift around him, trying to insinuate themselves into his brain. Tut's life force fought back as it had before: with a swirl of evasive lunacy, impossible for the clouds to control. If ever they came close to conquest, a flash of mental purple beat them back. I couldn't identify what the purple was—maybe some core of sanity within his madness—but it held the *pretas* at bay. They contented themselves with merely nudging him forward, guiding him to keep pace with Festina and the diplomats. Later, they might make an all-out attempt to turn Tut into their absolute puppet. For the moment, however, they only needed that he stay close enough to be available if they decided to use him.

So we all proceeded south: Tut through the bush . . . Festina, Li, and Ubatu along the shore . . . me on the current in the river's deepest channel. I had no trouble keeping my head above the flood—partly turned to moss and missing half a leg, I was light enough to float high in the water. And unlike rivers back home on Anicca, the Grindstone had no snags where I might get caught: Muta was millions of years away from having trees, and therefore millions of years from having significant deadfalls blocking the stream. If a tree-sized fern fell into the river, it would rot so much faster than conventional wood, there wouldn't be time for obstructions to form.

Which gave me clear sailing through the night.

17

Satori [Japanese]: A sudden flash of enlightenment; a spiritual breakthrough. Strictly speaking, satori refers to a life-changing experience of seeing the world as it truly is. However, many people also use satori for smaller "Aha!" moments and for any burst of insight.

WHEN Prince Gotama left the pleasure palace, he wandered through cities and countryside, seeking truth. He listened to many teachers; he practiced spiritual disciplines; he fasted in the wilderness before deciding that ravenous hunger was not conducive to inner calm. At last, he seated himself beneath a great tree and vowed he wouldn't budge until he achieved enlightenment.

The good gods rejoiced that this time had come. For all their power, they were no more free than any other living creature. They longed for Gotama to awaken—to become Tathagata—so he could teach them the path to liberation.

But one god feared what Gotama might achieve. Mara, god of passion and delusion, knew his power would be shattered if the prince won through to ultimate truth. Therefore, Mara summoned his sons (the Fears) and his daughters (the Desires), and together they tried to break Prince Gotama's resolve by using threats and temptations. Some say Gotama was so focused, he didn't even notice this assault; but others say Gotama had to summon all his mental strength to fight back and would never have Awakened if he hadn't been forced to make a supreme spiritual effort. Perhaps an all-out confrontation with the sources of turmoil is the only way to become a Buddha.

Whatever the case, Mara failed—Prince Gotama couldn't be intimidated or lured from his goal. The god and his children slunk away in defeat. Throughout the hours of darkness, Gotama passed through the four stages of Awakening: remembering his past lives, seeing the world without delusion, understanding the causes of suffering, and finally (at dawn) achieving nirvana . . . which is not some spacey state of bliss, but a simple unwavering clarity so perfect one can never fall into error again. Gotama, Tathagata Buddha, hadn't become some miracle-working superman; he'd just purged himself of all his own bullshit.

What transcendence could be higher?

I thought about Gotama as I floated through the darkness—about the night he faced Mara. Maybe I should try the same thing myself. Not that I was anywhere close to enlightenment; my earlier "So what?" moment was only a small upward step, not a leap straight into the heavens. But maybe I should confront my own version of Mara. As the Grindstone propelled me southward, I finally had the time and space to think. Slowly the depth of my situation sank in: the hollowness that would dog me down the years if I couldn't reach out and communicate.

"Balrog," I said. "Can we talk?"

Water rushed around me. Darkness filled my eyes.

"Balrog. We're joined, you and I. Merged. Closer than husband and wife. Can we talk?"

Only the river and the night.

"I've given up a lot," I said. "You've got the better of me over and over. The things you've offered in return . . . you've helped when I asked, and even saved my life, but . . . do you understand loneliness, Balrog? You're a hive creature. Maybe loneliness is beyond your comprehension. But if you and I are going to be together—for the rest of my life, till death us do part—I'll shrivel inside if we don't connect. If I'm just the lowly human and you never ever share . . . please, Balrog, don't make me live like that. It's too cold."

Blackness. Silence.

"When Kaisho Namida talks about you," I said, "she makes you sound like a lover. She makes it sound like she loves you, and you love her back. I don't ask you to love me . . ." (Oh, would no one ever love me? I yearned so deeply to writhe with passion, and would even open myself to the spores if it would ease my longing.) "I don't ask you to love me, but please . . . please. Meet me halfway so I'm not alone."

Nothing. And yet . . .

Floating gently, my eyes slipped shut. I dreamed.

Once again I was at the pagoda: the gravesite of Fuentes civilization, with its fountain and orchard of minichili trees. Once again I saw statues of heroes in the arboretum—one coated with purple jelly, another surrounded by sandy black grains, a third turned to glass and lava—but in my dream, the statues had changed.

Now the marble figure enclosed in jelly looked like Tut . . . the one with black sand had become an Arabic man carrying a huge four-barreled gun . . . the one in glass and lava was no longer Hui-Neng the Patriarch, but a beautiful naked woman . . . and all the rest within sight were similarly changed, some to people I recognized (students and professors from the Explorer Academy), others to people I couldn't name but who seemed familiar, as if I'd met them in other dreams. Or other lives.

I turned toward the fountain in the middle of the pagoda. False memory said the fountain had contained a golden Buddha overlaid with Balrog moss. My mother said she had seen Kaisho Namida in a wheelchair. Now . . . now I saw both Kaisho and myself, the two of us sitting in lotus position, facing each other, knees touching. Our eyes were open, gazing on each other as we floated in midair two meters above the fountain. We both were moss from the waist down: glowing a warm-hearth red that filled the space around us with light. Kaisho's hands made the mudra gesture for Birth, while mine made the gesture for Enlightenment. The pair of us smiled with sisterly gentleness.

Comfortable with each other. Not alone. Reassurance.

I dreamed this as if I were a third person standing in the temple's doorway: with a view of the arboretum outside as well as Kaisho and me inside. No one else was part of this. Just the statues of heroes, plus a levitating Kaisho and Youn Suu. Did it mean something that I saw the scene from the threshold between the temple and the outer world beyond? The boundary between the sacred and mundane?

"It means whatever fits," said Kaisho. She and the duplicate Youn Suu turned, rotating in air until both could look at me. "None of it's really predetermined. At least we hope not. We throw a lot of things your way, but only you decide what to use."

I asked, "Who's 'we'?"

The Youn Suu in front of me smiled. "You want to know who's pulling the strings? Irrelevant. The important thing is what you do once your strings are cut loose. I'll have to remember to teach you that."

"You're going to teach *me*?" I said. "You *are* me."

"No. Look at yourself."

I did. My hands weren't my familiar dark brown, but a much lighter shade that showed multiple scrapes and scratches. My clothes were Unity nanomesh, but not colored in motley Mutan camouflage; just a solid sheen of black stretching down to the white boots of a Technocracy tightsuit.

Festina had taken the black nanomesh. Her tightsuit was white and her hands, gouged and nicked in her trip through the bush, were exactly like the ones on the end of my arms.

"You're having her dream," the other Youn Suu said. "She can't have it herself—she's awake."

"Besides"—Kaisho chuckled—"Festina would *hate* receiving messages in dreams. Such a rationalist! If she dreamed two plus two equaled four, she'd automatically mistrust it. You, on the other hand, will pay attention. Oneiromantic prophecies are in your blood. Literally."

"You mean my veins are full of Balrog spores?"

"Shush," Kaisho told me. "There's one universal rule of prophecy, recognized by every thread of human culture: you don't get to ask clarifying questions. You just listen and suck it up."

"Then," Youn Suu added, "if you've got a milligram of sense, you interpret the message like an intelligent mensch, rather than some self-centered oaf who's never learned the concept of 'double meaning.'"

"I know how prophecies work," I said. "The wise benefit, while fools work their own destruction."

The second Youn Suu turned to Kaisho. "Pompous little bint, aren't I?"

"She's quoting," Kaisho replied.

"I knew that." The other Youn Suu turned back to me. "Are you ready to hear the message?"

I nodded.

"Okay," the Youn Suu said. "Give her the message, Kaisho."

Kaisho frowned. "I thought *you* had the message."

"How can I have the message?" my double said. "I'm just Youn Suu. I have no words of wisdom, and I certainly don't know anything about the future."

"Well, *I* don't have a message either," Kaisho said. "I've been the Balrog's meat pasty for decades, but do the blasted spores tell me anything? Not bloody likely. I get sent on errands all over the galaxy, and most of the time I don't have the slightest hint what I'm supposed to do." She glanced at me. "Get used to faking it, sister. Our mossy master loves us dearly, but he never spells things out."

"So we go to all this trouble," the other Youn Suu muttered, "for an honest-to-goodness dream visitation, and we don't have anything to say?" She looked down on me from her place above the fountain. "This is a great steaming mound of embarrassment, isn't it?"

"I get the message," I said.

"You do?"

"I do. But did you have to lay it on so thickly? *I'm just Youn Suu. I have no words of wisdom, and I certainly don't know anything about the future.* Spare me the gushing humility."

Youn Suu gave me a dubious look. "That's the message you think we're sending? Some crap about having faith in yourself? Sweetheart, if tripe like that was all we had to offer, we'd send you a goddamned greeting card."

"You've stopped talking like me," I said. "I don't swear, and I don't use words like 'sweetheart.' "

"How about words like 'fucking smart-ass'?" My own face glowered at me, then turned to Kaisho. "Come on, moss-breath, we're done here."

Kaisho gave me a piercing stare. "*Are* we done? Do you know what you have to teach Festina?"

"How would I know that?" I said. "I'm just Youn Suu. I have no words of wisdom. I certainly don't know anything about the future."

The thing that looked like me made a growling sound in its throat. "Buddhists! You can have them, spore-head. They're all yours. Give me a hot-looking glass chick with legs and an attitude, and I'll make the galaxy my bitch!"

The Youn Suu look-alike winked out of existence. Kaisho looked apologetic. "Sorry. He can never resist putting on a show."

"Who was he?" I asked.

"A friend of the Balrog's."

"Some great and powerful alien?"

"Of course," Kaisho said. "He and the Balrog are working together on a project. Along with a good many others in the League."

"What are they all up to?"

Kaisho smiled. "You'll figure it out. When you do, tell Festina. It's time she knew."

"No hints?"

"Sure, here's a hint. Become enlightened. Then you'll know everything."

"How do I become enlightened?"

Kaisho shrugged. "It's easy. Just wake up."

I woke up. Dream over. And despite the lack of direct information, I felt I'd learned a lot.

I'd learned that when I reached out to the Balrog—when I needed the solace of contact—the Balrog was ready to answer.

Oblique, frustrating answers . . . but enough to assure me I wouldn't live my life in numb solitary confinement.

I rode peacefully on the flooded Grindstone. The rain had stopped. Above me, the sky was full of stars.

An hour before dawn, I reached the lake created by the Stage Two station's dam. The current was slower but still perceptible; muddy water poured thick as cream over the dam, taking with it leaves and other debris floating on the lake's surface. I could easily swim against the pull. Taking my time, conserving my strength, I stroked toward the station.

My skin had not turned to moss; that hadn't been necessary. When the nanomesh uniform sensed my body temperature dropping to unacceptable levels, it had puffed itself up: from a skintight sheath to a thick layer of fabric filled with air bubbles. It held my body heat like foam insulation, even stretching itself to cover my hands and most of my head—just the face left bare so I could see and breathe. I offered my thanks to the Unity's foresight, giving their survey teams all-weather clothes.

The outfit reminded me of a cold-water diving suit I'd worn during scuba training at the Academy . . . except that the Unity uniform was still colored in multihued camouflage patterns matching the local foliage. I attracted much interest from plant-eating fish who thought I might be a tasty mat of ferns floating on the surface. My slow swimming kept them from coming too close (even mid-Triassic fish were smart enough to know that plants didn't do the breaststroke) but I accumulated a crowd of followers who wistfully hoped I might prove to be food.

Onshore, Festina and the diplomats continued toward the station. Their journey wasn't as easy as mine; walking through semi-jungle gets tiring. At least they had adequate light for traveling—Festina carried a number of spare glow-tubes. The Bumbler also helped. It could scan ahead for trouble, letting them pick better routes and reducing the need for backtracking. Still, they hadn't had a pleasant time. Ubatu was injured and weakened from blood loss. Li was in decent physical shape for a civilian, but came nowhere near matching Festina's level of endurance. He whined . . . demanded frequent rest breaks . . . didn't push himself to keep up.

Once Li stopped and refused to go any farther. By sixth sense I heard him say, "This is absurd! We're stumbling around in the dark. I'm not budging another millimeter till morning." Festina took her time responding: probably deciding what tack to take with a stubborn diplomat. Ubatu, however, just grabbed Li by his pricey silk shirt and shook him, making incomprehensible sounds of rage through her ruined mouth. It worked far better than rational argument—a few hard cuffs, and Li started moving again.

Deeper out in the bush, Tut was also on the move. He had to be: if he slowed down, he'd die. A beanpole like him, with little insulating fat and no clothes but masks, could only survive the cold damp by staying active. By dawn Tut was racked with shivers, despite his constant capering. The foliage through which he moved was soaking wet, drenching him whenever he bumped against a rain-laden frond. Once the sun arrived it might warm him a bit, but the season was still late autumn. The day would remain cool for hours . . . and if Tut collapsed in exhaustion, even the heat of noon might not restore his body to a life-sustaining temperature.

For the time being, though, he was still on his feet. *Pretas* surrounded him, urging him on. They'd helped him through the night, jolting him awake whenever he came close to dropping from fatigue. I was sure they'd keep him on the move until . . . until he did whatever a planetful of frustrated ghosts wanted him to do.

We were all alive and moving—Tut, Festina, Li, Ubatu, the *pretas*, and I. All of us converged on the station, like actors approaching the climax of a VR melodrama. I wondered whether events had been planned this way from the beginning . . . by the League, the Balrog, the purple-jelly Fuentes, or any other godlike aliens who liked playing puppet-master. But as the Youn Suu in my dream had said, it really didn't matter who was pulling the strings.

The important thing was what we did with whatever small freedoms we had.

The first gray light of the coming dawn glistened on the water—a perfect time for a swim.

At the far end of the lake, the station rose above the beach. It was built in the shape of a Fuentes head—black marble skin, bright glass eyes with hundreds of facets, huge chrome mandibles framing the mouthlike entrance—but the forehead was circled with a crown of golden spikes: not pure gold but some gleaming alloy, each spike ten meters long, square at the base and tapering out to a point as sharp as a lightning rod.

The lightning rod resemblance wasn't accidental. If the station had done its job sixty-five hundred years ago, bolts of power should have shot from that golden crown, uplifting every EMP cloud in the neighborhood. But I perceived no energy being emitted. In fact, I perceived little from the station at all. My sixth sense encompassed the building's exterior, but stopped blind at the doorway . . . as if the world ended there, and the station's interior was part of some other reality. A pocket universe like the research center in Drill-Press.

I wondered if even the Balrog knew what lay inside the building. It might be as blind as I was. Or perhaps the moss knew exactly what the station held and wanted to keep it secret; the spores never missed a chance to spring a surprise on lesser beings. The Balrog had a childish fondness for catching people unawares . . . unless there was some deeper motivation for the moss's actions. Zen masters also loved springing surprises, in an effort to shock students out of conventional patterns of thinking. As one sensei famously said, "Sometimes a slap is needed for a newborn child to breathe."

Kaisho Namida had been a student of Zen. The Balrog had certainly jolted her out of conventional ways. Were the spores trying to do the same with me—not startling me for the fun of it, but doling out disorienting shocks in the hope of Waking me up?

"Just for the record," I told the Balrog, "my form of Buddhism isn't like Zen. We prefer the slow but steady approach . . . *without* undue surprises. Trying to achieve enlightenment in a single lifetime is considered needy."

For a moment—just a moment—I imagined the Balrog laughing.

I reached the station before the others: swam ashore, pulled myself above the waterline, and lay on the beach letting my clothes dry as I waited for Festina and the diplomats. Drying didn't take long—the nanomesh channeled excess H_2O molecules to the surface of the fabric, then formed a seal to prevent drops from seeping back in. I sloshed most of the moisture off with my hands. Muta's predawn air did the rest.

The station's front doors were only a stone's throw away, but I made no effort to enter. Better to wait for Festina—I couldn't help notice that *pretas* clustered thickly on the beach, but not a single cloudy particle ventured nearer than ten meters to the building. Those that got close moved on quickly, as if the proximity made them nervous. In fact, every cloud within range seemed anxious or outright afraid; their auras fluttered with agitation. Were they worried our group would cause trouble inside the Stage Two installation? Or did they fear that something in the building might be disturbed by our arrival and cause trouble for *everyone?*

Such questions would be answered in time. Meanwhile, I experimented with ways to get around in my low-mobility condition: crawling stomach down, sitting up and going backward (bouncing along on my rump), trying to walk upside down on my hands (impossible because my limp legs flopped around too much to keep my balance), rolling lengthwise, various ungainly sideways maneuvers. . . .

At last, I paused for breath. Lying on the sand, breathing deeply, I considered other means of locomotion . . . like asking the Balrog for help. My alien parasite had spectacular powers. On Cashleen, the spores had formed that mossy carriage to whoosh me through the streets of Zoonau . . . and the navy's files were full of similar incidents, including a time on the planet Troyen when the Balrog picked up the entire royal palace and used it as a battering ram against a mass of soldiers. If the Balrog could telekinetically move a building, why couldn't it move me?

But I knew that wouldn't happen—not on Muta, where the Balrog had gone to great lengths to hide its presence. Yes, the spores could construct glowing red carriages . . . and perhaps they could lift me into the air, or teleport me instantly to another continent. But they wouldn't; not here. They'd do nothing out of the ordinary unless their actions could be concealed from the outside world. The Balrog might amuse itself under my skin, romping through my tissues and reshaping my brain; but it wouldn't miraculously restore my half-amputated leg. That would give away the game to . . .

To whom? The *pretas*?

Or to whatever waited inside the station? Was *that* the threat the Balrog hid from?

Pity I couldn't see into the building. In the meantime, I watched the horizon brighten and let myself fall asleep.

I woke as Festina and the diplomats became visible to the naked eye. They walked along the beach, all three glum and apprehensive—right up to the point where the Bumbler chirped to indicate it had sensed something interesting.

Me.

I lay on the outermost edge of its scan. Festina soon realized the little machine was reporting a human body sprawled in front of the station. She set off at a run, leaving the others behind . . . but she slowed to a casual jog when I waved to show I was alive.

The fear that had blazed through her aura shifted to beaming relief . . . then, because she was Festina Ramos, the relief darkened to suspicion. When she got within earshot, she yelled, "How the hell did you end up here?"

"I swam. Saved you the effort of carrying me."

"We thought you'd been attacked by Rexies."

"I was." I reached down and raised my left leg with my hands—showing her the stump. "One Rexy wouldn't leave without having a bite."

Festina swallowed hard. "Do you want me to look at your wounds?"

"Better not. The nanomesh closed up around the damage. You wouldn't want to open things and start new bleeding."

Festina's eyes met mine. I'd spoken the literal truth—the uniform *had* closed up around the damage, and she *wouldn't* want to start new bleeding—but Festina was smart enough to grasp what I'd left unsaid. The nanomesh couldn't have plugged the spurt of a major arterial rupture; that had to be the work of the Balrog. Festina realized there must be some reason I didn't want to talk about the spores now that we were close to the station. She knew how circumspect the Balrog had been since we'd landed on Muta. Besides, she may have thought I was equivocating to hide my condition from Li and Ubatu . . . who'd hurried to join us and were now close enough to hear.

"You look pretty damned comfortable," Li grumbled at me. "Must be nice, not having to walk all night."

I said, "Must be nice, being able to walk at all."

Li glared at me, but held his tongue. Ubatu, unable to speak, also remained silent beneath the bandages swathing her face . . . but her eyes, peering out between strips of gauze, glinted like black diamonds. I was still alive, and therefore still a prize to be seized for Ifa-Vodun. Perhaps even now she was praying to the Balrog—trying to project her thoughts to say, "Great mossy loa, come ride me, come *heal* me." I couldn't be sure that was what she had in mind; but her aura showed ferocious hunger, fierce to the point of obsession, as she gazed fixedly at me.

Meanwhile, Li had turned to contemplate the gold spikes protruding from the station's crown. Wan predawn light reflected from the polished gilt surface. "So this is the place that'll save us from turning into smoke?"

"No," Festina said. "This is the place that'll turn the EMP clouds into gods . . . at which point, we get the hell back to *Pistachio* and save ourselves."

"What if we can't do anything? What if some machine is broken beyond repair?"

"Then we become smoke ourselves," Festina told him. "The Unity and Technocracy will research their asses off till they find some way to protect landing parties from Stage One microbes and EMP-shooting clouds. Once they've figured that out, you can be damned sure they'll come back. They won't pass up the chance to get their hands on Fuentes technology . . . especially the process for becoming transcendent. Sooner or later, they'll bring in teams to get this station up and running, even if it takes a complete rebuild. We might spend a decade or two as smoke, but eventually someone *will* activate Stage Two. Then up we all go to heaven." She made a face. "Godhood, here we come. Yippee."

"You still don't like the idea?" I asked.

"I've been thinking about it all night," Festina answered. "Why am I so against it? What's so great about my current condition that makes godhood feel like diminishment? It must be . . . you know . . ." Embarrassed, she gestured toward the birthmark on her cheek. "I'm comfortable with feeling beleaguered. Always forced to struggle. Even when I succeed, I mistrust the success, so I run off to find another fight. I don't know who I am unless I'm up to my eyeballs in shit."

"I'm the same way," Li said. "Sitting around is exasperating. I need to be on the attack, to charge into the slavering horde—"

"No," Festina interrupted, "that's not what I mean. I'm no adrenaline junkie. I'm an Explorer, for God's sake. We don't seek out trouble; that's unprofessional. But I just feel I have to . . . like I'm being called to exercise my humanity . . ."

She blushed—her good cheek turning red. "I told you, I've been brooding all night. Never a good thing. I start composing soliloquies. Trying to rationalize my contradictions. Why can't I believe that advancement might work? Why does something in my head keep saying, *Human, human, human, I must remain human* . . . as if being human is the most sacred state in the universe and anything else is sacrilege. That's bullshit. *Homo sapiens* are barely beyond monkeys. There must be something better . . . whether it's achieved by microbes and dark energy, or by meditating over a thousand lifetimes until you find enlightenment. Run-of-the-mill humanity cannot be the peak of creation. No. No. A thousand times no." She shook her head fiercely . . . then let it sag. "But I bristle with mistrust at anything else. Becoming more than human seems either a false promise or a genuine evil. *Human, human, I must remain human.* That voice in my head won't stop."

"That voice in your head is Mara," I told her. "The god of delusion and ignorance. Or if you regard gods as metaphors, it's the voice of ego."

"If gods were metaphors," she said, "we wouldn't be having this conversation. It's the imminent chance of becoming a god that makes me feel this bleak." Abruptly, she broke into a laugh. "Hell, Youn Suu, maybe some people deserve to be gods . . . but me? On a heavenly throne? I wouldn't know what to do with myself."

"If you became a god," Li said, "you'd know then. There's no such thing as a god with self-doubt."

"Another reason I don't trust gods." Festina turned her gaze toward the station—the giant alien head with its insect eyes and mandibles. "I look at that, and I ask how a whole world could choose to abandon their very flesh. Everyone on Muta planned to ascend . . . and if the experiment had worked, other Fuentes planets would have repeated the trick as soon as possible. In fact, the other Fuentes *did* ascend eventually; they found a different way to elevate themselves, and damned near the entire race chose to take the big leap. They were so eager to run from everything . . ." Her voice faded. "I don't understand it."

"Maybe they were bored," Li said. "Like the Cashlings. So jaded with existence, they'd do anything to liven it up."

"Are you bored, Ambassador?" I asked.

"I'm cold and tired and hungry," he replied . . . as if that answered my question.

"In any civilization, some people are bound to be bored," Festina said. "But the whole species? Bored to the point where they'd rip their bodies into smoke in the hope of becoming something better?"

"The Unity does much the same," I pointed out. "They're ready to engineer their bodies, their DNA, their language, their religion, all in the name of becoming more than human. The Technocracy is heading that way too. We haven't gone as far as the Unity, but that's because we're in denial—publicly pretending we don't believe in gene-splicing babies, while privately spending billions on the black market. *I* was engineered. Ubatu was too, right?"

She nodded . . . and looked grateful I'd involved her in the conversation rather than treating her like some speechless wad of flotsam heaped on the sand. I turned to Li. "Did *your* parents build you inside a test tube?"

"Of course," he said. "Otherwise, I couldn't compete with engineered children. Everyone who rises to the top has boosted DNA."

He glanced at Festina as if he expected confirmation. "I have no idea whether I was engineered," Festina muttered. "I was adopted."

"So?" Li asked. "The adoption agency must have supplied your genetic history when you came of age."

"There was no adoption agency." Festina had dropped her gaze to the sand under our feet.

"You mean you were found on a doorstep?" Li asked.

"Yes. Literally." She lifted her head, and defiance burned in her eyes. "I was left on the steps of a church, all right? Presumably because my real parents didn't want a blemished child." Festina jutted out her chin, raising her birthmarked cheek higher. "My adoptive parents weren't so picky."

Suddenly, she whirled on me. "Why the hell are you smiling?"

"You were adopted," I said. I was more than just smiling—I was trying not to laugh. "You were adopted."

The exhilaration of comprehension. In the blink of an eye, I'd seen the truth. Why the Balrog kept filling my head with the Ghost Fountain Pagoda and the Arboretum of Heroes. Why the statues had become Tut and other Explorers, each one marked by an alien presence. Why the Balrog only infected Buddhist women, and even why that voice in Festina's head kept repeating, *Human, human, I must remain human.*

I knew. I understood. Gods and Buddhas, demigods and myths. The Balrog and other powerful aliens working together on a project.

"Festina," I said, "you came out of nowhere, real parents unknown. You can jog half an hour with me on your shoulder and have enough strength left to fight two Rexies. You're devoted to struggle, and refuse to rest on any sort of victory. Wherever there's trouble in the galaxy, you happen to be in the neighborhood. Really, Festina, don't you see?"

"See what?" she asked, her eyes fierce as lightning.

"That I'm not the only ringer in this fight." I gave her a rueful look. "We really *are* reverse mirror images."

"I don't know what you're talking about."

"No. You don't. That's your nature. Facing down the universe, not sitting back to understand it. Prometheus, not Buddha. You mentioned Prometheus yourself while we were talking to Ohpa. You're the classic Western hero who defies the gods for the sake of humanity."

She rolled her eyes. "I'm scarcely a hero, Youn Suu. Explorers who try to be heroes end up dead."

"You don't have to try," I told her. "You just are. So am I. I'm an Eastern-style hero; you're the Western version. Eastern heroes know; Western heroes do. Eastern heroes learn to accept; Western heroes fight to their dying breath. Eastern heroes are born with great fanfare in royal pleasure palaces; Western heroes are found floating in baskets and brought up by shepherds. Grotesque clichés, but that's the point of the game."

"Game? What game?" Li grumbled.

I ignored him. "The players choose their pieces from threads of human culture." *Threads of human culture:* Kaisho had used that phrase in my dream. "The Balrog, for instance, picks Buddhist women. It seizes us, reshapes us, transforms us into our own cultural ideal. Bit by bit, we approach Tathagata. As for you, Festina . . . you've been chosen too. By some other powerful alien who's working with the Balrog. Except that *your* patron picked the ideal embodied by Prometheus . . . and Hercules, Ulysses, all the god-defying monster-killers. You get the sword; I get the lotus. Meanwhile, someone else gets the plow, someone gets the scepter, someone gets the divine madness . . ."

"She's babbling," Li said in disgust. "None of this makes—"

"Shut up!" Festina snapped. "I think this is important." She leaned close to me. "Who's saying this? Youn Suu? Or the Balrog?"

"I don't know," I answered. "Maybe the Balrog planted this in my mind; maybe I figured it out myself. But everything's clicked into place: everything I've ever seen, every class at the Academy, all the files I've read about what's happening in the universe . . ."

I lowered my voice. "Listen. We're chosen. You, me, a lot of others." I remembered all the statues I'd seen in the arboretum. "We've been selected by high-ranking aliens in the League of Peoples; they're grooming us to be *champions*. There's something in *Homo sapiens* . . . or maybe in human culture . . . something the superior races care about. Maybe something they lost on the way to becoming powerful: we have some potential the League no longer possesses. So they have this project—this game—to push humans beyond normal. Not beyond the limits of humanity; it's our humanness that's valuable. But if a set of us are pushed to become embodiments of time-honored human ideals . . ."

"Like the Balrog pushing you to become a living Buddha?"

"Yes. The Balrog picked that particular aspect of humanity, and it's taking me down that path. Now I've reached the point where I've finally gleaned a few insights." I gave a rueful chuckle. "Good thing I'm becoming the sort of ideal who understands the universe. If I got chosen to be, oh, the Ultimate Thief or the Ultimate Drunkard, we wouldn't have a clue what was happening."

"What about me?" Festina asked. "I'm no goddamned ultimate."

"Not yet. But you're being put through your paces by whatever alien is molding you into its champion. You're the heroic archetype, right down the line: beginning with a mysterious birth that hides your real identity and going on from there. The alien left you on a doorstep where some family would give you precisely the right upbringing. Probably watched over you as you were growing up and secretly nudged you in the right direction if ever you slipped off course. You aren't more than human, but you're . . . exactly what you need to be, mentally and physically."

"In order to be a champion."

"Yes."

"So I'm engineered?"

I shrugged. "Your genes could be all-natural if your alien patron wanted it that way—choosing two exemplary parents and trusting to chance. Some patrons might avoid direct genetic intervention, for fear of splicing out whatever crucial element we humans have. But one way or another, you were created to express an aspect of humanity your patron thinks is important."

"A goddamned hero."

"A European-style hero. Knight, monster-slayer, rescuer of innocents."

"Fuck that," Festina said. "And fuck this whole business of competing with you or anyone else."

"We aren't competing," I told her. "The game isn't about who's stronger than who, it's who achieves the final goal. Which type of champion will realize humanity's potential. The puppet-masters behind the experiment will keep bringing champions like you and me together until we crack whatever secret we're supposed to reveal."

Festina stared at me a long time. Her aura said she was thinking it over: hoping it wasn't true, fearing it was. Finally, she whispered, "Is there some way to recognize these champions?"

I touched the birthmark on her cheek. Then I touched the ooze on my own. "We're marked for easy recognition. The whole damned Explorer Corps. We're the champions—every last member."

* * *

Festina gaped in horror. "You mean we were all . . . tampered with . . . by aliens . . . from birth? *Before* birth? Everybody in the corps?"

I wanted to answer, *Look at me. Look at you. Could it possibly be an accident we were born reverse images of each other?* But the words that came out of my mouth were, "Sorry. Can't say more. The Mother of Time will pull out my tongue."

"Bloody hell!" Festina roared. She grabbed me by the arms and jerked me off the ground. "You are *not* going to leave things there. You're going to tell me everything I need—"

"No," my mouth said without my volition.

"Don't give me that shit. How do the aliens influence the Excorps? How do they control who does and doesn't become an Explorer? Good God, were they even responsible for creating the corps in the first place? And maintaining it all these years? I need answers, Youn Suu."

"No," I said again. "You don't. Too much information would jeopardize the final outcome. It's all about what's inherent in *Homo sapiens*; champions have certain traits emphasized, but nothing human has been excised. What you and I are has always been possible in the human species, even if it's seldom attained. But learning the whole truth now would ruin our naïveté. It would make us more than human. Prejudice the experiment."

"Forcing you to become Buddha doesn't prejudice the experiment?"

"The Buddha was entirely human. Anyway, the Balrog isn't forcing me to become anything. It's accelerating certain parts of the process, but I've taken every crucial step on my own. That's the way it had to be, or the effort would have been wasted." I put my hand on hers. "You'll have the same opportunity, Festina. I can see you think your whole life has been a lie—that you're a rat running through someone else's maze. But you've always had choices. Real choices with real consequences. They have to let you choose, or the rest is pointless."

"I thought you said they nudged me to become what I am. They bred me, they birthed me, they controlled me . . ."

"They didn't control you," I said. "They influenced you. They arranged for you to be raised in a certain culture. But look at it this way, Festina: ultimately, you have the League of Peoples, the most powerful beings in the universe, ensuring you have free will and a free choice. *They can't let anyone mess with you.* They can guide you to the entrance of one rat maze after another, but once you're inside, they can't interfere. They *can't.* Past a point, they have to keep their hands off." I brushed her cheek, pretending not to see a tear in the corner of her eye. "We hold the missing pieces, Festina—you, me, and the other Explorers. The League of Peoples needs us; they can't fulfill themselves without us."

"Just what I want," Festina said, easing me away and lowering me to the sand. "To fluff the League of Peoples because they can't get it up themselves. Damn!"

She turned, took a few steps, and kicked at a loose stone lying on the beach. Kicked it hard. The stone was lifted off the ground and sent flying to the edge of the lake, plopping loudly into the shallows. Small fish fled from the noise; larger fish swam closer to see if it might be food. "You realize what you've done?" Festina asked. "I didn't want to be a god, but you've made me one anyway. Prometheus, for Christ's sake! You think I'm predestined to live out a legend . . . so even if I dodge ascension here on Muta, it doesn't matter because I'm already halfway up Olympus."

Her voice was so bitter, I wanted to touch her, comfort her . . . but she was too far away, and if I dragged myself toward her, she'd just pull away. "If it helps," I said, "there's always a chance I'm wrong. This could be disinformation planted by the Balrog to hide something else."

"Do you think that's likely?"

I shrugged. Some time in the preceding moments, I'd gone back to speaking for myself rather than having words thrust into my mouth. Hard to tell when it had happened; the line between me and the Balrog was no longer easy to identify.

Odd that I didn't feel dismayed—merging with a creature who was slowly devouring me and who'd darkened my life long before Zoonau. The oozing mess on my cheek . . . had it really been an accident by careless gene engineers, or had spores sneaked into the lab where I was created and subtly altered the embryo? I couldn't be sure, but I suspected the Balrog was responsible for making me an Ugly Screaming Stink-Girl.

Yet I didn't feel anger or outrage. After a lifetime of smarting at injustice, I was relieved to think my disfigurement wasn't random mischance or bad karma. My cheek looked that way for a reason.

I found that comforting.

Enough," said Festina. "Enough of this shit. We've got work to do."

"Whatever you've got in mind," Li grumbled, "I hope to God there's no more walking."

"You can rest where you are if you like," Festina answered. "But time's getting short. According to the Bumbler, we're damned near full of Stage One microbes. We have to get the station working fast."

"What does the Bumbler see inside the station?" I asked.

Festina played with the little machine for a few seconds, then shook her head. "Nothing. The place is shielded against scans, just like buildings in Drill-Press. I'll have to go in blind."

She started toward the entrance. I called after her, "You aren't going alone, are you?"

"Just thought I'd take a peek while you people caught your breath."

"I'm not out of breath," I told her. I began to crawl toward her, sand rasping beneath my body. Suddenly, arms wrapped around me, picking me up. Ubatu. She gave me a quick little hug before carrying me easily across the beach. "See?" I told Festina. "I can get around just fine."

"Youn Suu," Festina said, "this isn't going to work. No matter how strong Ubatu may be, she can't move quickly with you weighing her down. Besides, she's injured. And *you're* injured. You're both liabilities I can't afford. I have to go in alone."

"Not a chance," I said. "You'll need me inside. I'm sure."

"Why? What's inside?"

"I don't know. That's why you'll need me. I have to see what's in there before I can help you."

"If you get in my way, we all might die."

"If you go in without me, you'll be out of your depth."

She glared at me. "Why? Because you're an enlightened Buddhist know-it-all, and I'm not?"

"Because every mythic hero needs some brainy beauty to explain how to kill the hydra or escape the labyrinth."

Festina made a face. "I've always considered *myself* the brainy beauty."

"No, you haven't. Neither have I. We grew up thinking we were Ugly Screaming Stink-Girls . . . which is ridiculous, because we *are* brainy beauties. But now I'm wise as well as brainy, so you need me. Western heroes never wise up till it's too late, and everyone else is dead. Just ask Oedipus. Or Hamlet."

"Just you wait," Festina said. "When this mission is over, I'm going to study Eastern mythology so I can make cheap-ass put-downs about *your* metaphysical shortcomings."

"Ooooomph!" Ubatu yelled. Or some similar sound of loud urgency.

Festina looked around as if there might be some looming danger, but Li (who'd followed on our heels and eavesdropped) said, "She's trying to tell you, for God's sake, shut up! Eastern, Western, this, that, as if those are the only two options!"

"Mph!" Ubatu said, nodding.

"And as if," Li went on, "Eastern and Western haven't interbred to the point where the two can't be separated. Look at me—my father came from a colony that was mostly Chinese, my mother from one that was mostly Belgian, but both planets were so thoroughly mainstream Technocracy, the only difference was the street names. I suppose you people were raised on Fringe Worlds that still cling to vestiges of your original ethnicities; but let me tell you, the Technocracy Core is the proverbial melting pot. Everyone is a mongrel, and the lifestyles mongrelized too. East and West have blended with African, Polynesian, Aboriginal, and Inuit . . . not to mention Divian, Cashling, Fasskister, and all the other alien cultures in our neighborhood. So don't give me East and West. The terms are meaningless. At least they are now. Maybe back in Confucius's day . . ."

"Ooooomph!" Ubatu yelled again. Her arms clenched around me. For a moment, I thought she'd use me as weapon to smack Li across the face. But the impulse passed; her grip relaxed back to normal.

"Behave, you two," Festina snapped. "Behave, or I really will make you wait outside."

She turned and walked toward the station. When the rest of us followed, she said nothing.

18

Bodhichitta [Sanskrit]: The awakened heart/mind/spirit. Every living creature already possesses bodhichitta. The purpose of skillful practice is to remove klesha (poisons) that prevent one's bodhichitta from making itself known.

SINCE the station was a giant Fuentes head, its door was placed in its mouth: a curtain of dark energy centered between the four huge mandibles. By "dark energy," I mean a field of silent blackness—an intangible thing that blocked off light, but didn't register on any of the Bumbler's sensors. When Festina reported the lack of readings, Li said, "Stupid machine. What good is it?"

"If it can't be used as eyes," Festina said, "we'll use it as a hat on a stick."

She pushed the Bumbler into the flat curtain of blackness (making sure to keep her fingers safely out of the field). She waited a moment, then pulled the little device back. "No apparent damage," she said after checking it over. "And it still works. Let's hope that means we can pass through without our intestines exploding."

Festina stepped through the sheet of blackness. A moment later, Ubatu did the same with me in her arms. Immediately, I went blind.

I still had my normal vision. Light entered the building through two glassed-in domes overhead: the faceted Fuentes eyes high up on the station's "face." The general glow was dim—outside, the sun hadn't quite reached the horizon—but the tepid illumination showed we had entered a narrow corridor circling the edge of the building. The corridor's interior wall was as smooth and white as an eggshell. It curved upward to join the outside walls a short distance below the spiked crown. The actual contents of the station (whatever they were) sat in a great white bowl inside the Fuentes head. This corridor ringed the middle of the bowl, in the gap between the inner and outer walls.

All this, I could see with my physical eyes. My sixth sense, however, stretched no farther than my skin. I could perceive everything inside my own body—millions of Balrog spores, and what little remained of my own tissues—but I could see nothing beyond . . . not even Ubatu's life force, though she was pressed against me, still holding me in her arms.

A deep, abject blindness.

Within me, the Balrog stirred. Its life force wasn't nervous or dismayed, but it was definitely disoriented. Disconnected. Its glow had shut down the moment we crossed the threshold—as if it was saving strength.

Ah. I understood.

The Balrog was a hive creature: each spore linked with all others, a gestalt spreading through the galaxy. The spores shared everything instantaneously—thoughts, strength, brainpower—which is why they could keep glowing, even inside my body. For normal creatures, producing light where no one could see was just wasting energy . . . but for Balrog spores, such squandered output would instantly be replenished from reserves in other spores. Probably, the Balrog had trillions of spores doing nothing but soaking up sun on well-lit planets, then feeding solar power to spores like the ones under my skin. The moss in my belly could draw upon huge amounts of energy as needed . . .

. . . until we'd entered this station. Which somehow cut off my spores from their fellows. Not only were they blind, devoid of their sixth sense; they were isolated. On their own.

I could almost imagine bits of moss snuggling up to my own cells for comfort. As soon as we passed through the station's black entrance, the spores had ceased to be the Balrog. Now they were piteous orphans, not dominating me but *depending* on me.

From this point on, we could expect no help from the Balrog as a whole. As for the small supply of spores I carried in my body, I assumed they were there for a purpose, but I couldn't imagine what. They had limited brainpower, limited energy, and probably limited abilities. There'd be no dramatic feats of telekinesis to save us from the station's dangers. If I got injured, perhaps the spores wouldn't even be able to keep me alive.

We humans—we Explorers—we *champions*—were finally on our own.

What now?" Li asked behind me. He'd taken his time coming through the entrance's energy field, but had finally gathered enough courage to join us.

"Now we look around," Festina said. "And before anyone wanders off, let's use the Bumbler." She took a quick sensor scan. "No good," she reported. "We can't see through the inner wall."

"How about the Stage One microbes inside you?" I asked. "I don't suppose they decided to stay outside?"

Festina raised a questioning eyebrow. "The EMP clouds keep their distance from this station," I said. "It makes them nervous. Maybe the microbes that are trying to mutate you want to stay out too."

"Oh good," Festina muttered. "I love waltzing into places that terrify the locals." But she took more readings with the Bumbler and reported, "We still have our escort of microbes—around us and in our bloodstreams. They must be so eager to turn us into smoke, they don't care if monsters live in this building."

"They're microbes," Li said. "They're too stupid to care about anything."

He had a point. The microbes weren't *pretas*; they had no intelligence or emotions. They were just little wrecking machines, waiting for the signal to tear us apart. We could hope the signal wouldn't pass through the station's scan-proof walls . . . but that was just wishful thinking. The Fuentes would have done their best to make sure the signal blanketed the entire planet—*especially* into buildings like this one, which probably had a crew of maintenance personnel to make sure it worked when the time came.

"Let's get going," Festina said, slinging the Bumbler over her shoulder. "We'll circle this corridor once and see what there is to see."

We walked the circumference of the station and found two entrances into the central "bowl"—one on the north and one on the south, both curtained over with the same black energy that covered the front door. No noise came through either entrance; the building hung thick with absolute silence, as if the walls shut out every wayward sound. All we heard was our footsteps on the concrete floor . . . the rustling of our clothes . . . the beating of our hearts.

After our first circuit, we started around again. This time, Festina stopped in front of the first door we came to: the southern entrance, black, blank, revealing nothing. Once again, she pushed the Bumbler through to make sure the energy curtain was safe to enter; the machine came back unharmed. "Okay," she said. "Time to jump down the rabbit hole, Alice."

We stepped into a room brightening with dawn. I'd thought the roof of the station was opaque; it looked that way from the outside. From the inside, however, the room seemed open to the air: a sky of brightening gray, edging into cool, cloudless blue. The sun was too low to be seen, but its rays penetrated the walls, illuminating everything with a yellowed glow.

What was there to see? Ornate machinery: gleaming brass, shining steel, bits of copper and gold. The place reminded me of a Victorian astronomical observatory, with its open roof and collection of equipment below, bristling with gears, cranks, wheels, and levers. There was nothing so recognizable as a telescope, but numerous devices pointed skyward, some long and sharp like spears, others like bulbous cylinders or elongated pyramids. All of them made soft noises—one producing a hum, another a hiss, a third tick-tick-tick—filling the room with a background purr that suggested the station was still operational.

The equipment only covered the outer half of the chamber. The middle of the room was clear of clutter, with nothing but a low ash-gray dome set into the floor—the way humans might put a reflecting pool or a little garden plot in the heart of an open rotunda. But if the dome on the floor was supposed to add visual appeal, it didn't succeed. It was simply a mound of gray, twenty paces across, not quite rising to knee height in the center . . . not what I'd call an attractive architectural feature, but the Fuentes might have had different aesthetic tastes.

Then something fluttered in the mass of grayness. An infinitesimal motion. I looked more closely, trying to detect what had moved . . . and, finally, I realized what I was seeing. I should have recognized it instantly, but I'd come to rely so much on my sixth sense, my normal vision had lost its edge.

The dome—the gray heap—was fuzzy. Mossy. In fact, the mound resembled the mat of spores that had covered the city of Zoonau. It had the same texture, the same smothering weight, the same thick furry surface . . . everything but the color.

I was looking at the Balrog's pallid gray sibling: an anti-Balrog, faded and wilted and dulled.

Ever since we'd landed on Muta, the Balrog had carefully concealed its presence. Now I finally knew what it had been hiding from.

Festina stared at the moss. "Is that what I think it is?" she whispered.

"It appears so," I said.

"You don't know? You don't have any, uhh, feelings about it?"

"My sixth sense hasn't worked since we entered the station."

"That's disconcerting."

"Tell me about it," I said.

Festina pulled the Bumbler into position for a scan. "That stuff certainly reads like the Balrog . . . except, of course, the color."

"It's blotchy," Li said in a loud voice. "Like it's got mange."

He was right. Though the mound at first appeared a uniform gray, closer examination showed subtle variations in tone. Some patches were bleached nearly white; some were smokier, almost as dark as charcoal; other areas had ghostly tints, the barest touch of opal or olive . . . as if this wasn't a single type of moss, but a haphazard assemblage of slightly different breeds, with each individual clump squeezed against its neighbors.

Motley, I thought. Motley like the mishmash of colors in Muta's ferns. Motley like the mosaics on Fuentes buildings. Motley like the *pretas*, seeming to form single clouds, but to my sixth sense, showing up as multitudes of different beings crammed together—neither separate nor integrated, but tossed into a jumble, like salad.

Li took a step toward the mound. "Careful," Festina said. "We don't know whether it's safe. And before you say something stupid like, 'How dangerous can moss be?' remember what the Balrog did to Zoonau."

"*Is* this the Balrog?" Li asked. "Or is it something different?"

"Chemically, it's the same," Festina answered, consulting the Bumbler. "But that means nothing. Chemically, humans are nearly identical to slime molds. What matters is how the chemicals go together."

"With Balrogs," I said, "what matters is how the *spores* go together. I don't think these are a single hive mind. They're separate hive minds, huddled together for warmth."

"You say that because of the different colors?"

"Yes. And because it's what the entire planet has been shouting at us ever since we landed. Motley. Separate things unblended. That's the message."

Li gave me a disgusted look. "Planets don't shout messages. They just *are*."

"What they are *is* the message," I said.

Festina frowned. "Don't go animist on me, Youn Suu. I'm still getting used to you as a junior Buddha."

"I'm an all-purpose Eastern hero. Buddhism is my specialty, but I dabble in animism as a sideline."

"So when it comes to kicking ass, I take on the gods, and you take the pissy little nature spirits?" She looked at the gray mound. "Which of us handles natural-looking moss with godlike powers?"

"What godlike powers?" Li asked. "It's just a pile of moss. No big threat."

Festina and I winced. The Balrog would have taken Li's words as a cue for attack. But the gray anti-Balrog didn't react . . . except for a slight shiver.

Li didn't even realize the risk he'd taken. He walked to the edge of the moss and stared at it: perhaps debating whether to poke it with his shoe. Festina tensed, but didn't stop him; even self-sacrificing Western heroes can let fools walk into the lion's mouth, just to see what the lion does. In the end, the lion—the gray moss—made no obvious response. Li glowered at the mound a moment. Then he said, "Boring!" and turned to walk away.

An odd expression came over his face. "What's wrong?" Festina asked.

"I can't move my foot," he said.

"Why not?"

"I just can't."

Festina almost took a step forward, but I shot out my hand to catch her. "Scan with the Bumbler," I said.

"Forget the damned machine," Li snapped. "I'm . . . I'm paralyzed. Maybe I'm having a stroke."

I knew that wasn't true; Li probably did too. But he couldn't bring himself to admit he'd been caught in a mossy trap.

"I'm getting electrical readings," Festina said. "From the gray spores."

"EMPs?" I asked.

"Not that strong. But a pattern of electrical discharges are focused on Li, and they're interfering with his nervous system. Signals aren't traveling properly between his muscles and brain."

"If we get too close, will the same happen to us?"

"Probably." Festina shucked off her backpack and pulled out a coil of soft white rope. "I might be able to lasso him and drag him back . . ."

"No!" Li shouted. "Just come grab me. Hurry. I'm—"

His foot lifted. Li looked at it in surprise. I assume the motion wasn't Li's doing—electrical discharges from the mound were moving the leg against Li's will—but I never found out for sure. The next moment, Li stepped into the bed of moss. Then his legs buckled, and he toppled backward.

Li fell more slowly than gravity would dictate: as if he were in a VR adventure where the action could suddenly go slow-mo for dramatic effect. His descent took at least ten seconds, drifting through the air, millimeter by millimeter, a feather wisping its way to the ground.

All the way down, Li screamed: a prolonged earsplitting wail, full of anger when it started ("How can you do this to me? To *me*?") but flooding with fear as the fall continued, then right at the end, transmuting to sorrow—regret? maybe even shame at how his life had turned out?—only to be cut off abruptly as he reached the middle of the heap, and spores swept in to cover him. An instant later, Ambassador Li Chin Ho was nothing but a fuzzed-over lump within the mound of gray.

The rest of us didn't react for several seconds. Ubatu's grip was tight around me. Finally, Festina let out her breath and checked the Bumbler's readout. "Li's fall was slowed by something the sensors couldn't analyze. The effect left residual heat, but beyond that the Bumbler says UNKNOWN EMISSION."

"The emission came from the spores?"

"No way to tell . . . but if you ask me, that gray heap used telekinesis to drag Li in, slowing his fall so he wouldn't crush any spores when he landed."

"That's encouraging," I said. "If the moss was afraid of Li falling full force, the spores must be fairly fragile."

"Mmph!" Ubatu agreed, making stomping gestures with her foot.

Festina put her hand on Ubatu's arm. "Crushing the bastards is certainly an option to consider . . . but if they can telekinetically grab prey and reel it in, let's consider that option from a safe distance. I propose a strategic retreat and then we debate tactics."

"Strategic retreat sounds good," I said, and nudged Ubatu toward the exit. While Festina grabbed her Bumbler and backpack, Ubatu carried me to the curtain of energy where we'd entered the room. She hit the black sheet at a pretty good speed—unluckily for me, because the energy field had turned as solid as a concrete wall. Held in Ubatu's arms, I thunked hard against the black surface, then was squashed in by Ubatu's body for a moment before she realized what had happened.

"Mmph!" she muttered as she backed away.

"Festina," I said. "It seems to be a one-way door."

"Shit!" Juggling her pack and the Bumbler, Festina hurried over. She reached gingerly toward the black barrier. Her fingers stopped on contact. "Shit!" she said again . . . then she slammed out her hand in a palm-heel strike, as if brute force might shatter the blockage. The sheet of black made no sound when hit, but I could see the jarring impact travel up Festina's arm, hard enough that the recoil made her step back.

"I believe you're right, Youn Suu. It appears to be a one-way door."

From behind us came a cackling laugh. We whipped around to see the source: Li's head protruding from the mass of gray, spores flecking his skin like pustules. The rest of his body lay submerged in moss, but at least his lungs were working—he had enough breath to laugh again.

Festina groaned. "Am I the only one on this planet who *isn't* possessed by something?"

"Give it time," I told her. "The morning's still young."

* * *

"Hah!" Li cried. "You're trapped."

"Is that Li speaking?" Festina asked me. "Or the moss just using his mouth?"

"Likely the moss," I said. "Got inside him . . . infiltrated his gray matter . . . took over the speech centers and the neurons that understand English." I shrugged. "Eat someone's brain, learn a new language."

"The planarian approach to linguistics."

"You'll go the same way as me," Li sneered. "Soon, you'll all be eaten."

Festina gave me a look. "Isn't he supposed to twirl his mustache when he says crap like that?"

"He probably can't," I said. "The spores swallowed his hands."

"Pity they didn't get his tongue." She raised her voice. "Lot of good eating in a tongue. Mmm, yeah, tasty. I'd eat Li's tongue myself, if that'd save us from one of those 'You unsuspecting fools!' speeches."

"You *are* unsuspecting fools!" Li said.

"Aww, jeez, here it comes," Festina muttered.

"Usually, we only eat vermin," Li gloated. "Scrawny lizards and meatless insects that wander in here to make nests. It's been a long time since we dined on anything larger."

"*Dined?*" Festina said. "Who the hell uses words like *dined*? Not even a gasbag like Li would say *dined*."

"We are not Li," the leering head replied. "We are the Glorious Ones. We are the Divine."

"For God's sake," said Festina, "if you have to possess the poor guy, would you please search his brain for the *normal* speech centers? Li wouldn't be caught dead saying 'Glorious' or 'Divine.' "

"We're content with the part of his brain we've claimed. Contact with this inferior creature's mind disgusts us. We don't intend to access more than necessary . . . but it's been a long time since we had visitors, and we would speak with you."

Festina rolled her eyes at the phrase "we would speak with you." Personally, I thought we were lucky the "Divine" considered themselves too lofty to rummage through Li's brain. Otherwise, they might learn things we preferred to keep secret. What would happen, for example, if the Divine discovered that my body contained Balrog spores? I might instantly become the next meal. Yes, they intended to eat me eventually—or as they might put it, they'd "feast on my succulent flesh"—but for the moment, the patchy gray spores appeared eager to inflate their egos at our expense.

I wondered if the Divine were naturally pompous, or if there was something in Li's body chemistry that induced self-aggrandizement. Buddhists have always known you should be careful what you eat.

So what do you want to gloat about?" Festina asked the moss. "How clever you were to mess up Stage Two for the Fuentes?"

"What?" Li's spore-flecked head asked. "What do you mean?"

"My friend is implying," I said, "that you, the Divine, are responsible for this station's failure. She thinks your presence here indicates you sabotaged the Fuentes' attempt at transcendence." I glanced at Festina. "Alas, she views higher beings with suspicion. Magnificent ones such as you . . . she fears you may seek to prevent lesser creatures from achieving your own degree of perfection."

"*Magnificent ones such as you?*" Festina said under her breath. "Guess we know who's chosen to be the ass-kissing suck-up."

"I prefer the term 'good cop,' " I whispered back.

"Silence!" the possessed head roared. "It is not for you to judge us. You know nothing of our plight."

"Then enlighten us, that we may benefit from your wisdom," I said.

"We *shall* enlighten you," the Divine replied through Li's mouth. "But any benefits therefrom will be short-lived. When we finish consuming this man's flesh, one of you will be next."

"Take Youn Suu," Festina said. "She's bioengineered . . . all kinds of yummy extra vitamins."

"Bitch," I murmured (with a smile).

"I prefer the term 'bad cop,'" Festina said.

You're wrong thinking we sabotaged the Ascension." Li's head had composed itself into a smug expression—as smug as anyone could be while clumps of gray fuzz snacked on his cheeks. "We are the ultimate result of that process. We," said the Divine, "are what you would call Uplifted Fuentes."

"I've seen Uplifted Fuentes," Festina replied. "They look like purple jelly."

"Impostors!" the Divine howled. "Lying, deceitful frauds!"

"Why?"

"They claim we are not truly elevated!" Li's head made a snorting sound that might have been a laugh or a sniffle. "You saw what we can do—how we drew your companion to us. You'll experience the same power soon enough. Even if you run, we shall drag you back by force of will and munch with delight on your bones. But the Jelly Ones . . . they whisper . . . we shut them out, but they whisper . . . they say we are pitiful craven things who never really rose at all."

"Gee," said Festina, "how could they think that?"

I gave her a warning look. The Divine *were* craven things—whining snivelers without enlightenment—but like Bamar demons who could be fooled by Ugly Screaming Stink-names, the gray spores shouldn't be underestimated just because they seemed like buffoons. This moss had real powers: telekinesis and who knew what else. Their mentality might be deficient (perhaps just degraded with age), but they were still deadly. Just ask Ambassador Li.

"The Jelly Ones don't understand you," I said. "They're cruel to torment you with their whispering. Do they do it often?"

"They never stop. Never! When they get close enough, we destroy them . . . but mostly they stay out of range and plague us with taunts. They say they could help if only we'd let them. Liars! We don't need their help."

"I'll bet you hold others at bay too," I said. "Other creatures besides the Jelly Ones."

"Oh yes, many others. We have millions of enemies—millions and millions! All of them hateful and jealous. But we kill them if they get too close."

"What about the settlers?" Festina asked. "The Unity. The Greenstriders. They lived here for years, and you didn't eat them."

"We are the Divine!" they shrieked through Li's mouth. "Do we squander our strength on lesser beings when we must conserve power to fight greater enemies?"

"Ah," said Festina, under her breath. "The bastards have limited energy."

"Besides," the Divine continued, "why should we exert ourselves when microbes do the job for us? In time, the microbes turn all invaders to smoke. Then the newcomers cease to be annoyances."

"You're on good terms with the EMP clouds?" Festina asked.

"The clouds are beneath our contempt . . . but they know their place. At one time, they tried to steal our treasure, but—"

"*Treasure?*" Festina and I repeated in unison.

"Our blessing. Our inheritance."

"O Splendid Ones," I said, "perhaps you should explain what that means. We wish to comprehend your true greatness."

"We're glad to do so," the Divine replied. "Too long have we been misunderstood. Listen, and be amazed."

As the Divine began to speak, Ubatu laid me on the floor. That might just have meant she was resting her arms—why hold me during a potentially lengthy diatribe, when she might need all her strength later?—but I was still troubled by her action. Ubatu hadn't been carrying me out of courtesy or compassion; it was something to do with Ifa-Vodun. She saw me as the vessel of a particularly powerful loa. I'd thought she wanted to keep her hands on me and perhaps win favor with the Balrog through displays of worshipful servitude.

But now Ubatu had met the Divine. And now she'd set me down. I couldn't help wondering if she'd decided the Divine would be more susceptible to her pandering than the Balrog had been. They certainly seemed better candidates for being manipulated: powerful, but not very bright. If Ubatu abased herself before the Divine—if she offered to be their priestess—they might be gullible enough to accept.

Especially if she could prove her loyalty. Perhaps by offering Festina and me as sacrifices. And betraying the secret that I harbored the Divine's enemies: Balrog spores. If Ubatu had been capable of speech, she might have already blurted out the truth. As it was, she'd have to bide her time: wait for some kind of opening that would let her catch the Divine's attention before Festina and I could stop her.

Or not. I might be inventing ulterior motives where none existed. Ubatu could simply be resting her arms. I wished I could still read her life force, but my sixth sense had lost its reach. I had to fall back on my natural five senses, keeping a close eye on Ubatu to make sure she did nothing treacherous while the Divine talked.

Meanwhile, Festina took up a position leaning directly on the curtain of blackness across the room's entrance. If the energy field lost its solidity for the slightest instant, she'd fall into the outer corridor and perhaps beyond the Divine's clutches. Putting her weight on the blackness might also force the Divine to expend energy maintaining the curtain's impenetrability. If the gray spores had limited resources of power, why not compel them to use as much energy as possible?

I found it difficult to believe the Divine were as mighty as they claimed. They reminded me of a grandiose jungle tribe, hiding from modern society, claiming to be masters of the world but living on lizards and insects. If we could make them overextend themselves, we might find a way to avoid being eaten like Li. But first, we had to listen to them pontificate.

"Long, long ago," the Divine said through Li's half-eaten lips, "we were technicians at this station. The ones who readied it for

Stage Two of the Ascension. We did *exactly* what we were told. Exactly! We followed the scientists' directions to the letter."

"Fine, we got the message," Festina said. "You just followed orders, and you weren't the ones who screwed up. What happened?"

"The Ascension happened!" The Divine apparently liked to shriek. This particular yell sounded more breathy than those previous; I wondered if the spores had started snacking on Li's lungs. "It happened just as predicted. First, the microbes pulled apart our bodies. Then, the energy projectors in this station activated themselves. It was *glorious*."

"What went wrong?"

"From our viewpoint, nothing. In the form of clouds, we gathered at the energy projectors. We felt ourselves change—growing more powerful. New strength flooded through us, and we used that strength to feed on the radiation. We gathered it to us; we drank it in; we *reveled* in it. All that power for ourselves."

"For yourselves?" I asked. "What about the people in Drill-Press? Weren't they supposed to get their share too?"

"There wasn't enough to go around! The scientists must have miscalculated. After we ascended, we drove the others away; otherwise, they would have stolen what was rightfully ours."

"You'd already ascended," Festina said, "but you kept sucking up the power pumped out by this station?"

"The power *belonged* to us. Our treasure. Our due."

"Oh boy," Festina muttered under her breath. Raising her voice, she said, "Let me get this straight. This station could produce enough energy to uplift everyone in this part of the planet, including the entire city of Drill-Press and God knows how far beyond. Instead, your team of grease monkeys, who happened to be closest to the source, were the first shoved up the evolutionary ladder. You acquired fancy new abilities and immediately used those abilities to grab the energy for yourself. For the past sixty-five hundred years, no one else has been able to ascend because you're hogging the juice . . . and you yourselves are getting a million times the intended dose of radiation, which means you're—"

"Divine and glorious," I put in before Festina finished her sentence.

She paused for a moment, then said, "Right. Divine and glorious. Absolutely." She gave me a look, then turned back to the moss. "I suppose the same happened at other projection stations?"

"At all of them," replied the moss. "We're in constant mental contact with our counterparts around the planet. Our thoughts are . . . sublime."

"I'll bet. Because you guzzle sublime radiation. The more you get, the more you want, right?"

"The more we absorb, the more our majesty increases."

"We get the picture . . . don't we, Youn Suu?"

"Indeed."

Personally, I was picturing a group of people on Anicca called Crunchers. They caught and ate small snail-like creatures whose shells contained powerful hallucinogens. Crunch, crunch, crunch as the snail shell went down . . . then they'd pass out or go off wandering in a daze. Every few years, safety officials talked of exterminating the snails as a means of ending Crunch addiction; but monks and nuns howled in protest at any mass killing—even snails. Besides, the snails played a role in Anicca's ecology: a protein in their slime trails helped keep the soil fertile. The snails couldn't be slaughtered for fear of environmental disaster. Anicca's safety officials never carried out their threat, and the crunch-crunch-crunching continued.

Festina probably wasn't familiar with Crunchers, but she'd be picturing something else—a different drug, or perhaps wireheading, sex-melds, surgical deverbalization, or any of the other ways *Homo sapiens* embraced delusion. If life didn't offer enough opportunities for fixation, people doggedly sought more inventive obsessions. And the enthusiasm for honey traps wasn't restricted to human beings; these gray spores, these former Fuentes, had succumbed to a similar temptation. When the Stage Two energy flowed, they were supposed to let it wash over them, like bathing in a pleasant stream . . . but instead, they'd got a taste of uplifting energy and instantly wanted it all. They'd gobbled so much in those first few moments, they'd overdosed. Yes, they'd gained telekinesis and perhaps other powers too, but they'd damaged themselves in the process. Burned out their brains. Instead of gaining enlightenment, the Divine had become virtually infantile . . . but infants with god-like strength.

"So you're still basking in the station's radiance," Festina said. "I'm surprised the equipment keeps working after so many millennia."

"We are the Divine!" the moss shouted. "Do we not have the power to do what we will?"

"They were technicians," I reminded Festina. "Now they're technicians with TK. They know how to keep the machines operational. Anyway, Fuentes technology can last a long time without outside maintenance. Remember the research center in Drill-Press? Whatever kept the pocket universe stable . . . remember how well that equipment worked?"

"Ah . . . yes . . ." Festina said. "I remember how stable the research center was. You think the equipment here is the same?" She thought for a moment. "You're probably right. Wherever I go, Fuentes artifacts all seem in similar condition."

I.e., on the verge of falling apart. Just as the rainbow-arch research center had flickered constantly, perhaps the machines around us were ready for massive failure. The Divine spores could perform routine maintenance on the station's facilities, but how would they manufacture new parts when old ones broke beyond repair? Some time soon, there'd be a malfunction the gray moss couldn't handle; then it would all be over.

Perhaps that explained why the Balrog had finally come to Muta. The Divine might be vulnerable now. In the past sixty-five centuries, while the station still worked, the gray spores had been unassailable . . . but now when the system was weakening, perhaps the moss could be beaten. Besides, the Balrog might want to resolve the mess on Muta before this station suffered permanent breakdown; otherwise, there'd be no way to propel the *pretas* into Stage Two. Our arrival may have been timed for a unique window of opportunity:

when the station's output was precarious enough to debilitate the Divine, but still sufficiently functional to elevate the *pretas*.

All we had to do now was persuade the Divine to share the station's energy with their fellows: the EMP clouds, the *pretas*, the hungry, hungry ghosts.

"Where does the station's power come from?" I asked the Divine. "Hydroelectric generators in the dam? Solar collectors? Geothermal? Fusion using lake water as a hydrogen source?"

"All those," the moss replied. "There's also a sizable amount of plutonium buried beneath the building's foundations. Well shielded, of course, but it provides ongoing heat."

"Tremendous," Festina said. "What prevents a runaway chain reaction? Control equipment sixty-five hundred years old?"

"You need not worry about nuclear explosions, human. Your death will come as we feed on your flesh."

"What do you need flesh for? Don't you feed on this station's energy."

"We bask in that glory, yes. But we also require small replenishments of chemical nutrients. We can obtain simple elements like oxygen and nitrogen from the air, but we have long since depleted all nearby iron, calcium, and the like. We spend much of our time dormant to reduce our needs . . . but the flesh of four humans will allow us to remain awake for years."

"Glad to be of service," Festina said. She looked at the surrounding equipment: the metal spikes, barrels, and pyramids. "Do all these things project the energy you eat?"

"They are part of the chain of production. The actual emission center is directly beneath us."

"There's a basement?"

Li's head cackled with laughter. "No. The emission surface is embedded in the floor on which you stand. We have positioned ourselves on the primary projection outlet. Originally, the power was supposed to be transferred to broadcast rods on the exterior; but we couldn't permit it to be squandered on the world at large."

In other words, the Divine were sitting directly on the central emitter—like a dragon sprawled on its hoard. Or like a plug holding back the flow. If somehow the moss was cleared away, the Stage Two radiation would be released as originally intended: it would spark across the gap to the station's roof and shoot from the spiky crown on the giant Fuentes head. Nearby *pretas* would be uplifted. Clouds farther off would learn what was happening, thanks to their shared mental links . . . and *pretas* around the world would fly here as fast as they could, yearning to be freed from their smoky existence. I didn't know how long it would take for every cloud to make its way here and be transformed—hours? years?—but that didn't matter. If clouds in the immediate neighborhood were elevated, we'd be safe from angry EMPs. We could set up a Sperm-tail anchor and return to *Pistachio*, where standard decontamination procedures would purge us of Stage One microbes.

All that stood in our way were the spores, corking up the energy flow. Remove them, and the problems of Muta would be solved.

Festina must have followed the same train of thought, because she murmured, "All right, your Buddha-ness, any suggestions for a fuzzy gray exorcism?"

"We could try gentle persuasion. Show them the error of their ways."

"Or," said Festina, "we could kick their ass."

"The moment you try, you get eaten like Li."

"Never underestimate a Western champion, you Eastern also-ran. We always have a trick up our sleeve . . . a magic sword, a flask of holy water, or spiffy ruby slippers."

I wanted to ask what trick she intended, but the Divine might overhear. So would Ubatu . . . who'd listened to Festina, and now had a worrisome look in her eye. It occurred to me, I'd never told Festina about Ifa-Vodun and Ubatu's goal of toadying up to godlike aliens. Surely though, that wouldn't matter—Festina had never trusted Ubatu (or anyone else, for that matter), so there was no risk Festina would say too much with Ubatu in earshot. Right?

Festina glanced cautiously toward the heap of Divine, then said very softly, "Back at Camp Esteem, when we first searched the cabins for survivors, I found something. Something I took, just in case it came in useful." Her hand slipped into her backpack. When she pulled it out again, a small object lay in her palm: egg-shaped, no bigger than the tip of her thumb, colored in swirls of pink and green. "It's a Unity minigrenade. Doesn't look like much, but there's antimatter inside—enough for a good-sized explosion. Team Esteem must have packed it in case they needed to blow their way into some Fuentes security vault." She cast a sideways look at the Divine. "If those spores are as weak as I think, this should burn them to a crisp. We'll take cover behind all this fancy equipment." Festina reached for the Bumbler with her free hand. "Give me a few seconds to analyze where we'll get the best protection from the blast . . ."

She didn't have those seconds. Ubatu snatched the egglike object from Festina's palm with the speed of a striking eagle. I tried to stop her but wasn't quick enough—Ubatu moved inhumanly fast, beyond even my bioengineered reflexes. Either her designers had discovered some new genetic tricks, or she'd been amplified with illegal implants: artificial glands that could pump a barrage of chemicals into her bloodstream when she needed an extra boost. I barely managed to catch her leg as she was bolting away . . . but she shook me off and dashed across the floor, hollering, "Ooommmph! Ooommmph!"

Straight toward the Divine.

The gray spores rippled at Ubatu's approach . . . in fear? In anticipation of another hearty meal? But they took no obvious action. Ubatu stopped short of the mound and abased herself, holding out the little pink-and-green ovoid like an offering to an idol. Beside me, Festina turned dials rapidly on the Bumbler, scanning, scanning, scanning. Still looking for a place to take cover if the grenade went off? Was there really a chance of accidental detonation? I had no idea. I knew nothing about Unity minigrenades: not a subject we'd studied in the Explorer Academy. I didn't know a grenade's power, its volatility, the timing on its fuse . . .

Oh.

No . . .

Oh again.

Eastern champions don't always think quickly, but sooner or later they do catch on.

"Be careful with that!" I shouted to Ubatu. "Don't you know not to make sudden moves with a bomb?"

"A bomb?" The words squealed from Li's mouth as the mound of moss went wild: variegated patches of gray thrashing against their neighbors. The patches remained separate, but their boundaries blurred. I wondered how much they'd been mind-linked in the past few minutes; enough to coordinate their efforts in eating Li and speaking through his mouth, but not to deal with matters of life and death. A motley—a mosaic—individuals with no real community. "A bomb?" the Divine repeated, as if they'd never entertained the thought they could be threatened in their own sanctum.

"Ooommmph!" Ubatu cried. She pulled in her outstretched hands, clutching the little blob of pink and green to her breast for a moment, before hurling herself on top of it. "Ooommmph," she said to the Divine. Softly. Reverently.

"What is she doing?" the Divine shrieked, still rustling with agitation.

Since Ubatu couldn't answer, I did. "She's showing that she's willing to throw herself on a grenade for you. Demonstrating her readiness to sacrifice herself for your magnificence."

Ubatu nodded eagerly.

Even without my sixth sense, I could almost feel the gray moss staring at her. "Why would she do that?" the Divine asked.

"Because she wants to win your favor. She wants to worship you . . . in the hope that you'll share some of your knowledge and glory. None of the other advanced aliens in the galaxy will grant such boons to lesser beings . . . but Commander Ubatu believes that if she enacts the correct rituals in a spirit of true obeisance, you'll make her your priestess."

"Priestess? Priestess?" The gray mound shivered. I doubted the spores ever considered the possibility of acquiring a priestess. If sentient beings had wandered into this station anytime in the centuries before our arrival, the Divine probably just gobbled up everybody—no attempt to form a congregation. But now that Ubatu had made the offer . . .

"Is the bomb safe now?" the moss asked.

"I don't think it's going to explode," I told them truthfully.

"Then approach, priestess," the Divine said. "Approach and let us assess you."

Ubatu leapt to her feet, then bowed deeply. "Ooomph!" She straightened and took a few steps forward, up to the edge of the mound. Only then did she glance down at the front of her uniform. The gold cloth was smeared with a gooey blot of orangey yellow.

"What's that?" the Divine asked.

"Ooommph?" Ubatu said, still staring at the mess.

"Looks to me like egg yolk," I told them. "Better clean it off before—"

My words were drowned out by screams: sudden agonized howls from the Divine. This time they weren't using the dead Li as an intermediary—the cries of pain came directly from the mound itself. Somehow the spores, with neither mouths nor lungs, wailed like dying animals. "What have you done? What have you done? What have you done? What have you done?"

I'd done nothing . . . but Festina had. I looked back and saw her standing beside a brass pyramid almost exactly her own height. While Ubatu and the egg/grenade captivated the Divine's attention, Festina had used the Bumbler to scan the station's equipment. She'd found what she was looking for, then crept silently across the floor and popped open an access panel. Reaching inside, she'd detached a wire: a single slim strand of yellow that she now held in her right hand. Her left hand was out of sight, inside the pyramid's guts.

The room had gone silent—the hum and hiss of machinery dwindling to nothingness.

"Hey, Youn Suu," Festina said. "I found the off switch."

* * *

The silence lasted another heartbeat. Then the Divine cried, "Traitor! Deceiver!"

Ubatu was yanked off her feet and pulled into the mass of gray—swallowed with merciless brutality. She made no sound as she disappeared under the spores . . . perhaps hoping the Divine might just possess her rather than consume her. Or maybe she didn't mind being eaten; maybe she was so fanatic she'd revel in *any* kind of attention from "advanced lifeforms."

Ifa-Vodun's first martyr.

While Ubatu was vanishing into the heap, I murmured to Festina, "Pity you can't tell the difference between an egg and a grenade."

"Yeah," she said. "Real shame."

"You found the egg in the huts you searched?"

"Sure. One of Team Esteem's naturalists had gathered a nice set of samples—eggs from the nests of local lizards. I've always liked little colored eggs; I couldn't resist taking the prettiest. Breaks my heart Ubatu smashed it."

"Didn't do the baby lizard much good either."

"Don't blame me," Festina said. "I wasn't the one who sold out to the enemy."

"You suspected Ubatu would?"

"I suspected she'd do something stupid. Back on *Pistachio*, I read her personnel file. She has a record of irrational behavior in pursuit of advanced aliens . . . and flagrantly preaching some religion called Ifa—"

The rest of Festina's words were drowned out by more screams from the moss. They'd finished dealing with Ubatu; they'd ripped her apart because they thought she was a hypocrite, falsely offering to be their priestess just to distract them. Now they were turning to the real source of their distress: the woman who had shut down the station. "Put that wire back!" they shrieked at Festina. "Fix it, or we'll kill you!"

"You were going to kill me anyway," Festina said. "If you try it now, I've got my left hand around some glass thingamajig the Bumbler tells me is fragile as hell. There's foamy orange liquid inside the thingamajig; if I break the glass, it'll spill all over. I haven't a clue what the stuff does, but I'm willing to bet the orange liquid is a complex chemical you can't replace. I'm also willing to bet the liquid is essential for running this station—my Bumbler says this pyramid is a central hub for all the wires and pipes in the building. Mess with me, and I snap the thingamajig to pieces . . . splatter orange goo everywhere. That'll put this place out of commission a lot more permanently than a loose wire."

"Put the wire back, human! Reattach it now. Don't you realize the *sacrilege* . . .

"Sacrilege? Bullshit. You aren't gods. You're opportunists who were in the right place at the right time to suck on a magic teat. You've been slurping the milk of heaven ever since, but you're no more divine than I am."

"If we can't touch you, what about your companion?" I felt a wave of hate from the gray moss aimed at me—a palpable flash of loathing so strong it registered on my dormant sixth sense. "Reattach the wire," the Divine told Festina, "or we'll kill your friend."

"Honestly," Festina said, "can't you talk about anything but killing? First you were going to kill us for lunch. Then you were going to kill me for sacrilege. Now you're going to kill Youn Suu for extortion. The more you make death threats, the more you convince me there's no point striking a deal. You're lousy at negotiation."

"Perhaps it's because the Divine have just eaten Li and Ubatu," I said. "Neither of them were good at diplomacy either."

"If they ate *you*, would they get all enlightened?"

"If they asked politely, they could have the bottom half of my right leg. It wouldn't be enough to bring out their *entire* Buddha nature . . . but it might raise their IQ forty or fifty points, and it would even me up nicely."

"Bilateral symmetry is so important," Festina agreed.

"Shut up, shut up, shut up!" the Divine shrieked. "Shut up and tell us what you want."

Festina laughed. "What do you think we want? Get your fuzzy asses off the energy emitter. Let this station work the way it was intended."

"But we *need* the energy! We need it or we'll die."

"Nonsense." Festina held up the detached wire, still in her right hand. "You're already cut off, aren't you? And you're still alive. So don't give me sob stories. Maybe if you stop overdosing on weird-shit energy, you'll transform the way you were meant to: into *real* higher beings, not just psionic blowhards. Besides," she added, "I don't care if you *do* die. You killed Li and Ubatu. That makes you dangerous nonsentient lifeforms. The League of Peoples will give me a gold star for ending your useless lives."

"But . . ."

"No buts! Get off the emitter . . . now. Otherwise—"

Three things happened in rapid succession.

First, Festina's left hand was thrown back out of the pyramid. Somehow the Divine had telekinetically ripped loose her grip on the glass thingamajig without breaking the delicate mechanism. I was surprised the spores had tried such a risky maneuver—if they'd miscalculated, they might have smashed the glass and put the station permanently out of order—but deprived of their age-old addiction, the bits of moss were desperate enough to take the chance. I heard no shattering glass; the Divine's gamble had paid off.

Second, Festina gasped . . . not just in surprise at having her hand torn free from the pyramid. She was under some other attack: the Divine trying to kill her. Telekinetically crushing her heart? Squeezing her throat? Bursting an artery in her brain? The spores would want her dead, to make sure she gave no more trouble and to take revenge for the trouble she'd already caused. Without a sixth sense, I couldn't tell what the Divine was doing; but the sharpness of her gasp suggested the onslaught was fast and brutal.

Third, I felt power surge within me: the red Balrog spores finally making their move. Their strength was limited—their mass was no more than a tenth of the Divine mound's, and their energy proportionately small—but they had the advantage of surprise. The Divine spores never expected opposition on the psychic plane, so they were totally unprepared for the Balrog's intervention. Glowing red barriers sprang up around Festina and me, beating back the Divine's assault. Festina's gasp turned to relief as the Divine's crushing grip was repelled.

But the respite was only temporary; we weren't safe yet. The red spores in my body were massively outnumbered by the gray spore heap. My internal Balrog could only protect us a short while: I felt the Divine hammering on the red glow around me, trying to bash down the wall. My spores had no strength to spare beyond keeping the enemy at bay. Festina and I would have to neutralize the Divine on our own, before the gray overwhelmed the red and ripped us all to pieces.

At least we had one advantage: the gray spores couldn't draw on the station's energy. Festina still held the detached yellow wire, so no power was flowing. Even as that thought crossed my mind, however, the wire jerked in her hand. The Divine must have grabbed it telekinetically; their next step would be to reconnect it and bring the station back online. With the return of radiation to the emitters, the gray spores would gain all the strength they needed to finish us off.

As Festina fought to hold the wire back, I pulled myself toward her as fast as I could. The Divine didn't stop me; why weaken themselves by dividing their efforts? They were already concentrating on two tasks: trying to break the red fields that protected Festina and me, and shoving the wire back into place.

Festina held the wire in both hands now, wrestling it like a thin yellow snake. Her body strained with the effort, a desperate tug-of-war. It amazed me the wire didn't break under the tension; either it was made from high-tech material far stronger than conventional copper, or the Divine were psionically reinforcing it, holding it together by the power of their will. Millimeter by millimeter, the bare tip of conductor at the end of the wire nosed its way toward the electrical terminal where it was supposed to be attached . . . but before it made contact, I grabbed Festina's arms and added my strength to hers.

More precisely, I added my *weight* to hers. I had no legs to brace myself, and lying on the floor, I couldn't reach high enough to grab the wire itself. All I could do was grip her bent elbows and hang off them, letting my body mass drag her down. The wire came with us, pulling away from the connection terminal by our combined efforts. In the center of the room, the Divine howled gibberish . . . perhaps curses in the ancient Fuentes language.

Both Festina and I hung our full weights on the wire—pulling down while the Divine tried to lift the thin strand into place. Under other circumstances, the metal line would have sliced Festina's fingers like a garrote; but the Balrog's glowing red shield resisted the wire's cutting force as well as the gray moss's ongoing assault. Still, we were only fighting a delaying action . . . and we weren't winning. Bit by bit, we were pulled upward as the Divine spores exerted their willpower.

"Got any bright ideas?" Festina asked.

I looked around for inspiration. The pyramid's open access panel showed hundreds of complex components, from electronic circuit boards to sheets of spongy biologicals to crystal vials containing colored liquids and gases . . . but a faint gray fog lay between us and the machinery, almost exactly like the dim red glow surrounding Festina and me. The Divine must have raised that fog as a force field, to stop us attacking the pyramid's delicate innards. Not that we really would have tried to damage the fragile equipment—we still wanted to reactivate the station once we'd removed the Divine—but the gray spores weren't taking chances. I was glad they had to expend energy on the gray fog field; the more they used on unnecessary measures, the less strength they had for pulling the yellow wire. But the fog meant there was nothing within reach we could use to our benefit.

So Festina and I continued to dangle—the two of us entwined awkwardly, muscles straining, our breaths loud in our ears. "So," Festina said, trying to make her tone conversational, "what are the odds the Divine will exhaust themselves before they reconnect the wire?"

"I don't know."

"But you're an Eastern hero," she said with a smile. "Aren't you supposed to know everything we dumb Western heroes don't?"

"Eastern heroes specialize in the big picture. Ultimate truths of the cosmos, not what's going to happen in the next ten seconds. Although," I added, "hanging from this wire reminds me of a story."

"Feel free to share." Festina yanked on the wire as it struggled to make the connection. "What else do I have to do but listen to stories?"

"Once upon a time," I said, "a monk was chased by a tiger. While running away, he accidentally fell off a cliff; he just barely saved himself by grabbing a vine on the cliff's edge. So there he was dangling, with the tiger roaring just above his head and a deadly plunge beneath his feet."

"I'll like this story a lot," Festina said, "if the monk has a clever way to escape."

"This isn't that kind of story. The monk noticed the vine he was holding had berries on it. He caught a berry in his mouth and ate it. 'Ahh,' he said. 'How sweet.' And that's the end of the story."

"In other words," Festina said, "ignore your troubles and enjoy what you can?"

"No. Don't ignore *anything*. That's the point. Even if you're in desperate straits, berries still exist, and they're still sweet. The universe doesn't go sour just because you personally have problems."

"And the tiger doesn't go away just because you eat a berry."

"Exactly. Don't fixate on either the berry or the tiger."

"Okay." Festina said nothing for a few heartbeats. The wire in her fingers continued to inch toward the terminal. "Youn Suu," she muttered, "I'm having trouble seeing the berry here. Unless . . ."

"Grr-arrh."

We both snapped our heads toward the door. Tut stood inside the black energy curtain: still wearing the battered bear mask, sniffing the air in a gruff ursine way.

"Grr-arrh," he said again. "Grr-*arrh*!"

"Okay," Festina said. "Berry . . . bear . . . it's a stretch, but I get the point."

"Tut!" I yelled. "See the gray moss, Tut? The moss, Tut, the moss. Show the bastards you still don't care."

For a moment, he didn't respond . . . and I feared his brain had been damaged by the *pretas* who'd worked all night to possess him.

Then: "Hot damn, Mom!" He whipped the mask off his head. "You've finally found some fun on this shit hole of a planet. Swan dive!"

As he'd done atop the ziggurat in Zoonau, Tut threw himself onto the spores.

When the Divine pulled Li and Ubatu into their midst, they'd taken their time. They'd reeled the diplomats in, making sure their descent was slow—slow enough not to crush any spores underneath.

But when Tut plunged into the mossy heap . . .

The Divine weren't prepared to split their attention in so many directions: having to deal with Tut, as well as playing tug-of-war with the yellow wire, maintaining the gray fog to protect the pyramid's mechanical guts, and keeping up pressure on the red glow that shielded Festina and me. Tut's move caught the Divine by surprise. They were used to dragging prey in, not having it leap on top of them. Besides, the demonic gray spores were too fixated on reconnecting the yellow wire; they didn't react to Tut until a nanosecond before he plunged into their midst. Then, at the last instant, as Tut plummeted down like an avalanche of long-delayed karma . . . the Divine simply bolted in fright.

Pure atavistic instinct: jump out of the way. The spores forgot everything else as they scattered in all directions, fleeing to the edges of the room with the grainy sound of a sandstorm.

The tug-of-war on the yellow wire ended abruptly. Festina and I hit the floor as the panicked Divine let go of their end.

Tut landed on solid gold: a golden disk embedded in the floor, almost exactly the size of Tut himself as he threw out his arms and legs to absorb the impact of landing. He looked like da Vinci's drawing of human anatomical proportion as he posed spread-eagled within the golden circle. Then Festina, free from the Divine's TK, shrugged me off and slapped the yellow wire back into place on its terminal.

All around the room, machines began to hum. A heartbeat later, golden light flooded upward from the emitter disk, streaming around Tut's body like honey-colored fire. Gray spores howled and tried to scurry back to the radiance . . . but at the edges of the disk, they ran into a glowing red barrier. I could feel the Balrog spores inside me blaze with dying determination as they spent their last reserves of energy holding the Divine back.

Gold light filled the dome of the station. It built to a blazing intensity, then exploded outward through the spikes in the building's crown. For a moment, my sixth sense returned, showing me hundreds of *pretas* outside the station, permeated with healing bursts of energy. I waited to see them transform . . .

. . . but instead I went blind. *Truly* blind. No sixth sense. No eyes. The spores in my body—the ones replacing parts of my brain, the ones that had kept me alive through broken bones, hemorrhages, and even amputation—all of them reached the end of their strength and died en masse within me.

I was purged of my infestation . . . and left with a body no longer able to survive on its own.

Everything went black.

19

Prajna [Pali]: Wisdom; insight; understanding.

TO my great surprise, I woke up. More or less.

I was no longer in the station. I was no longer anywhere. My surroundings were neither light nor dark, hot nor cold. Just there. Peaceful and placid, undemanding, unyielding.

So, I thought, *the Afterlife Bardo. I'm dead.*

Tibetan scholars liked to contemplate the gaps between things—particularly the gap between death and rebirth. They called these in-between states Bardos. The Bardo of Death was sometimes pictured as a spirit realm where the recently deceased made choices in preparation for their next life.

As a non-Tibetan, I had my doubts. In standard scriptures, the Buddha never mentioned Bardos; I'd always considered them holdovers from some pre-Buddhist mysticism. At best, I'd thought Bardos might be useful metaphors for stages in a more metaphysical journey.

Yet here I was. Or so it appeared.

Balrog, I said, with soundless words, *you're manipulating my perceptions again. Simulating an afterlife. Must you keep playing these games?*

A point of red appeared in the nothingness. A solitary Balrog spore. It hovered in my consciousness—not speaking, just waiting.

This is all in my mind, I said. *What's left of my mind. Considering I'm missing most of my brain, it's surprising I can think at all.*

Silence.

You're helping me, aren't you? Working your magic from afar. For thousands of years, the Divine walled off the station from your influence . . . but the Divine are out of the picture. As soon as a few pretas *got elevated—truly elevated—they'd deal with the Divine, one way or another. So you're no longer shut out, and you can reach my dying brain. Right?*

The glowing red spore showed no reaction . . . but I felt as if it was listening. Hearing my final thoughts.

I am *dying, aren't I? When you came to me back in Zoonau, I knew this all might lead to my death. And here it is. My death.*

The spore dimmed slightly, then returned to its steady glow.

But, I continued, *you could still save me, couldn't you? If I invited you into my body again, you could patch me up. You could teleport spores into me from anywhere in the galaxy. You could heal me by infesting me again.*

The spore bobbed slightly.

For several moments, I didn't speak. Finally, I said, *I'm not afraid of death. True death might not lead to a Bardo, but I'm not afraid. Fear is unskillful.*

This time, the spore didn't respond. It was still waiting.

There's more I could do, isn't there? I'm not afraid of death, but living would let me accomplish useful things. I laughed lightly. *The Bodhisattva's decision—choosing not to move on, because there are still creatures who need help.*

The spore fluttered momentarily. I didn't know what that meant. There were surely an infinite number of things I would never understand even if I became enlightened. Enlightenment isn't omniscience; it's just freedom.

At that moment, I had a degree of freedom. Free choice: I could bid farewell to the Balrog and let death come as it always comes eventually; or I could invite the Balrog to enter me, once again surrendering to alien infestation.

Put it another way: I could run from the sufferings of the universe, or I could join forces once again with a quirky creature who'd called me to be its champion.

I had no body, but I moved toward the glowing spore. I opened my being . . . my trust . . . my love . . .

Once again, I woke up.

Festina was lightly slapping my face. "Youn Suu. Come on, Youn Suu, wake up. Come on . . ."

I opened my eyes. What I saw first was Festina's hand; it had ooze on it. She'd been slapping my bad cheek and hadn't cared. I took her hand . . . kissed it . . . wiped it off on my uniform. When she looked embarrassed, I just smiled. "I'm fine," I said. "I died for a bit, but decided that was too easy."

"What do you mean, you died?" By now, Festina had pulled back her hand and was wiping it vigorously on her own uniform. Wiping off my kiss? "I scanned you with the Bumbler," she said. "You weren't dead, you just fainted." She gave me a look. "If you'd been dead, you idiot, I'd be giving you CPR, not patting your face as if you were a swooning chambermaid."

I shrugged. Whether I'd really died didn't matter. If I'd rejected the Balrog, all the CPR in the universe wouldn't have helped me. But the dead spores inside me had been replaced by fresh ones, full of mischievous energy. I could feel them—feel their power.

My sixth sense was back.

Which meant I could tell what was happening in the rest of the station. Light continued to gush from the station's emitter plate . . . and Tut still lay on the golden disk, bending this way and that to make shadows on the ceiling with his body. His thin frame didn't block much of the radiance—certainly not as much as the Divine had all these years.

I couldn't sense the Divine. Perhaps when the first *pretas* were uplifted, they'd used their new power to eradicate the spores; or perhaps the newly elevated Fuentes had dealt more kindly with their centuries-long enemies. The *pretas* might have helped the Divine to ascend too, as should have happened from the very beginning.

Vengeance or mercy: often hard to predict.

I felt the Fuentes' arrival a moment before I saw it—a powerful presence blossoming in the room, a life force of dazzling vitality. The creature's aura blazed from a spot behind Festina's back . . . and suddenly, there was a small slick of purple on the floor, a sheen of quivering jelly.

How anticlimactic.

When I pointed out our visitor to Festina, she sighed. "Now the big boys arrive—to pat us on the back and send us on our way."

"Actually," the jelly said, "we're patting *ourselves* on the back." The voice was female: low and gentle, slightly amused. "We did an excellent job choosing our champion."

Festina glared. "So Youn Suu's theory about champions is true?"

The jelly laughed. "Admiral, you can't expect me to give a straight answer. Perhaps what Youn Suu said *is* true; perhaps every member of the Explorer Corps is the protégé of some high-echelon race in the League of Peoples. Perhaps each member of the corps was created or chosen in the belief that *Homo sapiens* have the potential to do something we can't do ourselves. Or perhaps we overheard Youn Suu expound that hypothesis, and we find it amusing to encourage such a ridiculous conjecture."

"I hate you guys," Festina muttered. "Every smug bastard in the League. I really hate you."

"Hypothetically," I said to the jelly, "if you *did* sponsor a particular Explorer as your champion . . . who would it be?"

"Not me," Festina said. "Please tell me I'm not the one. I'd hate to be created by something that looks like grape jam."

The jelly laughed again. "Rest assured, Admiral, you aren't ours. Neither is Youn Suu; she and her ilk belong to the Balrog."

"So if it isn't me and it isn't Youn Suu . . ." Festina's head turned, and so did mine: both of us looked toward Tut.

"Your legends recount many refreshing forms of madness," the jelly said. "Mostly, such stories are untrue to life. Genuine mental illnesses are seldom amusing; those who suffer from such conditions are miserably dysfunctional. But your folktales abound with wise fools and lunatics. If one carefully arranges precise metabolic imbalances throughout a child's gestation and infancy . . ."

Festina finished the sentence. "You get someone who's loony but still competent. Assuming you aren't just lying about this whole 'champion' thing."

No, I thought, the "champion thing" wasn't a lie. I remembered the flashes of purple I'd seen in Tut's aura, helping him fight off possession by the *pretas.* It was the same shade of purple as the Fuentes jelly: just a tiny flicker of aid from his "sponsors" to keep him in the game. The jelly couldn't actually force Tut to do anything—that would ruin the spontaneity of the experiment—but they could orchestrate events to bring Tut to when and where he was needed.

"If you're Tut's patron," I said to the jelly, "who's Festina's?"

"That will be revealed at a time of her patron's choosing . . . assuming, again, we aren't lying."

"And in the meantime, the patron just lets me sweat in ignorance?" Festina asked.

"Ignorance is necessary," the jelly replied. "If we influence you too much, we prevent you from acting spontaneously. That defeats the whole exercise. We cannot guide you, or we may unwittingly steer you away from . . . whatever you might discover. For the same reason, we cannot rescue you from every trouble that arises. Dealing with life-or-death situations is when you are most likely to make a breakthrough." The jelly paused. "Or at least that's one school of thought."

Festina growled. "So you just keep manipulating Explorers into one potentially lethal danger after another to see how we react?"

The jelly chuckled. "Admiral . . . that's what 'expendable' means."

EPILOGUE

If you meet the Buddha in the road, kill him: An adage that warns against one last fixation—you can become unskillfully attached to Buddhism itself. You have to discard this final dependency too.

POISED on the beach outside the station, Festina, Tut, and I watched pulses of gold light spread from the spikes in the crown. My sixth sense told me the radiation blanketed an area fifty kilometers in radius; any *preta* within that zone ascended after a few seconds of exposure. As I'd expected, the news had spread to every EMP cloud in the world. The whole smoky population of the planet was now on the way, simmering toward us at the speed of sound. Within twenty-four hours, every *preta* on Muta would be free.

"You realize," I said to Festina and Tut, "you two can still become transcendent. The microbes are working on your bodies. In hours or days, you'll disintegrate. Next thing you know, you'll be demigods."

"No," Festina said, "next thing I know I'll be purple jelly." She waved her hand dismissively. "No thanks."

"Maybe only Fuentes turn into purple jelly. Maybe humans turn into *green* jelly."

"Ooo!" said Tut. "Could *I* turn into green jelly? Or gold jelly. That would be even better."

Festina raised an eyebrow. "Do you really want to ascend, Tut? I don't see the appeal . . . unless you'd like to thumb your nose at the jelly Fuentes. Once you're jelly yourself, they can't use you as their champion."

Tut thought about it a moment. "Nah, Auntie. If I ascended, I might go all serious. Wouldn't want to wear masks . . . wouldn't want to eat cookies . . . wouldn't want to pull down my pants and—"

"We get the point," Festina interrupted.

She pulled a Sperm-tail anchor from her backpack, flicked the ON switch, and set it on the ground. Unclipping her comm from her belt, she said, "Captain Cohen, we're ready for home."

"Very good, Admiral. The Sperm-tail's on its way."

Seconds later, the tail whisked out of the sky above the lake. Small waves rippled placidly, glinting in the soft early sunlight. The tail seemed to play in the fresh air, flicking this way and that, admiring its reflection in the water's surface. Then it remembered its duty and flew to the anchor, forming a fluttering pillar reaching all the way to *Pistachio*.

"So that's it?" Tut asked. "Nothing else to do?"

"Nothing but fill out a million reports," Festina replied. "We didn't rescue the survey teams, but we've done all we can. They must have ascended by now . . . and I assume they'll be polite enough to inform the Unity they're safe."

"The Admiralty won't be thrilled," Tut said, "considering the Unity has just acquired a few dozen gods, and the Technocracy gets stuck with nothing. The balance of power's been thrown out of whack."

Festina shrugged. "Who knows what the survey teams will do, now that they're elevated? Maybe they'll help the Unity . . . but maybe they'll decide there's more interesting things to do than hang out with mere humans."

"Maybe," I said, "the uplifted survey teams will create their own champions in the Explorer Corps."

"It's possible," Festina agreed. "Assuming the whole champion business isn't bullshit. You have to realize, Youn Suu, the Balrog may have planted that notion in your mind as a joke. Or to mislead us from something else."

"You're going to ignore the possibility?"

"No, I'll investigate the crap out of it . . . but quietly. The navy treats Explorers badly enough already. The last thing I want is the High Council deciding we're dangerous minions of alien masters, planted in the fleet to do God knows what. The corps could end up in jail . . . or worse. So I'd appreciate the two of you not mentioning the champion theory in your reports. Let me look into it discreetly."

"Fine with me, Auntie," Tut said. "I don't understand it anyway." He looked at the anchored Sperm-tail. "Ready to go?"

"After you," Festina told him.

Tut grinned. "You two want to be alone?"

"Go. That's an order."

Tut gave Festina a sloppy salute and bent over the small anchor box. A moment later, he disappeared upward: sucked into the Sperm-tail's pocket universe and propelled all the way to the ship.

Festina turned to me. "Now . . . are you really coming back? Or does the Balrog have other plans?"

"The Balrog doesn't give me orders," I said.

"Not that you're aware of. How do you know your mind is your own?"

I just smiled. A breeze gently ruffled the nearby ferns, and waves lapped at the sand. Farther off, amphibians chirped in search of mates, insects nibbled on multicolored vegetation, and *pretas*—hungry ghosts—finally found the sustenance they'd been missing for six and a half thousand years.

After a while, Festina asked, "Are you coming back to the ship, Youn Suu?"

"What use does the navy have for an Explorer who can't walk?"

"You can do research," Festina said. "I could get you assigned to my staff. Then you could help investigate somebody's bizarre allegation that aliens are messing with the Explorer Corps."

"Would you trust me to do that? Or would you suspect every word I said, wondering if it was all disinformation planted by the Balrog for its own nefarious ends?"

She gave me a sheepish look. "I mistrust damned near everyone, Youn Suu. Even when they *aren't* infested with smart-ass alien parasites."

"You'd treat me as an enemy spy. An aggravation you didn't need." I patted her leg gently. "Don't worry about me. And don't feel guilty. I'll be fine."

"What will you do?"

"The Balrog can teleport me anywhere. I'll go someplace I'm needed."

"Where?"

"I don't know yet. Perhaps I'll contemplate the universe until an answer comes to me."

"Until the Balrog plants an answer in your mind."

"I choose not to see it that way." I held out my hand to her. "We'll probably meet again. I have a sense that when everything comes to a head, we'll all be there together."

Instead of taking my hand, she bent and kissed my cheek. The one with the mark of a champion. "Western heroes ride off into the sunset," Festina said. "Eastern heroes end up sitting alone in the dawn." She kissed me again. "I like your way better."

Then she was gone.